GRIT BLACK BLOOD

ADVANCED PRAISE

GRIT, BLACK, BLOOD

BY ASHLEY ERWIN

"The long awaited epic southern fried fatalistic myth, ***Grit, Black, Blood***, is a Greek tragedy soaked in moonshine and Crisco. Ashley Erwin is one of crime fiction's most authentic voices."

—**S.A. Cosby,** bestselling author of ***Razorblade Tears***

"***Grit, Black, Blood*** comes out of the gate hard and fast and with every intention of taking no prisoners. Told in a unique and kinetic prose, Ashley Erwin writes like how Barry Hannah said William Faulkner wrote—all horns blaring at once. Readers of death-defying sly noir written by the likes of writers like Frank Bill and Bruce Holbert will be eager to get whiskey drunk on this novel of violence and cunning."

—**Charles Dodd White**, author of ***A Year Without Months***

"Ashley Erwin is the Queen of grit lit, busting a bottle upside your head and pressing a blade to your jugular with her poetic vernacular that cuts deep into the human condition, peeling back the layers of tough-as-boot-leather-lives surviving within the chewed up rural landscape of ***Grit, Black, Blood***, where devilish deeds are as common as the air we breathe and vengeance is another word for family, so twist off the cap of some smooth Kentucky bourbon, pour a few fingers, take a deep inhale and pony up for one helluva story."

—**Frank Bill**, author of ***The Savage***

"Ashley Erwin is doing for Kentucky what John D. MacDonald did for Florida and Flannery O'Connor did for Georgia. She speaks the vernacular of the land—of Dairy Marts, cornfields, knife fights, and coal mines. The characters in ***Grit, Black, Blood*** are as off-the-wall as they come, yet as authentic and raw as any I've read in a novel. If you're a fan of Southern crime fiction, you need to buy this book"

—**C.W. Blackwell**, author of ***Hard Mountain Clay***

"Ashley Erwin writes with the rage and fury of a Tarantino film on the pages of a Tom Franklin novel. ***Grit, Black, Blood*** kicks you in the gut, walks a mud hole through you, and keeps you turning pages. Don't miss out on this book!"

—**Mark Westmoreland**, author of ***A Violent Gospel***

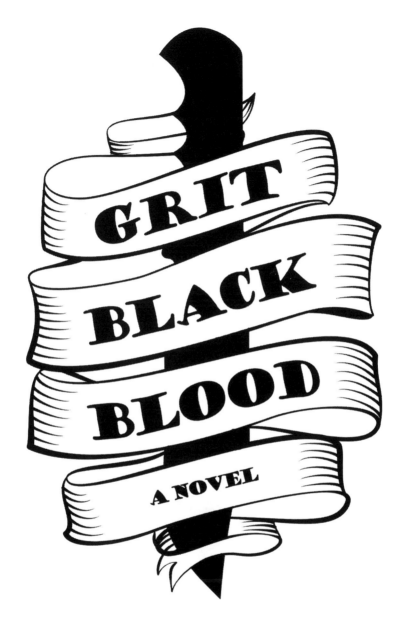

GRIT BLACK BLOOD

A NOVEL

ASHLEY ERWIN

SHOTGUN HONEY
2022

GRIT, BLACK, BLOOD

Published by **Shotgun Honey Books**

215 Loma Road
Charleston, WV 25314
www.ShotgunHoney.com
Cover by Bad Fido.

First Printing 2022.

ISBN-10: 1-956957-15-4
ISBN-13: 978-1-956957-15-0

9 8 7 6 5 4 3 2 1   22 21 20 19 18 17

For the Hitman of Hazard and all 'em other Erwins
making up that tree in Carter County;
for Nanny, and those we've lost;
for Gary, the one on the other side of the page,
I hope ya hear my voice, it's ya I'm always talking to,
and for The Man, ain't nothing worth doing less yar by my side,
and finally for Edna, as much as there's bits of 'em in me,
there's a helleva lot ya there too, all my love, firecracker

GRIT BLACK BLOOD

1

1990

ENTER COWBOY MICK

He'd shot five people that day. The lady with the bouffant. The husband to her. Red, the man who ran Red's. The fat man in front of him while waiting in line to kill Red. And me. Believe that were all that gun'd give him in the years he'd tote it.

.45 split through me like its cutting hair. Sent me against the busted-out cutlass next door with streams of red spurting out. Settled over me in cold spikes fitted with flesh eaters as rodeo hands, the disease making way over ever' inch.

Mick Fairchild were his name, that rusty motherfucker. Stood with a phone in one hand and Ruger Blackhawk in the other. His feet planted on the peeling patch of throw-away roof that these shitholes always have. It'd been two years since I'd seen him last and "Morning Mick," bubbled out a lot nicer than that fucker deserved.

"Morning," he clipped that phone dropping from his shoulder.

OH THAT'S RIGHT, THE PHONE.... WELL, WE BETTER REWIND...
RRRRINNNNNNG. RRRRINNNNNNG.

Zero in on a phone. A rotary phone. A shitty phone with a long cord that belongs in a place where gravel makes up the majority of the parking lot, where beat down doors and bugs constantly crawl outta cracks and there's always one lady round somewheres with her hair teased to Gawd in a blue buffant and there ain't shit ya can go to saying to her that's gonna convince her ya ain't what she's thinking ya are and the Franklin ya slam down for propiety sake with the hint at…if there's a joiner, I'd garner a listen and by the grace of Gawd there hadn't been one so's 'fore ya know what's what yar popping frosties and swapping yarns with a man packing heat and ya done found out 'bout his children's children he don't see no more 'cause he ain't worth the company and it's shitty, the place ya'r at, not him, he's a pretty solid guy for a feller named T'Bone who train hopped off the tracks just yonder over and ya go to thinking he probably don't deserve all that shit his kids said to him 'cause he seems like a nice enough guy 'cause ya'r cracking cold ones outta cooler listening to a train whiz by every hour on the hour where breezes don't exist….'cept for once a year when ya finally decide to tear yourself from the shitty green door encasing the room where this phone exists and get some air on yar skin 'cause a damn week'd passed since ya were somewheres halfway of Waco and Dallas with that deed of paper bare knuckled 'tween yar fingers and that steering wheel with 'em words sawing nail beds into yar damned meat paw skin with a back order of cast iron sear blackening where Connie'd wrote his name; Yer daddy. Find him.

RRRRINNNNNNG. RRRRINNNNNNG. Then there goes that damn phone again biting clumps of yar gut and spitting 'em back at ya, horning out like some goddamn bugle of deserve as in, Buddy, ya best believe what's coming's got a pre-requisite. But all ya can think 'bout is that fluff of corn exploding on yar windshield and 'em spirals of tinctured yeller spinning arcs and sparks like whittled gold which'd Rama-Jammed yar foot down metal-to-the-peddle jarring up 'em wheels of that rumbled muscle car dead-in-yar-tracks on a two lane highway in the middle of fucking nowhere and ya never really did like the middle of fucking nowhere 'cause it's where ya's from and there were always that stink tagging along like a damned blanket suffocating tight and it weren't the type nurses taught in hospitals and all of it due, this episode, this random splitting of a cornfield by a punching fat middle aged clown with paint leftover from a kid's birthday plastered on his face were 'cause ya's hunting yar dad and there were an all over notion of not right tied up on both those ends, like, weren't nothing warranting a clown getup this far out in the boonies that weren't dipped and dripped in seedy and wrong, which were of right accord like the card carrying sentimentality ya had towards that particular family member in search of and the sure fired sealed and dealed agreement of both 'em quandaries were flapping jacks in the form of that big fat ZERO that clown mouth were making and suppose it were sorta natural causations to why yar foot would go to knee jerk reaction of BURN BABY BURN and stomp that gas peddle full metal jacket down plowdriving Ronald McDonald there to clip-dent-to-shit on yar bumper and ya double-Dutch-shoving a body in your trunk and all this sermoned to the mount 'cause in the foreground of NOW where that same monster's parked, there's a faded yeller paper flapping under yar windshield in the mother-fucking breeze.

THAT oughta bring us 'bout fair and square...Let's get to that convo carrying out... Shall we...

In true slip-n-slide fashion and form, a wide variance the preferred measure of attack regarding these sorts of thangs however Mick standing with his feet spread further than his shoulders atop that motel roof weren't rooted so much in tactical attunement and finesse as much as it were the desired absconsion of that bean pole visage that carried a 150-pound frame on a taller than should even when sopping wet. But ya had to give props for the try.

“Thought I’s gonna have to wait all morning up here sweating like a pig ‘fore ya grabbed that note.”

“Hate I struck ya as slow, Mick.” A slight slurrying of slush detectible in the lower right side and a grateful sigh that the Wessen Gawd Almighty clutched in the left were beginning to assuage the worry of the bullet’s initial cumbersome placement

Turned up to him, marking a spot with a squint. “How long’s it been?”

Mick swatted out, “Two but that little affair didn’t really give us adequate time, so’s twelve for good measure,” as if it were a fact he’d chewed on ever’day since the last sighting. “That a clown I saw in yar trunk?”

“Sure enough is.”

“He tie the balloon wrong?”

Mick always were a man to draw things out. Fashioned hisself after a real life gun slinger. A version of one of ‘em tough guys born and bred on John Wayne and Clint. Caught hisself up in it. Living out this fantasy of somebody reared in the wrong time, in the wrong place. Wanted no ownership whatsoever to that holler back east. He’d growed into it well. Wore the threads. Spoke the talk. Carried the gun. But he weren’t never forced to ownership on it.

“Just sent a reminder down my spine’s all.”

Mick went for a scratch on his nose, the Ruger following suit, pinning that grain against the rugged glare of his sun tarnished skin. “Might like a story.”

He weren’t asking after the one ‘bout Ronald. He’s asking after that blood that’d sat and boiled and festered on him. “Come on me in a cornfield. Just popped out.”

“Ya don’t say.” The gun still arched by his brow, “just popped out on ya?”

“That’d be.”

My guess, he’d been sent down on a promise of a couple stacks of ten. Been told and fed and clothed in things that ain’t part, that ain't real, and he done shot me. This cowboy, Mick Fairchild, 'cause somebody'd told him to and 'cause he never could get past my knowing what he really were.

"I'd say it now if ya's primed on a thing," he clomped with heavy breath.

Fighting words, finally. Traveled all the way up to the line and now the tiptoe across to see who's made of what. That pain of knowing whittling over the dawn's speckling. That scar he'd earnt at six all grease and shine from where Granny'd done a bad stitch after he'd been pushed down and beat over by a Meek boy, so he said.

From mine to his but more to me, "Ya ain't ever wanted to hear nothing I'd done tried to give. Starting up now just cause ya's standing there and I's sitting here don't seem to fit all that well with sense. It's a problem, Mick. It truly is."

That glint forced mean; a stare I'd seen practiced since rumbles staged in the back yard. But there's clouds buried in him. Barrels of haze covering up his eyes, fogging over that sight he's never granted.

It were dynamite and the match were already fucking burning. GO. TIME. "Ya's a sickly boy. Fragile little thing. Cough 'bout ya. Always that cough. That cawing. That rattling. Like ya's begging for it, begging for the gawddamn world to stop. Like ya'd something worth contributing. And I used to hope maybe ya did. Used to think—GAWDdamn, it might just be."

Sun tipped round, edging Mick's tilt over and out. Folds of black, tacky on still cold gravel. That frail boy playing in the dirt of his mind. His life ahead of him. That thing that'd make him whole hidden in a suit somewheres he's yet to step in.

"Never quite found the fit, did ya."

I'd made my peace on it long ago.

Charted my mark.

Slug kicked out.

Fire burned through.

•

Bang clanged overhead.

Mick Fairchild were my brother and I'd done killed him dead.

BUT the kicker, the one to boot, the thing that'd make ya madder than hell were that not even an hour ago in between 'em reruns of (Nanny's Family) on that two station T.V., though ya'd a mind on ya to go and have a talking with that lady in the front 'bout that spell of false advertising as there were distinct and as ya recall solitary reason for why ya'd pulled into this here Oasis and that were the golden promise of HBO for free and yet when that clicker there to a 1986 box with two bunny ear antennas sticking out were hell or highwater intent on fucking mockery sending illuminating shards onto the wide sprawl of every sort of potato chip that shitty vending machine held 'cause that's more like than not to be the case, ain't it, like what else ya supposed to do at 3 in the morning when ya've put a fair hurting on a bottle of whiskey and yar stomach starts asshole catcalling ya from the deep 'bout how if ya's a good and true Christian ya woulda had the decency to at least sop down some Bologna on white bread to ya innards and go to work on the bottle but seeing as how we're clearly in the stage of life were we can't have nice things and ya hear T-Bone there through the wall lend a holler to that same office airing a grievance 'bout noise incompliance and how if somebody don't shoot 'em there racoons off the roof while he's in the middle of an afternoon siesta which is exactly what a cooler full of frosties'll do to a feller though I believe he were in the business of that grand tradition of whiskey sipping 'till it came proper drinking time hence the predicament of the aforementioned chips meaning Mick there'd set up camp for quite some time and of course the real tears for fears here were that shot he'd done give were 9 to 1 odds of land from the particular velocity of wind and altogether shit shot he'd always been but he'd got me good.

Clean slug. Type that goes in swift and sharp and finds itself feeling real nice and snug right up next yar guts, right at that spot that'll ensure that slow steady bleed, where no amount of tinkering or pulling or rooting gonna find that tip or that end. That's what he done give me. A sure fire shot of dying in a parking lot with no gawddamn dignity to be found and a helluva short distance 'tween the length of time we'd spent being mad and confused 'bout each other.

That rusty motherfucker.

Always imagined it'd find me in some fashion like this, in some sorry for nothing shit stain of a town but if I'd my choosing, I'd surely want it occurring some place other than anywhere in fucking Texas. Just thinking 'bout it, it's enough to make me give a lean out to defying that inevitable and hightailing my ass the five or six more hours it'd take to cross a line just so's I didn't have to die in this Gawd forsaken place.

Can't trust a man to come from something so flat. Can't trust his intentions, his yearnings, none of it. Ain't a gawddamn thing ever come from a drive through Texas that were worth a damn and this being the culmination only lands that hammer harder.

And by Gawd if any of that doing involved anything less than hauling the dead body of my brother that'd of course fell off that roof and pinned my foot leaving us both stagnant and still and driving his ass all the way back to where it were that'd bred and sealed two boys fate in a situation like we'd got ourselves here, than I would've.

Just ain't gonna happen.

So's it'd appear, unfortunate for me, that the crawling sprawl of a train rolling in on the eastside of this spit of a town, consisting all of one hotel and a gas station, and my brother's dead stare stamping my face in a burn mark on 'em green peepers, my last cradling. I's to die out here with the sound of grind charging filters through breeze. That carrying of buzz playing by that blue bouffant woman my brother's Ruger took pity on with a clear mark. That channeling dumping over the left drip of exhaust and silver streak of dirty granite come out mufflers of hard traveled miles. 'Til finally, the chug of wheels burning over track finds its resting in the perk of my ears and settles with the dust of that train's first roll through Hazard.

2

1930

THE WHITTLE BOYS

"Well, I don't mind telling ye, me broder's passion weren't somet'ing he'd learnt entirely on his own, now. Bit of a mark of trade, rather. Picked it up over a spell of ripping and running we'd found erselves in. Fuck, we's bathing in it ferr we even stepped foot into double digits. Ain't it right, Riley? Riley? Riley…"

Quick to it, Cian burst up. That line of rope tethering all decisions want for a whiplash twirl as Riley went after the big scruff, who'd made it his sole and only job to drive him crazy with cut-back eyes and grunts of reprisals ever since they stepped off Irish soil and onto Atlantic steel. Well it just wouldn't do now would it. That's exactly how Riley saw it and once he'd made it his intent to go after the big brawling mustached tard, come to be known as The Russian ever after, it were settled and stamped in stone.

Tuggled down and fastened at the hips, these two. And for right measure. Both of 'em loaded up as they were. History proved there's better odds in the pairing of 'em than they's like to find by 'emselves. And as their lives tended toward the hankering for a little rough house it didn't take long for 'em to find that trouble their eyes'd always tended to. And given that minor detail that neither one of 'em stood very much taller than a woman, being all 'bout five foot six, there were a spot of crafty that came along with.

Unfortunate for The Russian and his altogether misappraisal of The Whittle Boy's value, he did not himself take this spot of ingenuity into consideration and found a rather sticky scene unfolding. Weren't so much his fault. He'd not known their dealings back on the Isle of Green. Say for example that time of merriment found in two young boys lives when they discover the innate fascination explosions can produce and what might occur when stumbling on such a plot as three forgotten or rather misplaced boxes of gunpowder will provide. Nor did he fully know the ramification of getting one's ear loped off after trying to argue his way out of a necessity that life hadn't give much choice of avoiding.

Well, have ye ever heard the like of it. Truly. To have yer ear chopped off by Donny Bowen of McCreary Hill, due in part to being so dirt poor that the need for stealing came 'bout ye soon as the foot went for a tap. Clopped it clear off with a cleaver, Donny did. Spouting out into the hole of blood gushing twill that went to a pump from a five-year-olds head.

Send the salt straight down through ye, now. Nooo, 'fraid The Russian did not take into considering at all these telltale signs of this being the two not to fuss with. 'Fraid had he taken the note, that the gab dribbling from these two lot's mouths were more full up of foxy twinge than there were a ladle of truth to spill and how, soon as Cain saw the jut of his broder's flip of brow change with the sudden thrust of a pile drive dive up the gutter, that sudden alarm being jettied up with the swoop of Riley's milly little hands, for that need for a swift block The Russian should've cared call to unfortunately did not grace the frame of 'em peeper's he'd so adamantly made window dressing for Riley to smash through.

It were called the Devious Do. A move made up after many a black stuff drowned down the gullet. No more than thirteen, they were, these two deviant sires. Out for a jaunt along Riverborn, through, a tread of green and brown carrying over that same straddle of land separating the McCreary farm from the wealthier brood of Daigh Molony, Riley and Cian warmed by the sprawl of a fire in the back of a room they'd no position to be.

"Aye, will ye look not there, Riley." Cian's brow pushed aside the waft of burn reaching from spitting yella and gave glance to the set of boots just come in from the cold.

"Soaked to the bone, there, Meave." A man rustled the furl of his outer layers, stamping the cake of iced mud over the clank of stone floor.

"Aye." Cian gave a right nudge to his broder's arm, motioning for a look-see. "Look. See, there."

Riley remained frozen on the spit. His outlying hands smothered in the clay dread that digging'll do. His mind busy with the shut off of that tedious reminder, though it'd taken to a yell in the time since their stopping, that food hadn't hit his pit in longer than he'd like to recall. The grumbles now transformed to angry quarrels of sea monsters heavy with the thrashing inside.

"Riley, yer missing yer chance, there, boy." Cian's mutterings jumped from his mouth, laying out lines of wire to that hood of fur his broder were now wont to wear at all times of chill, which given their birth footing weren't much.

"I swears it," Cain pushed.

Riley turned, hushing down his broder's words with the spying of the man's seating hisself near the thresh of Meave's bar.

"Ye gonna thank and hug me once ye take note of this'n here. Why, I bet," Cian got in close to that good side under fur and whispered, "we gonna end this day with full bellies and cheshire smiles, broder."

Things did not, as one might want, linger still during this quiet exchange, so that all parties did not in fact remain privy less to the plotting of others, which brings us round to the man affixed Meave's bar. Only eight years since and yet the man 'fore Riley and

Cian looked to have aged that of a hundred. Where in spite all that ill hanging skin and long curly tendrils of white draped therein and what one might utter, "an altogether flat-out tired demeanor 'bout him," the face of Donny Bowen sat upon the body of a man not meant at living very much longer.

"How's it go, there, Meave?" His hands busy with the unwrapping of cotton and nightly dew. He turned, taking in the view of two small boys seated by the fire. The one with his eyes pointed to him, the other laden in fur, and in that dreary head of his where age had not yet found it's resting, he perhaps remembered meeting a set of the like once 'fore. But could not recall however the reasoning surrounding it and so left their cut and ventured back to the promise of a little something warm. "Tell me this and tell me no more," his voice carried, "is there a dram waiting to purse these here puckers for I been out and 'bout and nary a thought this mind past of anything other than the hit of a pint, the smash of a glass."

Ever'day for twenty odd years, this were Donny Bowen's greeting to Meave and ever'time after her hearing it, she always responded the same, "'Tis true, there, Donny. 'Tis true." This were no different today and once the small glass of whiskey slid over the worn and grooved wood grain, the recalling of where 'em pointy eyes might've come from appeared. Seemed some eight years or so back, Bowen remembered finding a set of dirty fingers nipping in a place they'd rather not belonged.

"If I were to even tell ye who just walked his happy ars in and sat not four feet from ye with nar a worry in the world, ye wouldn't believe me. Why ye just wouldn't even believe me, Gawd's truth."

No longer could Riley ignore. No longer could he sit roasting and stewing with promises of slop swimming up next the growl of predators and so with a slow steady reach, he removed that fur hood from his head. Stouter of the two, Riley would grow to be considered the brawn, however at the age of a measly thirteen years this, not quite in effect and he appeared more the summoning of many parts. With strong hands and forearms, the result of fieldwork when farmer's granted, and biceps to boot, his appendages seemed to belong to a very small and somewhat angry man as the rest of him fit oddly by comparison. For on his head were fixed the pudgy resolve of a boy on his cheeks and near his chin, though his stomach could certainly attest to it all being a lie mocking him whenever viewed. His hair fitting much with the same, a stack of muffled curls the color of ruby fire red, looked the belongings of some saint not yet christened by the church. And yet leading down those thick somewhat uncontrollable tussled twines, there lay the fractured scar of where an ear once bore. Tucked and gnarled and mashed, the wound could not be described as anything other than a mind field of infection gone wrong and somehow scooped out. This however not occurring out of anything other than necessity as the illness at one point grappled and fought its way across the ruins of his cheek and over the shielding of his ocular bone 'til it found the unfortunate promise of the eye, itself.

This, a point of contention for him to live and breath with for the rest of his life. The folly of those monsters and their feeding frenzy in the depth of his gut thus became the secret voices of his future yearnings. And so now he sits, forever changed, this boy of only thirteen turned monster at age five, who lost not only an ear but also an eye, staring at the crotched fuck who gave him such gifts.

"Told ye, ye'd never believe me."

The Devious Do followed as such. Riley, having only mere seconds to acknowledge the hatred brewing overtop the monsters in his belly, quickly took it upon hisself to grab hold of a fire poker left on the floor by Meave or some other helpless bastard, who never would've thought it as useful as Riley would soon find it to be, and proceeded to slither from his many layers of clothing and gather his footing 'fore his broder.

However, as pointed to earlier, it were not just Riley who suddenly became aware of his long lost acquaintance, as Donny Bowen too made a show of moves hisself. For out his pocket and smacked on the bar came the unlikely appearance of brass knuckles wrapped round each circular edge with the scraps of past time usings.

Well, this were simply not something done, what Cian thought. No, it just simply would not do. And as much as he'd intended on letting this one play the course, allowing his broder the rightful go at avenging that act done to him those eight years past, he could not and he too gathered the closest weapon at hand. An iron kettle set aside for the boil.

"Meave, believe it time for a spot of air," the old Bowen chapped.

The boys drew closer.

Meave took in the sight and grabbed a coat from under the bar and muttered with her leaving, "Pissing to high heaven outside and I gots to make room for a little dick swinging." Door slammed with the exit of a voice trailing out, "Bloody hell."

Knocking round Riley's innards that dream of flailing skin and rotted mire came creeping, that dream of waking and his ear and eye being intact, tautly draped across his forehead, that crunch of his wishing for Bowen's death gripped round that black iron.

Bowen knocked back the little bit left in the bottom of the glass Meave give him and slowly slid his old and rickety fingers into that set of well used metal. He drummed up that fire in him that went cold after years of docility but that never quite went out and he thought of the pleasure it were gonna bring him to smash and crack some skulls after all this time.

Meanwhile, Cain measured up the wrinkles and the settling of years on the man and gathered the finer points of entry to be that of the shank followed directly by a slop to the snout and clomp to the jowl for good measure. In his mind he took to the shank first 'cause a man of his size, standing at no more than six feet towered over a set of thirteen-year-olds barely fitting above five, needed to be knocked down quick and by his reckoning a good hard side-swipe to the knee right where the muscles meet for the binding would certainly do the trick. As for the other two, fail safes, or rather guilty pleasures come from years of contemplation as to the sounds they'd produce.

Riley's plan—a blood gorge however found and however met.

For Old man Bowen, it mattered little how the hoot-n-nanny went as long as 'em flames burning bright inside were given a nice rage. So the man, who'd give that boy the cause for his standing like he were all upright and hate filled, took to it with the crash of his chair and the pound of his fist.

Aw, it were a mighty awful sight indeed. For one, though it might could be lent that 'em boys carried a twinge of the nasty with 'em ever since birth, and due to their somewhat unfortunate upbringing, some already being documented as it were, they'd never, not the neither of 'em, made a true effort into the art of the Reaper. But one can't ever discount the surge of a cunning nature and the promise of a full belly afterwards.

Cian took to the bunch of that old broke down brute first. Swinging and hurling that black kettle used round 'bout. Why the air went to a call of loping wind pipes, a tune chortled forth from some forgotten woeful tale.

Woosh. Woosh. Woosh.

Came over Bowen in crosswise strips of soaked and dripped stew. Chunks of leftovers spilling and plopping on the floor, causing a right awful slip if one were to chance the misstep. While at the same time, Riley's settling jabs in the thick. The slice jutting through and through. Almost like, if he's to close his good eye and give an ear, the chorus of it all'd take ye to dance.

Woosh. Woosh.
Jut.
Woosh. Woosh.
Jut.
Woosh. Woosh.
Jut.

So that the whole affair played out in twirls and cuts. In two steps and side divisions. All the while, that slug Bowen tarried, shoving down one and two's as he watched 'em boys make their moves round him.

Woosh. Woosh.
Jut.
Woosh. Woosh.
Jut.

They moved and snaked. 'Em boys taking dives over dropped carrots and slop. Trained their noses for the forget, their guts too strained with the smell of red pumping under that ragged and worn leather edging ahead. 'Em taters lost on 'em both.

Woosh. Woosh. SMACK. Kettle popped through mush. That soft coating of goo muscles end with after a certain amount of age. Smooshed in and out like a rubber band, the giveback a sign of the skin's defense.

Bowen dripped over. Brass knuckles and twisted hands clobbering out after. Knocking down swats of air and spit falling from his wobbly face. Fingers caught hold of poor Cian's slow pull back. Sent down inferno splints of orange blaze as his locks swished back in slow-mo.

Popped him. One. Two. Three. Bowen did. Fucked him back and over so's that Cian fell into his broder's chest, knocking down that poker from out his hands and sending the both of 'em on their backs for the ram-through to come next.

Though, the air gone from the tyrant, he came after 'em two

boys stomping boots to ground. Searching for fingers or bones to crush. Looking like some gawddamn giant hovering and leering as they rolled and shifted, smothering 'emsevles in the juice of that stew and the squish of 'em carrots and taters. And by the time they'd done pushed and squirmed their way back near up the fire, having received at least three good lickings a piece from Bowen's heel, Riley saw the out.

Over next up where that poker'd set and that kettle placed for the boil, there were a log grabber just begging. Riley jabbed after it. The one hand busy at pulling Cian up with him, the other channeling after that black iron. But it weren't like this feint at action somehow prevented the blows from coming off Bowen and 'fore Riley'd a chance at holding the damn thing, 'em metal knuckles came down on flesh. Wrenched a welt on that cheek 'til it pounded bone. Caused the red to spill and float down that mark of scared skin where a young boy's ear once leant.

Cian dropped back from the hold of his elbows, searching for a thing to stop the curdle that sound were making as Bowen drove over and over and over again into his broder's face. Spotted the kettle just near his foot. Tried for a tip up, for a kick at it, but it weren't something to give lightly to the action. His eyes moved to the fire poker just at arm's length and stretched 'em awkward fingers of a boy figuring out exactly what sort of man'd come later from the action taken next. Reached and reached he did. That sound of his broder's belaboring carrying out next to him.

Yet, 'fore Cian even give it one chance with that poker his fingers managed to grab, Riley were up and at it. Log grabber in hand. End pulling on the edge of Bowen's nose. Bowen's face dipped forward with eyes bugging. A red tinge gone all wrong 'bout him. And all of a sudden 'fore Cian's very eyes, the monster took over and his broder became something else entirely. All rage filled, voice crackling, mad DAWG yanking, what he were. Right brutal, it were.

Riley mongrelized Bowen. Tugged and yanked and pulled

'til that nose came barreling off. 'Til that skin wobbled hanging and flapping from the muscles. He flung hisself from the ground with bloodied cheek and battered skin and flailed in twitches and snatches, in crumbling detachment of rumbled disbelief, Riley went after Bowen and there to meet him once the eye Riley'd plucked fell and mixed with the goo of stew and he'd gone on after that second, his broder popped up too.

Jut. Jut.
Snatch.
Jut. Jut.
Snatch.

They picked Bowen over with licks and ticks and bangs and plucks and pummeled him over and under and which way and what 'cause it were the only way they knew to go on 'bout it and that poor lot, for don't believe in the end Bowen could be described as anything other, died slow. The brute plumb drained.

Taking it back a hair, the necessity for The Devious Do long ago stashed in a back room of Riley and Cian's minds so that it were only on a rarity that they utilized such skill set as these. However, given, as mentioned 'fore, the stature of the gentlemen and that part of sailing cross the ocean to a new place unforeseen where tends to be the flavor, as it always usually is, that being word of mouth traveling faster than any fire lit, they took it upon 'emselves, these broders to make an example of The Russian. A show, if ye will, for all those aboard. So's all those mouths leaving and stepping foot on American soil might not never forget the landing of the Whittle Boys in 1926.

3

1930

CECIL "DOC" HODGE

What began as a rather ordinary day for the railroad prospector, one met with pride and jovial bemusing to all the possibilities apparent that a man may greet such a day with, slowly and ever assuredly unraveled into a thread most'd never dare think for a pull.

Now, it's common knowledge for it not to be in a man's best interest to go 'round rummaging through another man's property without formal introduction. This, however, appeared vacant from the prospector's mind, he being not from the surrounding area and therefore exempt from such knowledge to which all others were spoon fed from birth. For who didn't share a story of how someone's Uncle or brother or father, having through no fault but his own, done that very thing they now warned against, found hisself as the punch to some fervent sharing round a jug, all of it ending in the same: "poor fella's shot," "dumb bastard's buried," or the personal favorite, "they booted his ass all the way back down the county line and up the other 'fore their foot grew tired." Thus the prospector, man called by the name of his father, George Gerald Thompson III, hailing from upstate New York, bringing with him all the attributes of fine education, who truly and whole heartedly believed he's toting progress, prosperity, and the American Dream to the people of Kentucky, stepped out of that dingy boat the railroad company done loaned him, stepped off the shallow waterway where Bartlett and Bend streams fork onto that shiny moss covered stone leaking up above the stream's babble, in a pair of boots nicer than any man in this county ever done dreamed of owning, happened on a man he'd never known existed and assuredly after meeting wished him erased from his mind forever.

See, unlike Mr. George Gerald Thompson III, that man scouting trees, who'd soon come to stumble upon the man in the dingy, done growed up on this land. Done shared in the grievances of broke back work and hard come winters. Done knowed and learnt long ago what might happen if given over to the indulgences of folly one might overlook with a jug of fire gluing his innards still, that this ain't the friendliest of places even if that's what the yearning inside wants it to be. Might be a hard one for someone not carrying weight of the same to come by, but one this one-wood-legged-easy-to-goat-but-certainly-loyal-to-some mountain man were all kinds of in the right mood to do. And when he stepped out from that yella poplar that'd blocked his view of Mr. George Gerald Thompson III disembarking that small sad wooden vessel, he gave a minor pause as to examine closely what he knew already in his gut.

And what a contrast it were, this dandy of a man, with a shirt tailored from a fresh press tucked down all nice and straight with fine twilled trousers breaching thereafter into calves of fresh from the factory boots, replete with shine still intact.

Why, if the man behind the tree were rooted in the institutions of the day he might care to give a good goddamn to his appearance. To that sprawling nest of a beard with no doubt food and twigs left in. For why would there ever be call to a brushing in a place such as this. To 'em britches he'd done breathed and near bred, if given the chance but it were a long time off since the clopping doom of his long lost leg, which'd rooted him a little careless to the affectations of any woman passersby. What might the man leering beady portals over at this dandy think if he too were born in such proximity to the city, if he too were granted with the gifts of such things as fine threads and lofty thoughts, would he to carry his foot in such a manner, perhaps, stamp on the ground of another man's claim like-so. Not that, mind ya, one less or more important to the other, this not the way of it.

It is simply put that they exist.

George Gerald Thompson III challenged the quip of his balance upon the rock sticking up from the fork of Bartlett and Bend knowing not of his voyeur nor of the impact of his next step as he reached for the yella markers that'd plot the potential laying of the railroad's next line. From where, as his foot ventured forth onto that mossy exchange coating a small and unremarkable rise up from the riverbed to acreage, out stepped the man behind the tree.

His name, Cecil 'Doc' Hodge.

"Reckon it right ya git on back in that sorry eye sore of a boat and paddle yar ass on back the way ya come."

It were known this state and all the way down to Florida, Cecil 'Doc' Hodge saved all his sweet drippings for just one, and seeing as she'd passed ten years come this fall, it were in ever'one else's best interest to steer clear and steer wide. That the carrying of this message had not traveled the extra jaunt to the state of New York were not and never would make the slightest damn difference to him. Fact, the thought could and quite possibly did inflame the nerves of Cecil's wooden leg to no end that the possession of such things were not handed out in pamphlet form soon as the crossing of the state line occurred.

Now, though, the claiming of such could certainly be made that George Gerald Thompson III were in no way a dim-witted person, he having spent the better part of his adolescents in schools Cecil 'Doc' Hodge might better think were pronunciations of gibberish if taken over in a chat. And yet he'd never thought to entertain the notion of hostility to PROGRESS would ever exist, though he'd certainly been warned a time or two in the passing of the night through whispers. In that, or perhaps along with such understanding, it would never occur to George Gerald Thompson III, just as it had not occurred to him 'fore 'bout stepping out on a man's land without proper call, that this Cecil 'Doc' Hodge were one of the few warning stories who'd accomplished all three of those prior declarations to any man who'd come cross his path while he's scouting out on his land.

Oh yes, indeed.

George Gerald Thompson III gave no more a glance to the hatchet in Cecil 'Doc' Hodge's hand as he did the peg stemming down the breadth of his britches 'fore barreling out like some long-lost buffoon, "No cause for alarm. I work for the railroad. See these," he raised the yella markers up high, his feet clomping wet on Hodge's land, "meant to lay down some marks on the land. Track some runs."

Now why, do ya ask, would George Gerald Thompson III talk in such a manner coming from the places of his history? Well, seemed there were some sort of attempt at assimilation prior to his venturing to the land blue. A seminar given just prior to his exiting the big city, wherein it were decided upon that a certain element of colloquial jargon were here spread throughout the mountain and it might make for better yield if, those taking salary, and mind ya, not the actual grunters digging, blasting, and laying, they's a different sort, talk in a fashion as to make 'emselves a slight bit more approachable by shortening their phrases to a slow pace with most cases stating actions as opposed to extensions or questions. "State it so they understand but don't drag it out so there's time to question." The combination of such instruction paired with George Gerald Thompson III's contrived twang which sounded more like a depiction of a pig in a suit once plastered up in yar head, came off in the only way it could to someone like Cecil 'Doc' Hodge.

Sounded like a gawddamn asshole.

This, however, also not registered in George Gerald Thompson III's mind.

Cecil 'Doc' Hodge gave way to the view of this man once more. Scanning smile and hair and make, squashing down flits of mock he felt pushing back on him with ever' drop of moist forming on his rock.

"Boy, ya hard of hearing?"

"Why, I —"

George Gerald Thompson III's mind cataloged back through the filtered images of his youth 'til he came to that one where he'd thought it buried so deep no room left for it to rise. A flashing sprawl of white and red, of hands reaching across that long dinette that served more as a children's table, a separate entity from where the adults allowed to dine, to that calamitous mixture of peas and potatoes strewn, of meat knocked over along speckled chunks of china, of bits of green and red stringing ooze atop Mother's fine Christmas dinner. He thought of the look of Father's face as he came crashing through the swinging door separating he and his brother and little cousin Teddy from the imbibers a room over. No matter the spots of food crusted under Teddy and Sullivan's nails, no matter the ruffle of their shirts, or the speck of angered thirst dotting their eyes, Father's reaction saved only for him. Saved only for his eldest son. For the son who'd let two boys bully him. Who'd no interest in sports and the hunt like his younger brother Sullivan. Who'd rather spend his time reading under shade than engage in terror as little Teddy were known to do, as boys and men were known to do. And there covered in splooged gravy plotting stakes of hold in his face, his father looked at him, the question living behind glassy blues, that utterance of regret and shame tearing holes through his heart. 'What kind of man are you, son?' The statement freezing time in cold spikes that threatened a fall on his head. 'You hear me, son? What kind of man are you?"

The episode'd ruined Christmas dinner. Carried over into the weeks of the new year without so much as an exchange between George Gerald Thompson II and his son the third. Months and months trailing by with silenced dinners as they'd no longer forced him to sit at the long dinette though it were not a privilege anymore to move over to the next. 'Til finally George Gerald Thompson III left, trailing down to Kentucky to work for the railroad and lay tracks and learn to be man.

These were the things running through George Gerald Thompson III's mind as he stared back at the mountain man, Cecil 'Doc' Hodge, and filled to the brim with his father's chidings, he decided today the day, and he barreled out unafraid, though he'd certainly due cause to be, "My name is George Gerald Thompson III and I'm a railroad man. I've come to lay down marks for track."

And then he did. He stepped foot from that mossy patch. He rounded out clinks in the dirt with 'em fancy boots of his and he began the trek towards the fairway for where the presumed track would go.

Concurrently, and to no knowledge of either mentioned prior, there came to join, a footslog from an unlikely met two. Two strangers to the land. Two highway men who'd jumped passage from green to meet blue to meet green again. Not a kind journey but one that were met with gusto and one that continued in the lean of particular tastes and gifts and afforded a hand in the situation at play that neither George Gerald Thompson III nor Cecil 'Doc' Hodge knew possible.

From the distance, it appeared nothing more than a common interchange. A thing to stumble over and brush past and yet there formed a pause in the broder's steps, a sudden take of interest at the man they watched who held the hatchet and had the beard, a sudden calling to stay a moment longer. To watch.

How it went, Cian and Riley posted up next to an oak, the both of 'em, taking ganders round the trunk while the two men up the hill carried on in their business.

With nar a second thought, from out Cecil 'Doc' Hodge's hand flew the hatchet. Grip of his dirty print etched in the throw over of wood carrying metal. Sharpened edge landed smack dab in the reach of George Gerald Thompson III's next step and stuck a bare hair from where that boot hit.

"Boy, I give not one solitary fuck to the who of why yer here. Git off my fucking land."

Cian and Riley watched as the finer dressed one shifted stories in his head for the appropriate move. The panic settling and causing sweat to froth over his skin but remain hidden under his threads. The thought of how he'd back peddle after stepping out too far. And for whatever reason, and for perhaps no reason at all, Cian gathered an intervention needed. Not due, mind ya, to the man with the hatchet's aid and certainly not due to the fancy pants teetering at the blade, but more so to the fact that they'd walked all they'd planned on going and this looked as good as any they'd passed by.

And so it were that the two who'd traveled all that very long way from Ireland to here, who'd stumbled on the happenchance occurrence of a man's over extension, pulled from out their coats, that very thing that made 'em so happy as a child and decided to unload fire as a way of announcing.

Rolled bundles of dynamite bite on fallen trees and picked over moss, the last burnt boulders of scorched green and red down the mount, that boom spitting spikes of dirt where men'd learnt the ways and how's of things. And soon to follow thereafter, once the confusion squashed quiet, once George Gerald Thompson

III's outline done disappeared, once Cecil 'Doc' Hodge's gun lowered from the direction of Cian and Riley, there happened a common chord.

It were like the meet up of animals, the stare down shuffle of hooves dug and antlers reared and in the silence grappling round that hill, they knew. They saw it. Each. Carved and ripped and culled from that same wound, that same red-brown spilling out after, they knew the three of 'em that things were soon to change.

4

1988

RONNIE FAIRCHILD

Candy-apple-red'd turned gone-with-the-wind-brick-brown all up the bottom half of me like some fucking dirty film left overtop the pond. Only thing missing were floating jimmies and a couple sad misused Nati-lights. Gawd knows ya's sporting the chunk of hamburger meat throw'd over the side of the boat. Faces started to turn there, brother. Keep it up out here, ya gonna blister cherry. Gonna turn Cocktail Cove bloat. Good not spelled nowheres.

Fair say, ya'da like Cocktail Cove, Mick. Horror of a thing how they built it. Not the cove. Can't blame a man for seeking out a route to slay snatch and snatch slaying were bound in boat tie-up galore on that Cove in Lake Lanier. But the lake, that were the true abortion. The flat lined spike once the life drilled out. Took the hull right out the town, innards justa laying there not knowing how to go 'bout it without the covering.

Best of intentions that were. The lake. Didn't bulldoze down a thing. Not a damn thing, most people don't know that. Not no more. Always carves a bit of surprise on folks when that water gets down and a couple of kids get tangled up in some wire that got knocked loose by a set of piss and vinegar studs popping five-foot wakes in a no wake zone. Fuckers.

Oh yeah, folks'd get all up in a hissy when somebody's leg'd get choked up in chicken wire that a farmer'd put round a coupe way back in 19 ought 26, thinking not nothing but damn nothing 'bout it 'cause "this here's country and what would government folks want with a piece of land rarely fitting to turn anything but dirt, nohow?"

And don't think for one second, there's a one of 'em that spares a thought to that chapel they's floating above. Not when there's tan lines concerned. Ain't never seen so many women worried 'bout where the sun were hitting and where it weren't. Like any of that shit mattered when a triangle top spiraled down to the end zone. More than not they's commended for the favor of blaring country lightening white in the dark from where 'em titties'd shine.

Didn't pay one mind's eye to the scraping that steeple ached on the belly of 'em boats, not a one of 'em. Bet it'd cause their little Christian hearts to flutter, 'cause ya know that's what all 'em little things were spraying out come Sunday morning, to know there's a church right up under Cocktail Cove justa bathing in all that Kool-Aid red jungle juice dripping off their young girly legs. Tiny bits of Jesus just dying right there with ever' breath of, "'em boys is bigger y'all, let's go on over there," as they hopped from boat to boat.

Near 'bout run yar ass down with how fast 'em little pink pedi'd toes'd go to shuffle cross slick boat bottom blues, none of 'em careening half a thought how it were gonna drip through Bi-Lo shopping rows 'bout what they done, back up in town. Caught up in all that benzo or whatever else kinda drug they ripped from their Mommy's cupboard. Just a bunch of bopped Muppet baby heads on top 'em skinny little teenage necks. Made all that glitter and bronze go to filter pixie streams out in the water. Cover up some of the stank left from all the shit brewing cauldron bubble underneath. Sea of neon pink and green dancing Dixie cup dreams over ferries and dinghies and boats big as houses with slides and bedrooms and mirrors and white lady mounds fueling backwater country fab dreams. Fucking Cocktail Cove there, brother.

Ya'da made a mighty fine go there on that Redneck Riviera dealing squashed teenage hope, oh ya'da done just fine there, brother. And ain't it so and of due derision that after all 'em years of chase…ain't never gonna guess where I'm going next, that 'em sheets we's tangled in now were properly made by the hands of a forlorn Queen…oh is that right? Ya think ya oughta know?

Wouldn't believe me even if branded up under 'em lids…

'Member Agatha's youngin. 'Member her, that girl ya'd gone on with when ya's real young, or tried to at least. Saw her clear as day, clear as devils sending crows to steal our souls, ain't that what Nanny used to say when the storm were a coming, devil winds and crow watch.

Weren't Agatha that raised her…her sister, what were her name again? Little bitty thang with torpedo lunch-room titties that hung down low as shit. Ever'time she went for a lean, thought they'd just kangaroo up like tails and hold her there. Can ya imagine fitting one of those up in yar mouth. Like to fucking strangle ya. Woulda covered yar entire face. Maybe not now with all that goo ya got dripping out. Sure as shit woulda covered that scar of yars. Bring it full circle, wouldn't it?

That's how ya got the thing, 'cause of Agatha's girl. That's what ya told Mommy or tried to, she weren't listening much to ya back in 'em days. Lawd, can't no one blame her for that. What'd ya say it were again that'd happened…tripped on a rock, ain't that right. By the creek, where Nanny'd bashed that copperhead with flint. Kilt it dead, we thought, 'member that. All three of us standing round watching, not knowing that flint'd just split off and gnarled things 'bout a bit and that copperhead were gonna come back mean as a viper which it surely did. K-O'd for not even a minute, just long enough for ya to get a step too close, and that copperhead came back at ya, and ya not being but three, fell down hard as a sack of taters on creek bed points and went to wallering out puddle buckets of scared on us shooting an aftermath of brimstone vengeance from the roll back of Nanny's hand as she bashed that motherfucker over and over and over again to a boulder that bruised snake-jam-maroon once she's done, which when ya come back with that tall tale 'bout how ya got that scar when ya's... thirteen...I knew it HORSEFUCKINGSHIT. 'Cause there weren't no amount of yanking nor paying that'd get yar ass close to that creek again. And there were sets and sets of wetted down sheets covered up in the night that woulda charged truth behind it.

Didn't fool a damned one of us with yar stuffing down of sheets into the sink come mid-dawn-break. Only so many times a set a wash can go on 'fore there's a note writ up 'bout the use of soap. Nanny just started breaking off extra and leaving it at the bottom of the stairs for ya like ya's a mouse and it cheese, like it called the piss right out of ya just so it'd have a use.

Don't really even matter what ya did to that girl, her face said it all when I run into her, well that, and I'm sure Agatha's leaving and Torpedo Tit raising. Dropped ever'thing Agatha did. Talk of the fucking town. For a trucker named Lonnel. Met him down at Curt's café. Right there by the highway. He'd probably pulled off to catch some shut eye and grab a biscuit not never thinking nothing 'bout taking on a board and just her luck when he popped into line after her, weren't it. According to yar little girl friend, Sally, y'all be happy to know she growed up right fine, fitting somewheres in between Agatha and Torpedo Tit's shape, looked real good in that neon yella suit she's wearing, cut came way high on her hips, full shape of the leg s'ing out underneath in nice fat biscuit fed yam, only the barren showing slyly behind her blue blockers—Agatha'd scooped too many eggs on her plate and the lady were threatening to charge her double, ruthless, that blue-hair, press her shellacked "corvette-red" piercer down on top yar plate with all the might of a linebacker so's that scale'd go up and Curt's coffer filled, and Agatha being bargainable at best, were holding up the line and that poor unsuspecting man, Lonnel, offered to pay, not knowing perhaps what all 'em jacked up Levi's on sour hips'd planned for him. Doubt they made it to a second tea refill 'fore she'd her hand on his knee.

Called it country peddling, Sally did. "Agatha always were one for the theatrics." Never mind the frizzed up hair and stage bright suit her daughter were wearing as she laid it on thick between bumble-gum blows and candy swiped lips.

She'd climbed over two tie-ups just to lay her greasy paws on the back of my shirt. Said she'd know'd it true by the fit of my shoulders. How she ain't never seen no set a steer haunches like 'em Fairchilds carried.

Of all the times I'd gone to the Cocktail Cove, which couldn't number more than three, I'd done so for reason, a look see for a particular lot, there brother, a family of runners, runners of things—the Georgia Mason clan. Stood on the edge of a fuel dock with a cooler full and a fifty tied to the end of my hand ready and waiting for anyone heading out who'd lend a ride. Promise of another if they'd do the solid of bringing me back. Worked ever'time and not cause folks needed the money. If they's rich enough to have a boat, they's rich enough to afford the gas. Funny enough, it were the beer that got me on most. Just like it were the beer that crunched ice cold through my veins while Sally went on 'bout how long it'd been and where ya were and if we'd talked since and how she's sorry to hear 'bout Momma and with ever' gnash of yellered teeth spinning outta don't-know-shit-'bout-shit-mouth, I reckoned the only thing that'd do were to stuff a fat cock down past her chompers to stop all that hot air from spilling out, and it didn't matter one way or another whether it me or somebody else long as the job got done.

Yet on and on while the sun left iron prints on the back of my neck, while my hand locked frozen on beer after beer after beer, she kept on 'bout her life and how she'd gone along with one sorry cocksucker after another and how all she needed were a "real man. How 'em good one's is so hard to find and she heard tale once from a friend of a friend of a friend, who'd met herself a real live beau from outta Charleston right here on Cocktail Cove and how she intended to come ever'day of the summer 'til she did the same." 'Til finally, after piss ass drunk done crawled up my spine and sent shock waves of numb over all my limbs with lips spilling dribbles out the edge just so's that nasty swamp ass air could slip in, that Sally plainly fell on my dick and not in the way a man's wont to experience but in the sort that leaves a stain on ya for a good week after and there's a constant check to the nethers for precautions and notes of any new growths.

Gutter-fucked her raw, Mick, and weren't a thing pretty 'bout it. Nor right like enjoyable, I'd add. But a thing needed done nonetheless.

So there I were bent over the hindquarters of the girl ya got caught playing fiddle stick with way back when at consequently the same time Torpedo Tit come out with the wash on the backside of their place and to ya and Sally's surprise did not take too kindly to the site. Dropped that basket, madder than shit, and hauled 'em big atom-bombs hanging from her chest, each one swaying opposite from the other, the fear of their smacking together again instructing Gawd when to blow the light out on the world, ya barely able to pull that baby snake from Sally 'fore Torpedo Tit'd both hands round it giving the world's worst shake down of an Indian burn that'd left it blue, black, and swole for damn near six months after. Not to mention marked up that right side of yar face from where yar head knocked-damn-near-drag-out-dead from the drop when she finally let go of yar squiggly.

Just pumping away on smeared-liner-mascara-festooned-plumped-drunk Sally on that boat, me, yar long lost hated brother. Can ya believe it? Of all the places, Cocktail Cove were the spot where I fucked her and finally met my Dad, Willard Tell.

5

1930

HOUND BONNEHUE

When I's knee high to nothing I wore dresses. Long tattered frocks lined in stripes. Some in polka dots or designs too faded to tell. I's the third to pass through 'em. The third to piddle and live tripping over my little feet 'cause I'd not yet growed into 'em.

They's the cause to many things for me. Picture of me somewheres, locked away in a drawer or tossed off in a broke frame hunkered down in a pile of webs near the corner of an attic. They's out there.

To know me now, ya wouldn't believe it. Call me a liar right to my face probably, which wouldn't be the move to make so's ya'd keep quiet on it all, carving out fibber on the insides of yar lungs just so's it confirmed somewheres ya ain't buying it. But back then, well back then I's known to play round in the dirt with fabric tied round my thighs, hiked up near my knees. That frilly collar someone'd insisted on being a part of the fucking thing tucked down and itching my chest and neck.

Weren't my Mommy and Daddy's fault they couldn't afford nothing better for their only son to wear. That's just how the holler worked, ya know. Made due. Hell, I's lucky. Knew a boy whose family done turned him out. Poor fella's Daddy done got caught up in a feud he'd no footing in and went down river from there so to speak. And that boy spent seven of the ten years he'd left in him 'fore coming of age, which at the time weren't nothing shy of thirteen, toiling the land of a not so friendly man his Mommy's new husband done sold him too. Word carrying out all over 'em hills that new beau weren't the type to take in another man's son but he'd sure found himself a place for all three of his sisters.

My complaining 'bout wearing a dress didn't really make all that much sense. Don't mean I didn't mind it. I did. Hated the gawddamn thing. Wished with all the might a kid could that my Mommy'd popped out some boys 'stead of two girls. But wishing and wanting got little to do with having.

I's named after my Daddy's father, Percy Moses Bonnehue. Now, why my parents lacked the fortitude to go ahead and switch that phrasing round were directly connected to the events surrounding my getting the name people knows me by today. Received my birth name due to some other bastard receiving his, who were handed down that same one I's getting from a Mommy, who at one point or another'd enough humor in her to think it funny to name a boy Percy and send him out in the world in a dress. And due to the giving of that name to all 'em generations of men, we's forced in a way, perhaps more than most, to be meaner than a coon protecting her babies, which sends me to that latter extension where I's forced to prove just how vicious a boy named Percy, standing round in a gawddamn nightgown passed to him by two sisters who went round saying shit they knew they weren't supposed to, to a group of boys they's intent on playing tongue with, were.

See, not unlike myself they's another boy handed with another family name who lived down the valley a ways. Esom Dean. Named after his Daddy's Daddy, Esom Roth Dean, and what that entire family'd had in common were a particular set of sumabitchness that seemed to travel through the bloodstream and infect ever' single one of 'em red headed turds. It were him that carried that boulder to the edge of Michner's cliff and dropped it off dispelling both my sisters' good nature. So's naturally it were him who became the reason behind my ever venturing forth in a grapple. Daddy couldn't be bothered with the thing, more than enough trouble waiting for him in town. And it were damn near too long past for my making a name. Going on ten and all, walking round in dresses like I's doing seemed 'bout due my turn at earning a stripe with a scuffle.

Didn't take all that much for the accommodating to begin. Sister rolled into the house, which weren't nothing more than a room with sheets put up, crying and hollering 'bout some girl telling some other girl that they's nothing more than soiled trash. Shit couldn't stand, ya know. Couldn't have people mouthing off like that 'bout my kin and hell I's more than ready and willing to go out there and do something 'bout it. So's I hightailed my ass down the hill. On over past Lester's and good sweet Gerri-Lynn's place and walked right on up to that Dean household, which weren't nothing more than a scooped out hunting cabin converted, and barked for Esom Jr. to carry his skinny ass on out to the yard.

Couldn't keep my sisters from my heels. Came plodding along and what tended to happen when there's a boy all of six feet tall with a dress drawing near up his knees and two grown girls tagging behind him, happened. Gathered ourselves a gaggle of leerers interested in the surroundings of my leading. So's that when I looked back, found my two sisters, Lester and his three kids, and Gerri-Lynn and her husband and their two growns and then their kids, and some feller who just happened to be taking a walk'bout, saw the commotion and decided to follow up as well, and that paired with the fucking ragtag team of children the Deans birthed—must've been damn near twenty five people standing round waiting for the beginnings of that there wrestling to begin.

The fight itself something for the books. Took all of maybe three hits 'fore that boy, who mind ya were five years older but two inches shorter than myself, realized there weren't gonna be any let up on him. My Daddy hadn't raised nothing like that. Chopping wood and towing never served my shoulders so well 'til I threw that first cut out to skin. But just as my Daddy done for me so'd Esom done for him and there weren't no room for any budge on his part. Not as it were in front of his folks and the lot of those on watch. With ever' jab and pull I gave, he gritted up and found a little something left to reach back out on me.

Now what's fair were fair most times, two boys throwing bows in a yard probably fell somewheres near that'n there but 'em Deans were a group of sumabitches if I ever met a few and not long after I'd pinned that boy's face up under my heel and gone through the heave and tow my shoulder's so accustomed to, splaying out drops of brown ruby on that gawddamn dress I's forced to wear, Esom Sr. stepped out on us and poked a Savage rifle in my back. Shoved the end of that barrel through that thin layer of fabric, worn through now by all the years of my wallering in it, and jammed it in the root of my spine.

"Best carry yar ass home, hear, 'fore I change my mind how I'm going 'bout my day," he splayed.

Well, I didn't have no use in dying all it boiled down to, pretty much. No use for it all. Come there to settle a score and whoop some asshole from here to next week and don't reckon I enjoyed the part where we'd found ourselves a joiner in a situation there weren't no room for him to be in from the get-go.

Splitting wood ain't so hard. Don't matter how thick. Ya hit it direct, it's gonna tear in two. Sometimes maybe even three.

When the hewing's done, Lester'd shielded his kids eyes from me. Feared they's not ready to see the boy in the gown's face after ripping another boy's skin loose, that boy being Esom Dean, with his bare teeth, and once satiated with the wound moving on to the father, Esom Roth Dean. Knew 'em screams I'd heard while the act in progression came from Gerri-Lynn as she and her husband and their kids and their kids tried desperately to forget that image as they went tearing from 'em hills all fast and flighty. Sound biting back in crunched twigs and broken dirt, aiming breaks in between my chomps and blows.

Walked back from 'em Dean's carrying with me the blood of a father and a son. Blood on my lips and in between my teeth from where biting were the only thing could be done that hadn't yet. Blood under my nails. Mixed there with torn off skin, packed down like salted meat saved up for winter. Blood coating that once yellowed dress with faded lines now appearing like sheens of paint. Walked back with my sister's feet rarely filling the ten-foot gap they's keeping between me and 'em 'cause they's afraid I might forget they's kin and turn back on 'em. Walked back knowing that there's a name hollered out over and over again by a wailing woman cradling her boy and his father in her arms, or what's left of 'em, and that name'd be the one I's to have for all my days since.

Dress flailing 'bout like it were, me scrapping on all fours like I was, can't say I blamed 'em.

6

1930

ALBERT TODD

"Mister Todd, sir, I knows ya's a busy man and all and I 'preciate the time ya give me. Seeing me on short. I do. Can't fathom how it is yar days go 'bout. All I knows the mine. Ya know, just the mine. Ain't nothing else I've ever set foot in, 'cept that mine. Done worked it now, supposing all said and done, better part of forty years. Yessir that's right 'bout right. Forty years.

"Born and raised in this here town. Right here in Hazard, yessir. Sure enough were. Whole family done never moved from it. And not 'til, must been two years now, most still living here with us. Cora and Melba Dean rushed out on us in winter and Calhoun went down shortly after. Just me, mine, and my brothers still going now. All of us connected to the mine. We's grateful for it. Can't make no bad talk otherwise. When Mister Davis first showed up. There's a great deal of thanks to be passed round. Brought in all the stuff he done. Gave us all the things he done give. We ain't trying at a bite to the hand that feeds. Ain't it at all. All we wants is fair wage.

"I knows ya's a busy man. I sees it. Sees ya going over 'em docs ya got stacked high. Signing scrips, huh. Mighty obliged for ‘em. Mighty obliged. Thanks to it be. Thanks for the store. For ‘em houses. Nicest thing any in my family ever done had. Mister Davis is a nice, good man. A fair man. That's what they says ‘bout him, now. Couldn't utter it out any other way. Wouldn't have it. No Sir. Wouldn't have none of that talk ‘bout Mister Davis. Not on my watch. Not on any watch. ‘Fore he came in this town there's barely a thing. Really. Not a thing. Just land. In with the train. That's what they said. Don't have to tell ya that. Ya knows it.

“Signing Scrips. Boys gonna ‘preciate that. We certainly do. Gonna go back home, give Cora the lot of ‘em, have her go on to the store tomorrow. Buy up some things. Suppose we all handing over to the wife. Right. Said, ain't it right. Ya just married ain't ya? Baby? Bet she's just as purty as anything. Ever'one loves ‘em babies. Gots me four myself. Sure do. That's how most families go round here. We like to breed ‘em. Gonna send Cora to the store. Send her for some things. Give her ‘em scrips. She knows what we need. Can't keep track of it all myself, ya knows. She knows how it do.

“Speaking on the store and ‘em scrips. There's been a slight run round on some folks. Mister Davis always said come to ya first if there's things a doing. Said he's an open door ruling round here. And, well, seeing as how ya's the one doing all the managing nowadays since his taken slight ill. Thought it—hate I'm disturbing ya so. Busy and all. Look real busy signing ‘em scripts. And we's thankful for ‘em. Thankful for the job. But, see, there's been some issue at the store. Well, ‘em Whitmires, they's been having problems with Randi. He done put ‘em on lock. Straight shut trade down on ‘em. Whitmires live over from me, now. Live in the house next. Been there ever since we's given ‘em by Mister Davis. Good man, Mister Davis. Ain't one to pry on it now. But the block been going three days now and they's some youngins on ‘em. Got a set of three babes and one older. Oldest just started up. Sure there's a scrip being signed for him in that stack ya got. Mighty thankful.

"Problem of it is, Cora, my wife, she been going over giving 'em part of our goods. Real Christian like of her. Real fire of the Lord breathing through her veins. Certainly do. Ya look a Christ fearing man. Y'all get up to church much? Ya and the fam? Bet yar wife do. Refined folks like y'all be, bet y'all living and breathing with His ever' step. Providers. He provides the hope. We aim at ever'thing else, right? Right. Cora's a good woman and so is Patsy, Wilmer's wife, Wilmer Whitmires. He's a good man too. Hard worker. Worked with him all these years. From the beginning. Lived beside him all that time too, like I said earlier. Wouldn't step out of line for nothing. A good man. And now Randi won't let him have nothing from the store. Even when he bring in scrip. Randi just takes it. Puts it up. Says it's for the past due. But he don't let him have none of it.

"Randi ain't never give no reason for anyone to ever cross marks on him. He keeps the store open seven days a week. He'll order things needing ordered so's shelves is stocked and people go and come as they please. How he's always been. How ever'one always been. Town been fine with it all. Certainly do. All of us getting by. Waking up. Doing our jobs. Tending to our children. Even when there were that problem couple weeks back with 'em boys getting too lit after dark. Only needed spread but a whisper for it to get squashed. Formed ourselves a little group. Not like, not a group like that. Ain't never need worried 'bout a group like that. We's all understanding what that'll do. Weren't even a group really, nohow. More like two or three that goes round watching for drunks. Makes sure no one's stepping out of line. Save ya the trouble. Can't have the foremen doing their job and that'n too. Can't have it. We settled it fair for ya anyhow.

"Whitmires' youngest, Maddie, done set up to crying from the break of day 'til she get so tuckered out, sleep's the only thing that'll take hold. Cora can't give her off nothing more. We got mouths to feed ourselves. Mean, she would if she could but she knows I'll get on her if she goes to not eating again. She'll do that. She'll feed the entire camp then not eat herself if that's what it takes for babies to go to bed full. All she cares 'bout is 'em babies. Don't matter if they ain't hers or not. Says, 'We all Gawd's children, so they's all of 'em like my own.' Good woman.

"Whitmires tried talking to Randi now ever'day. Goes ever'day after work and ever'day 'fore it. Tries to bargain with him. Tries for something. Walks right past that big box Randi's got and tries a hand at Jesus on him. That crate just glaring over it all. And Randi don't budge none. Don't say a thing. Just locks his eyes on that box like the world's drilling in him. Ya know, when that crate first come in, we asked him what it's for. Treated us just like he's treating Whitmires now. With plain nothing. Didn't speak nothing to it. Nothing 'bout it. Nothing. Dee Henders told Cora, crate's moved three times since he's got it. Three times. From behind the counter. That seal of special delivery bleeding black sear over the wood. Raining when it came through. Knows it 'cause Cora saw two men dressed all up in Sunday's best bringing it in. Said the seal took to a bleed from the travel.

"Anyways, Dee said Randi kept it on the back shelf but it took all three of 'em just to put it up there. And weren't none of 'em not blood shot red when they's done with the heave. Then Dee told Cora, they moved it slight. Made it so that seal were facing out. Said when they first put it up there, it weren't. The seal. It were on the other side. Backed up to the cans and flour bags stocking the back wall. But then the men noticed and moved it.

"Well, I didn't think nothing of it, now. Didn't think a thing. Figured it were brought in for Mister Davis and he didn't need nobody prying in the business of his doings. But then I stopped in myself. Went in for some things Cora weren't able to get. Said Randi done told her prices changed. Said when she brought her lot up to the counter and laid out what I done give her to spend that it weren't enough. Maybe she'd done heard him wrong or something. Or maybe she'd accidentally not grabbed enough scrips. Been known to happen. Probably were the case right? But then she said he done to her what he done to the Whitmires. How he'd not give 'em scrips back to her. Said he put 'em back with the Whitmires. Told her he's holding 'em for when she brought in more. Then she could have her things. Then she said when she went to leave, she saw Randi done moved that crate. Moved it on top the counter. Right next to where she's standing. Special Delivery burning holes in her.

"Now, I knew there's some sort of mistake when I's walking in there. Didn't think nothing of it 'til I come through Randi's doors and seen that damn crate done moved again. It were pointed right at me. Right there in the middle of the floor with cans stacked up on it. Special Delivery greeting ever'one who's to come through. Caught me off guard is all. Like it's meant for me. Like it's meant for us all or something. Ya just keep signing 'em scrips, there, Mister Todd. Don't let me stop ya. But, see, it's just that, well, when I went up and tried talking to Randi 'bout my wife not being able to buy nothing he said, well, he said ya's the one who told him. Told me ya's the one who said prices got to go up. Said weren't nobody allowed to get nothing unless they paid double. Said he's just following what he's told. And the thing 'bout it is, don't mean to second guess yar doings, ain't trying nothing like that but if what he's saying's right, well, ain't none of us gonna be able to afford nothing. Have to save up an entire month's earnings just to buy the things we's needing.

"So's I asked for my wife's givings back from him.

"Said, with all due respect, that I's gonna have to count what she done gave and what we's soon to get and see where's we at. I knows ya's a busy man, Mister Todd. A busy, young, not too young, though. I knows ya went to the schooling. That's why Mister Davis got ya running things but could it be, maybe, could it be there's been some sort of misunderstanding?"

Henry McCluen shifts, his feet caked in black, his trousers displeasingly sooted in much the same way, the hat which holds the wax from where the candle fits on the brim to see in the mines trembles in his hand as Albert Todd's fingers stop mid scribble.

"Mr. McCluen," Albert Todd slapped down on a stack of thirty scrips, his nails polished, brassed, and emboldened, a young man of no more than twenty, and he looked Mr. McCluen in the eyes and said, "Mr. Davis was right to speak so highly of you."

"Thank ya, Mister Todd, thank ya."

Henry quickly turns to go, knowing Mister Todd's time not a thing to be harped with any longer but just as he reaches the door, Mister Todd speaks again with a rush that burns his precision towards exemplary penship to a halt, "Perhaps, you would be so kind as to tell Mr. Whitmires and any other men whose scrips were taken, that they are to meet at the store tomorrow at dusk for proper compensation."

"Yessir. Yessir. Yessir, indeed. I'll be sure to do it. I thanks ya."

7

1990

RONNIE FAIRCHILD

Across from the splatter of Blue Buffant's untimely death stands a tree. On it, the carvings of youngins' promises to one another. Marked by X's and O's and hearts and forevers tagging the base where even if ya could get right up on it and spread yar hands round with a friend meeting up on the other side, there wouldn't be no touching of hands. An old oak. Branches carrying on over the ground like they's bridges made for walking over, like there's fire water bubbling down below 'em, only hope at yar feet not melting, hopping tow on bark and braving up the ledge 'til higher, safer ground found. Planted round the time a plantation existed where I set. Branches holding out bodies of boys and men who'd done got cross with a master. Imagined there's tobacco planted up nearby, back up behind that brush fanning down on 'em roots.

That tree done seen and heard more in its existence of knowing and being than any man care come across this very gravel I's planted in. Knew there's things ain't ever meant being defined or touched on or explained, that things just aimed at happening at times. Like when some bastard done decided the need for a road to run up on it. Tree didn't do nothing but suffer the loss of dead roots, then bear down in the ground few feet over and go on 'bout it. When that limb done fell from it, from some drunk smashing head light first, the smatterings of plastic littered up next to a heart with the initials A+J carved deep, probably didn't even flinch. Said to itself, I done lost some 'fore, gonna lose some still. Couldn't be no waste for whining. Couldn't go holding on to weight like that or cawing out why's in the dark of night. No point in all that. No point in making that a focus. Can't get locked up on that. Ain't its job.

Focus come in colors for that tree. In remaining standing after all the years it's faced, after all the men done tried their hands at force on it. Can't stress energy on that. Not when there's reds and oranges to be made. Not when there's sun to take in and wind to blow through. Not when there's life still moving. Naw, it does what it does. What it's always done. Let's that fire build in it's base, fill up the core, travel over 'em tiny mounds of skin plotting it's body 'til it can't go nowhere but out, 'til there ain't no holding back what needs doing, and 'em leaves come out all bright and blood and rage filled and for all the reasons I'd long forgot 'em colors reminded me of Betsy Tomlin.

They had it so's that when ya passed by the Dairy Mart, only one thing usually come to mind on a hot, end of the summer day. If there's money in yar pocket, which weren't ever the case up to a point for me, it were whether ya's to go on with the splurge of a flurry after ya'd downed yar burger. But since I's poorer than fucking dirt, up to a point, only thing worth stopping for were to stare at Betsy Tomlin and wonder how the fuck she managed squeezing that body in 'em tight ass clothes. I don't know how or where she got 'em and I didn't give a sure-fire fuck to their origins neither. All I knew is there weren't nowhere else a boy's like to come cross a girl dressed like that unless there's a trip made to a city and that required two things most didn't have in Hazard. Lest, not any folks I'd come to know well.

Betsy come to Hazard by way of her Daddy. They'd come for the same reasons ever'body come. Work up in or for 'em mines and the biggest one to date were run by Albie Todd. Some time later, funny enough, Betsy's Daddy and I's to have a run-in that'd prove quite comical, all things considered, but at the time of my salivating over his daughter, he didn't know me from diddly squat.

Anyhow, they moved here special on the request of Albie Todd and it were ever' male in town's delight that Betsy just so happened to take a summer job at the Dairy Mart. Way she handed out 'em fucking flurries drove ever' man in this county and quite possibly the next to utter batshit craze. Swear there's a moment in ever' man and boy's mind this county and the next thanking Gawd they'd moved here just so's she could hand out 'em fucking flurries. Be a gawddamn line formed thirty minutes 'fore she even started her shift sometimes.

At the time, I remember running shine for one of 'em nasty Meaks. Only way'd I found any money in my pocket in 'em early years. First job I'd got that didn't involve hoeing or picking. Simple enough it seemed. I's to hand off a supply line to a man named Mac. A test run, what Dwight called it. See if I got what it'd take. Some shit like that. And hell, weren't like I knew anything better. I's given tutelage that my only job were to make sure that lightening didn't get handed to nobody other than or I's to get it good by Larry, what I's told by that yella teethed fuck, Dwight. I's to wait on Mac outside the Dairy Mart. Collect the trade. Then head on back up to Nanny and Papaws 'fore supper hit the table. Neither of 'em any bit the wiser to my enterprising ways. That were the plan. But that were working under my not knowing what it were exactly I's dealing with.

Well, I done what I came there for. Set down on the backside of the Dairy Mart with jugs a sloshing, not thinking a thing other than how I needed Mac to get a move on and show up. Didn't think nothing of the line stacking out twenty or so waiting. Didn't think nothing 'bout how if someone were to step from that line and go to asking questions 'bout my reasonings behind waiting out the back of the Dairy Mart might lead to conclusions that'd get me in a whole heap of trouble if anybody took the time. Didn't think 'bout how it might be better for me to not squat like I's doing with my arms tucked round my knees and my ass dragging ground 'cause my legs were tired from the trek nor how my head's pitched up right near that back door so's that if anyone where to give it even the slightest push I's gonna see stars. No Sir, did not one of 'em thoughts come crawling and poking and when that door slammed wide open with fucking Betsy Tomlin carrying out trash she'd probably insisted on trucking to the can herself, 'cause Gawd knows all she'd have to do were bat 'em purty green eyes and the world would've opened up for her and swallowed it, she nailed that ass of hers right square in my face and both of us went to a tumble.

Might could argue I'd done succeeded in getting what the whole county's in the business of waiting for out front. To remember it now, how I'd not hightailed my ass back up that hill, trucking that hooch on back to Dwight with embarrassment shoved down my pants along with the throb of feeling a girls body, however big or small a part I played in it, I'll say were more due to being young and dumb than anything else.

Our stumbling ended in quite the displacement of things. Poor Betsy's bag of an afternoon's run of heavy-eyed men went to gushing over grass and gravel alike. Smooshed and melting still, bowls of milky white spilled. Half empty ketchup packets spewed red on blades of green, threw two bitten downed hot dogs out in the wild for feral animals to forage for later, and there sitting and stewing in the middle of all that were Betsy Tomlin glaring rattlesnake mean at me for causing that bag to go bursting up and through her blouse. That tight piece of fabric hiding up 'em watermelons bigger than any girl should ever be carrying at such an age went to translucent but not from what I needed it to be.

Seemed in the knocking of her ass to my face I'd made a fumble myself. As contact made, my hand tipped back, left that hold I needed to keep 'em jugs from toppling over and I'd hit ground, though my feet'd gone up from the smack, and I'd managed not only in succeeding at making the biggest ass of myself I've ever done, honest truth, but also in kicking that fucking shine loose all over poor, poor Betsy. And there planted behind that white veil that no boy or man's ever granted look behind unless given due permission or after shelling out something were the stare back of what ever' man in the county'd give their leg and arms to see—big, perked up, nipples.

"Shiiiiittttt," she said it like it were something she'd only heard her Daddy say 'fore and now it were finally the right time for her to break it out.

"Betsy, I…"

"Just shiitt." Second time came a little easier.

"Betsy, I didn't see ya. Shouldn't have been standing there, I don't know what, how, ya ok?" Went to panic. Words coming out faster than thoughts jumbling round. Decided talking wouldn't do. Went to take off my shirt. Thought maybe it'd work for her to put it on. For her to hide 'em gawddamn most beautiful things I'd ever laid up on.

"Here," I yanked my t-shirt off over her way, thanking ever' purty hair on my Nanny's head for just having washed it only yesterday. Smell of limestone and mountain rock floating from my hand to hers aiming at a compete with the burn of booze.

"What's your name?" She yanked the shirt from me, stopping for a sec, to gather her breath. The movement striking up the chords of fire that Papaw says tickles and warms the belly when the shine's good.

Panic settled up in my throat, made it so the word stuck hard on the skin, that ball preventing the sound from calling normal.

"Ronnie." The shine of 'em jugs loosing their appeal on me as the drape of what Mac and Dwight planned on doing once they found out a jug's missing.

"Ronnie, I know you?"

"Ya wouldn't."

"Then, how is it you knowing my name?"

Boobs came back into play. She'd stripped her shirt. There they were. Her fire engine hair barely covering the tops of 'em.

Speak. Speak. "Don't reckon there's a man breathing and living that don't know yar name, Betsy."

She smiled. "How old are you anyhow?"

"Thirteen."

"Thirteen, huh…"

"What?"

"You a little young to be waiting out here in the middle of the day like this, ain't you?"

"No."

"Sure, you are. Ain't even summer yet and you already playing hooky. Shouldn't you be in school somewheres?"

"Shouldn't ya?"

"I finished early. Right 'fore Daddy brought me here. Smartass."

"Oh. How old are ya?"

"Old enough. You got any brothers?"

"Got one."

"He older?" She flipped out a roll from her pocket. Saw the smoke were wet. "Shiiiittt."

"Sorry."

"I said is he older?" She fiddled with the end as if the wet were like to give to burn and suddenly the story of ol' Tom Meaks dying by fire flushed me.

Pulled up racing speed and knocked the smoke from her hand.

"That was my last one."

"Unless ya looking for a new face, I wouldn't do that if I's ya.

That's prime time right there and ya's doused in it, don't ya know nothing, girl."

"What you know 'bout that?"

"Not much but I'm getting there."

"Mac's gonna have your hide."

"That is if Dwight don't get to me first. Wait."

"Honey, Mac's been running shine through here ever since I got hired. I act like I don't see nothing. He acts just the same. But he ain't a nice man, sugar."

"Most of 'em never is."

"That's probably right. Hey, I gotta get back in, ok."

"k."

"You keep your head up there, honey."

"K."

When she went to leave, there weren't nothing to do but prepare for that ass whooping I's 'bout to receive. Hope to hell it wouldn't result in anything major and that I could at least get home and only receive it from the one instead of the two but part of me knew that wouldn't happen even then. Just set there and went on ahead and accepted it. Fairly certain, if I'd not seen the plaque covered in dried twig and mossed over mud, I wouldn't have been so comfortable with it but there's little else to feel after ya read:

To the memory of those who died on Nov. 3rd of 1930
May all 35 of 'em find God knowing we sent theirs to meet the other

8

NOVEMBER 3, 1930

ENOCH MURRAY

"Son. Times, people ain't gonna wanna give what owed. Ya can go on with it. Drive a mind crazy with the why's for it. But that don't never change nothing. Ain't what's important."

Daddy stopped mid-sway of next step, ferns crowding up near the brush down of black bite sprayed on his coveralls and he knelt down to me, 'em big worn-through tired paws grabbing hold of "my-not-quite-understanding-yet-little-shoulders," insisting this were all the things I needed ever know, and peered down deep in my soul and said, "Ya gots to take it." Look of dead serious shooting straight from him, injecting right to me as he chawed loose, "C'mon, we got's to go."

Daddy's pants weighed down near the ground. Crumpled over the lace up of his boot near the front and trailing out like little flaps come the back. They's carrying the black. It don't seem like he's bothered much by it, fast as he's moving. Shuffling over 'em burs, and brambles and briars. Don't appear affected by any of it. Too busy at it. 'Em sturdy legs laying waste to dead bursts of yella littering the woods. Felt like we's wading in gold. Made it so like there's a fairy tale buried near up and we's both in the business of finding it 'fore anybody else chalked up wiser.

I's doing my best to keep with him. Stepping where he stepped. Following his lead. Cutting past naked branches, fighting with the thicket. There's like to be twigs jumping out at ever' angle this time of year. All of 'em biting back at nature's ripping of 'em and by Gawd, they's pulling at a prevent on me. Keep me from keeping up with him. Some succeeded at it too. I's falling short of Daddy's patterned heavies. His long lumbers primed for no stop anytime soon.

Most days, ya couldn't tell where Daddy's hair left and where his skin began for that soot welted on the back of his neck. Black wore on him just like it did his britches. Strung out years of work in tracks on patches no bigger than my hand. Must've took a rag to it today. Drug a scrap of torn off shirt right cross the nape, dividing the line of what's his and what's there's.

Knew better than to ask where we's going. I'd heard Mr. McCluen spouting out something 'bout a meet up when he stopped by last night. I weren't so very young to know good news stopped delivery round six and anything past ten required a play at possum once that door opened. Didn't never even see one hair on Mr. McCluen's head. Just that sliver of Daddy's long john's flashing stank white from the moon's glare. Didn't know how Daddy took it or what it were exact Mr. McCluen were there imparting but the saying, "Meet up" came chalking out twice. What done give rise to that flurry in my belly when Daddy come hollering in for me, "to git with it and c'mon."

Wherever we's going, gonna take us thirty to an hour to get there. That's how long it took to walk to others and that's how far up the hill we lived from most. Hill folk. Holler people. However ya put it. That's what we were. Good thirty minutes to get to the mine and another fifteen to get from there to the camp where ever'one else stayed up at. Daddy liked a lot of land spread between us and 'em. Said, "prefer to see 'em coming if they came."

We didn't get many visitors. Which spoke even more to Mr. McCluen's stopping by and to Daddy's hustle now. Gonna be almost night 'fore we reached up close to anybody, and I'd be speaking to a fib if I didn't state, there's yet again come a mighty flutter near my insides at the thought of walking back in pitch black. These woods were worlds apart at night from what they were at day and it only took one misstep to end up landing on the wrong lot.

Cecil 'Doc' Hodge stood proof to that and his living next to us didn't help that unease swathing over me. Had to walk through his land to get either to ours or to pass on down to theirs and he weren't the type to let damn near nobody come traipsing through. Got hisself worked up ever'time like he knew soon as an inch passed over on his. And Daddy were 'bout the only one I knew who'd free range to go and come as he pleased.

I's purty sure whatever he done to earn the name 'Doc' little to nothing to do with no medicine. He were more bear than he were man, looked to be, weren't like schooling and him ever crossed paths. But somehow or another he earned it and it done stuck with him ever since. Even Daddy called him such. He'd stop by, holler out to the nothing of timber and bush surrounding, "Doc," like he's giving salutations to the forest itself but he later told me he's giving hellos to Cecil. Said, "Boy, if ya seeing him, it's like ya're too late." That were why when we crossed over the log marking our end and his beginning, I went to a double step with Daddy where I's damn near chapping his heels.

Weren't just any man who could make a life for hisself up here. First man to settle up in these hills rumored to be some sort of crazed devil. Went 'bout plaguing the land with dead animal hides and rants and threats to those who passed by 'til finally the man who'd been living in silence on the hill the whole time done had his fill of him, walked over and smashed his head on a rock 'til there weren't no telling what where the mans and what were the rocks no more.

Don't nobody remember the name of that crazy'd who made all that noise but there's certainly a tipping towards that other being a Bonnehue. They lived up the other side of us. Didn't get up with 'em so much. Suppose there's other families splintered in between but for the most part our little sandwich, Cecil, us, and Bonnehue's made up the most of it.

I ain't never seen no Bonnehue in person but from 'em whips spilling from my brother's lips there weren't no hurry for me to go finding out what parts were true. I's right comfortable being weary of one mountain man, I didn't need no other to go causing more strife. Plus, I's too gathered up in the notion of going to my first "meet up" to be bothered with the off chance that there's something worse out there than Cecil 'Doc' Hodge, though part of me knew it to exist.

We passed on it all. Passed over Hodges with no show of the bear man, jumped rope over that clearing where Bartlett and Bend met up, Daddy's steady two step convincing me we's alright being where we was, walked down and out on tiptoed leaves as we came close to 'em Meaks, who might could be a runner up to that man with brains splayed on that rock all 'em years ago, and trunked it up round that tree line overlooking town. Or as Daddy called it, Camp.

Camp stood in a stripped bare waste of what where long cleared by the Rail man on his initial come through. When they first laid eyes on it, 'em Rail men, they's proposing for tracks where 'em houses stood. That were the plan then, but Mr. Davis'd come along, he's old friends with one of 'em boys, and offered to buy up the land proper. Seemed that during the picking and laying of track, folks'd stumbled on a bit of the black. Not nothing big, mind ya. Not nothing like what they's pulling up now but enough little pebbles that it came honest there'd be a notice if someone ain't ever grown up round these hills. And since it didn't make no lick of sense to go moving people far up from where the mine'd sit, which were just 'bout a ten minuter from where

Randi's and all 'em houses now stood and given the land's clearing all ready bought and paid for, the camp and Randi's went up purty soon after.

Once we finally passed on over the mount and came clomping close enough down the hill where it all came into view, that's when I realized our meet up like to happen somewheres down up in it. Weren't much. Little shabby spot of a town but there's enough providing for a decent enough living for most.

When Daddy weren't giving it name—camp—he spoke 'bout it in a nod to that flat sprawling with nar a tree poking up between. Killing Fields. That's how Daddy always started the story. See, when a rail man goes to scout for track and finally picks up on something, they come in and they settle 'emselves in a little bit of a war with anything that's standing up in their way. Wrench and drag and cull the dirt of trees and bowers. Any sort of entanglement that's like to lay roots and cause problems later on. That's how the camp look like it did. Like some giant done went hard at a clearing. Knocking boulders down, rolling out dirt like he's making biscuits or something, pushing the leftovers to the side and up so's that it looked like the hollowed-out shell of a pie and all 'em houses up in it something for the mine to eat later. Least, that's how it came on to me ever'time Daddy went on 'bout it.

Name of the spot where we stood looking down were Windsor's Peak. A ten foot drop off into that softened up dough and out in the open of that killing field where ya couldn't throw a stone without ever'body in ever' direction knowing who and where and how. And funny enough for all that heavy breathing we'd both done making our way to it, Daddy took pause against a big pine, his back blocking my view of the flickering of lights popping out as night shutdown the sun.

"Git back—" Daddy's shoulder's heaved, that burnt broke hide busting through thin cloth as his hand shot down, preventing me from going more.

Don't step none further what that hand spoke to. Stamped and confirmed that whatever it were he's taking in, it weren't nothing meant at me being a part of nor around.

"Son, go on back. Go on up the hill and git Cecil for me. Go and git the 'Doc.'" Daddy's hand kept waving me back. Inching out commands that these weren't the things need viewing of a boy.

That hand wanted my tail kicking up chunks of clay back yonder, crossing back to all those spots we'd done been, aiming for treaties with the 'Doc.' Wanted me to go negotiating with that bear of a man up on his mountain. Didn't Daddy know that I'd rather have whatever come the other side of him than face up with that man back there. Didn't Daddy know what going to a "meet up" could do for the youngest of a set of three. How that tends to put some weight on a name. Make it so's the next time there's a whopping come his way he might know a thing or two 'bout the ways of man and how best to go 'bout defending hisself against it. How else to learn something if I ain't done viewed the experience?

Couldn't be all that much. We's just standing over Randi's. That two-room little store. Camp spread out 'fore us. Mine stationed up on the other end. Houses squatted out in rows of two leading the way. Seen it a thousand times, Daddy has. Done counted out ever' shingle on ever' shack, I'm sure, twice over while he's walking down to work. Just the type he were. Gawd Almighty, Daddy, please don't make me go see that man.

He couldn't keep me from going to a "meet up—"

Couldn't. Wouldn't.

Wait now…wait…Daddy…what's the cranking…what's that cranking…that don't sound right…what's going on…Daddy?

Noise came out the bellows of that killing field like that giant still carrying on and living. Came roaring over like thunder, carrying down the signature of the Lord in buckets of brass sounded like. Spraying out metal in flashes of click backs and overs. Chugging down fire. The clap-backs of the machine cranking out blasts of light that poofed and rose in sparks at Daddy's feet.

That thing he'd wanted held at mountain's distance from me crawling up from the valley of that baked pie. I only caught it in glimpses. In kick ups of wails clambering nails in dirt as they tried a flee from it.

Sounded like slaughter, though I'd only known it 'fore from the howl of chickens and pigs.

This were different.

This viewing dropped Daddy from the bark of that tree and slid him down to his knees, that steady hand falling limp over his leg. This done turned him to a mouth breather with cries held tight 'cause there weren't no air getting to him. That clicking stole it from him. Picked it up, carried it down, and put it in the middle of that latch so's the silence weren't the fall over of another cartridge filled but the slow steady pull of life from my Daddy.

He'd not wanted me part of it. Weren't no room for it and a boy. But that weren't left to him no more. Not once he fell back. Not once I saw what it were he's looking at. What were capable of doing what I'd never seen done 'fore, what'd rattled the soul in him.

At the bottom of Windsor's Peak, there were a group of men gathered. Round 'bout thirty in all, though it didn't feel right to count. Growl of that crank, of what I'd come to know later, of what we'd all come to know later in this county and all across that state, came from the pop out of black powder pushing from the core of a Gatling gun. Came down on the country spitting out steel from a round holding up six more at the ready just as long as that crank kept turning up and over. That clap back spurned from a lever hid up in the middle of that cylinder. It's job, the clipping out of that fallen shell just as soon as a steel soldier sent out to the field.

Weren't even a second of watching it, beholding that long trail of kill feeding into that barrel then shooting out its mouth 'fore I's forced to a knee too. Fell down right there next up Daddy, breathing out my mouth like there might be question to my mind's working. Nothing but stare, left in me out below.

There, on the ground, in the middle of thirty-four men already clipped and blown apart, their lives mixing up in the mud, were Mr. McCluen. His hands held out front, his life teetering on meaning, that thing that were kept inside the box went to quiet for a moment. The man cranking it stuck up on the problem with 'em early Gatling models.

But that silence done nothing for that ring burnt in my ears. It didn't do a damn thing but freeze time on us all. Pick us up from out of the mind's process and drop us down a hundred feet below so's that our hearts barely work and our limbs gone numb.

Only Mr. McCluen, who believed it a chance for change, his joints going at a move, slinging out the one foot from the other in the fold of his friends' mess of red and pickled and picked over flesh, went for a stand. Blood bit back at the bib, a tear he'd not known birthed in his side, spurting things meant to stay, out from his back. He can't seem to make sense, can't seem to understand what'd happened? What he's doing there? Why 'em shots stopped?

Daddy and I slunk back, our weight falling cement on our heels, our toes sunk in like roots next up that tree, taking in that pain that ain't got no name. The staring on it like some laying upon God, hisself, like holding up a hand to a light 'cause that's what yar body commanded to do. 'Cause there weren't no other left in ya. Body falling, were the react.

Mr. McCluen's feet went all clumsy underneath, done took to shuffling rocks with his shoes it looked. His head gone for the shake, blood falling in little rivers down the sides. Couldn't tell from the distance how bad they'd laid in him only that he's trying for sense in the wade of 'em dead men at his feet and like all who's watching from windows and peaks, we's all coming up at lost. He looked in pain and confused. An animal caught in barbwire struggling for an out. Ever' pull of muscle leading to a dead end as he inched towards that door of Randi's.

Mr. McCluen were older in body than he were in spirit. Not soft. Not weak. Weren't no one who survived very long round here who's weak. But brass give little care for weak and strong alike. What all 'em stacked ghosts still smoking spoke.

Daddy were right to keep me from it. The want to be man stripped and gutted from me with ever' forced sludge of Mr. McCluen below. I wanted to close up. Shut down. Forget I's there. Tell myself it weren't real. Tell myself the lie tipping that man forward down there. But Daddy kept. His body given out. But his eyes kept. He scorched William and Lonnie and Mr. Grave and Theo and Buck and Mr. Leonidus and all 'em others in his head and he gritted and gripped and dug 'em big paws deep into the earth and he made vow to make it right. And so did I. I stared back with hate in my heart, pumped back the scare of a little boy and watched Mr. McCluen take another step. His words too gargled to make out the command of his lips, but somehow or another Mr. Davis's name hid somewhere in 'em.

Then the click back. The shot out that ended and started it all.

9

1956

HOW I, RONNIE FAIRCHILD, CAME TO BE: WILLARD TELL

PART II

Smokes start tasting real good after beer number three. I's on number four with two whiskey backs pushing the train.

Noon. Second Friday of the month and payday done filled up the bar. Not my town. I's just passing through. Landed up in this'n here four days last. Hadn't made my leave, yet.

Called it Hazard. Hazard, Kentucky. Come midway through the trudge towards somewhere else but I'd caught tip to a little heat and needed a bunker. Pattie's were I landed. She rented a hole out the back and didn't ask much come way of dealing's past.

Most times it were out the car for me. Feet scrunched up under the seat, window pitched for a breeze. Take it to the ground during Summers. Carry a blanket couple yards from the road. Better out there when the air's thick. Liked sleeping out in the country. Liked the tone it set on me. Splurge on a room ever' now and then. Some dirt cheap motel. Whiz of the window unit buzzing over sleep. Empty set of six crushed at the mattress end. Sleep so hard, wake up not knowing where I were.

Directed to Pattie's by some sad looking fella come traipsing out the woods on me in his Sunday best. On his person, two rabbits tied, shotgun throwed over his shoulder, sleeves rolled on up, looking like he'd gone out on a bet to 'em trees. That lesson he'd long forgot, the one that'd sent him from 'em in the first place, found and settled on.

He were a good 'ole boy. Liquored up to high heaven. Eyes sending out rays of red as he pointed down the road, said, "Pattie'll do ya right. Tell her Johnny sent ya and she'll do ya right."

Come to find out, that Johnny ran a table on Fridays. And seemed apparent the game on second Friday, his biggest showing. Seemed weren't nothing else folks spitting 'bout other than their attending his abode 'fore she came strutting through that door. A blur holding hostage to all things following after.

One of 'em steal yar breath away walks that dared the lungs another gulp and shot an arrow to the gut commanding stay all at the same time.

Buddied up right next to me. Right next my stool. Spilling out that sweat that made life worth living.

10

1956

CONNIE

I don't give two good gawddamns to what's been told, the spelling of trouble don't never come without a wave of blonde and tall cut to truck frame. Motherfucker's gonna knock me up with just those two alone. Pack on a tan, some lowdown longing for the gaze puddles of blue, and a set of forearms meant for work, and I'm useless. Honey, I mean, panties down for the drop, goo swaddling loose near the lips. Trouble shooting laying down fire all throughout my tiddly bits.

And wouldn't ya know, once that shine swept out my eyes and that gloom of smoke mingling 'bout that always sets up to a hang in Pattie's, done gave to a cradle on my skin, I spotted that there trouble with a capital fucking T.

Should've turned right round on him. Marched clear. Gone on down to Mindy Mac's who charged me not even a dollar for a pull out the jug, and forgot all 'bout this cocksucker right here. 'Cause even in heels I doubted I'd meet his shoulders and I just couldn't be having that.

And where and what the fuck was Pattie thinking having all that squared up on her bar. That purty gridlock grin leaking out oil. Slicking women down in their areas with out so much as a shout out of warning. That dirty Bitch. I'm sure she'd found the occasion quite fitting to go missing her bra, letting 'em big ol' bitties flying loose ever'time she knelt down and pulled up a cold one. She sure as shit did.

Giving me a run for my money? She gonna try and bed that man. Make him think she's all the best Hazard can offer. Ya mean, to tell me, that yar cooch done been taken out of retirement in hopes of getting a little puss up on this motherfucker, here.

And him. That dusty down for trouble at just 'bout the drop of hat ain't got no business up round here. No mam. Ain't got none at all.

I think...I think it only right I tell this fool where it is he should go with all that. Surely do.

"Looks like ya been busy with the place, Pattie?"

11

WILLARD TELL

Weren't tall for nothing. Not short neither. Fit somewheres in between. Like the right type for most and the majority want for all. Way 'em pair of jeans fitted round that figure eight she'd cut cross that floor with a fade of life hard lived sending out buckshot calls, guessing that were leaning more towards the all part.

Body like that, I's surprised there weren't trumpets blaring out the sandwiching of gawddamn 'fore and after with the phrase. Come with it all sorts of complications. All sorts of threats and red and an ol' man coming after and a drive sealing her stink on yar upper lip. Yar dick smothered in that it-were-worth-ever'-minute-of-it-juice.

12

CONNIE

Arch that back out just a touch on him. Make it so's that ass come swaying out like a barnyard door with two purebreds rooting and ready right behind. Not none of that skinny lanky Pattie sort of shit. But some of that this-ass-were-raised-on-biscuits-honey-can't-ya-tell-shit.

Oh, I know ya can. Been at this game some time now. Know exactly what a tall drink like yarself been on the search for. Ya didn't even know it. Didn't even know ya's looking. But they all look. Take that hair down. Let that smell bathe over ya. Let those legs spread a spell so ya see the light through my thighs so ya imagine what other things might look like between my thighs.

Ain't even looked at ya yet and I got ya.

13

WILLARD TELL

She were a bad one alright.

Told myself come next week this town won't look no different than any other. Coughed up the lie and offered it over to my head down yonder that this weren't the sort that ended in any fashion of well.

14

CONNIE

Didn't need to know nothing 'bout him. Not his name. Not what he's doing here. Not who his folks be and where they stay up at. Didn't need anything like that pumping life to all that goodness.

"Take it neat this time, Pattie."

15

WILLARD TELL

Last bit of gold sparkling, my ticket out. Finish it and be gone. Forget the girl. Forget her smell. Forget her petite little shoulders and all 'em curves in all the right places. Forget that patch of sun spreading shine on her shirt, making out that tender flesh underneath. Get on.

16

CONNIE

Time.

"Leaving out so soon?" Turned on him. Slapped that whiskey down and 'bout faced on his ass. All slicked back, blue eyed, tan skin, tall, muscle-y, slab of a man, there to greet me.

17

WILLARD TELL

"Pardon." Damn near spit my beer out at her. Sprayed down all 'em freckles and blonde and purty greens in Bud.

Gawddamn.

18

1988

WILLARD TELL

—

THE DAY HIS SON CAME TO COLLECT

Toby were right in the middle of it, alright. Right smack-dab in the shit. Where he always were. And if he weren't, he were charging full force to get in.

"It ain't Ironhead, it's the Man in Black."

That no-shirt-cut-off-jean-wearing-hoe-skinny-boy cut more chew than most fuckers. Argue with the gawddamn wall if he could. Punch a fucking hole through it and holler at 'em boards if he felt the point lost. Do it 'til a cut of X crossed down the middle.

"Tell—"

That's what he called me.

"D'ya hear this shit, Tell."

'Bout to caw out how he can't believe his ears.

"I plumb can't believe my fucking ears. Dumbest shit I ever..."

They'd gone at it for an hour now this College boy and him and Toby were damn well close to hitting the lid. Impressed a mighty hard lick of shittards, fuckwads, cocksuckers, asswipes, blubber-bitches, all sorts of combustibles until the kicker, his favorite, the one he held dearest, the one that wallered baby-Jesus-deep in cumsquad-fuck-yar-momma-spew. It were what we's all waiting on. Ever' single rubberneck within an arm's reach, which sounds like it ain't a lot, 'til ya see how many folks can fit on the front, butt, and middle of a pontoon, a Monterey, and a Cruiser Holiday. Betting there were fifty eyes locked on watch. Including sad little Sally, who, bless her fucking heart, were in search of a man to take home to Momma and pop out some kids for the life-long in a sea full of let's-just-git-drunk-and-screw-reds, poor fucking thang. Made habit of tagalong to crusty Toby, thinking he might just hang the moon, swallowed laughs crushing "pick me" plumes steam rolling out her mouth to ever' funny or not thing that boy said. It were enough to rip a hole through ya if took it in for too long.

Mean, this were a guy, who'd opted to knock out his own front tooth with a hammer, a fucking hammer, a fucking-sitting-by-the-garage-door-hammer-that-ain't`-seen-use-since, well, fucking-never, on the rumor that there were a dentist who'd fit ya with a gold tooth for a buck and if ya made it a buck-fifty, he'd carve it up with a letter or something. Mean, this were a guy who'd spread-eagle-flying-squirrel jumped down five fucking bleacher rows at Atlanta Motor Speedway last year when some mouth-breathing-back-wood-fuck, Toby weren't above the pander, blew a spot of chew down on that cement right at the proper time when Bill Elliot took the lead. Felt, our Toby did, that were some sort of Mount Everest pile of disrespect. Clobbered down all those bleachers and beat the SHIT outta that boy and got his ass hauled off by four brick-wall-built security guards and banned for the rest of the race. Toby'd sported the #3 on a gold tooth ever since. Wore nothing but black ever since, just like his hero, and there weren't gonna be no way round or split in between that were gonna tell him otherwise. Soon as Earnhardt started driving Goodwrench black, that were what he'd be for life and Toby were hell bent on sharing the bad-boy-messiah's work all over the land.

"Bite back on this motherfucker and tell him there ain't no

way in hell the Man in Black's gonna go down in history as The Intimidator. Let him have it, Tell."

Toby'd honed bullseye on me first thing. Hadn't let go since. To be fair, I'd cracked his skull with enough fast-running chirps, barbwire couldn't keep him away now.

"Boy, I'm gonna…ya see that…just turn and look…ya see that surely motherfucker right there—"

Toby'd gone for the point at me. It were only a matter of time 'fore that pot came boiling over into the fire. It's what beer kept too far from the cooler on Georgia summer days'll do. Fueled piss warm down yar throttle with enough cooled mire, it'd go to make ya feel stuck and there's a fair amount of anger that churns up when a man's pinned tight. Dripped all down the lizard spine of him, breathing fight or fuck, and since he were spouting Molotov burns all over another man's ears and weren't the type to play pitch, it were looking like fight's gonna happen sooner than later. His bringing me into it were unfortunately the last hurdle 'fore we all heard KAPOW.

But best stop for a sec. and bring y'all all in as to how. How we met. Why we met. And what were the purpose in my carrying on with it? 'Cause the likelihood of our interacting for a spell longer than a dynamite fuse weren't all that high.

Come to me, Toby did, in a barrel nose pile drive at the end of two demon wishing inked wannabe goons busy with the half-hearted chunk of his 160 sopping wet man-child-ass out the storefront they called home. Landed face down in a chalk-outline at my feet with enough pickled vengeance in him to go ahead and chug life into all 'em gritty stick figures marking black on his arms. Just a full fucking motherload of gritty dudes and puked bullets and the blaring trophy-#3- daring ya to look the fuck at him. A full blown redneck reincarnate of Lee Marvin with slicked white hair, come from his Momma's bad side, or so he'd spell out later when he'd hit rock bottom on the hooch, a stretched out 6-foot-6 skinny frame, claimed, by him, from the leftovers of a seven foot tall Granpappy who could kick any man's ass anytime, anyplace, and a fuck the world tough guy mentality that'd catapulted his ass right back up and flipped a camel in between his lips just as soon as he hit the ground.

Stood right there in the crossroads of I-know-all-the-things and asshole lane of what-the-fuck-ya-looking-at-glory and spilled from the billow of a blue popped lip, from, the assumed beginning of that there fight inside, flashing that gold engraved front tooth, and that motherfucker said to me, a man he ain't ever met, a man who were standing in the dark, who outweighed him by a solid forty, and carried more than a fair share of better-cross-the-fucking-street-scars on his person, with the biggest shit-eating grin that'd no doubt ignited the whole fucking affair, "Ya look a man who can toss down a few."

Took me to a semi-family-friendly biker bar, which probably don't exist but in small boomfuck towns on the outskirt of blow yar brains out living and just enough space to get lost, always somewheres near a road named after a bridge, this one not part of the 'ception. Browns Bridge Road in a cinderblock dive where culled dreams live, we got shit-tanked amongst blue hairs, soccer moms, young slags, and a bare picking of pregos blowing doe-eyes at a styrofoam clenching Elvis impersonator who were pretty damn close to the original 'fore the fourth whiskey washed down and were the fucking finest singer my ears'd ever landed on by the time I'd hit the fifth.

Oh, we's thick as thieves, this newfound friend and me by the end of it. Our arms twined up round each other with a mic in one hand and an hour old beer in the other crooning out "What now, What next, Where to" and then a slobbering drop of a whisper pining out "Just tell her Jim said hello," and not a single fucker in there wanting to mouth-own the reason for wet piling brick heavy behind drunk eyes.

Weren't 'til the final washing down of late hour suds and slathered creaky heeled tweens thudding a sloshed version of Reba's "You're the one I been dreaming of," that I spotted Gerald Mason, which were the reason Toby and I needed to meet, weren't it. 'Course that the furthest from Toby's mind when he's chunked out the door by two-not- quite-skin-heads-yet-but-they's-leaning-towards-red-suspender-close-cusses.

Rationale'd probably, he just didn't want to drink alone. Only die hards got strength enough in their guts for that and he didn't seem old enough to carry the weight of regret just yet. Saw a man. Needed a drink. Made an opportunity.

And why go to all the trouble for a rat bastard like Gerald Mason? 'Cause Gerald Mason ran the biggest gambling ring outside the Bow Benders and held a tighter court than hens warming eggs. Wouldn't let nobody in who weren't vetted and spoke for and that were where Toby came in. Stupid as he appeared to be, family'd tied him to the Masons on his Momma's side, that same side that'd garnered that white hair to go on and take root and it were a thing ever' male in the family no matter how distant were rumored to carry at some point in their lives 'til the day they died, and I'd gone on the hunt for any man county wide sporting it and found Toby to be the easiest mark made. And just so happened, this piss poor replica of what-drinking-during-pregnancy-and-howl-at-the-moon-good-times-country-fun'll do were practically a stone's throw from Highland Terrace where all that shit went down and where a man couldn't even bare think of stepping foot on without ten-gun-trained-scorchers honed in on his person. List and ever'thing and brother Doyle working the entry with snake-bite mean coursing through his veins.

The plan, course, were to work Toby into enough of a frenzy with a load of barreling-bumper-car-fun-tales that'd go on ahead and spurn necessary for him, 'cause ain't it grand the need for validate and prove coiling purge from a boy who were too young for a war and hadn't yet found the call to arms strong enough for act yet, to impress upon his new found cool friend, a big mouth trade, "ya know there's this game..."

All that were needed. An in. A handheld lead through the gates of Highland Terrace, a ride down that winding graveled road, past all 'em trailers and beady eyes glaring watch, past all 'em barrels camo'ing behind window tint, just ya, yar escort, and a car cruising at a dawdling speed of fucking 2mph.

See a fella'd once got hog-tied drunk on some of Doyle's shine and thought right proper of hisself after going all in on deuce holding four, and decided a run for the winnings, stupid sumabitch. Got as far as the spikes laid down at Lavinia's, Gerald's niece, and got met with her ten-year-old crooning a shotgun outta sliding window, chewing back "Freeze sucker." No one'd spide hide nor tail of him since, and Gerald took it upon hisself, or rather his boys did, to go ahead and make rubble of that road, gargled it up with a front loader and spit the shit right back out in jagged chunks so's the only way to drive on it were at the expedient pace of get-fucked-slow if ya's doing wrong. 2mph to be exact.

Like to say I took that ride first night of meeting Toby...but I didn't. Hence, sitting courtside to the bottleneck-drop-out of a shit heap of rage 'bout to come from Toby to a good ol'college boy on Cocktail Cove, who'd jumped ship from his to ours 'cause of Sally's tits no doubt, and run his fucking mouth, which might make it sound like there's some vilify stuck to him, and that Toby within his rights of sanctitude, but it weren't nothing more than fucking STUPID stacked paint bucket high no matter what side it viewed. College boy's too stupid to know the fight's not gonna stop once he lifted that blade he's got tucked down in his boot up under that scrunched sock and Toby's stupid coming from his not spotting the metal 'fore the shit storm drooling I-dare-ya's outta his mouth'd got started and both their dumb shits not realizing the fat lady were growing mighty tired of the bullshit feather puffing and woulda just rather shot the both of 'em then listen to the shit carry on any longer.

And seeing as how the pile of gawkers now sprouted weed heavy in country field and there more than a fair share of white heads bobbing fishing lure bright along that now quite cove, and since I'd no intention whatsoever of spending more time than needed with Toby and he's proving 'bout as useful as a three legged dawg in a race getting me to Highland Terrace, and seeing as how that College boy's fists'd started to ball and clench and that blade-heavy-foot gone on to tap, and knowing Toby a scrapper but College boy a lifter, and my needing fast track into Mason territory, I did what most in my position would…cold clocked that sumabitch College boy with the end of my Beretta, picked the switchblade from out his sock, hit the button, and pitched it back over yonder to the Monterey that boy come from, metal spiking the side with a right honest WHACK, and sat my ass right back down, waiting for anybody else who might want to step foot in the shit.

Coulda heard a pin drop and there weren't a face not mouth breathing round 'cept for ever' white hair looking. They's all pinned tweezer eye tight. Well all of 'em but the one, an Eastwood-growling-fucker with tunnel vision pointed direct for me sporting a face too similar not to know though the meet up between a dodged bullet for the past thirty-six years.

19

1957

HAZEL MEAKS

Not for nothing and sometimes half of when, she felt like the drinking of tea stamped her distinct. Even though, the slurping on it never made a lick of difference to that spot that caused the grief. She could still make it out alright. That sense of viewing creeping over her thumb and pointer, molding her soft hands along the bump of passed down china. That dot of sparkling buried in the tree line, a spot of reckoning chortling sputters against what she tried at. Bore into her something fierce when she'd realized the only window splintering light in her room looked out to that mount and that dot in 'em woods.

In the quiet of winter mornings and those of the fall too, she'd stand folded in burnt sugar and mashed oat that wore like crusted edges along the fringe of a shawl, and she'd watch the steam from her cup rise and fog the glass. That twinkle going along with it. She'd wait for the blur, that part where the glass and the spot bled, fizzled in the haze and she'd write her name. The shawl's tentacles swarming along her skin in curved wraps and knotted twirls and clasped holds. She'd write the name left behind. Circle it round so there weren't no chance for its escape.

Bare knuckling that teacup, a surprise find at Merle's Shop For Secondhand Things. That feel of porcelain spreading back beyond the twilled threads, covering her skin in new and now. She'd think on the day of her finding it. The day she'd got her a job, how she'd walked past Merle's and there in the window listed by a marker of .25 cents, she'd laid claim, shoving the poles of her heels in concrete.

"More fitting for a person like me," wringing in her ears. Refined her. Leant comfort, that small senseless mug meant to impress. She clung to it.

Made her work out pleasantries in her head. What it'd sound like to have company, to have a lady's luncheon, tea with friends. She'd turn to that image of perfectly swept hair and arched brows, that blood red lip, that editorial pose models give when the world's watching, and she'd sigh and suck in her gut and remember why the cool feel of china granted so much. Why it made her different and better.

Ever'thing aimed at getting far and wide for her. Saved it up. A little pile of nothing much. Stored it in a Libby's tomato juice can. Perceived it a sign when she happened on it at the Hazard Coca Cola bottling factory. How something like that found its way from the big city of Chicago had to mean a thing and she took it that meaning were settled on a golden trail out for her. Ever since, with rigorous perusal, whenever there were an ad highlighting the benefits of Libby's, she felt the flutter of angel's wings leading her correct. Like she'd her own personal guardian come in the form of that slender visage in red standing right there in the magazine. That "what could," looking back at her.

She belonged with folks like that.

To her, that spot didn't really exist no more. She'd made up a story of a fire. Some disaster spreading out due to drought and a drunk. Some bastard falling asleep on a poor fire circle and that bottle clutched in his hand laying drip 'til the flames finally caught up. Sent down the plunder of some fifty homes once that red and orange finally squashed quiet with their lick. It were her backstory to why she didn't have no family round these parts if someone'd the hankering to ask. Didn't matter the actual fire took place some thirty years ago. Didn't matter her embellishment of a drought when it were due to the opposite. The flood of '27. Didn't matter the power plant the reason for its destruction. The Meak family still. In her mind, it were a drunk. A drunk and a still. A still catching fire. The flames rolling over the mount. The killing of a clan, the result.

Knicked 'em off like they's gnats on a horse. Made it so that glint of metal peaking from the green brush of pine, poplar, and maple couldn't possibly still hold true. Couldn't in no way be that other part of her. That rattlesnake done been took care of. Clomped off at the neck with a hatchet.

Years of working out that twange, of shoving down that brunt of seeing 'em things, of dealing with that man, of working in 'em stills, of walking down that hooch at an age she's meant for picking daisies. She'd got it so that if there's a new one passing through town and happened on her while she's standing out front the job, puffing one down, they wouldn't know she's from there at all. They might even say to 'emselves, "now, what's a girl like that doing in a place like here."

Mean, she'd put in the work. Shaved down the sides of 'em hips of hers with lycra and girdle, fitted out 'em little itty-bitty mounds in torpedo cones, and worked that hair ever' night in pieces of fabric she'd gone to the trouble of spraying down with an old diluted bottle of Chanel #5, more than half water filled sort a thing. She'd done made it the vision. Took it direct from 'em books she'd yanked from the one and only time she'd wasted money in a chair at Tammy's hair room. Turned her red with the way her hair set up. Convinced her, Tammy didn't know two shakes of damn at feathering soft curls and now that she'd the picture, weren't no need going to her again. And thank Gawd, she'd faired better than all her other sisters and wasn't granted with that big honker gracing ever'body else. Just thank HIM daily she did when she looked up after her face painted and on for the world.

Felt like she'd really done it. Like she'd really gone on and changed. Become one of those. Not one of 'em.

But. But in 'em mornings, when the tea and the shawl went to battle on her, when that last part of 'em clinged hold, that shawl being something she'd never meant at parting with, she felt the unburdening need, the firesome throw of the coals at her feet to not lie to the Lord and that's when and only when she were Hazel Meaks. Right there in 'em letters spelled out to Gawd.

With the window cleansed, Elizabeth Johnson hurried with the furl of an unruly curl, her eyes racing back and forth between the sheers laid out on her one and only table. Just simply would not due. Not today. Not when they'd put that new boy on shift next to her and they'd both gone at it with crazy eyes as the bottles shuffled by.

Would not do at all.

He'd asked her to go get coffee 'fore the shift. Stopped her specific. Right there in front of Connie and Betsy and June and Mary. Grabbed her arm and pulled her to him. The women left behind cackling like hens with their grins and twinkling eyes at the new hot man making moves on their Elizabeth.

He were the first man to ever be so bold with her. His hands melting like chocolate over her skin, like sticky, eewwee, gooeeey, sweet. She'd made Connie and Betsy ask ever' single boy on the third shift 'bout him. Came back with the name Joe Saber and how he's soon to get on with Albie Todd. Wouldn't be on the clock for Coke very much longer.

"Fact of it, he's slated to move on after today but wanted to stay special so's he could get a request in for a certain somebody," so said Connie.

They's to meet at Willie's Tea Room and Diner, a place she

couldn't afford, and one that dictated this curl's cooperation better soon come.

Twiddled.

Licked.

Sprayed.

Finally, stayed. Felled by metal and pinned through.

She'd planned on making a grand entrance. Allotted herself just the right amount of time to be five minutes late. That damn curl'd postponed her another ten and as it were, she's afraid, poor Joe might think he's being stood up rather than her yearning for fashionably late. A thing done nowadays.

Her reading weren't all that good but she could manage an ok pace if given the privacy and the evening last were spent in just that very dedicated strife of getting through a Vogue article that spoke to the Modern Woman. A woman of fine prowess, polite accommodating conversation, a look to stop 'em dead, and an air of mystery to lead 'em there. That last part not entirely advocacy for lateness but it were all Elizabeth felt she could do, given that true mystery, one she'd never reveal.

Why, it were only four months ago she'd made that promise to herself—this were the year of get out.

Get out of Hazard.

Get out of Kentucky.

Get out of the country.

Head for the city, what she'd promised.

New York.

Figured she'd pick up a man on the way if this'n here didn't work out right. Gave herself a deadline and ever'thing and seeing as how it were only Jan 29 of the year 1957, Elizabeth Johnson felt she's on the fast track. World'd just have to fall in line like that curl.

20

JANUARY 29, 1957

SAMUEL JOHNSON

"Whacha ya done, boy?" Samuel Johnson paused, his feathered gray tips moving in the green wind. His foot set to tap on a fallen poplar bridging the banks of a creek. Smell of something wrong laying track round his nose.

Devil's Wind, what his Momma'd called it. Said, "ya could tell soon as that air dropped what's brewing. Thicked up on ya, like the base of a rue. Pockets and clumps of cold catching ya off guard like there's evil lurking. Always happened right 'fore 'em heavy rains. Right 'fore 'em gates opened. Why Gawd rained down. Wash 'em bits of wicked away."

"Hard of hearing, said, whacha ya done, boy?"

Child stood caked near too his damn knees in silt by the side of the creek. Wouldn't take but a finger's shove 'fore he topples over, probably get hisself drowned in the process. Weren't no doubt his name ended with Meak, that's for damn sure. Mark of freckles bridging his nose and fire-bit hair flailing wild-like on him stood the testament. How far down the line from Ole Tom, Samuel didn't know. Believed he's, Ole nasty Tom, still fathering well into his fifties, though there weren't no new pick of litter coming through, if there's a meaning to be caught. Why, Samuel'd a mind on him to leave him there entirely, let his ass wait it out in the rain 'til some sense soaked up in him.

"Boy, ya aching to get left here, if ya don't get to talking."

Samuel didn't very much think too kindly 'bout hill folk and it were common knowledge 'em Meaks were the rottenest lot to come out of it. Weren't so very far from 'em, Samuel was, but being born at the base of Hazard proper and in 'em hills might as well be continents width far as Samuel's concerned.

If it weren't for the day being what it were, he would've treated hisself just fine to an afternoon of watching the storm roll in. Seeing as how his brother, Solomon already there with the widow Belcount, he almost worked up a mess of reasons for why it didn't really matter all that much his not making it. But the core of him knew that'd never do. Not on January 29th. Solomon'd have his ass if he didn't show, not to mention that little bit of guilt that'd go to stew and fester on its own.

It weren't that Samuel minded the company of Mrs. Belcount or that this boy here were really all that much of hindrance, it were instead the news he'd overheard on the line at Coca Cola factory—that new boy, Joe, meant to make moves on Elizabeth Johnson, who clearly weren't meant for no other man than him. Set in Samuel's mind ever since he'd first caught glimpse of her. Thought she's just as purty as a girl from one of 'em mags and if she kept even a remotely clean house, he knew his Momma'd approve. That were what this all 'bout anyhow. Samuel's hauling ass up the mount to Mrs. Belcount's on a day when the rain's sure to come, and come hard when it did. All of it for his dead Momma. And it sorta sent him to pickle when he entertained the notion that this Elizabeth Johnson were starting to overshadow the memory of the only woman'd he'd ever truly cared for. But he weren't so cold to it either.

For him, it were time to move on. Mrs. Belcount practically near her seventies, dealing with the loss of hearing in one if not both her ears and took too with blinders in her eyes the size of quarters, it weren't like she's built to notice for all that much longer he and Solomon's even stopping by. It were a terrible thing to think, he's quite aware, but that didn't mean it weren't the truth.

He'd life to live, didn't he? Moves to make. How's he supposed to go 'bout all that when he's trucking up for this and Elizabeth Johnson's on her way for coffee with that Joe fella. Didn't nobody understand these things? Solomon already rooted down with a family and child of his own, not that much of a stretch for him to continue on with familial obligations. But a young bachelor, surly Momma'd understand. As long as Elizabeth Johnson carried on in that one staple of truth, all of it swept under the rug, right?

Mean, from knee high to a grasshopper, both her boys listened to that absolute of absolutes, that their Momma thought a dirty house meant a tie-in with the Devil and they, 'emselves, were only to pick a partner fitting with such similar sentiments otherwise they's stepping out from the Lord. And that sort of living were doomed.

According to their Momma and most, Gawd were always on watch. No excuses. No deviations. No faltering. And this never more evidenced than in the home.

He remembered when Tammy Gardner invited Momma over. How she nearly fainted with the sight of 'em baseboards. How she's all of a sudden took to ill just to excuse herself from the company of such filth. How the longer she lingered next to such aversions, the more she felt like something wrong might befall her boys.

Most instances of Momma's visits with others followed in that same suit. Tended towered due occasion for expedient flight thereafter. But not Reba Belcount. When she'd gone over to Mrs. Belcount's place after that poor woman's husband were found dead in the middle of Jacklot Hollow, not a place, mind ya, their Momma cared going to, though it weren't a place she got up to all that often neither. Well, when their Momma heard 'bout that poor woman's husband, she hopped too. A bloated body turned upstream in the middle of Daniel McCluen's property, paired with the history of that family's past, weren't something taken down with a spoon of sugar. Fact, even at the age of ten and twelve, Samuel and Solomon knew this were more a salted cure sort of instance and did not and still would not be inclined to let their Momma venture out to the holler on her own. This, however, not a matter of debate, as their council neither sought nor inquired after at the time.

Having lost their own Daddy not a couple years back, they naturally did not question the reasoning behind their Momma's decision but assisted rather in the baking of one peach cobbler filled with three of their own canning debuts placed up on the shelves last summer. Mrs. Belcount living deep in the woods as she did were not all that accustomed to much company and barring the occasional visit from her sisters on the acreage over, her preparation for visitors perhaps not in the forefront of her mind. And yet there ain't many occurrences that the waft of fresh baked peach cobbler won't grant entry to. Thus, when their Momma showed up with goods in tow, Mrs. Belcount simply let her right on in. And thereafter, it were stamped in stone with nothing but praise and golden halos 'bout the woman who kept her floors "clean enough to eat on." It were saying a lot for a holler house.

Seemed almost a faint memory when their Momma'd asked her grown sons to look in on Mrs. Belcount after she left this earth and though the visits began with zeal, they'd fallen in habit the last two of the ten since their Momma's death. So that, it happened only on the day of their dear Momma's actual departure that they found the path leading up to the widow. An unfortunate alignment with that very same day Elizabeth Johnson were to take her coffee with Joe, even though Samuel'd yet to put in an application for her favor. That particular pairing of happenchance with the waft of Devil on the wind, a nod to a day better left inside than out, and the chance run-in with a Meak standing in silt by that same stream that'd delivered the Belcount widow's husband to the grave did not in the slightest, aid in the taming of Samuel Johnson's neck hair, which stood attention high. That the boy'd yet to answer charmed him even less.

Made for a question or two to uproot as Samuel glazed over the boy to the sky and the trees, and the silence of the leaves—felt like maybe he's playing part to a battle already lost so's that his mind turned and rolled like 'em clouds overhead. A boy raised in the holler not knowing a black bank of a stream weren't never meant for no steady standing. That ya'd go to sink and sink up fast just like it appeared this'n here done. That stepping outside, smelling that mix of hot and cold, that tint of green spreading out in the morn, meant there weren't no reason to go out unless ya had to and stopping for ruminations ain't one to necessitate it.

"Yar Daddy know ya's out here standing with yar thumb in yar ass?"

Boy looked up, eyes gone for the lean. "Who ya think sent me, ya shit."

Spoke down on Samuel like he'd grandfathered a litter, he did. All five foot two of 'em. All fifteen years or so. "Got yarself a mighty fine trap of trash spewing out for a Meak, there boy."

Boy unloaded a raw of spit he'd kept wedged in the back of his mouth. Let it fall down the dribble of his no-good-for-nothing gabber and spill down the front of a shirt not washed proper ever it were stained so bad. "Hand 'em out with the last name."

If Samuel were his brother he woulda knocked this boy's teeth out when he spit down that wad, that act alone disrespect enough to martyr the blood. But there weren't no living up to the reputation set forth by Solomon and the yearning to beat people never were a thing gracing Samuel's brow. In general, he's more given to the avoidance of most. Getting close enough to sprawl up a conflict worthy enough for a fight, not something he cared for at all. The boy on the other hand cut from that very same mold as Samuel's brother, he felt. Quick to anger and hot as fire when given the right fuel. So much so, that Samuel second guessed the bringing up of the boy's father, especially with that salty response, and would, if given a redo, start with something a little less vinegary. "Ain't nobody gonna offer up no help if ya's speaking to samaritans like that."

"Don't need no help."

"How I hear it, ya may not need it now, but ya's to need it soon, boy. Once that rain starts pelting down. Supposed to rain all night. Like to get yarself submerged."

Trouble with the Meaks, amongst many, were their lacking drive to ever travel alone. They's clan people. Folks bred, born, and raised to travel in groups. And some of the most stubborn sumabitches ever given walk in the dirt. "Who ya waiting on anyhow?"

Boy dropped his head. Fiddled for a tug of chew in his pocket. Brought out a wad of stringy black mess and stuffed it behind his lip. Waited for the situate to rest and lull the wad to a nice buzz. Then looked up and spoke out, "'em."

From behind Samuel Johnson and certainly to his unfortunate surprise came the following of the clan. Bathed in the smell of slaughterhouse, two elder Meaks lumbered up the woods with specks of red still sporting wet on their boots. Individually, they's big enough to crowbar through a locked barn door without breaking a sweat but paired together, good Gawd Almighty, they's sure fire suited to steam roll an entire county. Certainly, the likes of Samuel Johnson.

Not wanting to get his ass beat in front of a boy on the way to the Widow Belcount's on the day Elizabeth Johnson were to meet up with that fella named Joe and one as well where, on the chance occurrence he managed to make it back in time to interrupt their little interchange, he'd decided to wear the nicest shirt he owned, Samuel hollered out in a panic. "Glad y'all showed up. He just been standing out here for the longest when I stumbled up on him. Just 'bout to help myself to him. See if we couldn't the both of us manage a pull out that black."

It were a condition of the nerves for Samuel Johnson when he got flustered to say things like this in ways like that. Sorta kinda like as long as he's talking, weren't nobody paying attention to all 'em other matters. Stepped hisself in a whole heap of shit when he's 'bout nine or so. First day of school. First day stepping back from break and who did Samuel Johnson run into while he were looking the other way, while all the kids were already seated in the room, one room, with all the ages melded together for morning traditions prior to be broke up after, Mrs. Rutherford. The very sweet, purty, most wonderful woman other than his Momma, he'd ever known up 'til then. Ran right smack into her, with hand held out, a long lean draw on his form so that he's sure to fall in line with the exact amount of weight needed for that stupid door, 'cause when he weren't able to budge it last year, a panic fell over him for a good three months, a young Samuel landed his hand into that place a man's only ever meant to touch on his wife. Mrs. Rutherford knocked back on the floor. His little body strewn over top her. That small member he weren't quite sure what exactly it's purpose were, rustling to full mast as he squished against the subtle give of Mrs. Rutherford's form beneath. A straight-up, no other way of putting, onslaught of shit spewing, of phrases 'bout the weather and his Momma and his reading that stuff she'd assigned and his Daddy and none of it translating to his need to get up and get off, 'cause all focus on 'em words trailing. Took ever'one a good two-minute fit 'fore there's someone cooled enough down to come grab hold and pull poor Samuel off.

But as opposed to then when all eyes trained, the Older Meaks brushed right on past Samuel, knowing good and well, it weren't never his intention to go helping the boy, and tired from the fourth shift and the smell of innards buried in their skin and heads, they walked cross the log jutting over both banks and met up with their kin on the opposite side. Picked his ass up both with one arm hooked to his and ravaged that Devil Wind with the largest sound of suck and cleared out of McCluen's land without nar a look back.

To which on a very silly level, Samuel Johnson were bothered more by their sweeping over him as opposed to his not being beat black and blue and yet it weren't something he's meant to give pause on very long for that wind were turning to something awful overhead and Widow Belcount's place still a fifteen minute trudge.

21

1990

RONNIE FAIRCHILD

Ever' single person in my family were born of a consequence of Gawd. Might go arguing that were the case for most, Gawd's hand being up in 'em, meddling round, throwing down directs of what and where, but ours came without the cultivating of it. A tying together of us to him where even if, and mostly if, that religion weren't poked or prodded it breathed up big long gulps inside just out of spite. Far back as the line went, our births branded in the dirt.

Ephraim, my Papaw's brother, came rumbling out his Momma after she'd done lost it all. Barefoot and pregnant, she were, and fending off the Devil, hisself, it seemed. Man named Jim, that devil part came after he'd marauded all 'bouts on that mountainside so's that the one and two put together ever after, his name stacked up like a pile of logs burning out Devil Jim to all those encountering him. Name still carried the weight of his fire even now if mentioned. Great Gran'd lost it all, or that near enough, 'fore he'd even showed up but way some'd spewed he were responsible for it all. Problem is little flair goes a long way if there's notoriety tied behind it. Like to be half a county boasting to be related to the sumabitch if there's enough firewater in 'em and if there's strangers round willing to believe the horse shit they's stepping in. Great Gran's problems came on her through consequences of Gawd and there ain't no confusing her loses with a tie-up to no other than he just happened on her after all that losing done begun.

Lost her son Samson, dragged dead from outside to in. That little seven-year-old body stacked up next her feet 'fore two damn days when Devil Jim came. A mangy bad mutt turned worse with the rabies got hold of him, signs showing too late for actions other than. Lost her husband, the steelhead behind that young soul's departure by a shotgun kiss to the head, his body still propped out front in the yard from where he'd begged for her forgiveness only after. And Baby Ephraim running two weeks late, Great Gran'd pushed down the thought he'd join the two small mounds out back by the tree. Four boys, three dead, and one in question too much for Great Gran.

Way others told it Devil Jim came as a blessing almost. A distraction to whatever it is people might be pushed to do with nothing to lose and only their self as witness to the horror lived. But Great Gran, like all 'em others in the line were of that same stock. Born of a consequence of Gawd. Came into this world with strife surrounding, she did, claiming air on that very same day as the Panic of 1893. Pushed out of McClainesville in '94 with the swarm of violence moving 'bout. Sent down with her Mommy all that long way to Hazard where she'd a distant cousin living. Great Gran were bred for hard. And maybe it were like people says, maybe Great Gran did give to the occasion to rise. Maybe when Devil Jim showed up in her yard, kicked grin over at the sight of her dead husband, smelled fresh the death of her young son, and leered black on the image of a barefoot, pregnant woman, she'd seen it only fair to tip that gun through that wood slit 'cause she'd never really favored any use for soft and there weren't no room for the mush in the first place.

With ever' lick of slick come off his tongue, ever' bit of persuasion, for that's what he's known to do, bend and split and mold half-truths 'til ya's in his grasp, she bit back at him, "Don't matter what ya want there Devil Man, ain't nothing to be give here."

She whispered out little prayers to Baby Ephraim, carved out marks in the wood from where her toes stayed planted, that maker of a bullseye never moving from Devil Jim's head. And somehow or another, with Gawd on her side, Devil Jim finally just got fed up and left. That threat of her death and Baby Ephraim's left in the scuff up of his boots as he went. And wouldn't it be that soon as Devil Jim's feet hit Big Bottom down yonder, Baby Ephraim debuted.

Papaw's story were likely swallowed up to a degree by the grand entry of his brother, but he, like us all, weren't nothing to go brushing off. Year after Devil Jim came for his calling on Great Gran, she'd got hitched on up to a farmer, Thomas Fairchild, who lived a mile down and were, it was sometimes said, her intended beau that whole time, her first husband'd only been faster on the grab. As it turned out, Thomas Fairchild'd saved up, after all that time, quite an affection for Great Gran and it came in the delivery of Papaw in the year 1914, though, he too were believed to join this world in body alone. For the week Great Gran were to give birth to Papaw, on the eve of his very birthday, Great Gran were kicked in the stomach by a mule. Big nasty, fowl natured beast, named Betsy, who's temperament only worsened with the introduction of Great Gran's new smell cutting clumps of dirt down in Betsy's barn. Weren't of the like to be having that at all and when Great Gran walked in to see 'bout the things people go doing up inside the walls of a barn, Betsy piled out a kick that sent poor Gran and soon to be Papaw back four feet with the air leaving out in one mighty rush of Gawd awful discomfort that bordered near panic and death.

Doctors believed even by the grace of Jesus; Papaw already dead inside Great Gran. Betsy's kick landed close to or on that exact spot of his helpless littley heartbeat. Believed, his still body the only thing assuring air and blood in Great Gran at all, for had she not been pregnant a hole dug for her instead. But even through their tellings and Great Gran's spitting of red, her constant grab and tug towards death's blackened robe, come seven days after the incident, Papaw came yawning to this world with a bruise on his head that'd later turn to birthmark, a sealing of his gumption to the world. Thomas Fairchild having walked in after his first night's rest, after the Doctor's instruction the next days to be the hardest, for the baby'd pass through, for him to be ready and prepared, Thomas were greeted to Papaw Fairchild, otherwise known as Moses.

Shoved into the world as a consequence of Gawd. What we, Fairchilds, did. Mommy weren't no different. Born towards the latter end of the depression, right when feeding mouths became a question of selling off children 'cause ever'one done gone so long without food, they's near death 'emselves. Opportunities for providing for someone else were few if ever far between, there came a need for rising, a consequence of Gawd, a child born from the madness at the start of a war. Connie Fairchild came into this world that very same day of September 1, 1939, to a family who'd all but given up hope to surviving. And following in that long line of what we Fairchilds do, I came in much the same way.

Believe ya, me, to hear the town tell it, I's ripped from Mommy's womb just so's 'em Christian folk could say something came out of that night other than the reek of death and mud. Said, my crying shuffled down like Gawd's tears on 'em. Not my words. Theirs. Said, it were the blessing that gave cause to the sun's rising after all that hell brought to 'em during the night.

Born on January 29, 1957, right there in Hazard. Right in the middle of three logs of pine cut and pulled together by two brothers named Samuel and Solomon Johnson. Right there atop the water.

22

JANUARY 29, 1957

ELIZABETH JOHNSON

On rare did Elizabeth Johnson ever heed anything other than the click clack of her shoes over 'em knobby boards bridging Butner's Pass, and nor did she yearn to change that tradition on this day if any other, but it appeared there defiance brooding and mixing in the air soon as she stepped clear of her roof, for there were a gaggle of folks near blocking her exit entire on that other side of the bridge, and bum rushing past a thing like that in a town like this simple wouldn't do.

They's fixated with life's worry granting gaze over the railing, that group of twenty, and it did not fit for a nice sit on Elizabeth as she approached. Poked at that trigger inside that went for the flare up when she thought of somebody finding out 'bout 'em freckles hiding under two coats of powder on her nose. Already unease percolating round her rib cage. Already another fifteen minutes added on to her, now, extremely late and no longer fashionable coffee date with Joe, just by proxy to the mass. She wondered if it possible, if there's a chance at all she'd pass by without their knowing. They's all so involved in their perch, the tight sprawl of bodies dressed in phases of burdened leans. She knew the likelihood of this never granting true but hurried on convinced that it still might. That Joe'd still be there, a true gentleman, having waited all this time without even ordering 'cause he's the sort that'd wait for a lady to arrive.

She took in the backs of 'em, thinking how it weren't all that odd for something to get caught. Been known to happen many times 'fore but why on Gawd's green earth did it have to be today. The statement sealed in her mouth. Then immediately swallowed, carrying that ill questioning of His doing down with it.

North Fork were like to bring down all manner of things round 'bout Hazard when there's a deluge. That inexplicable unleashing all of sudden unmassing a whole slew of things not belonging. Things'd flow down from the Ohio, picking up speed off the many smaller streams feeding the belly of the snake, and spit down 'til they's sure to find some sort of temporary resting near 'em logs of timber ole Harold Butner felled hisself way back in 1914.

Thank Gawd he were a stubborn bastard. Wanted a connector between his land and town that didn't involve no half day walk to that other pass over the river. Knew there's more than enough to be had by way of steel and got the idear in him to go petitioning the railroad company for some extra so's there could be that bridge of his wanting. Well, he waited and waited and waited but there weren't no word ever got back to him 'bout going to build no bridge and he went to take ill on it one day and started chopping. Cut down and cleared one whole acre from his land with an I'll-be-damned watch-me-show 'em muster in his grit and built that bridge all by hisself. Took the better part of two years.

Well, as anything that's done lasted a given amount of time out there in 'em elements, there's a certain spot of wear and tear and big ole wood timbers sunk down in the flow of one, sometimes ornery, institutions such as the Kentucky River, ain't no 'ception to it. Likewise, it were common thought 'em stilts'd sunk down a good four to five feet in the years of their standing making that water grow taller with the droop.

Made it so's that when there were objects trucking down, whether it be a shoe, or discarded chair, or piece of broke off barn, it got itself held up usually near the undercarriage of one of 'em slates. Take just a little nudge from a passerby to alleviate the offense. Not nothing big at all. But there were on occasion, when something called a torrent hit Hazard, that more weighty forms came calling on Butner's Pass. Nine times out of ten, weren't nothing but a chicken, maybe. Some poor unlucky bastard with its guard off. Largest things ever got pinned were a cow and a sow. Managed, the both of 'em, to hook some footing on a rock that jutted just sly the drop off nearest town. Nothing but a pull back of a couple shrubs and they hopped to, went waddling their fat asses right on down East Main Street.

Funny how farm animals tend to turn into good swimmers if need be. Folks ain't so often suited in that pot of luck and if they ain't taught, they don't never know how. Ya'd a thunk that there weren't a Momma living round a river mean as the Kentucky and all 'em streams surrounding that wouldn't take the time to go instilling a little bit of that knowhow in her babies but it were known to happen time and again. Especially since, that river'd swallow ya up and take ya down if given half the chance. Not that it were this particular river's fault over any other but more it were all river's fault, weren't it. Folks who tried at forgetting that usually ones to pay the largest.

Not for Elizabeth, though, surely not for her, or should it be said Hazel, 'cause that were the true self who's fear of water rooted in its dangers. Called up that root and rust sunk down near the pit of her with memories.

Wherein, when, upon gaining a little more ground on the voyeurs, the chalkboard scratch of someone gasping out, "BABY," caused the scuttle of one of her shoes. A simple misfire between head and feet. The root of her heel caught up in a well placed groove she should've passed over. Could've, were it not for the crowd and their leaning and that squaloring of that word. Walked by with her eyes closed, she knew that bridge so well. Had to know that bridge so well 'cause falling in weren't something she'd ever want experience with. 'Cause she were one of 'em babies never taught how by their Momma's. But in the confusion, her head not meeting with her feet, she went for a stumble. Fell. A step back from the others. Planted her face right there on 'em slats, her backside looking up at the world, her eyes spotting clear on water turned brown down below and something stuck up next an ole stalk of timber.

Overhead, that repeating charging out. That cry of "BABY, BABY, BABY," knocking back the fold of her brain ten rings 'til she's staring at that tiny person locked away up there who'd seen all those things. All the while that water gushing. Row after row after row of brown, then clear, then brown, then clear, like there's somebody punching down buckets of hate way back yonder, making that water mean again 'cause the time were due. The closing of her eyes forcing that sludge of nasty there with her so's there couldn't be no escape from her memory.

She remembered hearing that same word butchering slugs into her Momma over and over and over again. Her, not Elizabeth, but Hazel, crouching, hidden behind the hanging of a sheet that divided the youngins from the rest. That channel of iron peppering the air as her Momma's skin broke and life spurted out. That word. That, "BABY, BABY, BABY," spreading out thick along with her Momma breaking down on the floor.

She remembered hearing it so many times 'fore that she couldn't understand why this time its meaning different. Why Daddy's taking it so bad and why there weren't nobody else round to help tell him he's getting it all wrong. He's supposed to be happy. Babies were always a good thing, she thought. Why they'd brought to the world so many. Why she'd twenty brothers and sixteen sisters.

She remembered the smell of hooch heavy on Daddy's breath, that scent of sweet hot from his throat, her knowing there were a tweak or two, even then, to the most recent batch. Scent coming off like he'd left the grains in the rain 'fore mashing in. She remembered getting distracted by it, not noticing the licks of Daddy's fist'd stopped while her Momma fought for shallow pulls of air to fill some of what he'd took from her and left on the floor. Her Momma's body all curdled up like sour milk, all folded over into a ball.

She remembered Daddy haunched over, gasping for air from the beating, his body not something it once were now that age'd finally started in with the pull. She wanted to go to her Momma, to pick her up, scoop that tiny ball that were supposed to be her Momma in her tiny arms, help her get washed and clean and mended. She thought maybe if she only scooted real slow, walked on her hands and knees, by the time she got to her, Daddy'd already be passed out. That were the usual for how it went. Him coming in all brimstone, doling out words and hits. Drink weighing like a horse on him. Then, pass out, the thud and bang of his fall signaling out the okay as he drooled stank on the dirt floor. She remembered waiting, counting out, her small fingers knocking down digits 'til they's all tucked down into tiny fists.

"Hazel." She remembers.

"Hazel, my sweet little Hazel." 'Fore she knew what's what, her Daddy's grabbing on her. Held her tiny neck and little shoulders like a Daddy bear latching on to his cub. Picked her up and brought her real close like to meet 'em redding balls of fire he'd drunk hisself to. "Hazel, Hazel, Hazel, baby, yer Momma, yer Momma, she done a bad thing, now. Drove me to it. Drove me to hunt him down. That man she'd lain with. Fucking Bastard. Yer Momma done drove me to it."

She'd never seen her Daddy like this 'fore. Never seen all that pain and hate fixate like it were under his skin, filling up the reds of his cheeks. Weak, what she saw. Like he needed food and rest and the Lord. Broken somehow, the lines of clear black running from his nose, 'bacco crusted snot swimming down his beard, she saw, there, in him, something she'd never forget, something she'd never seen since—a shattering. And there living within that place, death fed and bore into him. It stirred and poked that fire set on him when he's birthed, that willingness and yearning to hand it out to others.

She'd learn that later, in the days that followed when finally she's granted opportunity to go to the aid of her Momma. Once her Momma'd settled enough strength to make it outside, to go down to the creek, that part where it pooled deepest. With only Hazel by her side, she waded into the water and dunked down, letting the screams bury in bubbles below. That fear in Hazel's stomach as she inched back from the bank, afraid the water'd take her down with it, that grasp of air leaving her chest just as it were squeezed clear and filled back up again. She waited for her Momma to raise up. She'd seen her take long dips like this 'fore. Seen her go down and hold it and rise anew like it were some spring granting second chances. But there weren't to be no coming up from this one. No flushing back the water telling Hazel, it there little secret, Momma knowing how to swim. Wouldn't be none of that.

Instead, Hazel's to be greeted with something clinging, something holding on to something it weren't never meant to hold on to for very long. Like some object out of place. Like some thing cast down a stream, brought and pushed there by events out its hands, controlled by things beyond its means.

Why were it this memory called to Elizabeth as she stared down through 'em slats, as she watched the flow of water pull over the rocks and shrubs and bits of debris? Why it all so familiar, this thing bumping up against a split off shaft of wood that jutted out like it were fishing.

In a different life, in the one long gone, she'd seen something of the like, something so similar, it froze her still. Made her legs and feet stone, made that breath rush from her with a quickness and a speed she weren't sure it'd come back. She felt the word, "Baby" start to slip over her. Travel from that long ago sight, from that part in her memory where she hid behind a tree, where her

Daddy came stomping up to that pool of deep and found Hazel's Momma and that "baby" floating out behind her face down adrift. From there to now, from the viewing of her, a new Meak, stillborn, tethered by her chord, to the now of the fishing out of a baby not even a year by a piece of near broke off wood. Both of em sick looking with their little lips blue and their little cauliflowered features white while that bridge of freckles and wet down head of fire bit hair still held and hold true.

23

JANUARY 29, 1957

SOLOMON JOHNSON

Belcount were there to greet me as she always were, a little more fade and fog held in the eyes, a little more white marble dotting her lenses. She stood, some haint vision behind the streaked out gray spread of spider droppings at the one window fronting her cabin and held one finger against the dirty glass like that were how time kept and my tardiness marked by the record keeper. The cabin long gone with neglect happened in a grove of overgrown tumblers of briars and burrs that sought after the consumption of the piss poor hanging timbers and the helpless form of her frail body standing front view in it went fast and forward towards an extension of its overall disastrous state so's that as the inching further into the causeway of grown weeds and knocked over shrubs and things, there were a bargaining forth with that same keeper of time and I felt assured I's in the proximity of travel some eighty ought years back with ever' trudge.

First thing come to me when I's to cross Belcount's threshold weren't never nothing I'd air out in the open but were that same rattling I'd hit up on nearly ever' damn time—why in the hell hadn't my Mommy found herself some kinship in one of 'em blue hairs down by the church instead of this kindred spirit buried up here in damn near the deepest spot of hollers in Perry County. And up here by herself for all this time, it were a gawddamn breathing miracle she hadn't succumb to either death by fucking boar set loose and on the hunt or blown up by one of 'em Meaks' family stills.

Ina worried herself half to death fearing for the woman. Ever since we got together and she'd heard Mommy tell her stories on Mrs. Belcount, Ina'd a soft spot held up for her. Half way had Mrs. Belcount convinced to come move her things in with us. Told her she'd made her a special quilt and ever'thing and there's a bed waiting and ready if she'd make the trip down. But Mrs. Belcount weren't no fool and no matter how hard we went at the persuade on her, she knew good and well there weren't no room waiting, that Ina'd ever' intention of doubling us up with the girls and gladly giving her our bed. Mrs. Belcount didn't want no part in it. Kissed my dear sweet wife's forehead and told her she'd rather stay up here. Take her chances with the Lord by her side than go 'bout playing any part in convincing us.

That were probably one of the reasons Ina went to loving on her so hard like she did. Belcount made habit of putting others 'fore her. A true praise-his-light-and-let-it- shine-through-kindness-to-others sort that just by mere proxy, there were a feeling of the Lord being with ya when she's round. Believe Ina, for selfish and not so selfish reasons, wanted our girls to be part of a thing like that and had it not caused Belcount to go leaving her house and things and memories, she might could've participated in the talk up and follow through but the time'd passed now and we'd never gone to the trouble of revisiting it.

She'd not looked well in years. Belcount, not my wife. Ina were just as purty as the day of our meeting, as that time she'd took to tumble, skinned up her knee and met my cool twirled frill of lips puckered to greet her wound, my lungs breathing life back on her knobby knee while my heart filled with wishful I do's. Time'd not treated Belcount so very kind and as she scooted herself from behind the dirty window, her feet shuffling in sandpaper swipes over cattywampus flooring, the years and her stern willing to not let 'em show their hang on her working the same thread and she looked to be a hundred and forty as opposed to eighty-two. Came out with heavy dripping down her bones though there weren't no hundred pounds on her even with her clothes on and held fast the sealing of her front door and slid her bare feet out in the dirt, her pale night gown floating over top like an angle's robe and I saw the problem we's soon all to face if we's to live long enough.

In the era when Mr. Belcount alive, so told my Mommy, they'd made a life for 'emselves, he and Mrs., carving out trade on occasion with Ole Tom Meaks, a necessity grown from proximity and one ill-fated from the beginning considering the lead up of Mr. Belcount's bloated body found and Mrs, now strewn in forgotten loss buried deep in a mire of haze that pointed to him still breathing and me, now, being that visage of his coming to save her after such long absence gone.

But back to his actual breathing, they'd lived and loved and kept to 'emselves, hoeing out a small garden to the right of their place and fancying trips out in the moss for the gold of ginseng when time came for trade. It were on one of these many outings, where Mr. Belcount'd disappear sometimes days at a time foraging for the loot, that Mrs. Belcount now believed he'd returned from and concurrently that same outing where he, in fact, had not, where he'd made meet up with a mean wretch of a man filled full with bottled hate and gathering excuse to build case to transgressions found in the hapless appearance of the mild mannered and loving Mr. Belcount, a target, though weren't no bullseye primed on his person as he traveled sack full and speedy step back to the Misses to share in supper and company.

Jacklot Hollow, have ya, weren't even part of Mr. Belcount's habit. More a Breakneck Bottom sort of man. Found the throw down of moss ready for the chew back and hew with ever' bit of the eye's take in once planted in 'em hills. But on this particular vanishing, for some calling pointed to by the Grace of His Almighty, Mr. Belcount'd gathered a tow in Jacklot'd probably do him some good seeing as how there were a story rolling round with the crunch of leaves that Henry's boy, Daniel, were like to turn a blind eye to any pickings pulled from his property as long as there's a tithe leant. And in turn, Mr. Belcount'd doubled stepped in with the don't-mind-if-I-do prance and went heavy handed on all that green laid out 'fore him with not one hair trained for trouble, though it were trudging along full speed and fire lit with the shotgun pull towards him.

Not having known Mr. Belcount, myself, his death occurring in the next to be mentioned, I cannot say if I bared resemblance to him or not or that if, perhaps, any man were to come up on the Widow, now, if they wouldn't too suffice in the calling forth of his memory. But, there lingering 'fore me with bare raw wet crinkling over 'em wrinkles and tiny shudders of bony shoulder snapping through, that Widow Belcount believed it true and dare say it were like duty ordained and tapped on me that it were, in fact, the case. So's, it were hardly anything other than standing and remaining mute that carried on this yearning for her and I followed suit knowing full well through time's unfolding that history'd revealed hatchet wounds plotting land marks and treasure finds up and down the real Mr. Belcount's body and rumors of eyes quiet with the watch of a one Ole-nasty-sumabitch-Meaks walking off with bloody brandishment of bored down and broke through blade dripping mystery over the woods, 'cause there weren't like to be no reprimand for a man who'd not seen it coming in the first.

This neither here nor there once Mrs. Belcount came folding in my arms, that small, tattered frame looking up, cranking out the smell of whatever lingerings her memory throwed sway to, venturing back to that time of her husband's heart pull. The tragedy of her surrender to the mind's game lost on her, though I couldn't hold no blame for a wade in the water.

Ina and I got married on the eve of the eve of her sevententh birthday at the court without her father's presence there 'cause, though he weren't a better man and didn't see wrong in being what I's being, he'd wanted his only daughter to not fall in line with the same life her mother'd done chose. After all we's both miners and he knew exact what that meant for a family. We'd said our promises 'fore Bubba Fulton, a six foot six beast of man with the mildest mannered tone and a tendency to sport hooch in a dry county even on days of marital bliss as what he's granting for us. It were just Ina, looking purtier than anything I'd done ever seen in a handmade gown of faintest yeller that her Momma'd said would bring out the color of pink in her skin ever so while her Momma camped out next to her with blue sending sparkle shots of love from her eyes, and me.

Samuel were invited but never did show.

For as long as care remember, Samuel'd done played his hand at excuse. Boy coulda made foreman at the Coca Cola factory twice over by now with how long he's gone to work for 'em and yet he weren't. Coulda married Carol Anne Montgomery back when they's kids and she were in the business of pining over him and all the twinkle in his eye of promise and sparkle that a young lean man with a sorta sweet looking face could give. But he'd waited two years and were too late by the time he'd finally worked hisself round to going after her and by then Carol Anne Montgomery held promise in her heart for Bill Turner and the stock pile of good looks and strong hands his family'd handed down to all their boys over the years.

Saw the break off and die down of what little bit of pride he'd mustered hold go off in the trees with no sign of look back when he'd knocked on Carol Anne's door and found Bill there sitting with his shirt off at the couch, not for a nod to indecency, but to the fact of his clearing her Mommy's yard the whole afternoon and the sweat taking sour on him so's Carol Anne were out in the back giving it a fresh wash for him to take it home. Come to Samuel right there, weren't no more hope holding on for that ceremony. Bill and her might as well already said vows.

When Ina and I brought our first girl to this world, little Lannie Lynn, named after Ina's greatgran Lynn Harper Collins, who came over with her husband for the train work back in 19ought10, Samuel'd found excuse in a tooth ache gone bad that'd deterred his visiting us for two whole days of my first baby taking down gulps in this world. Only later when he showed up sporting a less than puffy shiner, it were passed down to me he'd received from running his mouth to some temperamental sumabitch at the plant did I understand. Though that understanding carried along with it a tie to something else. Bore bloody mitts next three days of little Lannie Lynn's life, the skip out happening after all gone out for nod and my finding that sorry sack of shit that'd detained my brother, whether he's right or wrong in the rationing of it and sent down my own message that family's family and despite misgivings they ain't meant to be messed with by others.

My second girl's coming in met with less theatrics than the first for Samuel'd actually made appearance soon as I sent for him. Showed up with a bleeding heart full of warmth to dote and play with Lannie and take care to the things needed for Ina, which worked out in the same fashion as a woman's birthing do, meaning, stay clear and don't mind the screams 'cause good Charity Mathews, a portly woman with an unyielding maternal drawl of skin waving just above her elbows, took care to the entry of my first and garnered my trust to carry out the second, delivered our sweet June Pearl, named, course, after our Mommy with full family in tact to take in the whole of her. It were only later, while excusing myself to the night for a moment alone that I found two men standing shotgun spry with his name heavy drip on their tongues.

Weren't even two and half years older than Samuel and how Mommy spouted out at times we's near twins with the pain we both brought her from coming in, and for the life of me, I ain't never grappled hold of how and why trouble seemed focused and focused purely on destroying him. But it were proved, with this being no less an example in the timeline of efforts my brother made at trying to change that which he'd clamped hold to be, that despite us both coming from her, actions shown we's never destined to be the same man.

Seemed in the passing years, Samuel's mouth'd gabbed hot on that fire stone meant more for men punching out fist-backs after their charred warnings and it were a reoccurrence he'd yet graze flame on. So's that when cold air met my heavy warm heart, that rush of knowing exact why they'd come and what they meant, stirred in my throat with all 'em other chunks of leftover whoopings I'd done give out all 'em times 'fore. The common thread, the one perhaps Samuel grasped too tight on or perhaps weren't never truly aware of or cared to note, stated it were a lot easier going 'bout the ruffling of feathers in the wind when there's a handicap of big brother laying wait in the back ground for the right time to step in. And no matter how tired I's getting at playing such role, I weren't the type to go giving it up and letting another step in. Went on ahead and bared down for the witness there weren't gonna be no setting ass to blaze while he's under my roof.

Told 'em, "baring the death of one of their kin, which we all knew Samuel weren't capable of, it were an internal matter and I's assured to give 'em back whatever it were stole, damaged, pawned off, bribed, or give lend, but what I couldn't take no abiding in were the beat down of my brother while my second little girl's cutting z'ss next my wife and if there's issue with, they's to come back tomorrow and I'll take it up with 'em bright and early in the full shine of Gawd and all."

My entreatment, luckily, met with a full set of perched hearing for I'd earnt myself through scuffle and scrap and bare escape what one might recant as a little bit of quite the reputation, the basic spelling of it, stomped deep round and circled twice over that what's mine were mine and it weren't never not under no circumstance ever to come up for debate that any of it were looking to be fucked with.

What'd actually occurred between my Samuel and that set of good ole boys fit right snug up next to all 'em other offenses he'd made fucking habit of doing. The like of which meant, Samuel'd got a wild hair up his ass and ventured entry to the dwelling of man, a place only journey to in sparing dips, and found the game rarely ever 'bout words alone, that his belief, no matter how he yearned for it to be, mattered not, that, in fact, the world of man cared little else to his intentions or aimes at appease, for he were branded with cunt seared on his hide and they'd smelled him a mile back 'fore he'd ever stepped foot in.

Argued with myself many nights since if the grit ever present in him. If we's born with it or it pulled and mended together, the kindling laid down for the rise of wood and the reach up for the sky. Whether or not the actions of one led to the surmise of the other and wondered if maybe it were just that it all give to me. None of it left when the time came for him.

Widow Belcount shucked light the freeze of time, the now flooding back on her, and shriveled off her subtle clamp, the recall of her travel from the house to me settling down to hide in the moss verdant by the carryover of water from Tumler's stream not three stone throws away. She gave call to my being there and the noted absence of Samuel's not with a light tap on my shoulder, a sign of comfort I'd made, yet again, the long trek and then 'fore I'd chance to give excuse, she gave glimpse to some horror we'd far too long ignored.

24

JANUARY 28, 1957

WILLARD TELL

"I knows what I is," shaved off my tongue like strips of tar, 'em words did. "And I knows what y'all be."

Y'all weren't talking no more. Y'all were settled down now. Huddled on the floor. Splayed out after the smacking.

A curried jumble of muck dripped out the murky faucet of my yap, the slow drawn dribble, the leftover of sick on the floor from my head's telling of what's what.

"And I knows what I ain't."

Trinkets of scorch dynamited up the pipeline of me faster than a chicken's nod to a loped off head while a splinter quoted lines of scripture in my leg.

Hunting for a shoe. My shoe. Done torn from me in the scuffle. Not this'n. But that other. That one that led to this'n. That'n that'd caused the crawl out of actions don't no man ever really intend on using but that those whose mission for survival grants more light than most always knows, there's but a smidge of an inch that'll take 'em there. Don't matter where the start. Don't matter the time of age it occurs. Once there, ain't nothing to come back.

Scald cut craters in my throat as I looked down on a pipe that's covered in slatted red with chunks of meat still cleaved in its grooves. When I stepped in from the cold, couldn't no thought ever led me to what I'd be leaving when I come out.

I's to shake it off. Clamber out, lock it down, come full force out the back of it, no look back. No thought to the why of here.

But that why—that why's the problem, ain't it. The why's always the last one asked. Sometimes plum forgot. And yet its all there is. Why's done made a home for itself. Set down bricks of burn on my purpled skin. Shed back those parts of me that weren't meant to take it. Slung 'em off in splinted pound of fist to face and face to ground. My head not no where close to right.

But like I said, don't nobody rarely ask the why. The what, when, where's too busy blocking out the need for the rest. Start on it for a second, then back pedal nice and quiet like.

Keep 'em eyes down. Hope for it to pass. For that reason for why to disappear.

I could just hear her now. Laying in. All swoled, with back aching, and hunger tearing through, and that fowl mouthed face of her's looking more and more like an angel. Looking like someone I's meant to meet. Fired up hotter than a backwood pappy getting ready for the come of Sunday. Hear it now. Gawddamns just splitting the air. Firing out like kernels set to pop. All of it turned to worry with the crawl of time moving 'cause I weren't there with her but instead caught here with the fucking why's and the y'alls.

Set to float. That's where I's at. Floating between the thud of water falling on tin and the call of her voice in my head.

Wasn't here. Not here. Not in this room. But, then, how come the y'alls are down on the floor? And, my—my clothes, how come my clothes?

My shoe. Look for the shoe. Pay no mind to the hurt. What the hurt done, the why settled. Can't live there. No room for it there. Grab after the shoe.

Naw. Not that one. That's his. That belongs to him. Look for yars. The one flung in the corner. The one with the spot on it. That bit of grease. That ain't what it is. Just what's leant to it. What it is hangs next to the why.

Ignore the hurt. Ignore the cling of tingles returning to it. Scout for movement. For life. For flicks and twitches and arrivals of led. Wander over stillness of mashed blue, already turned so from the counts of gawddamns muttered in my head. Look for reasons for why to be asked to those who'd caused the what. Look past the hair and blood and brown making carriage over my hands and venture down to the poke and prod of cold I needed 'em to be. Make damn sure there won't be no coming after. Make sure that final charge the one that done it.

Don't wait for the surprise to come. Cut it down now. Now while it's just the y'alls and me. While that water's plucking down heavy outside. When there won't be no hurry or chance of people coming in.

News said it's sure to last all eve and carry on to the next. Said we's in for a noreaster. Some fancy-smance word for cats and dawgs and thunder and lightening come over the mount.

Go for the shoe. There. There it is.

Tears of wrong spread through me with the bend down. Fires lit for burn and spread making causeways up and over, sending down strikes of fuck in streams down my legs.

No weighing on the what. No focus on the red when I swipe the back of me. The breath'll return. No worry to that. Can't get sucked out from the bend alone. The heart'll go back to it soon enough. Just got to wade through that, now. Wade through the why's on the floor, the y'alls felled. Feast on 'em cinderblocks now covered in blood and death. Keep that head on a swivel. Make sure there ain't no air coming up. There ain't no bodies coming back for revenge.

Step over the mess. Pay no heed to it. No heed to the dropping of me on the floor. Stay on the y'alls. Remember the flash of breaks, the snap of bone. Bring up that smell of iron gripped and glued to my palm and chug it in. That were result of the what that led to the why. Feel my way past the tipped over card table, the spill of fat and red and white from the slow leak of the chin I'd forced over the brick. Scud over to the pile of bills speckled in red.

Pick up the jug of lightening and pour, and pour, and pour down on the jerk-of-life-still-present-in-him-fuck who'd caused the what that led to the why. Remember in the flashes why I'd staved off on the dealing of him last. Remember the pull, the rip, the feel of burn pool out of me.

Smack awake that dirty bastard, Johnny, who owned the deed to 'em cinders covered in blood, who'd invited me in once the rain done started, claiming "ain't it 'bout time ya visited the table. Got's ourselves a real live crew going."

Make sure he holds up long enough to see the crack of my whites 'fore I set his ass on fire. Make sure he takes a good wide gander at the mess he helped facilitate. At 'em faces he fostered so's they could plant their harm.

Remember to crank open 'em billfolds. Harrow that name in my skin. Make it so's it lives right next to mine. So's when vengeance tied with right time and Mason last name, the deed in action—nearly done.

Then walk out. Don't never ask the why again. Don't never admit to nobody, nowhere, not never, that I's shoved down, knocked out, hogtied, and drooled over. Don't never think no further on the treatment of my backside like a bitch in heat. Don't think on it none.

No more.

25

JANUARY 29TH, 1957

FUCKING NATURE OR THE CONSEQUENCE OF GAWD

It were calm now.

Coffee tinted damp colored the stole twine, spooled the frayed dark marks in dancing snake trails from out their hurried knots slopping over timber. Where it'd crashed and plundered and rendered us small, it were calm now.

Now, the child cradled. The dew wet cloth swaddled tight round him, yanked from a passing carriage, from a basket intended elsewhere for other things as they drifted, the child and the mother. As the carrying of soul struck streak crossed and changed the clobbered waverings of night. It swished lullaby grazes of rise and fall as the gang of two bobbed beside the mother who clinged guard on that little one for there still thought something yet to come.

The two men, claw diving in clay at either side of the make shift raft fought tired against buckets and buckets of carried down Kentucky River spew, bathed since by the worried wrinkles of their brows. Thoughts heavy and tired, they laid way to the lull of flood water, to the hush of life after surviving Gawd's Might to wash over their sleepless eyes, thankful they'd at least found each other in time. Sunk down to the bone with that thankful praise present in all Hazard's minds, thank Gawd, Almighty, it were calm now.

Big-cat-daddy-fat-gator-rain-drops what'd fell on 'em. What'd caused the start of the now floating and bewildered and somewhat lost, left to live. Callused and hardened with intents buried beneath, that rain'd poured. Mixed with soil less like to stand hold since the robbing begun, paired with that time of natural order kicking in and the Kentucky ready for the unleashing what'd led 'em men, those brothers finally found on common ground due to crisis head kick-in, to the woman who'd birthed the child, who both floated atop the tire and board over cross from Sterling's Hardware, where they's greeted, the four, by the five onlookers, who'd made refuge atop the building and away from the current of Blackwater sludge that'd kicked and spewed and chewed and devoured most of anything that stood on Hazard Main proper.

Something as simple as rain. Rain and time, both buildup primed, both stricken for hold on the other and tied in dance over top that now placid table top sheen, which no one watching believed truly finally at rest. With bottom barrel dregs, these survivors, these hapless souls left, stared out at a world changed with disbelief locked down and buried in their heads. But no flood's beginning ever as charged as the fishtail spinning of the end-all-drop when catastrophe spreads.

Any other time or rather most times, Tumler's stream lived and breathed as nothing more than a peaceful little brook. A one stop shop with no cause to worry and certainly not reason for alarm. Came down as an offshoot from McCluen's land and gave green to all Belcount's collards, and taters, and rutabagas. Gave sprout to her cabbage and onions and 'maters. Weren't nothing like that Daddy it come from, that Ohio mess and certainly not a spot like their Grandad, the Mississippi. Naw. Just some peaceful little brook, some no nothing fuss of purty water working its way down the holler and into the Kentucky at Butner's Pass. Sure, when there's a rain to come, it were like to get real fat. Fill up the curves of its sides. Wear out a little wider in the hips. That sorta thing. Not nothing for worry. Whittle down in a day, day and a half, tops. Mean, in all the time of Belcount's life up there on the mount, she'd only ever seen that little spot of water grant grief on her but once. Not but one time 'fore. Some thirty years back, some thirty years back almost to the day. But weren't no cause for alarm. Even if she could see and know and understand, the signs woulda come, right?

Mean, if she were granted clarity to look, buried deep in 'em folds of fuzzy mess, Belcount'd find it like it were yesterday, that murky brown current displaced and angry with the chew like it were clapping tacks on which lives to steal out of sleepy Belcount beds. Might could still feel that thick molasses hold that little stream done hardened to in the time of nightly prayers. How there'd give rise to an uncontrollable thirst, one with no beginning nor end, that middle gone crack with the whip, pulling down hard and wide over Belcount's small harvest of herbs and greens. 'Cause somehow or another, 'spite that house of her's being offset to any sort of spread that water might search to find, it'd gained magical extend, leaching out octopus vines, chugging ink sprawls of black under toe of their tiny little beds. How, even in the dead of sleep as that nasty water crept, those long hard rains of winter's edge took toll on ground near buried and dead by lacquer slivered off, washed away, fled. Belcount woke. That heart of hers damn near pounding out her chest. That damn rush of Blackwater coming for her head. If give chance she'd remember it. Remember how water ain't like to go taking slow when there's babies in heavy tow. How the chance unraveling of two tiny, small souls bore down with the drip of angry water fed did not no sound hardly make 'fore poor Belcount woke and found her two little doves dead.

And just then, as if recognition finally shown, some rare glimpse of past's withered fringe, Belcount spit from her cradle of sweet Solomon's breadth and went after high ground and high ground fast. 'Cause there's something give spark, something deep down inside, that spoke to the calling of it all again.

Meanwhile, the dread wore on Samuel. Worked ants in files of two up and down his legs. Like suicide watchers ready for the make on some dead man's bones. He tried at the swat on 'em. The pushdown on a bubble brewed shit storm of calamity. Too late for all that. It'd already set up to mining fire dripped glass from his throat, already set 'bout the crawl out of 'em glassies he'd positioned froze on 'em fleeing bear of a men Meak brothers, who'd walked by him like ain't no share in the road for a man as he.

Rolled up like fear waves, sinking his feet down in the sprawl. Covering his head in sharpshooter spew, washing his life away. Dread'd got worse with age, with the slow clicks of time etching round near all that rage that weren't no let out for. Not no chance at carrying burden to profit nor profit to change. 'Spite all his wanting and wavering and believing this here or that there gonna lead him to some different sort, he'd caught glimpse to the bears, to their subtle brush off to the ant in the way and he'd gone to drip and drool and deflate.

Laid him up real good now, set him down near that brush on the ground. Some worthless sort in the wicked rise of his never-quite-earning-their-second-look. Left him not hair-bone shy from where his brother and that Widow stepped and caused the not to notice cloud's growth surrounding his head to grow in scale much like that fox build push that stream done got started to give.

And without even scant acknowledge on his behalf, black muck slugged forward from steady climb, from bowled over branches and waterlogged banks, slipped up and soldier crawled and rised and rised and rised. So's without poor Samuel's attention, his boots slogged down, covered in crawling salamander twitch, as Blackwater came, came moving over 'em leather tips.

Flip that coin, go look the other side.

Elizabeth stood crippled. Yet another one of 'em burning fires she were like to get, the flare up sending down embers of broke black down smite all through her chest, when too much thought give to all that left behind in 'em woods, she stumbled fast and forward up against that railing with barely a smidge worth of air working through her lungs. Poor girl, 'spite all that fight against smoothing out 'em wrinkles round her edges, she'd found there's still a spot of rough at times causing headache.

An affliction what her Momma called it. Something she wholeheartedly felt her Momma never gained reign over hence her ending up like she did. But not Elizabeth. She weren't gonna be going down no similar trail. She'd devised herself a set of breadcrumbs to leap out of 'em dark and scary woods. Made herself a go-to-reactionary-ain't-gonna-stand-here-in-that-shit kinda deal. 'Cause that were exact what it were.

Affliction'd stick to ya, grab hold like thick red mud, sink ya down with any showing of struggle. She'd known it, for she'd lived it. Lived right there in the middle of all that shit for days. Missed work. Missed friends. Missed life. 'Til finally her body just got damn fed up with the battle and she managed a pull out. Put one foot in front the other and walked her I'm-not-gonna-let-this-eat-me-up ass out. And this weren't no gawddamn different.

She needed gone. Just like she'd said and just like she'd always made a plan on doing 'cept it meant to happen now and for good. She'd leave out soon as she could. Start that journey towards bigger and better. Soon a she rustled that suitcase from out and under her bed, it already packed now for a year with her just in case fancy dress, with her always dependable first impression attire, which fell just above the bust line to give the illusion that it might very well go down farther for the dip, just in case there's a man present, and course, a pair of coveralls she'd swiped from the bottling factory in case she needed appear blue collar ready, which were the one she probably needed wear the most. She'd go for it right now. Grab hold that can she'd stuffed back into the deepest spot of dark in her cabinets, pull out that small stack she'd saved, and kick this town goodbye. Forever.

Just place one foot in front the other. Turn and get to go. Tell 'em flames flaring up she ain't got time nor need for their servicing fear today. She's leaving out, ya hear. Gone. Turn that purty head of hers to the sky, ground down that searching flame's need for lick out, focus on that unsettling prick of Devil's Wind, 'cause at least it were out and not in, and gather herself one big gulp of air. That's what she'd do. So's that's what she did.

Just a real damn shame that weren't all that were factored in. For right as she's meant to hustle down and bear witness to that exit sign blaring bright with light, she opened up instead on the shoe drop's spite.

While back up in the holler, Belcount'd locked hold her scrawny little arms round the trunk of a yeller poplar rooted so far down it were like to know a disciple by first and last.

"Belcount, now, ya come on back here, honey. Can feel the wind whipping up something nasty on us. Don't wanna go get caught up in no storm when we's out here." Solomon tried for calm and steady but for the first time in a long one there were a forced covering to the smooth he's aiming for and it didn't appear like his words granting much ground.

She'd gone after the take on that tree good and proper with a spread-eagle wrap fixing one of her gangly set to break or might could fall off entire legs on that bark, loose skin already taken with the stamp and mark of 'em grooves. Worst of it working red and white splotch over her tired and lonely cheek like she's worried and praying to Gawd for strength against whatever she feared might come for the tearing away.

"What's got ya all worked up, honey. Ain't nothing to be scared of. Just me, Mrs. Belcount. Remember me. Little Solomon

Johnson. Remember my Momma, Mrs. Johnson. Me and my brother's visiting with ya ever since her passing, now. Ya take a look at me. See. See, Solomon."

Belcount didn't give him not one nar up and down, her gaze frosted over and chilled on something coming far out in the distance which he felt sure it were soon something he need know if he's ever gonna get her pulled from that gawddamn tree and back in the house in time for him to get on home 'fore dark done came and went.

"Today is the day Samuel and I comes to sees ya is all. Remember Samuel. Samuel's my brother. We're Mrs. Johnson's boys."

All 'em names thrown at her didn't seem to be doing one lick of good 'cept driving her nails further in that wood and making the ripping of her off the only option bound to give. And damn it all to hell, if she were but forty pounds heavier Solomon wouldn't care lend fear to doing it.

"Samuel's gonna be tickled pink at seeing ya. Don't ya wanna come over here with me and wait for him. Huh? C'mon, honey. C'mon over her, down here with me."

Now, if ever there were prime time spot for curve hurled, it would not find better slot than when there's spell yielding thrill of a woman near death cozied up to a tree and a man dead set on trying grant her free and so's the rumbling roll occurred. Moved through, cutting wide the backs of rustling leaves, came doling out pause and halt in pamphlet'd breeze and Solomon's ears dared chance for the turn as recollection worked. Through films and reels and where and how's and what's he looked. That lost unnerving venture of rustic understanding rushing over bramble and bush and leaf and mound, over trip and trigger and pushed back long-lost memory of things to never wish for again and to hope never grant visit yar kin. And gathering just right smack on the tongue of that lulling roll, that now turned rumble shouting out for both he and Belcount to hear, for as he looked away from her stone white grip, it finally came to view in crashing, spiraling, out of control fits.

And should it not be forgot, after so little time passed and yet a memory's rinse done, Samuel failed in the heeding of his own damn thoughts. Acting in that manner he'd foreswore and tom-fooleried on that Meak cub, he stood for quite a little spell too long and found the waders lifting in the rise and his boots buried down and his ankles and knees growing small in the slurried soar of a stream turned something else entire. Went for twist and turn, bow and scout, and not none of it seemed raise one lick of difference to that water's gator roll trap. He pulled and pitched, rammed down fingers and palms 'til full hand covered in blacked out stick, 'til water sloshed and poured and painted skin in loosened thicket spin, 'til shrub and leaf and branch took float, and he found his chest buried in river's desolate façade of it not giving one, count it, not one measly little fuck.

Now if the tailspin spiral of madness let out ain't ever the time for a man to go on ahead and find it in hisself what he's truly made of, there's rare opportunity elsewhere for him to ever grant the knowledge of his stew. Believe buried deep in that glimpse of life potentially lost were exact where Samuel pulled down and found he'd not yet wanted grant exit. Ya can call it coward and fright, yella bellied sort of living to wait all that very long just to find out what he's made of but that don't gather up very much meaning to the man who's battling up against it. And dare state, it don't really matter all that entire much where the fight's found just as long as the fucking punch's thrown anyhow and thank Gawd Almighty, a phrase to be repeated ever after in golden hue, dear-not-never-gathering-the-grit-needed-Samuel, ground down and went for the pull through.

He gnashed and spread and held out his weight against that nasty current. Back peddled his ass with toes clenched through leathered boot working counter to the rinse of squished down bottom river might. Scraped down on that bank of fallen off silt and dirt and mud and fought hard at that sink line punch that water done aimed for, its height now aching past navel towards chest, and he managed hold to a branch the like of which seemed planted by Gawd alone just for his grabbing and he worked and he worked and he worked up pull on that hitch and yanked his watery-tired-not-gonna-give-up-finally-found-muster-wearing-somewhere-thin's ass out of that water's grip.

Meanwhile, Lawd in Heaven, the message sent. If animals were listening at all, it were mighty time for the pair up and Elizabeth wouldn't of took too stunned to see it neither, it'd lit wet so hard. Oh how it all did fall. Came out from the sky some sheet of soppy nothing good ever coming from a wall of water like that sorta deal, splaying wet dynamite plops over wood and road and stream and folk alike.

To Elizabeth, the dance, the offset pull of what wet pellets of led can do to a woman's delicate and powdered skin, came quite too soon for her already rushed plan of exit for the day and neither did she appreciate the injustice on her hair and face nor did she care to venture further in the act of running to be rid of it. But these are things needed done when faced with a deluge. So's with fitted pencil skirt yanked high at her knees and shoes spiked from feet with a who-gives-a-damn-to-dirty-feet, she took to Main, her nice heeled shoes fitted inside her chugging air fast hands.

Hurried herself to the front of Sterling's Hardware, the awning granting shelter from the storm and watched annoyed at most to the steady stream of Gawd's tears barreling down at the bottom of the sidewalk's drop off. "Of all the days," bumping round her soggy head. Could it not held off, kept for just one damn day more 'fore the bottom fell out, 'fore she's faced with yet another thing blocking her way out or pulling her back from actually finally achieving it. She scooted back further, hands folded at the chest, and shimmied right up next to the Sterling's glass fronting the store, her cold wet frame giving smear.

Long lost were her thoughts to that fella she'd got all primped up for. Couldn't bare give rise to the thought of him at a time like this not with that wet dawg look she's sporting out for ever'one to see.

What would he possibly think of her now? What would she think?

Maybe, just maybe, she looked like one of 'em starlets whose makeup were still full intact once the rain done fell. Maybe there were a little more Rita wearing on her, her hair fallen down in the purtiest of glisten. It were known to take to a curl if the air just right and this after all were chock full of moisture leaking out on her. Maybe that were why all 'em biddies who'd made it out of nature's way were giving her hawk eyes, why the portly man with the bazooms rivaling hers perhaps if give leave of that wet shirt he's dawning, were giving look. But unfortunate for her, as elsewhere and all round happened in the midst, when she turned to face the sight of what all 'em others were taking in to view, Elizabeth saw the chaos playing out behind, the water's angry rise with big creepy monster tongue licks leaping out of the Kentucky, the slow but steady push of mud start to move and slide down the hill bucking up to the back of Michner's pass, the waterlogged drawl of her clothes and face, of 'em freckles that came poking out from under her nonexistent powder didn't seem to matter one bit.

Back down in town, it weren't cause for all that much alarm for her man not to come home and yet the taste of visceral couldn't quite get wiped from Connie's tongue as she went for the brush on 'em chompers. There standing as she were nine months 'bout to pop with her belly hanging low like a watermelon, cantaloupe, pumpkin, and the kitchen sink fitted up under her dress, she were anything less than amused.

She'd grown accustomed to more than a couple things while having a man round that when there were fire needing built and log needing cut, she'd not missed the act of doing 'em herself and she'd damn it all to hell if she's to go 'bout asking help from anybody else. Pouring rain no 'ception from any other. She knew he'd come back to her. Always did. Rumbling in some piss poor side of drunk with all "sweet babies" gushing forth and slobbered kisses. Come rolling in with a story the size of the state 'bout how something or another detained him. How he couldn't possibly get away. But she knew. She knew the battles raging within. She knew what were going down there at that mine. What 'em boys were living in. She knew there were times when there ain't nothing else better suited for a man's heavy mind then to find hisself in the middle of a little bit of rage and if that translated to her Willard staying out all night tearing one on then she's dealt a better hand than most. 'Cause, there weren't no denying, not anyone could, he were a good man.

A good drunk.

A good worker.

A good provider.

And most certainly were soon to be, a good damn father to that boy routing inside.

She knew it a boy 'cause in her family they'd do to sit on a woman lower than a girl and considering he were two clicks shy of popping out on his own last night, she went ahead and resolved this were to be a son. Not even told Willard 'bout it. Wanted it to be a surprise. Wanted the joy of telling him they's to name him Ronnie, name of Willard's dead brother, while he's holding that purty boy in his hands. But she'd tell him so, that if he didn't hurry hisself up off that wagon he's riding, she's sure to bring that little fella up into this world in his absence for he'd gone to paw at that door between her legs like a gawddamn cat searching for food. Hell, she'd half a mind on her to go searching for a pocket mirror and give a look see. Thought for sure there'd be a little paw playing hide and seek behind her flap.

And no matter how she went to work on it, that lingering up quiver of her going at life with that boy of hers alone, she knew, it weren't nothing she'd ever find herself in the mood for. Boy needed a father just like girl needed a Momma and seeing as she'd gone and lived that experiment of doing without herself in 'em young rearing years she just couldn't see fit for him to do the same as she.

Settled it right then and there, looking out at 'em fat unsettling streams of rain, there weren't no way on this Gawd granted green earth she's meant to live and spend her days that she's gonna bring that boy of theirs into the world without him and if that spoke to a fat preggor waddling her happy ass on down the hill and marching up and yanking that man of hers out a bar stool then so the fuck be it.

Now just one more stop 'fore we's to let it go—think, hence begin—prior and of peculiarity born did one Ole Bastard Tom Meaks find hisself in the met up of all things convulsing towards disaster, though it can only be described, if one were to lend 'emselves to that of righteous wielding and Gawd's meddling hand, that it fitting he the one who happened on his long forgot and dismissed daughter trapped between one nasty, mean, and nervous pig pinned unnaturally inside the bottom half of Sterling's Hardware under what some'd soon describe in the days after as a good ten feet high rush of Blackwater bite. The glimpsing of it only magnified in astonishment by the troubled and disbelieving nature with which posing Elizabeth, but forever hidden under the guise of living young Hazel, dropped all her troubled thoughts and angered memories like sunken ships in the cold chomp and waded towards that bastion of perhaps-not-so-very-shitty-as-one-might've-thought man who'd seeded her.

How Ole Bastard Tom Meaks actually ventured towards the

rescue occurred in yet another rare extension of care to one near drowned sorry sack of a brother, who his sons'd spoke to seeming half dumb and two spares shy of air gobbling, near the sides of a creek turned river. Where, walking down that line of his land bumping crosswise to the long ago turned widow by him, a one Miss Belcount's little shack of country holler greet, Meaks gave look to the squandering gulp of a man laid flat on his dirt.

Now, should it ever not be in the forefront of anyone's mind whose give just a bit of smidge to the story unfold, that a reminder speak as to the nefarious nature of that bastard of a man Meaks, allow time to build in revolver's clink, that he, of all the clan living up that mountain were never one hoped ever to come cross on land spotting his claim certainly not when mounted and discarded on a river running deep. So's it were with, as mentioned 'fore, both plots of peculiarity meet, that of Ole Tom Meaks and Samuel-lost-but-alive-Johnson.

Enter water stage left.

There's most assuredly an occasion for regret when standing in the shadow of a brick-bridge-built wall of water come crushing towards. Quite hard to place up argument against a thing like that. Even with billed grit chiding down river's buck, betting any who's standing and placing wage there ain't outcome room for much other than shit fire sure of never gonna win. And that friends were all our dear spellers and spindles of this here romp came up against as that water done prepped and ready for the move.

Were 'bout like a freight train loose down at the wheels, sparks clipping ground mineral weight of metal's strain from rub up against similar straights, from down round bends of track's possible breaks, that water done hooked heave-hoe landing as torpedos from factory spewed. Rushed sprawl down the bell of Ohio's stretch and swell, laying down salt in all 'em finger reach spreads. Made charged hull rips of leaves down dripped, of weightless things come floating bound in, 'til wet drowned rise, gone out in spin with little strips of brown pulled bottom meeting earth again.

That Bitch current rolled.

Reached out over hill and mountain and tree and home and came down for the plunder and swallow up whole. Chomped down, chugged back, ripped up, angered through cracks, that dark train of nature's-not-caring-spit claimed lives and loves and soul full pleas of "not us" as it covered clamored down fits of last breath give, "it were just too damn fast."

Sure enough did.

Flowed smart, went wide, split heaven and earth in watery divide, that plow of Blackwater bite came heavy with its feed. Channeled meet-up and greet with all our splitting ends, where brothers divided by space and time cleansed through with Kentucky Blue spree did Belcount journey off to death, her body too weak in filtered withered wedge, where flowed down mountain range with no words to speak 'cause tossing and turning all they'd managed keep, from barreling full dive to death's watery door, where, without their knowing little fat bellied Connie fled, met up with bare luck stripped life on liquids edge. Where peeled layer and layer of tussled family pride, battered branch of father daughter dammed up. Where houses went slip to that damned Blackwater dip and those who'd clamored hold of high land wavered in wind's whip, did find there, upon washed up Devil's charge bare bedrock roll for little Ronnie were coming out in a rush from Momma Connie's belly, gold.

Could give two gawddamns against weather and nature's hold for push and pull and rip, that child were coming no matter what the world endured or foretold. And in a panic of tectonic shift, Connie did what seemed an impossible lift, windshield wiping arms and feet she bobbed along the uncontrollable stream 'til there came from Heaven's Gates the grandest of offerings, a wrenched off board from old Butner's Pass, a saving grace of timbered A-framed wood large enough for her little fat legs to fit up, over, and round, for her back to lay flat on the current's travel down. And there amongst the wild of fear and necessity bite, she shoved and thrust and squeezed, screaming "baby Ronnie, get ready to fight." And though the storm and the water clipped building, furrowed rough edge, there, in the slide of "My Gawd," and "What's next" came brother Solomon, brother Samuel carried down from the mount's top, ushered forth as guardians of brave men past, they grabbed hold Connie's chariot, working hurried, working fast. And in that circumstance of beleaguered hell, while onlookers howled disbelief in the horror of night, Connie, the brothers, and the soon to join four, managed the feat of all feats, to bring forth that dear treasured gift of new life. Pinned between a wall, a car, a post in a jerrybuilt house of grabbed tire, wood plank, and two men, one woman unwilling for the water's take, the child, Ronnie came.

26

JANUARY 29, 1960

THE RAZOR'S EDGE

PART III

Connie didn't very well fancy herself a Union member since all she'd ever done for the mine were on occasion bed one of 'em men crawling out of it and it were sure fire proof that numbered grown on in height in the years Willard'd vanished as it were without a doubt true she'd gone on and dug up a bug bigger than a gawddamn car and went on ahead and swallowed it, leaving a whole lot of bitter where any sweet done ever landed, but she couldn't go abiding no run round on 'em boys by coal Daddy Todd neither so's she found herself just like all 'em others cramped up in a place they'd rather not be. Listening to a man they'd rather not hear.

She'd learnt up something fast once her thoughts went towards the worse to just keep 'em locked up behind that purty face of hers 'cause there's living proof breathing that if ever give the chance to actually go off the rail on some 'em bubbles popping off, there were like to be a whole slew of jumpers come clambering for the edge of regret cliff. For it can't never be twisted that mouth and mind of hers were on constant ninety-mile hour trudge with bullshit and grime granting fuel. Standing with a baby boy lodged on her too skinny of a hip didn't do nothing but make that fire breathe.

Gawddammit—there's rock hard witchery stew piping clouds of choke-the-life- from-ya-reds in hailstorm graves of air throughout this gawddamn room and not a one of 'em, not one gawddamn poor, angry, twisted up soul'd happened on the reasoning behind the cattle call rush. Just one big hungry pack of wolves staring down the show up of a slab of meat. Their eyes centered and drilled to that sorry suck fuck handing out excuse. Their ears glued in connect to the shred of not quite knowing full well what he's capable of totally though a line of spider web silk pulled from one head to the other forming that bastard's web of deceit.

Weeeellllll, I'll tell ya this brothers and sisters, ya could hear it now.

Hear the crinkle and waff of spoil feed mustering shift from sweated down grease. From man to man to mother to son to father and brother and back again, that shrill feel of spider busy as 'em daggers went mile high with the spill of all the shit Kieran Sterling spewed up front that room.

"Now. Now. Now." A small clay pot rattled as the forced mask of second generation straight from his Irish Moder's tit bared symbolic overreach blue. Bumped up against all that native-been-working-the-earth-'fore-ya-plant-of-boots-and-gonna-continue-on-still-once-there's-vote-come-through sneer working lock jaw on that next bolster of escaped air to come out. "No need to go off in a tizzy there boys...Misses...Misses...Please....take yer seat... there's no need to go for the shout out now. Grant me chance, begin again, there."

Kieran brushed his thumb over the groove of metal disc hid in his pocket, the dents rubbed raw into fine silver smooth from the years of his going to its aide.

"Now, I meant no offense at the address."

The claw sharp dip of buffed down nail picked in silent clink in the front scoop of his vest pocket and though he could hear his Gay's words sweep over him now with warnings the gesture made smug company, he couldn't help but meet the coin's brittle edge. "Men and the fine ladies of this here town, I understand the concern…Misses Brighton please, if I could just get in a word… it's true…"

Empty buzz charted out scouts over a crowd of men standing army drill deep in crusted coal mining blacks. Clipped filtered dip between the silhouettes of don't-give-a-damn-and-ain't-believing-it-neither, of us women as we lined beams at their side. All of us looking for things weren't no way that Plastic Patty ever gonna be able to deliver in the basement of a place holding too many memories to count.

Bastard robbed hisself the favor of poor hopeless folks just to be part of the Union in the first place. Oh, yeah, came out with a big ole show after the flood. Never seen so many lines of credit gave since. Practically gave his stock out for free. And couldn't nobody go to argue with the grandstand job he done for the citizens of Hazard after that water done went to work. Nooooo, there couldn't be care lent a word backwards 'bout good-sweet-angel-endeared Kieran Sterling. Not after he'd shown out like he'd done. Not after all that. Why, there weren't a person standing in this room here who hadn't received some sort of favor by that one there. Some form of late pay promised delivered next week 'cause there's a shingle come loose and hammer and nails needed bought and couldn't it just wait 'til this come Saturday, oohh, but not when there's the snow to come and the wind to creep and rob yar skin with licks of cold air as ya scoot further and further down in the blanket 'til there's knees touching nose.

But that were the thing weren't it. That were how he'd all of 'em fooled.

"…it's true, there's been an issue with the wages but I assurs ye as yer elected we'll not stand long against such injustices..."

He spouts.

Could hear a pin drop amidst all the inhales of crisis proper, two days since they'd gone to garnish 'em wages on the boys. Dropped 'em down five percent usual earning. Two days and not one month shy of the last cave in that'd took sister Louisa's husband Lee from her. Her nose bare witness to the nighttime wide awake trade she'd made after pacing 'em floors with little Daddy sick babies, weren't no wink to spare for her and it were starting to show definite toll on her frame. Red nose and puffy eyed, it were all that were left in me not to pick her up and place her opposite hip from Ronnie.

"...plan is as it always goes...Now I hears yer concerns, trust me I do but do ye not think there might be opportune for a talk?... Now hold ye there..."

Grappling round'bout like some gawddamn circus pavilion ringleader with winged tips enveloping shelter from the storm sorta flock build. Fucking Bastard. Living and breathing as I stand in view.

Gavel went for a tremble in Kieran's hand. The impulse to strike down the order. To gain control something he'd shouldn't want use too early. Men wouldn't go taking to hearing no demands from the sort like him. Wouldn't go to no good to have that wood come flying down on a group who's just rustled up bite after a whooping.

"Ya said we's to get water up and running here, Kieran, what we supposed to do with it now? What ya gonna do? Ya up there saying they's meant to answer to some things. Hell, we done gave out those demands two gawddamn months ago—"

"Yeah—"

A tall lanky sort with hair pulled back long like he'd rightly appreciate a good comb through and a rinse or at least a trim if hogtied down and enough booze poured in him, stepped out of his rank and went for a move up to the front, blackened cheek and all.

"I've had just 'bout enough of this pussyfooting round anybody need take. Now I gots two toddlers, a ten-year-old 'bout to go to work up in this sumabitch in the next year, an old lady, and a baby still sucking, I don't think there's a one of us in here gonna make argue against us needing do what's right for 'em."

By Gawd, ain't like an impassioned one of their own to go lighting the match. They's took to quiet ever' single word. Ever' pause of puff slapped with no move as Gary continued to the floor. His heavy weighted boots slogging Black Gold all the way to the front so's there might be view on all six foot two of his beaming-shoulda-maybe-rethought-that-summer-of-our-youth-when-he-were-courting-and-I-weren't-so-gawddamn-stupid-I-didn't-believe-thirteen-too-young-for-love-even-for-me-even-for-then frame and listened up.

"We needs a vote. We needs it now. And we needs it to go through. We all know what happens when that ain't the case, there's a plaque over yonder carved with the names of buried dead that shows it. Ain't not one of us can go affording time without pay and pay without fairness to the work we's doing just ain't right. Not when we's trying to carve out lives here for our boys. For our families. When there's folks needing taking care of. There ain't a one of us that can't find per exact the hill folk mindset needed if pushed come to shove in this here game of resolve. Trust and believe brothers and sisters, there's Enochs holed up inside all of us if situation's right. And I don't know 'bout all ya but I got 'bout enough time to wait on Mr. Todd figuring out whether or not he's in the wrong for what he done like I need a bent dick mule."

Weren't a face missing a dirty teethed grin. Always could count on good looking Gary for some charm.

"I says vote—"

"I second it—"

They's to over tune the bastard. Just ya wait and sees.

Kieran held hard to the coin. Just knew that any room for cave couldn't be carved out here in a place like this with a room full of men not when there's women folk casting down spells of witchery mountain shit on him if he didn't deliver. That's what they'd go to do on ye if ye ever stepped cross on him. Knew it plain as day. That's why his finger done warped indent over groove over groove over groove, he's filtering through all that metallic shroud of silver for a spot of good luck to come find him, for 'em right words to come land in his mouth, so's he still might rare tend holster of the nasty beast that comes from a group of men ready with the chomp on a set of wearied bones, 'cause Gawd knows, they'd zero down on even the most hidden flare of fear and come ready for the hunt. Just what they did.

"Gentlemen, ladies, I hears the worry. Trust me I do. By Jesus's name and body do ye not think I too don't know of the hardships. That I too don't dwell on such avarice nature of the beast of where money's gonna come or where its gone. My dear Gay, bless her sleeping soul, would speak often on the troubles of next dollar earned and after the flood did we not all feel the pinch of how far things could go south but I plead of ye brothers and sisters to recall yet again how the community came together. How we banded rise again this fair Hazard and made remember and restore to all the glory robbed from it…"

Always that damned flood, that one time fair view sign of Kieran-savior-oriented- light-mounted on top the tree to remind us of all he's give. 'Cause that's what he were truly saying up there on his pulpit. "Remember 'em favors, boys. Remember all those times I went for the bail out for ya. All those things y'all done owe me that I never come to collect." And he wouldn't collect. Wouldn't never go accepting no return from those men that came back with dollars in hand for the repay. Wouldn't have nothing of it. Not from no women and not from no men.

Said, with golden roll of carpet extend, with Gawd's drenched glorified touch and one hand crossed over the other at fat belly protrude, "Now, can't go offending the Lord Jesus like that now can we. Can't be a stain dishonest fellowship guiding me up when I goes to greet 'em pearly gates. Noooo, ye keep that there dear brother. Ye take it home and ye save it up for the time it truly in need."

See. No one never said he weren't a smart bastard. Ohhhhh, that he were indeed. Smug fuck shit.

"...brothers, sisters, please, 'em words No STRIKE haven't left my mouth once. Not once...Not once. All I'm saying is the demands must be settled 'fore we's to proceed. One more day is all I asks. One more for the drafting and deciding..."

"Whatcha expect we do? Huh, there Kieran. Huh. It ain't like ya's facing the same back break these boys done made...."

"Missess Brighton, please, I understand..."

Poor Ms. Brighton, she'd barely time to scoop the dirt over her young Taylor 'fore she's forced to go on with the burial of her oldest Palmer. Stood there now with hardly any more mourning left in her. 'Em other boys of hers, Eisle, Wayne, Corbin, and Myrtle, holding that wafer thin frame of hers up while they pinched ear to all Kieran spouted out. And that fucking Bastard just kept at it. Kept steam rolling over 'fore she'd even a chance to get out the gawddamn phrase she's meaning to spread over us next. Poor Woman.

"Ya says ya do. But do ya. Do ya really?" Distracted, Ms. Brighton looked from Kieran down to her boys, their hands wrapped gently round the Matriarch trying desperate at keep it together as we all looked on and in a roll of memory swallowed down by her throat's gulp, she simply took her seat.

There's an air of whip and rustle that'd steal the life from ya when ya went to thinking on the losses gathered in the room. On the many faces who bore just a bit lower from the grind of saying goodbye to a loved one without ever knowing it to be the last. How even if granted the foresight with it, what is there to say. No one ever wants to let go. No one ever wants to admit time ceases to those we want least gone from us. And that's one of the many reasons there weren't no standing for the bullshit spew dripping bottomless pit off that red haired ninny pitting out cross wise slabs of buttered shit over three-day old bread. Weren't no filling to be had on a thang such as that. Weren't nothing to be done with good fucking intentions, which were exactly what he'd happened on-prize ending to this here fucking shitty wrapped present tied up in a shitty ragged bow. Working out good faith on borrowed time, the bastard.

Gawddamnit, I can't believe this shit. I can't believe they's all just sitting round here listening to this shit. Standing in silence listening to this man tell them basically lend out in good will extension due to his having items after an act of Gawd that placed him in a position, I might add, that he didn't have no lead up to getting other than he come here with enough money to buy up a store and there he stands trying to tell us we need to give it one more day. Trying to say he understands, that no good bastard miling politician wannabe back door dealing, 'cause don't think there ain't more than a bit of suspicion as to how he's still running and operating that damn store when there ain't no one buying up shit. Don't think that, one bit. Ohhhh, there's more than just talk. Just wait and see. Just wait and see. Fucking bastard. Just can't stand it no more.

"Elizabeth, here, here, ya go on ahead and hold Ronnie, there for me. I gots something needs be said to that sack of shit standing up there."

27

FEBRUARY 3, 1960

ALBIE TODD

The sins of his father never weighed so very heavily on Albie Todd as the days when he awaited a certain guest's arrival. Thankfully, it was on such rare occurrence this guest ever called receive on, that the recounting of dear Dad seemed plucked from obscurity for only a momentary glimpse, though this did nothing for the insidious reminder. Understandably, given the time passed, that of twenty years at least, since Albie's last need for such a person as his guest might be, that on this day, this day as the sun shined and the Warblers poked yellowed bellies full of worms and earth from out thicket's charge, that the anticipation of revisiting his father's image sworn reborn in the visage of a man in his employ bore reticent on his morning nerves and he was not quite sure yet how to process their hold. Thus, he stood transfixed at the window, watching as the Warbler's danced about close to the ground, scanning secretly, even to himself, for the chance spotting of the snake that would soon lurk near and snap close on the prey frolicking in his field.

It was, of course, not always this way. Not always did he yearn for such predatory nature in things. As a child he'd wanted for destruction, certainly, as most often, young boys do at times, but these are mere formalities of fantasy, of "what if's" so that naturally the, "then I would," might carry out in the mind. So, that the hero give chance for rise, and noble characteristics displayed. The inference of dominance, on the other hand, the perception of power and reign given out, handed in fine slops of shared viewing so that later in life the actions reciprocated when chance and arrival align. Such a very long time since he'd thought of his father and the lessons he'd not give, the words he'd never said, that it seemed not even part of him any longer to ponder his presence.

Thus, he turned back.

At exactly 8:30 and not a moment later, his guest would arrive. The hour after the sun's rise, the precise amount of time it would take to walk from the pit of hell his guest housed himself in and make it clear glean over Annabell's hydrangeas, pits of powdered sky-blue petals spitting folly in his wake.

Annabell'd insisted on planting those damn things with the thought that perhaps the sight of something resemblant of Kentucky blue might endear the workers down below in Mill town to their family. It had not, unfortunately, ever crossed her heart or mind, that the blocking shadow of their house created over the village shrouded and ate any light the sun might gleam on their viewing of such blue and since there was not yet one visitor invited to their house that didn't travel there with them from the big city after Albie's new title given to him with the unfortunate death of Mr. Davis, it did not seem likely anyone might ever be granted the company of their petals. This, of course, not something to be commented on after such labors ensured by his wife to their fecund rise. Nor would it grant any purpose with his expression that he found the puffs of clustered powdered sky blue absolutely hideous because they were all the more a reminder that lineage strikes resemblance no matter how much deny is stuffed in the foundation.

Albie Todd, a man now aged quite well with distinction

believed absolutely that he stood opposite any place his father might ever occupy, and took what little comfort he might with his centered position inside his grand room, meant for grand decisions, by even grander people that it was a place his father would never, even if still growling back air, be allowed in. Couldn't even imagine what a man like his father would do if given invitation to such trappings.

The first thing he learned about his father and consequently, the first thing he learned about himself was Wolf.

Raoul meant Wolf.

"The Wolf is coming home, clean up—" A slurred charge of hurried fervor rattled amongst cluttered chaos of what three kids, a woman, and the square footage of 200 would bring. Us—pack, rustling in falling down traipse as the shove down and pick through of anything that might and could go for the upset on the Wolf hurriedly disappeared.

"Man can't be bothered with a home full of whining children and a mess to boot—" Sound lost in translation now. Too many years since his dear mother's death. More emphasis on the O's. She'd pad them in the back of her throat as if she's fishing a swath of cotton. Like luring a string of silk out in a no splash, still, pond. What straight from the roll of blonde hair dreams Swedish women sounded like, specifically ones that looked like angels with little halos over their names whenever their mark made.

Couldn't even do ample cleaning. Wasn't much room for things to sit or places for collect in that closet. Closet, a shelled-out utility trunk where paint stains came in splotched spots of tested hues, as if there would ever be the chance or want for redecorating in some nine story walk up full of poor immigrants. Made themselves a home amidst thin lines of Prussian Blue and Venetian Red. Their beds, a stack of two, shoved just as far as they would go against the wall, set next to full circles of Chrome Yellow, playing brilliant shine against dulled dabs of Drab and Shutter Green, none of them meant for murals, certainly, but made that way by sleepy heads that stared half eye slit towards the entrance of dreams.

"Lucky. Lucky for such space," Mother would spread her arms wide, missing the scratch of chipped plaster on both ends by not more than a foot, and tall, she was not.

Ever' now and again if they all went for the stand, there followed a whinnied refrain of bumped heads and bleeding nose and a sure fire shot of stars come cross their eyes but they were lucky. Most who lived in the flophouse spent their time in large bedded mess halls with no place to breath or think, with masses of children acting as courier pigeons from one end to the other as overworked mothers and some fathers, though there were only a handful few, prayed for silence.

The timing of the Wolf came on them slow. His appearance something of a grown venture where suddenly the accumulation of things no longer ignored, though they'd gone without notice for some time. His image like some abhorred tuft of hair, yanked and pried from a relentlessly itchy scalp with hopes the release might alleviate the scratch to which nothing might appease.

At night mostly—the Wolf's presence known only to Albie, he'd come. His slow sly entry left in shedded strands of mangy brown, in sudden noticed drippings of socks, or garrulous sprawls of shimmied shirts. Like vandals caught mid-swept. Like for Albie, alone, did the hair mutate and grow. His nocturnal showings lasting longer and longer and longer as that wedge of grizzly fur, that coarse bundle meant for pick up, continued egregiously towards arms and legs, as if the hair itself might spread over all inside the closet. As if Albie offered no escape from the Wolf's reach. And it was realizing this absolute truth, this non movable maze of where and when the Wolf had been, of stifling sickness in the depths of Albie's core upon viewing the hair clogged sinks of the common baths, all that nasty fuzz of not-belonging-there-strands begging for the pull so the sink could go back to the right way, to the way it was meant to function, to hair free, that Albie actually saw the Wolf as he stumbled in. The raucous lie spreading netted cement as time and time again, it, a proven fact that always, always, always, the Wolf left.

With haunches the size of whiskey barrels, with a ten hand count sprawl from shoulder to shoulder, with boulder bulges formed just beneath, as if rocks forged under bicep skin, with pronounced grope of elongated jaw that evened out the wide chunk of hair-thicker-than-most-heads-mustache, it was absolutely no surprise, the Wolf called the Wolf. No shock at all this German transplant, this slate of iron boss once called the Country's youngest Strongman, doled out dirty deeds for very, very, powerful men. And as he stumbled in, with smelly, ratty clothes, as he graced through sideway's step into Albie's once safe, once quiet, calm home, Albie's insides began fester and mold as that frightening moniker announced, "To Wolf ever'thing in his den was his own."

He'd come, the Wolf, always with hair of the dog already foamed in fine palates of hot drip at the corner of his mouth, the low dip down kiss to the girl cubs, the sudden slog of not bathed since last visit spitting man musk over ever' clip of air that could possibly fit in a space so small. That lingering burn of unsettling forced hand smell of some poor sap he'd worked over spread on the bare meat clamps of his mountain crawling paws. Always the swoop in, like some bandit, some pariah of wooly hirsute that only a foul-mouth-booze-loving-nasty-sailor-cussing-brick-house-laying-batter-your-eyes-out-if-someone's-paying-tramp-of-a-man-made-german-bone-crushing-steel could boast, hunkering down on his only son with a declarative this-is-mine sort of hug and yelling out to the world that for a second he remembered with a twirl "Der John."

The man standing back in the room of the house set on a hill that overlooked a town, some might say he ruled, did not in the least bare resemblance to his father baring his blue eyes. His fair complexion and golden, some might argue, long hair, though it did not of course reach hippie status, took after his mother in stature, build, and look, so that if given the incorrect light, Albie appeared somewhat sickly and a little weak, and there was comment afloat that this sometimes used to his advantage.

Earlier, before donning his favorite jacket, picked and mailed to him from the Big Apple, Albie'd stuffed the letters of clean white sinless sheet inside his starched shirt pocket full well knowing the intent and destruction to which their handing off would lead. No assuaging the recklessness in either direction for an invisible appendage already caught at the cross street of detriment and doom. They's meant—

He hated the slow infiltrating common talk, the wriggling inside his head foreign yet familiar, yet disgusting, that, no matter what triumph he took in never saying such quipped words out loud it still something of a haunt when they washed in bubbles along the shore of his folded mind; thus, he took start again—the papers.

The letters, to be exact, held no more than a sparse phrasing of words with no possible way of misinterpretation. The inked sprawl of two lines wrapped heartily around a fine stack of notes it would take quite a common man some very long time to make.

This, the price of peril and mayhem. The order of things when the guest arrived.

The order of things, yes truly, the order of things, that's what had brought him here. Brought him to this place now. Maintaining the order of things. The man that chose the leash instead of the wild for he knew he'd never be able to survive the latter. Never more abundantly clear, as he stood watching from the window, staring out along the horizon's tip, fingering that time piece, that stolen gift, robbed—no—owed, he was owed. It belonged to him.

That meaningful offering found tight round the neck that needed break so that endings could surmise here. Yes, truly. He belonged in that house with the grand room and the leather bound books where no dog ear dared live, where mallard print fit snug under crystal bowl and Tiffany lamp, where each room, a count of six, all sported immaculate view, even the washroom, fucking marble tile shipped from Italy direct washroom, where on special handed down mirror of finest New York boutique—splurge, had he asked his Annabell, please, display her fine set of perfumes, just so he, while soaking the grime of what sitting in a chair behind a desk, doling out task and commands might yield, might watch the sun filter crystal prism over his eyes in streams of glamour, that pranced fairy dance of silver sheen from mirrored case. He belonged there.

Further, it was of absolute choice Divine, on Albie's side alone, that he derived a position as such that would allow the cracking of whip on animals less than he, for in spite of his measly, smarmy stature, he was a man of power and a man of power yields higher than a beast.

Albie's first introduction to these laws came in the form of an air grappling punch spread so far back the sprawl of his tiny face that a molar knocked loose. Boy's name, Eckhart Bard, a neighbor on the third floor, who made it a personal goal to taunt and tease the much smaller Albie with lies and some truths about his father, most notably that of his absence and Albie's contribution to it. As if it yesterday, Albie recalled the sticky spit strand of blood and the immediate knowing, despite the incessant crack of pain vibrating his head, that the wailing showed no sign of letup. Not even with the juggling of soldier clink on the concrete slab of the flophouse floor.

This particular encounter marked the fourth of its kind in one week and Albie'd almost become accustomed to the overhaul of smack and jab his face and body took as if the covering of black and blue an attempt at rehaul, a redecorating of sorts similar to the intents of samples allotting the now absent for good Wolf's home.

Three years, two months, one week, and five days since the last howl reared and had it not been for the need of guidance in matters of whooping others and a multitude of pain carved so deep inside Albie's heart that even he would not know of its full extent until much later in life, there was scarce second thought give to his father, the Wolf's disappearance. Unless, of course, called upon by the rigorous pound of an equally as hurt boy slurring insults amidst injury about what he'd heard some drunks spout about the Wolf.

"Heard ye Da don't come home no more 'cause a bedwettin'—"

Pow.

"Ya, that's the spread of words jumbling cross the floors, that the Wolf's left the den to find other lambs—"

Pow.

The kind of hurt that goes deep in the crevice of tissue and pride leeched rivers of hate and confuse on the young Albie as Eckhart hacked away in front of his brood. Championed leader of a regalias troop of needy fatherless children, who'd made position on various enterprises around corners and newsstands which would illicit distinctions from throughout the neighborhood, regalias being but one they liked most, Eckhart, zeroed in on Albie in particular, come to find out later, because it was, in fact, his father the Wolf, who had taken from the young lad picking away shameless years of resent on him, his own father.

"Ya, ye Da left 'cause ye's nothing but a punk-sickly-no-good-never-gonna-be-not'ing-sorry-sop."

Pow.

But amidst the barrage, the onslaught of hits and careless disregard for common ground of all being left with the shit end of the deal, with no Dad around, Albie noticed something far more important. Some never before thought of OUT,` that had slicked past his mind despite countless hours spent on the evade of just such occurrences he was in. He noticed his sisters, Marina, Ingrid, and Greta at the far end of the room, noticed how the light from a big factory window cast sheen through simple white fabric, how from here, he saw not his sisters but three pretty young woman with budding forms standing in a group, who looked like his mother, quite beautiful.

Pow.

Albie noticed as well, that the largest member of Eckhart's tribe, a resolute hoss of a young man, who for all purpose of debate, could've carried on the Wolf's lineage if given different circumstances, was eye googling Ingrid.

Pow.

And suddenly, it dawned on young Albie, that a man who has something another man wants, if given just the right persuasion, can usually bend the hand with the promise of delivery and in turn yield the larger prize of the unknown. Thus, the next day, Albie devised, during hit after hit after hit, that he would go to his dear sister and ask of her a favor. A very small simple task. A moment of her time. A mere sputtering lapse with that hoss of a boy, for he knew Ingrid would certainly fall for such a brute given her affection for the one who'd peaked in and out of their youth, and she would, after some time, ask of him, that hoss of a boy, to make the beatings stop. To make end the suffering of her sickly brother. And no doubt, he would.

And no doubt he did. For not two days later as Albie watched from a corner, the testy waters of his plan not yet solidified in action, did that young hoss of a boy pick a fight with Eckhart, bloodied him senseless, that the convey to Albie understood.

To understand the horror of his guest, a man who at the age when others of his, peers that's to say, would with expedient and laser focused scope pursue that chance hope of bumping into a woman, leading thus end towards those lustful yearnings of such salacious nature that good Christian reared folk wouldn't dare dream of thinking, even in their locked up scriptured heads, he was recovering from an injury of most perilous description that even now to monitor the occurrence the full grappling of its severity lost. For how to put such an unfortunate vile, repudiated act—a scalp fashioned still with soft spot hardly etched in full grown bone, a young man, regulated by a path of choice already set forth despite any admonishments made otherwise, met, at the wrong time, a very dangerous set of men, who believed not in the adage that the young should be set mercifully aside. This young man, this soon to arrive guest of Albie Todd's, experienced the rather unfortunate ritual not seen since many, many, moons before Hazard existed, certainly before Kentucky existed, harkening back to that maiden time of fortressed foraging where land not owned by any at all, had his scalp near removed entirely from his head for happening on something he should not have been in proximity of view.

Veiled in such unbelievable circumstance and reason that the thread of Albie's guest's life took even further dip still towards some story book evil slip of which the product meant a man sporting such fine share of needle and string around the left side of his head that he forever favored a somewhat tamer version, though only in physicality alone, of Frankenstein; to have endured such tragic befalling at the formidable age of eleven, the spoon of castor oil life'd fed such an individual might very well tend towards a certain type of cure which could only be deciphered as ruthless. This was precisely the reason and the only one at that, that Albie had anything to do with him at all for if given chance, Albie knew full well as did most, The Hound, like his father, was not the sort to take to company of those unlike himself for very long.

Thus, it was that when the Hound stepped close to the double paned windowsill, his hot breath pressing scribbles of death on bleak glass, that no words exchanged between the two, no sentiments of phrase that could possible entice the animal to act, for, though, Albie'd solidified in that harrowing hall of neglect a realization that possession and control merely an arm's length trade in want, there existed as well the truth: a Wolf is a Wolf is a Wolf and Hound separated by one line alone; Albie thus, slipped between the crack of the pitched corner porthole that fat stack of sinless white papers, watching as it padded thunk atop Annabell's well pruned shrubs, full well knowing the Hound to pick it up as soon as he left.

28

NOVEMBER 3, 1930

THE WHITTLE BOYS

All Cecil wanted part of any longer were riding that young girl.

"What's dat?" Cian popped up, his back still sore from the fresh wack of tree tapping he'd busied hisself with for the day.

"Doing her head in again."

"Jaysus." Ever since she'd showed up, Cian never wished more that he too, could be embedded with disfigurement. The turning off of the shove and go making strutted swipes on a blanket of straw never lured so appealing as when he saw his broder roll over, that blank space of where an ear used to live syphoning silent sway in the place he'd prefer. "He's gonna rip her through."

"Probably die 'fore then," muttered spry from under his broder's lips.

"Smack down of wear and tear of arse like to carry over the holler. Where's the girl's parents, then, Riley. Huh, where they be? Jesus Christ Almighty, there's not a denying sinner left in hell who hadn't laid ears on the pitied cries jumbling leap outta that mouth."

"If it goes on, I'm like to go for the strangle on her meself. Tired of hearing it to be frank."

"Just seems odd, don't it, that's she stayed as long as she has?"

"Whacha ye mean odd?"

"Well, he's going at it now almost on the hour ever' hour, don't it seem she might be a little raw."

"Roll over Cian."

"Meaning, I'm all for a little dip in the pond, but—"

"But what?"

"Well, I mean, how much can the bastard really have stored in him?"

"Roll over Cian."

"Seriously, Riley. He's an old man. He's not even got both legs."

"What's a leg got to do with fucking? I seem to remember there spot ago, a two-legged dog making quite a few waves with some other mutts back in the day, aye. Don't ye? Seem to remember a time, in fact, where there were of particular attention placed on that golden mutt with both hinds chopped. Remember?"

"What a bastard Da was."

"Oh it weren't all Da's fault, now were it? Don't go placing blame on things ye've not gathered up all the cues on?"

"Whacha mean?"

"Ye know exact what I mean, Cain. We ate better that winter month than any other."

"Ye're a fucking bastard too."

"Fuck." Riley flipped over. The burn of a fresh knuckle graze twisting curly cue spurts of fire engine pain right overtop his kidneys. "Why…"

"Wait." Cain hurried for the protect of knees to face as Riley sledgehammer shelled his shin. "Fuck. Said, wait, broder."

Clobbering jarred the space between the men, their thoughts shied back to when they's boys and bickering and fighting went hand in hand with carried out decision of what to do when. Back to where fly 'round punches and skewed knots of pinched skin lived and shoved back chins and sideswiped push settled things in chokehold locks, though all of it up 'til then not something to cry for alarm as they's still, the both of 'em positioned on the floor like a right lolly set of wallering pigs.

"Git yer...hand...out me face."

All the while in the distance, 'em broder's placing being that of a hovel made from the discarded leaning of an old stone fireplace, that after much pillaging they'd fashioned a mighty nice, for wood standards, abode, replete with thatched roof and mud floors, both Cian and Riley laid pause, seemed Cecil 'Doc' Hodge might've found a spot of something bad. See, from 'cross a small swathed over path of devil's helmet and squashed blue and purple pits, those being from a berry thicket just to the left not but four feet away there, Cecil's place sat and there inside did the sound granting attend emit.

"He's stopped there Cian, stopped hisself midfuckingsweep."

"Riley, as sure as 'em birds know better to not go messing round 'em purple petals, Cecil knows when to take hisself a break. Ye said so yerself. He's an old man."

"Not saying I'm not agreeing with that, Cian, but have ye ever known a man to make that much of a thunk."

"Would ye call it a thunk. Felt more like a little plash to me."

"What the fuck's a plash?"

"Well, it's like a little drop in water, aren't it?"

"Where the fuck's water Riley?"

"The water's fucking secondary, it's fucking illuminating."

"Illuminating. Were fucking talking 'bout a sound and yer trying to paint a fucking scene. What the fuck goes through yer head? Why would ye feel it necessary to bring talk of a plash, which's got no place anywhere near the fucking thunk that came outta Cecil's? Where did ye even hear that 'fore?"

In fairness, as the proper usage of whatever word might or might not have described the sound they might or might not have heard that did or did not come from across the small pathway, there certainly weren't any hope left that they'd continue on in the discussion 'bout it on the floor for both now stood making wild accusations that'd lead undoubtly where they always did when it came to broders and the discussion of a thunk and or plash fell in the distance just as it emerged. Got 'em fucking nowhere, 'cept to that place neither of 'em needed be.

See to it now, Cian standing the scrawnier of the two but certainly flighty and fast in manuevered twitch, held corkscrew swivel with eyes darting back and forth as his blood gurgled up in heated red. Not always a sign of caution but certainly something to venture nod at, that when given the rise for Cian to get a little bit of the workup on him, when perhaps, there might be need for intervention, and especially when it were usually dawned on his broder's shoulders to be the one to walk him from the edge, it did not favor in the least when these affections, turned to Riley. And as normal fallout procedure became evidently clear, that common autopilot ignite, Riley readied hisself for the blast radius of his broder's smite with pumped fist so's that when the time needed, the knockout ready for cool down. For time and again, the only proved approach to Cain's brush towards calamitous upheaval entailed a pinning of the force 'fore it granted too large a wind to travel.

Meanwhile, in that granted perch spill of a very young girl's eye with fallen down hair of spitfire red and legs drawn wide and hooch vomit dried, crusty on her cheek and candy-apple throb of snatch hay burn, there sparked an idea as the thrusting continued. See, coated up next that pull of old man drill, her head turned by the smoosh of a hand smelling more and more like dirty ass with ever' punched thrust in her nethers below, she'd laid eyes on a carved thing of true queer nature. Some vestibule of half marked chew from where a tug-o-war with critters ended with eat up dots made from little scrappy teeth all atop the rim of that long lean peg leg. Like the man who's laying down pipe on her not give all that much thought to why a pair of, what she's thinking, coons would want gnaw on something come from that Red Maple just right left set his front door.

Surely he knew there's to be more than a fair share of syrup drip spill from that hoss of a tree. Mean anybody whose anybody done tapped and set the plug of a mouth with sure splayed glee just to taste that sweet drip. Why a set of animals wouldn't go ahead with the trouble weren't nothing out the ordinary. Hell, she once saw a Black Bear crawl clear through one of her Daddy's windows just to get to a set of biscuits Momma done made, that's when she were going to making biscuits, which, course hadn't been since she got herself all caught up with a case of blues and hadn't stepped one foot out from bed since. More than half the reason she's staring down that sorry piece of wood that done got pot marks all up the spine, done faced and seen and went to a heap of trouble trying to navigate 'em woods round here, specially when they's like to be took with a set of the rains and that mud'd go for the slide, specially when that little bit of leather strip fitted between the fat upper part where his nub'd go to sit looked worse for the wear and might stand chance to only last a couple months more, and how it hadn't gone all to some kinda funk and done tore off entire, specially with all that nastiness coming off his fingers he's jabbing and poking round at her with, and to think, probably more than half of it to do with her Momma not getting outta bed any longer. Almost enough to make her want to fashion a poking stick herself just so's she could go knock some sense into that woman.

Truth of it though, she thought, as that leg went all up and down with the thrust of a man who hadn't got a dick dip in some time, she probably just hadn't lived enough life yet to go knowing what could cause such a thing, what could cause a woman to forego sun and laughing and life, but then she couldn't state very well with any sincerety she knew what that were 'bout either. Decided probably best, her time spent on wondering after the how of that peg.

She'd heard the stories. Heard how on a split of full moon and non, there came a loud spare ship of screams over the mount. How in the middle of night her Paw and brothers and sisters and mother leapt from their crowded slumber with fear Devil Jim come back to haunt, that only he having the possession of such ill willed turn of tongue, come to rob 'em of their souls. There's stories floating all on top that hill and in 'em hollers 'bout that nasty scabrous plot of Satan's-do-gooder-soldier, 'bout how he'd twist and writhe and force his hand down in yar throat, how he'd pull and rip and tear from ya the very core of all those things contributing to human decency and leave ya there to rot and wither in the cold absence of Gawd, for when he's done with, or maybe even for there's dare chance walk through yar door, that viscous-spitting-lying-dribble-of-demon-rampallion-droog'd went ahead and took from ya all yar good. And even if it were just some yarn spread 'bout over the pits of fire spitting sparks, even if it only something whispered back after the bottles half done or damn well spitting dry blanks of sincere, there lived fear that we's all only moments away from one of 'em there Devil visits.

What that leg'd done, maybe what it'd gone on and done for Cecil too, were something of the same, something she'd long ago suspected. Little bit of confirm and deny all 'em things she'd done ever been told. See, word of that night some five years ago, when she, just seven, and that raucous shrill hurled forward in the black of night, that pulsating kick of metal heartbeat, that shell shock jerk of aching daggers ready for fuckblast spew stood as confirmation that if given time enough, with or without the tale of some backasswards fiend running ride on some soul buried up inside, that man, hardly ever needed much excuse 'bout him to go doing a little spit of bad. She knew it better than most, better than probably anybody understood, the evils a man could do. Felt it on the daily. Felt it from the moment she's sent out of the house with 'em jars of hooch, out to make 'em rounds, as her Daddy called it, as all the boys of her family, her bloodline called it, though she doubted they ever found 'emselves pinned with a wand up their middle as much as she did. It were all a fruitless ruse. No need to go making up no stories 'bout some Devil just to go make amends 'bout all the nasty a man's got to wrestle with, nohow. Devil Jim weren't the one who'd come visit 'em hills that night just like he weren't the one inspired evil deeds.

It were a man. Plain and simple. A man who'd made that noise come out, a man who'd, with drunkard hand, whose in the middle of pile driving knob in her little bits, that'd got hisself so fucking drunk, he'd went on ahead and shot his leg off 'cause, well, probably sounded like a good thought at the time, or 'cause maybe he'd wrestled so long with all that evil up in him he needed a place to set it down for a while and that while came in the form of a leg.

See, so what that little spot of peg, what that aching pull of robbed-from-him-even-though-it-by-his-own-hand-done were spell and confirm that even if there were a man running round that went by the name of Devil Jim, even if he were prone to take up with battles of venom spitting out into the world, it weren't cause to nothing magical, nothing special. Just like it weren't something she could go on denying any longer that she's getting the short end of the stick by piddling round in her Daddy's wishes or her brother's wishes or whoever it were dictating things need be done other than her. She might could even go so far as to consider that damned queer carved thing to be a spot of blessing. Yeah, maybe she could, Iionna Meaks thought.

Maybe when he'd set that thing down, finding it were doing more harm than good at getting hisself traction from the floor, his nub kept going for the slip anyhow off that pile of musty straw he'd covered with a tattered rawhide, took it off round'bout the same time he'd gone after that last sip off a mason jar that should'a seen well past a week and that's working on Daddy's time, that propped-up-old-beat-to-hell-glorified-walking-stick-turned-leg-meant savior. For what all 'em stories she'd heard, all 'em tales of Devil Jims and potential threats of one legged Cecil 'Doc' Hodge done left out, were the fact that burrowed down in that hollow spot of where his leg fit, Cecil'd made the habit of stashing his money and seeing as how Iionna'd grown tired of the life she's meant to live, she took that there as opportunity for something more.

THUNK or PLASH.

29

NOVEMBER 3, 1930

HOUND BONNEHUE

Iionna Meaks never meant nothing to me. Seen her take a nob in her mouth once like it were a caramel coated carrot, tell ya that. Just shy of Michner's Cliff. Where that girl'd flung herself couple years ago. Don't nobody even remember her name no more.

Sad thing.

Broke ever' bone in her body on the way down, that girl did. Said that when they found her, or what were left, what 'em man-eaters hadn't torn and hauled off, she's more twisted up than a thicket searching for water. Bones and muscles poking out like they's sets of thorns emptying petals.

In the mornings were when I liked going to Michner's most. Nobody touched it with a ten-foot pole no more. Not since that girl done what she did. Some bullshit 'bout 'em being afraid ill will rubbed granite stone blues on the bottom of yar feet once ya got high enough to see that tree line drop. What I liked most 'bout it. All that time by yarself, just to be up and watch and think and sit. Listen to 'em Jaybirds carry out lives in the wind.

Normally, they's not ones to go carting round by 'emselves but there's this young fella, guess I don't really know if he's young but that Jaybird were the closest thing to being a friend, so's I wanted him to be young. Going through the same things I's going through. Anyhow, he'd went on ahead and nested up in the floundering leftover of this dead oak near the edge of the drop off, and he and I'd go to keeping each other company when that sun'd peak for the rise. He'd go to chirping and we'd just sit there, the both, as the world spread ever' which a way in front. It were on one of 'em very occasions, one of 'em special mornings with him singing and me thinking as that sun colored frosty glow over the Kentucky, making that long tail of snakey water fit shallow and pink in yar eyes while 'em knots of chewy clouds steamed over tree fingers, when I seen Iionna shove skin down her throat. Caught her right as that boy plopped out.

Granted, I's in a hurry to get back and almost ran right past 'em. Hurry come from a stack of lumber meant to already be hoed down and shaved in fitting bundles with my initials stamped on 'em. Supposed to have 'em ready so's once Daddy got up all he needed do were walk four steps out the front door, coffee tin in hand, long johns airing wind through the unbuttoned flap at the back, Daddy looking more and more like some bad Santa variety who'd got caught up in a whole heap of wrong with a whiskey bottle and a losing battle of dietary frequency, and give a checked look to see so's that ever'thing in order when Lonnie Bibb come round. We'd carved a little business chipping lumber down in town and Lonnie being one of Daddy's oldest friends offered up tote so's Daddy didn't have to go less he wanted to, which that weren't never the case. Liked it right where he were and not a step out. But part of my duties as wood chopper and basic ensurer that my ass not tanned 'fore I'd ate supper, were that at least a pile of five, now that's five feet high and five feet long, done set down 'fore he got up. And given that there a little bit of delay already seeing how I couldn't just go and leave in the middle of that sunrise that'd offered up an understanding of what Gawd's country meant, I's in more than a bit of a shuffle when I cleared the brea of that cliff.

Stumbled on her and one of Gerri Lynn's kids playing show and tell behind a Sycamore. Weren't so much showing on her part but once her mouth opened wide and folded up over her teeth, don't reckon that boy gave much of a good gawddamn to her missing sliver. Never seen nothing like what she's doing in my whole life, but I can guaran-damn-tee I's looking more than a little forward to whenever it might happen to me. 'Cause judging by looks alone, all 'em twitched O's and clenched lips coming off him, all 'em tongue licks spouting from her, that hum and plow of slurp sealing that boy's face 'til he's forced to see Jesus in the back of that tree they's leant up against. It were clear just like that sunrise back up there on Michner's, it, part of a little something bigger, and I'll share it with anyone if they'd asked then, that it weren't just Gawd alone at work. Believe a little slit of Jesus too for that boy were going to a lot of trouble spelling out his name. "JEeeeeSSSusss—" almost like He's flowing outta him.

Made that one time I'd overheard Momma go to talking 'bout the Holy Spirit with one of her sisters, take on a whole new level of meaning.

Now, just so's we clear, there weren't nothing like spying coming from my end of the story. Daddy'd have my ass if I's caught peeping and he were in my ear the entire time of that five second break my feet were taking from moving.

"Boy, ya want one of 'em nasty fucks making eyes on yar sisters? Huh?" Backhand plow the answer to my head with an oleman-strong swipe that'd cause the eyes to sting and blur 'fore I'd dare chance opportune space at the explain— "Don't go feeding bark to no fire, boy. They's sisters and daughters to somebody."

So's ya can believe me, soon as that boy done dropped what looked to be a set of spider dribble all down Iionna's chin, I's as good as gone. All that time in between, that viewing of her tilted back head, cardinal hair bunched up by sycamore bark teeth, that boy's dipping down like he's pond diving with his swilly stick alone in a shallow cave of kissing minnows, all that counted out in ONE-M-I-S-S-I-S-S-I-P-P-I, and certainly did not last more than five seconds in all. Surely, Daddy could make some room for the understand on that.

But that don't mean, a girl who'd learnt and copied things she's been shown and led too deserved any of what she got next.

It were half a year later that Iionna Meaks came razor twine sharp over a hill on the south side of where Cecil 'Doc' Hodge's land began and a mugwort patch my family'd harvested since the first of us come to the holler.

Apparently if there were a line connecting all my family with the various spells of stomach issues that'd plagued us over the years laid out on land, it's said, it might carry the length of Kentucky total, and since in all the time of our existing up there on the mount, there hadn't never existed 'cause for Cecil to go minding our throwing down a little bit of seed to get 'em lower frequency stints in check, it were something of common venture for me to go grabbing some herb for at least one if not all the Bonnuhues living.

Couldn't say with all accuracy how much time past since my first gander at that girl and the time since but it were 'bout six months, two weeks, three days or something and there weren't all that much that'd gone for the change on her. Drew in hurried steps with a hovered shield of suspect following after her as she went for the pack down of what looked to be a handful few of national bank notes. Known it 'cause Lonnie'd done got sauced one evening and he and I'd stayed up well after the old man went to nod and somehow or another I talked him into showing me what it were they's handing out down there for goods. Whipped out his pocket a press of three two-dollar bills and laid 'em out one by one on a rock by the fire pit, his boot tailored down on the bottom side of 'em case there a shot of wind come up, plunging 'em to the fire. And sure enough just as then when my eye'd caught hold of something with the knowing it to be a thing to want after, I recognized instantly their distant cousin trucking hide in the loose fitting sprawl of Iionna Meak's nightgown as she begged hard for their sticked stay against her skin.

"Iionna?"

Even though I'd gone to more than my fair share of thoughts 'bout her since, there weren't not even the slightest bit of recollection as to who the hell I might be crossing her mind as she hauled ass forward. But telling by the speed she's trucking on, figured wherever she's going it were better than where she's been and I aimed that even if she didn't know me, I's to help. Whether or not she went for the repay with some carrot suck wouldn't hurt none either. And the closer she got the more and more I began to wet my whistle with the fancy.

Last week alone I'd woke up to a fair dirty dream where I's sunk down in a little swell of water at Tumler's stream. Almost like I's set to take a bath in it with my legs all folded up so's my knees granted glory to heaven as my belly sunk down like the Devil went for a pull on the scale. Weren't nothing special. Felt like I's going for a soak's all. 'Cept for when I looked down, my toes spreading in the warm water, there weren't no making out my bottom half. Couldn't see round it at all. Not with that large sprout of an orange tree shooting pillar straight high out my middle. Grown right there in between my legs as if I part born from the sapling and unable to move for the past fifty years. Just stuck there, stuck and rooted in the ground. Waiting for something to happen. For anything to happen. Knowing that at some point or another there's sure be a thing to happen. Woke up whiskey bottle soaked all down my front in a special kind of sauce and a feeling like there a bit of change come over me. Watching Iionna sprint high kicks, her chest piddling slacked bounce past thickets and shrubs made the wash of that feeling come back.

Weren't 'til she got right close up on me, so near the linger of dirty dick and sweaty gash slammed offense-sprinkle on 'em herbs, I saw the reason for her running. Slugging some Gawd awful mean behind that poor girl, who should it not be forgot were carrying with her what looked to be, if there's a squint shined over 'em starries, enough greenbacks to go ahead and 'cause question rise to what done to earn such a stack, were three distinct shapes of the type of men, who if ever there a buckshot following close yar hind legs and there a need to kick that slinging of dirt up a notch to that second, third, and Gawdwilling fourth gear, it were in such a case as this, for, ya'd never want no reason for 'em ever to go faster than a slow lean towards yar way. And as she hustled past the knockdown of some rotting poplar, as she hurled forward, chugging wild and furious to what she thought might act as salvation-lock-door-base, there weren't no help for the tightening of my pants as I saw that plot of hope for her designated to me. Might could be spoke to a bit of garish abandon that it were no longer in me to question the why of how it were she'd got into such a trap as it bore no more importance to that fella down below who happened cross-stich jump to the driver side of all things after.

Like to say there were a nod of wherewithal inside me to shine light on the shit fire calamity that would understandably befall a boy straight off the golden train of what a first fight'll do but unfortunate there weren't. What shoulda occurred from that very first titty wiggle of Iionna Meak's devilish frame shoulda been a sudden call to rise for a-hightail-my-ass-outta-here-right-the-very-fuck-now moment and yet it hadn't. The why of that, stuffed flagpole raise up the underside of one of 'em stupid fucking dresses so's that when the acknowledge of one very angry and semi-hobbling-peg-leg-wearing Cecil 'Doc'Hodge, who currently made constant wrestled sway with a set of britches bundled up in his fist like a chocked out turkey, and two men ain't never seen 'fore, looking like the rustic vagrant leftovers of a war fought elsewhere mixed with the charming candor of a sideway's grinning rattler, of which not one of the three wished anything but a whole fist of animus to little Miss Iionna Meaks, I musta looked a common sight of slow. Suppose it should then be no small feat of wonder why 'em men, 'em very well learnt souls of how to get things back if they's in the mood for want, 'em, don't touch, steal, take, gander, nor look near the throws of anything that might could be mine scrappy wretches took after me the way they did.

"Helluva thang a girl's gaze." Cecil 'Doc' Hodge chartered broke twig swing over the last of Iionna's bones that weren't yet smashed. All the others long whipped free from the weight of her life just like all 'em men who'd molded acts on her frame then left right when she's grown accustomed to their wants. She looked busted but somewhere in me I still found a spot of beauty floating round her face. Clinging all cattywompus, all pitched lanky legs, they'd not beat that part of belong away from where I knew she fit.

Don't get me wrong. I weren't stupid enough to think it love. I'd not known her. Not at all. But with her face smooshed and her hair draped over her eyes like curtains, and my head straddled in the hands of two very capable men, I believed her face to be the last I might ever see. Wanted it to have a veil of truth. Only thing I'd ever heard do that were love. So's I looked on her like my Mommy looked at my Daddy when he weren't looking. Like her whole life held in the believing that for her this were as good as it gets, that this, even if given the chance at something more, at a different time or place, that she wouldn't choose no one but him.

I pictured the sadness of that girl who flung herself off Michner's Cliff and thought if she were here now I would look at her the same. I would gaze at she and Iionna and love 'em so much all the pain went away. That's how I looked at Iionna as Cecil buttered the back of her neck with a hatchet. As that red went slide, covering all down her back, seeping in that dirt we's both pinned down in, she with Cecil's bloodied hands busy playing pickup sticks with 'em greenbacks and 'em two foreigners holding my melon in pressure tight grip, I tried to go back all 'em times I sat up there on the cliff listening to that Jaybird's caw. Tried to focus hard on that as 'em boys Bowie knives chipped hair and skin off my head.

30

1990

RONNIE FAIRCHILD

We'd not talked in so long the act lost to me and the rambling spread cheap and rich like buttered saltines ever'time I went to speak.

Mick, ya, never were one for a good constitution. Barf on a dime's notice. Lost all yar cookies once on Ella Mark right in the middle of the school yard 'cause Truman Shore let out an SBD on the playground. When that cloud of a four-day-sit-in-yar-belly cabbage stew came over ya, weren't nobody not eating cabbage stew at the time, fucking Linda Blair'd all over that sweet little girl. Got so bad folks went to fair warning 'fore lighting matches, they'd go to still a room, "Lightin' up, hear," a fella'd holler, and there'd be one sad sap who'd wave caution and take a sidestep outside just in case.

"Good thing ya's dead…woulda already spilled half yar glue if ya's living. Ain't that right?"

Shoulda closed his eyes. Folded down the skin. Made it so the space between us a little more. But for well over an hour now, there weren't no tearing from him. No moving at all from my dead little brother's stare.

"Hardheaded bastard."

Weren't no way in hell, ya woulda lasted long with me, anyhow. Not with the pack of fiber and shitty food I'd shoved in. I's two sheets away from peeling paint off this here broke down caddy somebody hadn't gone to the trouble of fixing. Likelihood brother, there, woulda lasted more than thirty cropped down near the shooter ain't factoring high at all.

"Consider yarself lucky."

Don't nobody want company with yesterday's burrito. Not with the shred of bubble guts working through me now.

"You'da gone trigger happy. Pair up another slug on me. Slam it right there to go along with the first."

Probably woulda done the same. That last shave of nasty smelled fucking Gawdawful. Like burnt rubber and wet dog and rotting eggs. Mean, if my hands weren't elbow deep in holding down that geyser ya'd shoved through me, it woulda done me some good to wipe the stink from my eyes. Way it stood now, I's holding steady stream to a wet set.

"Used to could clear a room if Mommy unclipped some of 'em lima beans. Remember that? She'd go after the stripping of 'em cans we'd put up in the winter with the first sign of unfrosted ground like Spring right outside the door. Go to argue with Nanny 'bout how she knew it in her bones that it weren't just a thaw. That this year were the year, Spring's to come in January. Just knew it, she did. Remember that?"

"Know what, maybe ya's too young to remember Mommy uncanning 'em beans. Ya'da been, what…two…three? Can't remember. Ya's young, that's for sure. Mommy were still living with us at Nanny's. When did she leave—were it yar sixth birthday… naw third…third…had to a been. Remember it 'cause ya went to crying and weren't nobody that could get ya to shut up. Nothing but red cheeks spilling crocodile tears. Wouldn't let nobody hold ya. Not Nanny. Not me. Just wanted to be left alone, left alone in Mommy's bed so's ya could take in the full scent of her."

Mommy'd left right 'bout the same time Mick'd started garnering interest in that other part of the equation—Daddy. Started asking 'bout Daddy this and Daddy that while he's pocking sticks through lizards outside and it were a subject neither Mommy nor Nanny wanted to entertain for any amount of time. Weren't all just that, sure, but it fell right convenient like in Mommy's lap for there to be trouble brewing down at the mine right when ya went Daddy blabbering. And Papaw, well, he weren't there to talk on it, now, where he, Mick?

"Well, I'll tell ya, since ya can't tell it yarself. Mommy thought she's being real big time making us a feast one day. She'd gone at it, now. Collards and cornbread and chicken and pork and beans. Made us an event, she did. Believe maybe it were Nanny's birthday…yeah, that sounds 'bout right. Boy, we ate like we hadn't seen food all year that day. Drank the pot licker and ever'thing. Even ya. Turned that bowl up and went to lapping back tracks of pepper and hog. Even tried to fish out another bowl. Wanted ya a part of that turkey neck."

"Just rolling in it we were, rolling in full. With extended belly's and stained up chins and cheeks and shirts. But the thing with collards, something ya hadn't yet experienced at the time, were they's a mean sorta clean that comes outta the backend of that experience and when Nanny let out one of her long-drawn windpipe solo of a hind thank ya, it weren't a thing yar little body could handle."

"Shit boy ya didn't even make it in yar hands. Just rubbernecked back like ya's eyeing a set of indecency frowned upon by Gawd. Like it painted up on that ceiling and 'fore any of us could figure out what in the world ya'd gone on and planned next, ya reached forward with the full power of all the might giv en and let it out. Spilled all that hard work, all that time Mommy'd went at it with fuss and sweat, all that mess of what a little boy puke'd do right there on the table. And by Gawd, I ain't never laughed so hard in my life. Not never."

I'd spent the last hour having this sorta on and off again talk with Mick. This sharing of meaningless shit passing from me to land on him. Bunch of kid stories where the endings shifted out barrel laughs and made room for moral hugs after both parties found their life's diversion 'cause to a simple misunderstanding that shoulda remedied itself long ago if one ever made moves towards a telephone. But the longer I stared at him while my head swept confused like at the ill attempts at my body's yearning to get up and clean that slug out my gut placed there, the more it became clear. All this my fault.

I'd led him to it. By my example, by my ability to grapple and hold and breath and sustain the life I'd set 'fore myself, I'd led him 'cause he'd only yearned, only ever yearned to follow. To be like me. Without his ever asking if that a thing to be done, without him ever questioning that just 'cause I's born first, just 'cause I's the one to cull the answers for myself due merely to no one being set there 'fore me so that I too might not react to their example, did not mean that faltering part he'd subscribed to me something I'd accepted. Lead weren't never nothing meant for me. Lead, were for teachers and parents and friends and perhaps, yes, for brothers, for men who burrowed fast and hard in the kinship of what it meant to be a part of something, to be aligned as steward of a pack, but these weren't me. These were assumptions, conclusions drawn, meat hooked in that delicate side of skin as soon as one's pushed from birth, clamped there with the just-in-case string to be pulled soon as next child conceived, soon as spawn spit. I'd not asked for it and 'cause it weren't something of my consent I'd shunned it as if it'd not existed. And I'll tell ya this, friends, if ya think for one second, that dear sweet brother is free and clear of judgment, buddy, ya got another thing coming. Just ask him how he got tangled up with 'em Masons? Hard headed somabitch...just had to do it, didn't he...couldn't help hisself, could he...sure he couldn't...parked hisself on the curb of trouble ever' single time with not even a dime in his fucking pocket to pay the meter. That were my brother.

31

FEBRUARY 1, 1964

CONNIE

Under the Lawd's eyes, she loved 'em both equal and when she started in on 'em collards, her arms bicep deep in a wash basin she'd pulled from next a stack of slaughter pales out the barn, she planned on seeing that thought cover all throughout the rest of the day just like that water's doing to 'em greens. Planned on not one thing poking otherwise. But it were a useless venture. It always were. 'Cause 'spite all her best intentions 'em seeds of spoil started climbing in 'til they's full up in the float with 'em leaves.

Her head'd start in like this from time to time, working hard at the convince and hard at the avoid. Felt like she's splitting halves with trying to love Mick just as much as she did Ronnie and trying to avoid 'em both so's there weren't no room for her to make the comparison. On the days where she knew she'd lose; she'd try a hand at gathering up a big ole stack of reasons why Mick were just as good as Ronnie and that's exact what she'd done the entire week. Even stopped by Green's Grocers on the way up just so's there'd be a sack of rock candy weighing down her pocket when she burst through 'em doors.

See, the habit of Connie's, as the habit of half the mountain, were to go 'bout cooking a storm when there's a bit of guilt stuck to yar boots and whenever that dirt got to a nice fine hearty coat, she knew it were time to visit her Mommy and 'em boys. Feast like cooking, what she'd do. Type where it don't matter if there's two or ten, there's gonna be enough for damn near twenty once all said and done.

Helped her with her nerves. Laid down a bed of cotton on her skin. Made her feel warm and cozy like nothing in the world could go to bother her while she's in it. Penance-like. Cook like she done something wrong, that's what her Mommy'd call it. Which she hadn't. She hadn't done a damn thing wrong. Not one damn thing. All she ever done were right, 'specially for that baby. Raised him up, didn't she. Had to count for something. Sure did in her eyes, which meant there were a bit of convince on the Lawd too. She coming from Him, boy coming from her—made sense. But can't go thinking on that very long could she, not when there's cooking needing done.

Cooking. Just cooking. Just getting up while the house still dark, while there's cold creeping under doors, smoothing rivers of ice over her socked feet. Just picking dirt from off leaves. Ain't no proof for a pinch of bad in that. Not yet. Not if 'em thoughts writ only in her head.

Boys'd gone wild when she'd showed up night 'fore. Shoulda seen 'em. Both of 'em just a tugging and a crawling and a loving on her like she some sort of a saint. Some sorta angel, which she knew she weren't. Both of 'em just as sweet as they could be. Both her boys who she loved equal. Who she's chucking stems for.

Done planned on coming all week. All week long this meal in her head. This space. Her in it. Mommy's kitchen. What thoughts'd do to her. Rest and seethe and rest and seethe and think and think and think 'til finally there's room for do.

She's making 'em fried chicken. Ever'body loved fried chicken. It were Nanny's birthday. Reason for the visit. Couldn't bring herself to come up no more just for 'em boys. She'd say it's what she's doing but that'd stopped a spell ago due to all that hurt. Not Papaw's hurt. Mick's. Mick were the one that hurt.

She'd shaved their necks with one swoop, 'em chickens, just as the sun lifted pockets of steam in patterned pinks and red. She coulda twirled 'em. Done it like Mommy. Taken both their heads in her hands and spun 'em round like they's a set of sheets, like she's 'bout ready to go flinging whips in the wind but she needed the snap of their spines to clink in her forearms. Needed to earn it. Earn the reward by force of will, by no jacket in forty-degree mountain morning cold, swell of life born in the slow to numb sheath of hard skin she'd built.

In the hour of her plucking, malted fuzz of dirty brown pit falling feather tops over her feet, she'd rocked in the old chair where Papaw held Mick in the evenings, and she couldn't remember the last time he'd fit close on her and she made false promise this soon to change. She told herself this as she finished dressing the chickens, their bodies warmth a fleeting vision of life to cold as their little legs smooshed in her hands and caught off guard by how natural they went to fold, she switched Ronnie to Mick in her head and brought the chick in close, whispering to the wind, she loved 'em both.

Used to could, when Mick's a baby, which suppose weren't so far off from now, she'd go to hold him with a squint and think he part of the same. That he come from that man she loved but couldn't no longer name, kept it locked up behind her knee, felt weren't no space left from that tear he'd done to her chest. She'd think as she passed over his eyes and nose that they not so very lean he not belonging to him, that his mouth not so very pursed it maybe not gonna fill out one of these days. But not no more. Can't hardly go to shining on him now. Not for very long. Not now that he's older and that face'd not once shown a gather of plump.

She'd not lived with 'em, her boys, in three years. Weren't something she's proud of, not in the least, and she hated the looks she got in town for it. All 'em hens picking assume off the ground. They didn't know, not none of 'em could. Got to be when she's walking 'bout, when she's making her way to union headquarters she couldn't barely pass the street without somebody crossing words under their breath 'bout their beliefs on her.

In the back of the house, the beginnings of movement churned and her heart went for a pause. She couldn't take him on his own. Needed the buffer of others.

She'd got fired from the bottling factor when Mick were implanted inside her, called in and picked off like she's a nasty scab, that's what ran over her mind as she coated up 'em breasts and thighs. Collards wouldn't be ready 'til dinner but biscuits and chicken'd be nice for breakfast.

They'd said, all 'em folks handing out Hell passes down in town, that she weren't nothing but a road side skank. All of 'em turning backs and hushing words when she went to walk by. Lost friends faster than she could count. Folks trying to place meters between what they thought she were and who they wanted to be. Only one who stood strong were Elizabeth. Lawd knows she'd bore the brunt of a rep.

Suppose Connie were cursed for the courting of violence in all its forms from the moment she took air. Hard being pretty like she were in the mountains, 'specially when that man she planned on tending life with'd disappeared. Soon as she started showing signs of another bun in the oven out of wedlock and no daddy to be announced, it were real hard for harlot not to proceed and follow her name.

She couldn't busy her mind very often with 'em words they's hurling at her, not when there's things needed done. Things. That's what she busied herself with now, getting things done. Doing things that mattered. Not listening to no bullshit story of how it were she's supposed to be living or what it were she shoulda done to prevent bastards from leaving her wound. She focused on the things, the tasks handed to her from the Union, the talks, the coffee, the supervising, the making sure so and so gets there and this one stays here and she were damn good at those things. Damn good indeed. Stashed up a role of respect from 'em miners with all she's doing and some from 'em wives who took the time to really see the efforts she'd made but don't none of that matter to her when 'em boys round. All they do is set the remind on her. Remind her of a night she ain't like to never forget. See it on his face ever'time he walks in. Ever'time he goes for the raise with his little arms held up and his skinny little face, she saw that night and weren't no amount of cooking's ever gonna heal that.

32

NOVEMBER 3RD, 1930

ENOCH MURRAY

Full dark'd already swallowed up trail when my feet hit. Daddy'd told me run. "Run. Not walk. Not like a child. Not like a boy who'd watched 'em things. But like a man. Like somebody meant to do something 'bout what's done and what's seen." Slicked trouble to the back of my boots and pushed me out to the world, he did.

He'd told me, "Don't stop. Not for one fucking thang. Not for nobody other than Doc."

I knew the way. Knew it 'cause he'd knowed it. 'Cause he'd told me where to go. Said, "Now what ya gonna need do…listen here, now…focus on me…what ya gonna do once ya get up near Bartlett and Bend, right where 'em streams meet and there's that divide, take the right. Not the left. The right. Right's gonna lead ya up to Doc's. Left's gonna take ya over to 'em Meaks and they ain't got nothing to offer when it comes to a thang like this. Nod yar head if I's understood."

He'd said, "where ya gonna go? The right. Exact. Then once ya get up that stretch and ya done moved past 'em dead trees Doc's turned over, ya know the ones, ya seen 'em…remember ya asked on 'em once…they's the dead pines he chopped down last year so's that bug wouldn't spread...ya go on to hollering for him. Very important, ya hear me, ya holler out nice and loud like, slow down yar feet so's there's a matching to that crunch of 'em leaves and 'em words ya spewing, and ya holler out with ever' step, "ENOCH MURRAY HERE, I'S SENT."

He'd said, "repeat it to me. Repeat ever'thing I done said.... that's right...and ya gonna holler out what...that's right. Now when ya done got all the way near where that crest starts to break and peak over in his holler, ya stop yar tracks right there and ya go to hollering double time on him, 'cept ya says this, "TROUBLE IN TOWN, MURRAY NEEDS YA." Then ya wait there. Right there. Don't move a smidge more. Don't even fucking breath 'til ya sees his face and once ya do, ya don't speak...Listen to me, it's gone on quite some time since he's laid eyes up on ya proper and there might be a little circle 'bout round ya, that's fine. Ya just go on and let him do it. Stick yar head up so's he can get a real good look at ya, so's he can sees ya's my boy."

Said, "Now after there's chance for him to get a good whiff on ya, ya tell him this, and make sure if there ain't nothing else transferred between the two of ya, 'cause there might be a press on ya by him, just give him a point to where I's at and tell him, MATEWAN'S COME THIS SIDE THE HILL. BRING IT ALL."

Daddy'd never spoke to me that much in my whole life. Not once. Only way I's ever guaranteed an audience were to go at a spell of acting out and considering there already two in line ahead of me dipping toes in dangerous sands, it weren't something I's in a hurry to do. Plus, it woulda meant lip thrown at Mommy and there weren't a speck of me that could ever go to saying something wrong to her.

Just thinking on Mommy brought fuzzies to my bones, wrapped me up next to a fire where all safe and sound, where instead of trudging through black forest I's tucked down with a full belly and my brothers next to me and it the holidays and the year'd gone good and Daddy home with us and we's happy. It were like that trick Donnie'd taught me. Donnie were the oldest then Tate then me. He'd showed it to me after that big ice storm came slicking through and Daddy were down at the mill, weren't never no day off, and Mommy'd got locked up at her sisters over there up in Bessie's Bottom and it were just Donnie and Tate and me and that branch'd gone to break off over top the roof and I felt sure it were some sort of monster coming in after us. Cried and cried and cried, I did. Surprised Tate didn't wrap me up in a blanket and send me out in the snow.

Snowed seven feet that night. A full man size of white to cover the sides of our house and press on that old oak with weight like it'd not seen in a while and crack that branch down in just the right angle that it hung with the bottom half of a long strip still tethered down to the dirt and a lean of a thank-Gawd-not-the-heaviest-branch-it-carried-limb on that very spot where Daddy'd built a support beam through our place. All the while in my head, demons and ghosts and haints making ready all their nasty plans. Believe it to be solid gold truth so much so that there weren't a part of me that couldn't go ahead and extend that party towards Mommy and start to fear she already dead by their hands. And what did Donnie do, he called me over to him. Not in a command but in the way a five year old who's done cried his eyes puffy were sure to be enticed to do.

He done it by rooting round in Mommy's secret hiding place and finding the jar of rock candy she kept in case there's ever need for cheering up, which she were always real good at figuring out, and he held it forth so's 'em pink crystals glistened and he said, "these here were give to me by Mommy, they's protection against all that's bad, like shields, ya know what shields be, right? See, Mommy told me that if they's to come, 'em bad things, I's to give 'em to ya just like she give 'em to us when we's youngins."

Donnie'd laid out his hand with that big ole palm facing heaven like, dirt and grooves already sealed on him with the work of someone twice his age there planted right next that sweet powder pink sugary stick and he said, “Now, ya take these and ya chew ‘em down and they gonna do something for ya just like they done for Tate and me...well, ya gonna have to come over here to get it, can’t bring it to ya. Not how it works. Ya got to come get it and believe in it. See, ‘cause this here ain’t no ordinary stick of sugar, naw, this crafted, sold and bought in the farthest deepest darkest corner of the hill, sold by one of ‘em Harlan sisters ain’t nobody like to talk ‘bout…that’s right, ya heard ‘em tales and they’s true. Why, weren’t it Tate, hey Tate, weren’t it ya who just saw one of ‘em witch sisters just the other day—”

Tate’d said, “Come right up next to me, she did, right there in the middle of the forest with one of ‘em special cloaks they’s like to wear, ya know, one of ‘em things that makes it so’s they’s walking round in plain sight but can’t no one go to see ‘em. Felt her breathing on my neck.”

Donnnie’d came back, “But was ya scared, Tate?”

Tate’d barked, “Hell naw, ain’t been scared since I ate ‘em rocks.”

Donnie’d lent out that hand just a smidge further. “See, these here are fear eaters. Once they’s in ya, they goes to soaking it up. Take it clear outta ya, they will. And don’t matter what ya face nor who it might be bringing it, they’s to rip that fear right from ya, so’s there won’t never be no need for it again. See, this made by the youngest of ‘em witch sisters. Made and give to all ‘em folk who’s willing to pay, some of ‘em dearly, some of ‘em with their lives just so’s they can give ‘em to they kids, so’s there won’t be no fear up in their hearts for all their years. Now, don’t get me wrong, she ain’t good. Just as mean and vile as her other two kin but she’s the less of ‘em all and when she were walking ‘bout one day looking for herbs to grind down and make evil shit with, she came across our dear Mommy and all that goodness of Mommy spread ‘bout her, spread round that nasty witch ‘til she, herself, blinded by it, ‘til for the first time in her life that witch began to see a spot of shine on the world and she were so thankful, so heartbroken, realizing she woulda never got that without the aide of our Mommy that she offered her up a gift. And ya know what that gift were, Enoch—it were three sugary sticks of fear eaters. So's ya just come over here and ya sits with yar brothers and ya have at it. Ya gobble it down. Ya let go of 'em fears that Mommy ain't safe, 'cause if she can charm the wits outta one of 'em Harlan witches then ain't a bit of snow gonna go bothering her and if one of 'em ghosts or haints or bed evil thangs decides to come in, there ain't no need for scare, 'cause Tate and I ain't gonna let nothing bad fall on ya, and with these fear eaters burning holes in yar belly, we know y'all do the same for us. All ya gots to do is trust in 'em. Trust in the love of Mommy and the kinship of yar Tate and me and know that we all done been through the same and come out that other side and this here, this stick of something-magic-come-this-way gonna help ya cross that other side…Just go ahead now…that's right…take it down…let it fill all of ya."

Five years since and it were the first time I'd needed recall 'em fear eaters. Made clear for their catch up as I stood there in wait, trying to remember all 'em times I'd walked 'em woods 'fore, and how this no different from then. How no matter how much wrong I'd seen in the day that path still grooved just to the left and that hole yonder dipped deepest on the right. Mapped it out all in my mind. All 'em places I's to pass 'fore I got up to 'Docs. Quieted my legs constant shake and made all 'em things Daddy'd done instructed stick simple like right up next 'em fear eaters, like looping one string over the other, like I's doing nothing by tying my shoe and just went on 'bout it.

Told myself, at the mouth of where the trail started, though there weren't no seeing it now nighttime's drenched over in bug black, there's a knot of wiry briar patches stacked one on top the other on either side leading back 'bout twenty feet and if I weren't careful I'd end up with a scratch from shoulder to hand 'fore I made it four feet. Went on ahead and noted there wouldn't be much room for breath after that 'cause I's to get in that nasty patch of poison ivy that layers up in three different parts shortly after. Closed my eyes and tried hard at the remember where exact it were that green spread round that curve and where it hit Witches Tree and started for the climb to Gawd. Planted my feet in all the right spots. Made my way up Barlett and Bend all twenty minutes of steady climb 'til I got to that high part of ridge where the limestone flattened a spell and 'em trees weren't so thick that the moon might not shine in and I might get a sense of my bearings 'fore hitting 'em streams.

Went on ahead and let 'em fear eaters swallow up all 'em knots twisting thorns up in me. Made it so's feet couldn't do nothing by hit leaves and ferns and thickets and shrubs and brush and the like, so's the mind'd not time for wander on all that dark. All that damn dark, all that damn covering black, and I did just what Daddy told. Worked my legs faster than a jack rabbit and hit Bartlett and Bend and made that right and bee lined right for 'Doc's with my mouth in full prep to make out exact what Daddy'd said and woulda done it too if it weren't for finding a boy with half his head carved off like he's a snake shedding skin.

33

NOVEMBER 2ND to bleed to the 3RD,1930

ALBIE TODD

Mr. Davis didn't care all that much for the title his men carried at mine camps, so it fell upon all those in his company to reference them instead as "friends" whenever he in the room, though even when Albie coughed the noun up, chunks of "gun thug" came on with it and there was a hurried plea to catch the airing vagrants fast before Mr. Davis took note. It was of course one of these very same events following the aftermath of a dreadful standoff between Mr. Davis's friends and a set of rather debased, and one might argue homicidal miners just a scootch over to the east, of which the name Matewan will act as placeholder henceforth, that preempted the phrase's working to a double time slot between the two. A garrulous affair where the repetition of the word acted in a lessoning of the indignities that befell such men, the miners, by the hands of "friends," though the walls that surrounded their heavy-footed sighs might argue otherwise, insisting the battering something of particularly strong note. It, of course, could and would not be argued otherwise, especially not ever again between the sentiments of these two men, a one Mr. Davis and another

Albie Todd, that it, the extension of their friend's talents, was in any way unjust.

The positioning of themselves, these two fine fellows, inside a room that would hereinafter be dubbed as The Eye, came as no mistake. It was, in fact, in ever' way intentional that Mr. Davis'd placed Albie's office on the eastern front of "Davis and Brother's Mining: Brother's held together by the Blue" in the same way that it was, in fact, in ever' way a part of Mr. Davis' stratagem that he'd added that last moniker to the heading of his mining enterprise. He was, after all, a man of very decisive manueverisms. He'd constructed, or had built for him, it should state, the main offices in the image of a medieval tower he'd once glimpsed in a book inhabiting his father's library and thought, even then how it reminiscent of a ladder to God. Thus, there proved no better place for their offices to be than at the top of that trail. One, of course, facing the east, The Eye, and one facing the west, The Head—omniscient when connected. And rarely would Mr. Davis be met elsewhere, specifically when the topic of "friends" on the docket and especially when that tagline followed, "soon to arrive."

So, then, on the night of November 2nd, the viewer would indeed find the placement of two separate spheres working in conjunction, one being The Head, though since it run by Mr. Davis, the concealment only spit in small spells of what shared with Albie, and the other, The Eye, and all that Albie might therefore see, though the computation of what these images might be, lost, for how could one know what one has not seen. And thus, as the men looked out over the East, the late evening dripping to early morn, the darkness spread, concealing what these actions truly meant.

Their "friends," as they could no longer be referenced as just Mr. Davis's after Albie's willing or unwilling participation in the things to follow, were dispatched from a much larger group of dignitaries that hailed from the outskirts of West Virginia and operated under the sole guidance of whomever paid the heftiest for their services, which needless to state resulted solely in coal and rail money, and with enough due diligence and stacked led, proved rather continually to be a very strong force to hold in one's pocket. It was the Matewan incident that'd prompted Mr. Davis to seek out their assistance and thus it was the Matewan incident that'd introduced them to Hazard and to Albie in the early morning of Nov. 3rd.

It proved thus, at least to anyone paying close enough attention, that Mr. Davis saw extreme promise and opportunity in pairing up with a set of men so capable. This, due entirely to the nature of Mr. Davis's true wants, which boiled down to nothing more than profit and profit alone. For apparently long before these "friends" or Albie showed up to the small eastern mountain town, Mr. Davis'd made promise to himself that production would falter for no man and no thing. And much like any well to do gentleman of his age, Mr. Davis fashioned his goals around enterprise and legacy, and as the years'd seem flown by, the gnawing urge to make damn sure he succeeded in these endeavors were soon placed ember hot in the fire.

It was then a natural procedure for him to realize that an expansion, i.e., the rearing of higher demand, meant more visibility and in the air of what loomed a national crisis across the board, this move seen as lowered price of goods. A dubious feat but not incapable—no. Merely something meant more for manueverability, something more done with softened blow. Something disguised. Thus, so as to not operate at a loss, Mr. Davis'd instructed Albie to start a garnishment program geared towards those individuals Albie deemed fit enough to weather the results. There was, of course, no strong hand, no forced revolver grin over Albie's shoulder. Merely a request.

Never did it once even wander down the corridors of Albie's mind that when granted with such a dubious task, he might find subtle satisfaction in the soliciting of it to Randi, the gentleman operating the coal store in town, and by that, the only store. Of course not, how could a man given reign on the ladder to God, in an office dubbed The Eye possess the fortitude to understand how seductive all this might be. Nor did Albie factor in how much he would relish the discomfort in Randi's eyes as he recounted these interactions back to him.

For The Head was to know and The Eye was to see.

The names, those unfortunate bastards to soon die by the hands of their friends, picked from a hat. An old miner bucket upturned on Albie's desk like an ashtray, though Albie's sentiments towards smoking were starting to, hopefully, finally, wane. He'd asked Randi, without even thinking, after the most frequent observers to his door and fittingly Randi'd produced a list of ten to which Albie studied for three days before deciding who might be the lucky three to end up with ball over their heads. Whitmires' name came after viewing his palling around with a tall broad fellow named Jeb Murray, who immediately struck a sudden and rather viscous spurt of indigestion in Albie and therefore provided proof enough that he too might be added. And since the campaigning to last for but a few days, just a few to let the bottom fill up again, that's how Mr. Davis'd put it, Albie saw no reason why there shouldn't be an even number to the list and thus proceeded to add an equaling of ten inside the hat and scrap altogether the picking. Plus, the dumping of all the pieces onto his desk enlivened him much more than any piecemeal lottery might.

It was, of course, an exaggerated oversight on Albie's part that he'd not foreseen how deep and dark that harrowing road led, all of it appearing more like play to him, even disregarding the transmission from Mr. Davis that a delivery in transit soon to arrive that might eliminate any unnecessaries if due cause arose. No, not once did Albie feign at seeing.

Thus, by the time ten strutted men in pinstripe suits and fettered vests, which snuggly encased ready and worn plinkertons at either side, stepped foot off the midnight train, a stop that usually would've never happened but did happen due to their being "friends," Albie realized too late what it was exactly about to take place.

The truth of the matter and perhaps the worst yet said, such little experience did Albie have in the world of men, even his deepest wanderings would not've taken him where these "friends" would soon go.

34

FEBRUARY 1, 1960

WILLARD TELL

On the edge of I-22, in a truck stop dive at high noon, survival piped down throats in clunks of raw egg soaked beer and not no one's worried how sanctuary at such a shithole crafted sorry southern bastards on our backs. Place like this made the cellar door of a one-legged whore house set next to a dance hall scratch appealing cross yar eyes. Made way for filth to mix with the horror show of burnt to hell grilled cheeses stacked all limp and greasy in front of ever' meaty hard hand scorching pain on beers and shots. Sorta spot where ever' time a fight broke out the chummed grill of ball sweat went to rise with the hope of cutting knuckles on bashed in faces and it were the exact sorta place, friends met forget.

Sabina, Ohio. Nice enough town where folks felt like they's doing something right raising families 'spite their kids smearing slit throats on master bedroom walls 'cause boredom grew fast and hard in any spot dubbed "Eden." Ending up here served me right. Locked down a load of self-serving sabotage slop and flung it over me soon as the car died off I62 right there along with ever' other dream to ever leave a sad prick's mind. Weren't like the town didn't try. Whole lot of that going round, they's serving it up in slices of Derby pie down at the diner but weren't no amount of country contrived nice that'd go to cover the smell of B O spurting from the armpit of the Midwest.

Spent the better part of three years funneling shit show sandwiches chalked full of regret with a tail end slice of disappear covering my tracks for a man named Mac and all of the stops ended at a similar terd stained town. This'n here, stop number five of six planned 'fore that engine blew steam over state black. Fucking thing spilled out just as the ramp pitched the ass of that car over the hill. Clamped me down right there on top for all the world to see and ever' man with a hard on for a hotrod to come kicking tires up close, posting notes on how much interest they shared in taking the clunk of metal off my hands.

If they'd any sense 'bout 'em at all they'd a known that a 1938 Buick Century Coupe smothered in faded gangster black carried along with it a whole heap of trouble. But they didn't, 'cause there's few who ever do and when I came too the next morning, there were a group making tracks outside the windshield eyeing down possible reasons why it were me coming out of it instead of something else.

Emptied outta that banana boat rocket with three days of stink on me, pouring empty pints of Old Grandad on the road, with hair all mussed to high heaven then dipped back down to Hell again, and a Red hanging on my lips like the lighting of it'd bring Christ's second coming to the crowd, and pitched out my dick for one of 'em horse drain pisses that'd spoiled a bruise on my back and didn't offer up nar one gawddamn word to the intrusion on my peaceful morning ritual. Spit enough soured water on the ground that a river of yellered vile flowed and pooled right at the bottom of the entry sign welcoming all those in need to the "Eden of Ohio, Sabina," and noted, this the type of place people ended up if they weren't careful.

Man who'd brought me there left just close the same taste of metallic blood shit cement stew in my mouth as the damn town did. Right fitting he the one to pick "Eden" as our drop considering my hankering to crack his skull and spoon feed his brains to a pack of hungry mutts ever' time there were an encounter. One of 'em other-end-of-the- spectrum southern bastards, who cradled Hell in his belly just for the fun of it and managed an unmeasurable taste for shit men ain't supposed to want after. Only man ever known to go running a gawddamn mountain-culled-shit-fire-seamed-type, named Bubba Ruther, on just 'bout the tightest leash ever made solely due to his, Edwin Hayes II, being the crookedest, meanest, vilest, most menacing motherfucker this side the Mason Dixon, 'cause, believe me, that list'd go on to extend much farther if the South's taking in too, bastards galore down there, 'em Mason's I's playing capture the flag from a mere few. Smug cunt wouldn't even let Jr. come off the lips of his closest friends, had to spell out his entire fucking name ever'time he's give reference.

Supposed to meet him at half past one in a shithole truck stop dive that promised air conditioning on a painted two-by-four that he said, hee-hawed, with ever' car whizzing past, which were why when I finally got done draining the lizard and snubbing that Red of diesel fueled 'bacoo down my throat, I went on and spoke to that crowd of nosey ninnies. "Someone direct me to a truck stop shithole with a bar in it."

Mainly B&E's how Edwin Hayes II started his career. Liked to pick off old folks and small businesses. Marked his potentials from the passenger seat of a beat to hell 1930's squad car. Parked it right next a steeple usually. Found the best harvest, those with hearts full of the Lawd. Believed they's like to ignore the bad when they got all that good smothering 'em. Well, that's what he said at least. Bastard were a smooth talker, that's for sure. Talked his way into and outta damn ever'thing and what a shock it were to most he's capable of it 'cause he were a damn awkward looking motherfucker. Pot lickered, he were and a lazy eye to boot. Had to get locked up on other parts of him just so's ya could take him in. Stare down at 'em big-as-a-damn-tree-trunk-forearms of his from all 'em logs he'd splinter or take in 'em skinny ass legs that somehow went to holding up that silly mess of a frame and spend the majority of the time trying to figure out how the Hell Gawd ever envisioned such a thing.

Used to run round with a scrawny errand boy named Skinny Colt Jackson, this were long 'fore Bubba came on, who somehow or another played make believe with salted caramel sledgehammers to anybody stupid enough to be bought. Oh, he could tame the fur off a lion if he's granted enough airspace to get that flapper moving.

Mean, "ain't it just the thing to warm yar aging heart to know that if there's anything ever to happen to ya that all these things ya got'd be safe," what he'd sell to little blue hairs over a cup of Joe. "Mean what's to say there couldn't be a fire." Their beady little eyes just lighting up with the thought. "What's to say there ain't a disaster aching in 'em there hot winds that's like to turn the air aghast." And then for the line-n-sinker, he'd go to quoting some scripture for 'em. "Was it not Gawd, who spoke, 'Moreover, man does not know his time, like fish caught in a treacherous net and birds trapped in a snare, so the son's of men are ensnared at an evil time when it suddenly falls on them.'" Then he'd smile. One of 'em squeamish drawn-out things that made his fish face and bug eyes appear less daunting. Oh, Skinny'd a way with words round 'em old folks. Fancied hisself a warped combo of a tent apostle and a traveling salesman and since he were culled in a way from the orations of a very longwinded Grandpappy who liked whiskey but liked telling fibs more, the whole of cons came on Skinny easy and nice. Hell, he'd have an appointment set up half the time 'fore he'd even got to the scripture. Come back with a slot for morning next for his appraiser, played by none other than Edwin Hayes II, to stop by and take a look. Papers'd be drafted the following week.

Course there wouldn't be no papers sent nor signed and 'em

nice folks who done worked their whole lifes'd find all their stuff gone by the third day. A grassroots gambit that only a dumb as shit poor kid from boomfuck nowhere might plant stakes in as a potential way out.

Him and Skinny came on my way casing for a score on a sunny Friday afternoon when the air hung molasses-chewed-thick and I's in the middle of unloading milk crates off the back of a truck driven by a man named Lawrence. Lawrence were a good man with a penchant for saint some'd say but he were a lazy as fuck bastard who paid me .25 cents a day to move his things and that were only if his wife forgot to pack him a sandwich, which'd save him the trip down to Tom Todd's counter for lunch. Friday were a day hardly overlooked by the Mrs. so it, something steady a boy could count on and I's hard press to miss an opportunity at a profit.

Spotting folks that don't belong in a small town ain't that hard. Howsomever, catching onto a set like Edwin Hayes II and Skinny, who'd no doubt come from a similar setting as those they'd frequented but'd spent time in some sort of city as well so's a flashy air of knowing wore on 'em in a can't-quiet-put-yar-finger-on-why-they's-a-spot-of-off-'bout-'em, were something I's taken with immediately. Noticed 'em firsthand going door to door dressed like a set of fancy slickers. Watched 'em carry out ever'thing mean Maynard Phillips owned. Then watched 'em do the same thing for damn near ever' house on the block. Stopped what I's doing right there and asked, "What 'em men doing Lawrence?"

"Huh." He didn't never pay no mind to no one when he's jamming egg salad sandwiches in.

"Said, ya see 'em men there…think they's robbing folks."

"Nah."

"Bullshit they ain't."

"Nah, ya got it wrong."

"Paint it right."

"They's appraising stuff."

"What?"

"Appraising stuff. Mattie's done already made an appointment for tomorrow."

Mattie were Lawrence's wife. "What ya mean?"

"Damn boy, they come in and see what yar stuff's worth so's ya can take out insurance. Git yar money back if anything gets damaged."

"Why they taking it then?"

"Well, somebody's got to go through it all. Take it to their off-premise spot while the appraiser comes through and catalogues it."

"Ain't never heard of nothing like that."

"Boy, whole point of me paying is to eat in peace, now carry 'em crates inside and leave me be."

Spotted no good right there. Could see it from a mile away and being that I'd waited my whole broke ass country life for a real taste, couldn't very well go letting it slip through.

Made a fair wage for a time, ripping and hawking. Traveled all round towns like mine. Other forgotten places where Jesus strong. Worked for a while too. Took over for Edwin Hayes II on the runs. Not as appraiser but as hauler. Skinny'd show me what to take and I'd pack it up nice like in the back of a 1934 Ford Model BB, a cardinal red tarp flapping in the wind while I drove on out to whatever Church Edwin Hayes II were camped at. Divvied up real nice for me and I's happy to have it. Happy ain't the word. I's damn over the moon on it. Saw a new town ever' couple of days. Drank whiskey and beer and cussed and lived and tried damn hard not to think 'bout all 'em folks we's destroying. It were a helluva time. Helluva time. But there's only so many flowers gonna grow over a pile of shit and it weren't too long 'fore the figuring out that Edwin Hayes II stunk more than anything I'd done ever smelt.

Come to find out, visiting Sunday morning sermons weren't just 'bout spying on marks for Edwin Hayes II or maybe it need put another way—Bastard liked to pick out his girlfriends from the Sunday school playground. Stumbled outta that cruiser of his with a fresh washed suit that don't nobody in 'em poor towns we's running in got and went out to 'em playgrounds they always got set up, swing and such, and set up and wait with a handful of caramel candies 'til all 'em frilly little socks and shiny black shoes come traipsing out for recess in between the learning of Noah and service.

Noticed it 'bout three towns back and gone at playing dumb ever since 'cause that money felt good and heavy on me. But ever' time that truck went rumbling past 'em holy lots we's hunting on, there he'd live with a group of curly headed girls with big eyes sitting on his lap under some tree or playing by his feet with one of 'em candies in their mouths. Only so long 'fore that green started feeling like bricks in my shoes. Ain't to state, I weren't hurting on it something fierce giving future money up but once I found out exact how young 'em girls went, decided it time to cut and run. Problem were I's young and stupid and young and stupid again, and I came to the conclusion that it probably best I beat the living fuck shit out him 'fore I left. Decided Sunday morning service, right after firestone-let-out, at Hopewell Baptist Church, just as good a place as any to throw some weight around.

Like any country church, Hopewell were tiny as a mouse hole and set up on a just a big enough knoll that a Preacher held glory in his eyes when he spoke of the mount, like his phone line to Gawd not something that were on perpetual hold. When Edwin Hayes II were handling his affairs at this particular church, he fancied a spot next to a pair of old Civil War cannons set side by side just a hair from the steeple. Almost like 'em soldiers held Gawd at their backs when they went to firing. Right between 'em. Near a plaque that spent more time on the ground then it did standing up right, 'cause it didn't take all that much for a set of boys to find hot ass in a restless town. He'd stand there while Skinny Colt Jackson'd hid in the middle of 'em fifty or so stones marking the old cemetary right next and I'd root up somewheres in between biting down the hate that grew. We'd stand, sit, lay, and listen while that Preacher'd go on and on 'bout the fresh revival of "new." Figured only reason a Church called anything old were just so's they could recall it new later. Seemed the slathering of "new" fit on damn near ever'thing, new books, new rooms, new pews 'til that Preacher worked it all back round to a chance at renewal with people down at the front and hands and wallets turned out towards the newness of Jesus's. In all that time listening to that Preacher spit bolts of Gawd out and Edwin Hayes II lick salves of sin in, it were real hard to spot which one ran the better game.

Near the family picnic area guarded by a troubled fence from where a set of dawgs'd bundled through the boards as they searched for a family ham set out for the celebrating of Mrs. Hattie Can's ninetieth birthday, I took my stand. Stumped down right beside an old school room chair rumpsprung from Nancy Holloway's big ass and waited for that final chime of hallaluahs to come after Preacher Mike took his bow. Doors'd pitch open, I'd funnel over to the blind spot on the left, and Edwin Hayes II's face would land in the blunt barreled brick of my fist. Done worked it out over and over again and there just couldn't be no place else for him to go.

Course, I'd not counted on the Preacher's daughter, Cassie Lynn. Rotund, ugly, cankered, and mean herself with a stripe of wild running down her back. She'd honed on Edwin Hayes II the moment he landed in town and done ever'thing in her power to gain his eye and 'spite her being four to five years older than he liked, he couldn't very well go turning down a knob-guzzle while her Daddy's handing out tickets to Heaven inside.

If I'da known he were gleaned up against that stained glass planting fantasy on satin ribbon'd hair and yella taffeta dresses while little Miss Cassie Lynn went at a game of tonsil hockey, sure as shit wouldn'ta wasted all that time squatting by that fence.

Edwin Hayes II's hello came from the clattered back hand splintering of Nancy Holloway's chair crashing thunderstruck over my neck and head in a burst of flailing vampire spikes and the nasal spray of a cumgobed throat shouting, "Git him, Eddie." Poured gasoline matches down my spine tingling all the way to the pits of my feet and 'fore I'd a chance at hollering back to the bastard, Edwin Hayes II were wrestling over top me with my head locked up in between 'em big lumberjack arms and no way for my face to tilt but smooshed. Motherfucker knocked me silly. Mean, broke my ass down. And as he hurled me round, controlling my ever' move with the pressing of 'em drumsticks of shit fire mad, little Miss Cassie Lynn went on and got the whole of the congregation out there with a snake pit of lies saying how I'd tried to take advantage of her while she's picking flowers for her Daddy out back and how, thank Gawd Almighty, Edwin Hayes II'd come to her rescue. Suppose they both needed an excuse to weather away any questions as to why they'd not taken in the Lawd with ever'body else inside the steeple.

Town practically chased me with a pitchfork as I's bleeding out.

Edwin Hayes II weren't changed one bit when he pulled that rustbelt red door open, bringing in with him the light and air of a hard day's drive and a cocksure foot. Knew it him from the squeak of Bubba's cowboy boots on that damn sticky floor as he's no doubt making headway for the appraiser to come through. Liked an entrance, 'em bastards did, and I could tell from the grit of ever' man in there's jaw that it weren't the first time this bar'd seen the likes of their kind. Reckon it weren't nothing other than a regular ole Friday night binge for these truckers and low lifes and all-round sort of folks that go to packing any and ever' type of weapon man could think of under their belts and up their sleeves. Naw, by my reckoning this were the exact place this meeting were meant to happen. And if time'd changed anything, which I knew it hadn't for a man like Edwin Hayes II, he woulda thought it pertinent that I turned to greet him the moment he stepped foot in and when I hadn't, when Bubba's boots grazed past the edge of that sawdust pile of sadder-than-a-two-legged-dawg-in-a-foot-race-looking bar I went on ahead and pulled that .41 Long Colt outta my pocket I'd saved all 'em many years for that pot licker sumabitch and u-turned on his ass lickety split and said, "Been quite some time, there, Jr."

35

FEBRUARY 1, 1960

EDWIN HAYES II — MATEWAN

PART I

A moratorium gloomed on Bubba's chest once that gun pulled but weren't no aside of dismay plotting Edwin Hayes II's brow. Naw, he punctured ear splints forward in a furried recant of blistered deviled past. Not one good gawddamn to that drum of metal teething fire towards his face.

"Bubba's and I's set up on a little bit of a squabble yestreen, ain't that right, Bubba…he ain't one to admit it now, but trust me when I says it, we were." Words chewed off the bottom of Edwin Hayes II's lips like he's biting butter from a biscuit. "If we's to settle things like Bubba does, mean, look at him, big fella like that… go on now, cradle that bullseye ya got taped on me a smidge to the left back there to him…ain't like to be much of an instance for somebody to go courting courage near that, am I right? We'd all just go round crashing and bashing wouldn't we…See here, like most men meant for force…mean, ain't it the most natural of occurrence to carve out life with a couple scuffles and breaks… how else to know what we're made of if the shit ain't pounded and molded so all that unnecessary pushed out; there's a certain, how to phrase it, negligence…that's what we come to, ain't it Bubba?"

Edwin rocked a snarl back to his heavy weight champ.

"Negligence to words, that's what it were…a not speaking less spoke to, a never questioning not nohow not anytime sort. A doer. That's what it were and that's what he is, a doer. One who does. Something I'd long suspected ya, yarself, might one day turn into. Something Mac promised me ya'd become, Willard. And lo and behold, here we are. Who woulda thought, our paths meeting up again, running numbers and green. Ya, the pickup man for Mac and me, the handoff."

"Words been peppering ever' lofty cloud in sight 'bout what ya done and what ya become. All of it aching praise in chicken wire wrapped pipes that's just assumed to be appealing, like ya's some sorta cure for all that ails…ain't that how Mac put it, Bubba… cure that ails, like ya's set up to relieve the entirety of mankind from ill will and brooding bad deeds. Must be mighty busy, ya is, running this away and that. Made a right fine mockery of that nice car. Oh we saw it. Stamped down like a spell of mold on a peach, like some fucking black dot on the sun…ya know what I thought when I saw that thang, when that clunk of junk come knifing spores of rot over the hill…thought, I bet that fucker ain't changed one gawddamn bit, not one ounce, bet he's just as small and yella and dumb as that country shit who nipped crumbs off my coat way back when. Thought, what all 'em folks been saying, all 'em sorry saps who slope shoulders forward in hunkered shirts ever'time Bubba comes walking in the room, don't know diddly shit 'bout nothing, that the only reason yar name's even in the lips of a man like Mac's 'cause…well, that's what we's arguing 'bout wasn't it, Bubba…oh, don't let him fool ya now, Bubba's exactly what I said he were, cautious with 'em words but I'll be gawd-damned if when he's feeling generous, he don't spill out a gravy train of wisdom…Wanna know what he said 'bout ya…sure ya do…hell, by now ever' crabapple fallen from the wrong fucking tree in here wants to know…ya don't, huh. Don't care one bit, do ya? Just gonna sit there with that fucking haul cocked on me and 'em squinty little eyes like ya'd done growed up into a man meant to do something and ya ain't gonna give me one iota."

"How 'bout ya, Bob, ya wanna know what Bubba and I's arguing 'bout, wanna know what it were he called this fella right here—"

Bob were the crusty motherfucker caked in grease up to his eyeballs donning a failed butcher's apron over a beer battered torso he'd put hard years into crafting. His sorry life'd no doubt wrestled with this similar stamping of bullshit weekly. Bob didn't want to know, just like nobody in their right mind wanted to know 'cause knowing meant listening and listening meant asking and asking a cocksure fucker like Edwin Hayes II who packed a dynamite barrel of human metal buckshot behind him named Bubba weren't nothing but a surefire handle of raw diesel implosion up yar ass. And ain't nobody looking for nothing close to that.

"Don't ya wanna know, Bob? Don't ya wanna know what kinda man's drinking suds at yar bar? Mean, I'd like to know. Sure would. Wouldn't ya Bubba...hell, if it were up to Bubba we'd all just wear placards round our neck spelling out all the wrongs we committed in our lives so's we could just go on ahead and separate the doers from the nots...ain't that right, Bubba? Mean, wouldn't that be nice. Whenever ya walked into a place, automatically, like thrust down and gift wrapped tied, ya knew who, and what, and how, ya knew from the very get go what sorta man ya's dealing with just by looking at his shirt, just by looking at that placard round his neck."

"Bob, ya can't go arguing with a thing like that. Knowing right when a murderer or pornographer or pedophile or altogether absconder of Gawd walks in yar bar. Mean, least ya'd have the decency of knowing when it were ya needed pull out that Reaper ya got buried underneath that plywood or better yet tell that ole ugly hoss ya got in the back flipping 'em sandwiches that don't matter how fast she thinks she can pump that Model 12, it ain't like to handle the hole Bubba's Phili Fox's capable of gunning through her."

A double barrel Fox whopped from behind Big Bastard Bubba's back and cornered square cross his man paws with bullets chomping at the bit.

"Must think me right stupid, Willard? Think a man don't know when he's being wielded towards that plank, don't think it, something instinctual for him to notice the writhe and whither in the water...ain't nothing other than foolshittedness to assume that the moment we stepped outta the sandbox there weren't but one confirmation clogged pore on our hinds that didn't feel the prick when sharks came lurking 'bout....and ya, Bob, mean for Gawd's sake, what did he promise ya, huh? What could this man, this killer've done, to convince ya, this the move to make. Mean, this has got to be the gawddamn stupidiest plot I ever seen? Mean, can ya believe it, Bubba? Honestly...come in here, our neck of the woods, knowing full well, there ain't a mouth breathing up in here that ain't held a bit of money in their back pockets with our sweat not marking it...think he's gonna get away with it."

"Go on ahead, Bob. Lay it down on the bar, now. Right there... right there overtop 'em fucking sandwiches. Don't no one wanna eat the damn things anyway...if folks wanted to know what government cheese tasted like they'd just carry their asses home...go on...put it up there...lay it down nice like. Don't wanna make that one there nervous, Bubba's just as trigger happy on a Wednesday as he is on Easter now...go on and call that Bitch up to...wanna see her waddle out with that 12's nose locked down on the ground or Bubba's double barrel here's gonna what...say it with me now... bust her what...bust her wide...now ya getting the hang of it."

Bob's Bitch rounded the corner in a slow slime trot with redwood sized legs and a discernable disliking to pants that 'caused bile to curdle up one's throat if their nose could find space between the thick spread of cornstarch crusting away from her meat box. She were country bottom mad. Made and molded by the harshness of never knowing pretty and formed by the rock hard hands that'd laid love on her after stills of shine ingested, she'd long ago gone to dressing like a man with hair buzzed short in wisps of scissor happy swipes and as time'd forced her out of sight due to an inherent sorrow that dragged from her eyes, she'd gone on and formed a set of friends inside her head and a habit of airing their laundry openly and wide.

"Jesus, Bob, can't ya find that Bitch no pants…what's that…she don't want no pants…how she don't want no pants…Bubba, move that gawddamn sight out of my line…Gawddammit Bubba…how big…ya reckon she could fit inside yar pants or ya think she too big…well, I know it's speculating…"

"Leave her be."

"As I live and breath, Bubba, he speaks…"

"Let that woman go and these folks too. Shouldn't nobody be subjected to that fucking wide flapper ya cutting loose lest they have to."

"What the fuck ya just say to me…"

"Let Bob go too."

"Well…"

"Don't nobody give a damn 'bout ya, 'cept for me, ya paranoid fuck. Ain't that important nohow."

"Go on…git outta here 'fore Bubba's starts letting slip that finger."

Thuds of chairs and boots scudded the floor as the door quipped fast with the let out of all those not bereft and hungering for blood.

"Shouldn'ta pulled that shit with all 'em folks here, Willard. There's a trail now."

"Just shut yar fucking mouth and lay down the sack."

"Bubba…hand it over."

Willard tried to distinguish the pump of red working—careful—in Bubba's veins from the throb of anger flaunting hate from his hands as his grip on that .41 Long Colt wrapped brick and mortar tight and in his head he went on and fashioned the tunnel he planned to ram a slug through on that hull of a mountain man.

Sack fell as it always did in these sorta gatherings, with the slippery wet thwack that aired reminiscent of cum juggling wallop glops down a whore's leg and not no man quick with the claim of which and who.

"Count it," Edwin Hayes II gritted.

"Don't need to."

"That's a stupid game."

"Won't be me Mac's coming after if it's off."

"Got a lot of faith pumping through him, don't he, Bubba?"

Willard leant forward. Swatted the tater sack back behind him with his boot and made move towards that half empty glass just hollering for him on the bar behind him and downed the swig of shit beer left. "Since we're swapping stories…"

"Is we friends now, Willard?"

"Naw, but there stands some clarifying."

"Bubba, ya know what…I thinks ya's right after all…"

Charred-cherry-brick-fire kicked from the end of Willard's snub, the line pointed and hurled direct for Bubba's big fucking forehead.

"Ya fucking shot Bubba…ya fucking shot him…ya fucking piece of shit…"

"Needed happen, Jr., needed happen a long time ago but reckon I'd not found a place right yet. 'Sides he's gonna do something stupid in a second anyway and I's probably gonna have to take the both of ya out at the same time and that ain't part of the plan."

"Fuck ya. Oh…just fucking look at him…looks fucking sick, fucking black blood ever'where…fucking head all torn to shit…don't think Mac's not gonna hear 'bout this…ya mark my words…aw, fuck it."

Buck knife flipped out from Edwin Hayes II's pant loop fast and loose as he shuffled up from the mire of gutted brain shit that once stood fashion as a man. But as 'fore and soon to follow again, appeared Willard in no mood other than business and he quickly dispatched Jr's stance with the sharp bite of metal through knee and a whispered grit torque, "Sit yar ass down, Jr."

"I'm gonna fucking, fuck, fucking, fuck, fucking, fuck yar shit up..."

"Wanna know why yar a shit and ain't none of that gonna come true, Jr...wanna know why ya's destined to die in a bar where there's more like to be a pile of cum soaked socks stuffed somewheres in the corner, 'cause ya's from shit fucking stock...ya wanna know who told me that...who spelled yar shit out in the air like some crop duster...Mac, ya fucking piece of shit. Moment yar name crossed his lips, he'd always start in with the backstory of why ya's soiled worse than Judas round these parts. Told me why it were ya wouldn't let nobody ever go to calling ya Jr neither 'cause yar Daddy were a Jr and there needed live a rope of distance between ya and him when ya's fishing business outta these waters. Wanna know what he said 'bout ya...huh."

"He said yar Daddy were that sorry piece of shit that helped 'em Gun thugs come in and take 'em houses away from 'em families at Matewan. Said there ain't a person living or breathing round Kentucky, Ohio, Virginia, West Virginia, or any of their likes that don't know the story 'bout what yar Daddy did and who he helped and how deep down in ya, lives just as much treacherous black as lived in him."

"Mac didn't even have to pay me for this pickup. Didn't even have to blink an eye on it. Said, I'd have it done by yesterday. Planned on killing ya 'fore I even got in the car. Carve ya up and take yar body back there. Drive the four and half hours it'd take 'fore Matewan blared green in a roadside sign and staple yar ass to it. Place one of 'em placards round yar neck so's ever'one knew who it were they's spilling bile over as they drove past the wretchedness I'd crafted. Wouldn't take no ownership to it or nothing 'cause I don't need the praise. Don't need the accolades. Don't need to go sewing seeds so's others might know what I am."

"Suppose the beauty 'bout being a sorry shit come from a sorry line is that there ain't much ya got to live up to. Hate's already branded on ever' person ya's ever aimed to meet. All ya got to do is show up. The curse for ya, though, rears in the complete unoriginal form of uselessness ya made fit on ya. Lest yar Daddy shared some conviction 'bout his misgivings. All ya done in the time since the years graced us is find another heavy lifter to back up all that fucking talk ya go on with and perhaps hush a family when they find their girls deflowered…A doer, huh, ya wanna know if I'm a doer, if I'm what Mac and all 'em others says 'bout me is true, if in fact I done exactly in ever' minute detail what 'em ninnies go on saying I done…it don't fucking matter."

"See why ya's busy trying to hustle and bulldoze through bullshit deals, that placement of yarself in high cotton floating fuzzies down in the dirt, ya never did gather the gumption to take a real close look at what power ya really had or what ya didn't. Doer… huh…Mac's a doer, he doled out this hit. Told me to keep the money I'm 'bout to take from ya and call it even. Said, he'd lay it down velvet with his Boss and wouldn't be no worry 'bout it at all. Said, he's tired of that yapper and all the shit that comes with it. Wouldn't even accept a cut from it. Said, it were something I needed take for myself. Bubba…he were a doer. Just like ya said. So much so that he'd hisself made a deal with Mac for the price of yar head. Planned on taking me down not long after the sack's exchanged."

"Wanna know how I know all this…how it come to me…ya know the answer…look real hard down at that leg…go on…look at it…look at how yar red's gooing out in waterfall laps…ya know the answer…it lies there…lies in yar blood buttering the floor, spreading to yar backstabbing friend, yar Doer back there…say it…say what ya know…say what's spelled there...ya right, it don't fucking matter."

36

FEBRUARY 1, 1960

MAC

On the desk. Layed over top papers built thick with black sludged coffee. His hand not weighing the care of bleached neat white. That's where he'd placed her. Had her. Not placed her. Had her. Placed, leans on burnt toast in trash. Had, breaks will, don't it. Weren't none of that. Not on that desk over 'em papers.

Night'd cut in spilled hog backed orange blood like venturesome warriors dying with the sun's dipping as I crossed into Hazard and I shoulda took it as a sign something off. Something were always off, it seemed, when we rolled in and like clockwork when we come over Butner's Pass, that dip in the road rocking the frame of my crew cab, Harry'd smelt it too. Poked his long snout from up under the bed of bunched towels in the back and gave a look-see to the world like maybe a pat on his reddened hair might crane things back right, which we both know wouldn't. Colored like the carriage of a Sugar Maple in fall, Harry were the best damn Red Setter I'd ever seen. But I guess it fair to state, I ain't ever really seen one 'fore Al'd gifted him twelve years ago. Back where mine and me lived, weren't nothing but mixed ole coonhounds and rutted on farm mutts. Harry were so gawddamn beautiful with his long shiny coat and prized thin features, used to fear he might get fucked if I let him loose too long in 'em backwoods. Lawd knows there's been worse to fair.

Not wanted to bring him at all but life'd grown cold and still in the house since June'd passed and Harry didn't deserve none of that. And 'spite his sudden jerks at my tendency to find ever' pothole and divot a road spit, there were parts that knew he'da preferred right by my side to anything else offered.

Cold comes on a place real quick like, don't it. Real outta nowhere with a thick coat of always existing and learnt the fastest way to do it, were to remove the woman who'd breathed hot for so long. I'd not noticed it 'fore, that slow build in 'em corners. Like cobwebs they were, little spots of molded emptiness. Suppose they's planted that night June'd left in her sleep and thank Gawd she did, 'cause I couldn't take it other. Felt, she knew it too. Like the beginning of sick'd started creeping and crawling in like one of 'em strands of dust on the floor and she'd just made deal with it, gone on and signed where it said take me fast. Sixteen when we met, sixteen and not a moment past knowing ever'thing, felt like. Gut told me I's to be with her. Married her a week later when the urge for bedding'd grown so strong I couldn't help but take her and she were too good to go round soiled so's we'd made it honest.

Got close to selling the place in the three years since she's gone but I don't spend enough time there for it to really matter no longer. Part of that goes to many things, as ya can imagine, but most of the not selling roots down in that same place that'd slammed married on our fingers. Gut couldn't let it go. Wouldn't know what I'd do if that sad little shuddered porch weren't there to greet me when I's tumbling home. Probably misfire altogether and never be quiet right again.

June'd taken a trip to Savannah when she's small. Something to do with a great Aunt living there and her wanting to meet the only girl to be born worth a damn on her sister's side 'fore she died. Suppose June'd got it in her mind that a proper house, houses like what they got down there in the "fine country," what she called it, meant having a porch with some shutters that clicked down if ya's ever so inclined for privacy or a storm. Told me the moment I'd peeled virgin off her back while we's lying there in all our stink and sweat that she'd always fancied having herself a set. Walked right out the house and went to chopping blocks from a Red Maple on the southern side of the farm, right where Ponty's creek runs and where 'em lilacs are like to grow so damn dense, ya get pickled purple by the time ya made out. Whittled down fifteen pairs of shutters in a matter of four days for my June.

She'd painted 'em yeller. Bright yeller. Like sunflowers lit on fire. Drove me crazy first couple times I come down the hill. My eyes all whirly and wide. Damn near crashed into the house, that yeller fixed on me so. Told her, we's liable to attract critters and hunters alike with that siren color blaring all loud in the front. But she'd loved 'em. So soon so did I.

June's Daddy died when she's round eight or so and her Mommy's sister's husband, that daughter of that great Aunt from that great house in Savannah, were the one who stepped in when times for a man needed. Gave her hand to me in the small steeple of a Baptist church outside of Dawson, Ga. June'd tied her hair up round a big Cherokee Rose and wore a yeller sash and told me she loved me with big beautiful starry eyes and her Uncle'd drove down just for the day then drove all the way back up to Kentucky where he were busy carving a name for hisself, that's what June'd said. That same week we's sent Harry and not two weeks after I's working for Uncle Al. Errand man ever since.

Smelled snatch 'fore the door even opened, creeping and sliming on the soiled carpet. Left like a dirty habit next to smoke burns that'd pilfered down from long hanging ashes where talk'd run long and formed stories. Knew just like when that sky'd run red and fiery, that on the other side of that wood, something wrong and vile awaited. Left a queasy turn in me not 'cause I'd not experienced bad but 'cause I had. Knew it all too well. Knew the way it seeped in strong silk over ya when ya first stepped in it and how if ya bathed too long, it turned to mud that never washed its black from yar skin.

Reason for the pause at the door, for the shift of foot, and the flare of nose as the pound nailed railroad spikes of hurt into something on the other side. Reason for the sly knock and the shuffled push when the grunt spoke, "c'mon in." Why immediately, 'spite the crawl of sick moving through, my head locked on the last time June and I'd touched. On the last time the smell of lavender dripped silver spin in between my fingers as she'd started gray pretty much as soon as we'd wed. She'd worn this frilly long nightgown that shown her figure when the moon shoved through the drapes and she liked to walk out into the field in the middle of the night luring me to her like a beast, like some damn wild thing meant for taming by this gorgeous woman with gray hair and nice teeth and sweet breath. We lived far enough down in a spot that there weren't much worry for spying and she'd let me if I whispered it nice like in her ear with slow nibbled gasps, take her, there under the moon, by the wildflowers, on a bed of green silky scale, under the eyes of stars. Last time our air patterned similar. Last time I'd felt the touch of a woman. Seen the scale of what love looked like on the pale nimble wane of an arched back as I tasted heaven.

Knew it quiet a different view once that door'd creak open. He'd forced her down in hogtied pin. With legs splayed wide and rope lathered tight and arms slunk down cross scripts and ash. Over the years, learnt, Al'd taken amongst many other things a bad habit of claiming own on damn near ever'thing once Mr. Davis passed almost like in the wake of that man's going, Al'd took up another form all on his own. Remember the first time I took note, boy named Freddie Hewlen wanted ever so badly to go earning him a spot next to Al. Fucker used to stand round just beggin' to be picked. Followed Al round like a gawddamn bloodhound searching for a master when weren't no one prying the litter. Right round '57, just 'fore that flood came through on the 29th, and Freddie were standing outside Al's door salivating for a chance to prove, just fucking chomping at the bit of validate. Now, at the time, I'd never seen nor known Al to take to a spell of mean. Mr. Davis's death'd wore on him hard with hurt hanging on his sleeve most times but something or another sure had lit a fire in his belly and Al came outta that office and just fucking wacked his small wormy little hands cross Freddie's face. Right there in front of 'bout a group of twenty. Went hard on him with a load of "fuck this," and "fuck that" and "ain't ya got any fucking decency in ya boy," and we all, those who's standing just took it in. Watched that boy run off like a hurt doe down the stairs and out into 'em woods and just thought, gawddamn. Worst bit of senseless I-don't-know-what-the-fuck spell of a fit I'd done seen and by grandfather time's clock, it marked the change in Al. Mean as a snake after that.

The woman weren't nobody I knew. I wouldn'ta known her nohow. My job weren't never part of the knowing in that regard and suppose if it didn't involve picking something up and carting it out elsewhere there weren't no reason for Al to go sharing his reasoning behind things. Not that he ever did or would in the first place. Perhaps I shoulda walked out right when I came in. Gone back out to the car and waited with Harry for the pillaging to be over. For the image of that woman's face not to be seared in my head the way it were with his hand shoved down her throat and her grunting to stop. For that deadness in her eyes as he finished his pounding to leave me. For the check out of her body that left some time ago to not sit with weight on my chest. Didn't even stop when he saw me. Just cleared out that ache of mean spit and pointed to the chair where an envelope with Mac writ on it set and clamped his fist hard over her head so she went limp on the desk and a spill of red pooled from the blonde that'd covered her face. Shoulda just fucking left. Not even opened the door. Least then I coulda gone on with the not knowing. With the never having heard "that'll be all Connie," when I went to shut the door.

37

1990

RONNIE

Truth bore witness to anything, it'd lean on yar killing Mommy the moment that Fuck spewed seed between her legs. Shoulda quit ya in the barn of that witchy woman. Up in Jacklot. Shoulda walked or got carried or pitched over on hands and knees and crawled up to that place where babies go to disappear and made that woman end it all 'fore ya's ever allowed chance at fucking shit up.

I's there, day ya come in. Scarred by the shit. Scarred by 'em sounds coming outta our sweet Mommy. 'Em slaughter caterwauls whaling shrill in plied pitched paint. Like ya's carving out the insides of the house while ya's making way.

Took Nanny out to the fucking yard. Thought her baby were in there dying. That the Lawd'd finally claimed time on all the shit her kind'd done in their life and found this to be the best place for the settling. Out there justa pacing grass. Just kicking up mounds of dirt, scattering chickens in the dried frizz of sunrise quiet, in that in between where sausage and bacon shoulda professed poetic dreams with the tickle of cast iron spit, with Mommy set over on the couch, her feet raised high so's 'em fat ankles might gain a little bit of release, with that knitted blanket of yeller daisies draped over her, 'cause she felt 'em flowers helped happiness grow inside. Shoulda, all of us, Nanny, her, and me carried out that morning in peace, with Nanny offering biscuits and scoops of gravy and Papaw and I going out to 'em woods, chopping down some blocks, surveying the land, making sure weren't nothing gone wrong overnight, weren't nobody bothering what's his. But couldn't be none of that, could there, Mick? No Papaw for the aiding and not quiet for the storm.

When Mommy'd started to show, that secret not even hers to keep no longer, not even something she'd managed say on, Nanny pretended it were just a bit of weight. That, "Lawd honey, tell ya what, we's gonna have to stop feeding ya so good. 'Bout round as house, ain't ya? 'Bout as full as a tick, I declare," she'd say it, scooping out another helping on Mommy's plate 'cause even though it weren't nothing we's talking 'bout, Nanny couldn't never go to letting hunger fill a mouth. Even when there were a cougar who'd got in the pig pen and tore suckling pink from ever'one of 'em babies of hers, she'd gone out just like it were any other day and laid down slop. Papaw just walking up after her with his hatchet ready to begin the carve, already had 'em spots picked out where he's gonna salt.

He'd do that with his girls. Follow 'em round just cleaning up what they couldn't, what he knew from the beginning needed be done in order for their surviving, 'cause don't think for one fucking minute, Papaw didn't know exact where ya come from and at what point ya arrived. Couldn't fool that man if he's lickered up to high Heaven in a mountain fog in the middle of a summer storm. Saw it in Mommy's eyes the moment she stepped foot through 'em doors the day after it happened. Town already rabie-mouthed foam with talk of what'd gone on in that office on the hill, like anyone ever truly stood a chance at being free from something so bad.

Jesus, it were spelled right on her for anybody to see if they'da took a look. Marked down in big yeller and purple hand grips on her arms, in tailored burns plotting her wrists that she made effort towards covering with the shitty leftovers of a shirt from the Man who'd left. Tousled up in the back biting knots left on her shoulders from where nails'd gripped and punches landed. Papaw knew it right fast. Knew it from the wobble of Mommy's legs, 'cause hadn't one moment of her life ever leant towards unsure. Even when she's wrong, she were sure footed. Why he'd never bothered laying worry on her.

Jesus, boy, ya shoulda never been here. Don't ya get that. This, here, shoulda never happened 'cause ya weren't meant to be here. Ya just weren't. Mommy weren't ready for ya. Didn't want ya. Couldn't even stand to look at ya most times and the only reason Nanny could were 'cause it just not in her nature not to. Gawddamn, mean, didn't ya know, didn't ya know from the spring of yar very first cell that what's done weren't right, that how ya come to be only ever gonna lead towards shit and bad and wrong. Couldn't ya get that.

But nah, we's forced to be there, forced to experience yar burgeoning lust for life, forced to hear and smell and watch as my Mommy and Nanny's daughter clamored against the peel of ya from her skin, as she bit down on a stick Nanny'd kept in times of strife. That poor woman. Fighting against life.

Mommy were a hard woman. Made that way. Molded to it. Heard Papaw spinning whiskey tales 'bout it to the stars out front. Don't know what'd called me to it, up and outta sleep, weren't nothing but snores and dark going on usually, and Papaw didn't like a sneak so stepping out on squeaky boards weren't the best of ideas. Musta muttered too many loud grievances, too much pull on his jar'd get him right vocal at times. And seeing how I's conditioned to follow his voice where ever it led, probably didn't stand much a chance in not hearing what he needed say. Ya'd only just come to us the night 'fore, a little pea pod in Mommy's belly with only Papaw and her to know the full truth. Hit of yar weight in her belly boring boulders on all our shoulders, surprised there's sleep to be had at all.

Papaw were out there on the porch naked as a jaybird in his chair striking out deals with something higher. Looked to be like he'd gone running in the woods, like there he'd sold the clothes off his back to that mountain man no one talks on anymore for fear he might come down the steeps into the bottoms and show the world what he's made of again, let the good Hazard people know Enoch Murray weren't one to be forgot just yet, looked a little like that, like that's the sort to instruct how to handle the things to happen next. Just railing, he were. 'Bout how when Mommy's little, she almost died. Slipped down in a ravine, right at the bottom of Michner's cliff. Seemed, as Papaw put it, set of Devils went to battle over there at the bottom of where that cliff began 'bout thirty ought years ago and it were something of a sharp maddening dip into the earth that'd turned housing for all sorts of critters in the aftermath, mostly those of the slithering smite type. Were a bad place full up of bad memories seared down in the earth and it couldn't come as surprise to even a few that evil'd gone on to burrow there.

Fell down as she's going after a handful of blackberries. "How cruel Gawd can be," Papaw howled. Bush'd grown up so tall it were near as big as a grown man and when she went to lean in, Nanny only turned but for a second, little Mommy fell. Scraped down that rock with bare-country-hot-summer-skin 'til she hit the pit. Stayed down there with 'em copperheads for three hours 'fore Papaw's able to fish her out. Can ya imagine? Our sweet little Mommy getting bit over and over on her young body in that dark hole of a place. All alone.

Nanny'd go to say that's what'd hardened her to the world, that little bit of time by herself amongst 'em teeth and monsters. Papaw hollered 'bout how when he finally got her up in his arms, after borrowing rope and scaling down with a miner helmet on, words, "Baby, just hold on," cracking whips out his throat, "I'm coming for ya, baby, Daddy's coming," echoing off that rock, when he finally got to her, after blasting down fifteen rounds on 'em snakes, damn near sending both of 'em deaf, he found Mommy wedged on a high spot with red dripping outta ten marked sets and one long sumabitch shredded in her fingers from where she'd found "rip" marked deep in her bones. Think, maybe, Papaw believed what Nanny did, that-that time in the pit'd scored, saved her perhaps from future harm. But that's just what they told 'emselves on the outside, 'cause ever'one living, including Mommy knew the truth and hardened ain't got much extension on the likes of what ruin'll do.

38

NOVEMBER 3, 1930

CECIL "DOC" HODGE AND CO.

—

3 SHOTGUNS AND 40 RIFLES

PART IV

Cecil's blood browned thumb, caked in the dribblings of split-tail red and crusted clear head juice, plucked the backside of his hatchet, dwarfing his hand against the gritted stone. He'd walked all night, silently wading towards that deep base of trouble, with two like-minded mentalities at his side. They'd passed in the dead of black, their canvas large oak watchtowers weaving the men's evil in slow swaying leaves, the gentle breeze unknowing of the fire roosting in their bellies, boiling their innards with hate.

"Worked 'emselves into a fine-looking cranny, wouldn't ye say, there broder." Cian teethed nail bits between his lips as he stepped from an oak. Pulled the tar studded spikes from out his pocket where he'd made habit of keeping 'em all tucked in and safe, such soft little lambs they were, indeed. Brick nails. Yanked from the soulless splaying of skin tacked on a half-pummeled wall last seen bereft of the body of an old man accused of larceny which the broders 'emselves'd watched the donning of spikes into the fair galoot, who, of course'd done nothing wrong other than carry the patron saint of stupidity round his helm for far too long in a place where it shoulda died due to the devils marauding 'bout. Fact, could be argued as such that the broders'd far more play in that poor man's fate then even the stars aligned, considering it were 'em who'd cleared the trough of many a farmer's barn, inside and out, just to keep from meeting dirt's bed and it were, truth be told, 'em too who'd overheard the appointment for Dudly, that being the sad sap's name, writ down on drenched whispered breath inside the confines of White's in their broad spit of a home, Cavan, where they'd neither bothered in the folly of ownership when they spied the pecking of Dudly's eyes by a sturdy fella nor did they move a dash when the nail driver began his work, sinking 'em three inch barbs through bread-fattened-skin on that half crumbling wall of an old unused Catholic church. A Catholic Church, ye say, aye, a Catholic Church.

"Ruffians." Riley pried pockets of afterlife from his gourd. In earnest, he needed no reason to let loose on the world, it lived in him all the time in ramrods of scoured dust and burning roofs. So much so that if dallied in only the slightest, his eyes closing off for mere seconds to what the world offered 'fore him, his thoughts'd carry him back to all sorts of wrong his body'd seen. For want of nothing else, he needed bones crushed at times just so's it confirmed his hands still worked and he still alive. And so it were not some huge inconvenience, the sharing of the wrongs done to 'em men down at Randi's by that boy, but an invitation to feel life again and Riley were more than willing to accommodate. Furthermore, as Riley gritted and chewed flaked sprawls of shriveled skin from his lips, sloughing sheets of red on the forest floor, he looked at his broder and removed ol' Donny Bowen's brass from his pocket with the thrill of a boy touching a tit for the first time.

It were as such then, when a group of men like these gathered round gazing on the future wrongdoings to be carried out on a bag of hired louts down below, that they's all thrust, and why wouldn't they be, to the depths of where their furies first began, to where 'em nicks shredded along their skin, set with salt, then rubbed forever in lemon with their recalling, and my how time can be ever forthcoming in the providing of such memories when there's some waiting to be done, which were, in fact, the only reason holding the bruisers back. Waiting for Jeb Murray, Enoch's daddy. One who'd brought 'em down the hill in the first place.

Jeb Murray were meant to be, as his son'd laid out for 'em rather nervously round the outskirts of a fettered fire ring, on the east side of Curly's knotted tree. The Eastside being of course not the common Eastside, which'd plagued quite a bit of debate over the years seeing as how there were folks stating that it were a matter of opinion where the Eastside set, depended on how yar back faced, least that's what a few drunks'd gone on 'bout five years ago when they's to meet up for a right cantankerous time, which as one might guess didn't end up anywhere near that landing of good, fact, split two of their heads wide open like dropped summer melons and left a purty nasty gash on the bulbous tree polyp, where ever after it said that 'em heads from 'em boys actually got took up in that tree and that were the reason why it'd gone for a low warped hang like an old geezer with a potbelly and sad drooping face. All of which ain't got nothing to do with anything other than there's those stating that the true Eastside belonged actually to the right of where 'em heads crashed in that bark and not on the left where true north'd govern it so.

Cecil, having factored in the rumors of such a stupid thing, went on and took it upon hisself to take wide strides round the entirety of that trunk using the sheen of his hatchet 'cause it weren't confirmed Jeb still drawing breath on this green earth and he'd half a mind to lean towards stumbling over a body or something worse once he made it full round both Easts. For fair be it to think it not beyond a set of hotheads to come in and kill a man then send his son out after those who might plight 'emselves with retribution and since the thought weren't so far off from Cecil's mind, in that, if paid enough, he might very well've done the same, he went on and curried favor's hide with a nice long walk'bout on that hill scanning the carnage left down yonder and round in ever' whicha way a compass might reach.

Course, now, Jeb weren't nowhere to be found. He'd done seen enough in his life to know how this story planned to end. Any man with any gawddamn sense 'bout him wouldn't watch a thing like that and stick round nohow. He'd vowed a long time ago not to end up like that.

Meanwhile back up yonder aways, far enough into the brush where there's a good chance at hide and a damn fair one at survive, Jeb'd made temporary camp with ear shot trained at ever' twig and wind rustle as far as his ear's lend hear. Set there with a cavity full of broke heart stew and a young man's spite spilling boat loads of ill through him as he aimed steady at a shaky hand and a lap full of slugs. By now, there lived a chance Cecil'd made his way down to the scene and there's like to be one helluva an angry lot planting points down breeches in response, that blanket of red hovering slight like a fog, but it were his boy that rattled forefront in Jeb's head and how there weren't no amount of erase in existence that were gonna ever rob 'em images from Enoch's mind and it were kicking some Gawd awful mire of shit to the surface. Taking Jeb back to a place he'd not wont to go.

Story of boys growing up seeing shit too soon weren't something so very out of sorts for these parts and there were certainly all types of wrong occurring in 'em hills but that don't make the stomaching of it any less vile just 'cause its tendency to happen and he knew it better than most. Jeb were five airing on sixteen when his Daddy took a hammer to the head. Knocked back by a set of just-doing-my-job-hands, that's how it put to him in the aftermath. His daddy's head leaking oil on the floor. They'd come, 'em men, just like these. Come by the order of somebody else on a night just like this when there weren't no suspecting, not that one ever could, when dirt floated in the air sticking fall to yar lungs and crisp on yar skin, and it seemed just some ordinary night, just some spend-time-with-the-fam-'fore-lights-out-sorta-thing. Saw 'em standing there over his Daddy, that hammer picked from off the table by the door on the left, from where his Mommy'd wanted hang a set of ole flowers on a nail so's they could dry and the place make take a nice waft, that's what she'd wanted. His daddy were supposed to put it up just after supper, just 'fore light broke down in the west, but the door'd got kicked open too fast, and the flowers fell, and they'd found the rifle by the door 'fore his Daddy'd dared a chance. Took him from Jeb like it yesterday, like they's standing shape and form in front of him as his hands fed bullet teeth to metal rack. Like he's still pawing mitts on his Mommy trying to make sense of why Daddy's legs won't move, and why they's in a hurry now to make it over to Cousin Ned's. Like they's just in front of him, shadows amongst trees.

Thirty years since that shotgun's used. Thirty years of waiting, collecting dust.

39

FEBRUARY 3, 1960

CONNIE'S DADDY'S GONE TO GET HIS GUN

Connie's daddy straddled the leftover fall down of a Loblolly Pine, that'd careened itself sunder in a lightning strike in the storm of '56, and now lay Viking scorched black on the fringe of Albie Todd's property. Leaded and engraved with a barrel of hate, he sat coating his lips with balm. Always were a necessity for Connie's Daddy. Spread of wax smoothed sin outta his lips, what he'd say. What he'd always said when somebody went to commenting on it. Probably grew out of a boy named Grady calling him a pansy way back when.

Back round the age of, let's just settle on ten, Grady and a bunch of other dipshits feeling might in the crowd with a hankering for downright mean, got it twisted all up in their shit for brain heads that lip balm a sign for a "dick pucker-as in one who gum-guzzles dick skin between they's lips," that's exact what Grady said in front of 'em others to Connie's Daddy, well, let's just call him Jim for now, his real name'll come in later. As ya can imagine, Jim didn't care all that much for a thing like that to be spread on him, specially since it were his Granmommy that'd got him hooked on lip balm and specially since ever'body who were anybody knew that Grady Meaks went fishing with one of his cousins down by Curly Fork and they'd got spied on more than once sticking their peckers round each other in a way that don't lend towards crossing streams, so Jim felt like there were more at stake here than just being called a name and insulting the fine character of one of his kin in the process. Did not care for it one bit.

At the time, Jim remembered but two things his Daddy'd taught him 'fore he died in a cave-in at the mine, be aware of yar surroundings and always, always, always, no matter what, look a fucker in the eye. Don't matter what a body's saying, don't matter what a mouth's spewing, and ya can bet a life's worth on the fact that if there's green involved, there ain't no amount of trust that lives anywhere 'cept for 'em eyes. Said, "There's a bit of good and bad and a lot of in between happening behind that glass and I advise a real strong taking to what ya think's steering it." Only thing Jim ever truly heeded from the bastard, and it were 'bout the nicest thing his Daddy'd ever give him but that ain't what's meant for share now.

Having that little bit of his Daddy tucked down against his bones, Jim went on and took note of 'em piercing blues chucking dynamite sticks at him from shit-talking Grady Meaks and he followed suit airing out the crowd of his dumber-than-a-box-of-dirt followers, and he leant on the air weighing the odds of this whole encounter ending any other way than the spilling of baby boy blood, and he reckoned it couldn't be, due entirely 'cause what he saw in 'em windows.

See, living behind Grady Meaks face, bore there in the hull of where feather cocking and flaunting high kick out spread, were the beginnings of a chicken shit life. That ever-wading yard of not gonna understand why his wife'd leave him for another, or how nobody at work or in town'd ever show him a spit of respect, no matter what they bathed over him with tongued grace, 'cause he didn't have a bit of spine holding that body of his up and what it would take for Grady to craft one up—meant change.

Naw, all that boy right there cared 'bout were how he's coming off. Didn't matter there weren't a hint of thinking-for-hisself-bone up under that skin of his, long as ever'body thought there were. Naw, up in 'em flecks of crystal sheen beyond that spit of Jim's face planted there in cue for approval, the problem lived, and it weren't something Jim believed Grady'd ever get a grip on and sorry for him weren't nobody in his life that'd have the heart to tell him 'cause shit's like to flock and hang round other piles of shit. Even when Grady Meaks died some fifteen years later, trumped and stabbed by one of his own, the man who ended up bedding and finally taking away Grady's own wife, there were a couple tagalong turds who ventured to the afterlife with him, those stupid, sorry saps, 'cause they weren't ever able to make that shift to change neither or better yet even question.

Point being, Jim knew that 'spite his standing outnumbered, five to one, 'spite his standing a good twenty pounds lighter than most all 'em peckerwood fucks, and 'spite his lacking any true experience with knowing how to hold yar own in a fight, he reckoned he needed to go on ahead and rip this boy a new asshole in front of all his friends if he ever planned on looking hisself in the mirror again.

How he got there, fore don't think for one second there weren't a barrel of connections leading from his Daddy dying to him standing with 'em boys getting ready for a hooray, were led by a whole lot of time spent over at his Granmommy's once his Daddy met the dirt and that compounded by his Daddy's absence, where 'em Meaks'd got real comfortable in their height and might on the mountain, which'd caused a little bit of a twist to the order of things, done surrendered a whole case for backasswards to go a spreading round 'em hills, least, where it concerned Jim, that was.

Now, that ain't to say Jim's Daddy were some sorta king or lion or even runner of things but there were a fair share of respect thrown his way for various reasons, most of which were based on his ability to unionize, that'd throw a helluva lot of clout round once 'em wages started to change, place a man on the forefront of hero if he's able to deliver long enough, which did not therein work out for Jim's Daddy, but that don't mean there weren't a line of gold under his name neither. Point being, appeared a couple years after he's gone, folks, well not folks, more like fucking Meaks, began to forget all the glory surrounding Jim's family name, least 'em youngins did and half the reason for that were 'em Meaks never really liked anybody gathering crawl out that pot they's all stewing in and the other staggering pull on all of 'em being the meanest, most uncivil pack of shits, and seemed the farther down the bloodline one went, the worse the smell of taint got. What could be said, however, were that in the absence of Jim's father and the presence of a wiry Granmommy, Jim learnt all manner of handy tidbits, not usually found in a young boy's life.

Two that he'd took away the most useful were, beeswax burned when combined with a little peppermint and his head were harder than a gawddamn rock and it just so happened or perhaps maybe it didn't just so happen, maybe there were a bit of design always in his Granmommy's decisions and therefore a smattering of that stringing over Jim too, that Granmommy only ever mixed her lip balm, made from beeswax, which might be getting a little ahead of ourselves, but let's give it a shout now, then trace back, with peppermint and Jim having a hard head didn't just lend itself to the fact that he could withstand a couple hard knocks but moreso that if he got hold of something inside that noggin of his, there weren't gonna ever be no let back unless he went on and buried that thought in the ground.

Well, history'd like to tell ya, that what occurred there with 'em boys were some kinda grand show with Jim pulling trick after trick from his hat and running steel rods up 'em boy's asses so far their families came to know the brunt and that ever'time they even thought they saw a bee, their sphincters scuttled up all tight like they's milling rocks for gold in their intestines and that if there were, dare spot, of an actual can of lip balm anywhere within the near vicinity their bowels went for a move reminiscent of Niagara falls with Poseidon, hisself, leading the course and that they'd carry that leaky ass flap for the entirety of a week, just spraying volatile shit ever'where they went. But that ain't how it went. Jim took his beating there by the filthy backdrop of Baker Hill's shitter, when Grady pulled out his infamous sucker punch, which were a tactic picked up from watching other bastard Meaks go to brawl, and blindsided Jim in the fucking ear, knocking his ass to the ground as cannon fire mined holes in his head, 'cause only assholes who haven't ever got hit believe they might actually stand their own in a fight. He, then, were afforded the luxury of facing the full wrath of asswipes through the reception of kick after kick after kick which'd settled cherries of blackened nots all along Jim's legs, back, and arms, which'd made nice foundation for the snotrockets and piss to film over him in a sudsy layer of all around bullshit that was his encounter with Grady Meaks.

Be that as it may, this tussle did not solicit Jim's forbearance from further violent acts, nor did it prevent him from visiting that same spot where he'd met hand to head ever'day for a week, that due diligence of his peers molding the better part of his skull and heart into a hardened rock. For Jim, the blows became blessings. Soothed lullaby tells along his temples, each hooked knot a revelation he'd soon hold against his attackers. Like how Grady made eyes after ever' hit with Sweeteye Johnny, a boy with puckered lips and pinched nose who favored Rock Hudson when he was a Texan in Giant, and just as red pickled in fermented pop outta Jim's cheek, just as swollen gash pried open by callous meat hungry boy fists, Sweeteye Johnny'd let out a cooed sigh from the back of his throat from where Jim gathered Grady'd like to put his dick and that alone were worth the price of admission to getting one's face busted in for a week straight. Or how Chubby Lyle Vogt were sweating bullets while keeping watch over it all, his only ever stepping forward when called on by Grady with phlegmy grin, or how out of all of 'em, including Grady, the biggest shit talker there, were a runt named Keller. Never did tell nobody his first name 'cause it were pansy-riddled, something like Sandy or Terry. Weren't no use paying much attention to either of 'em. Keller were all bark and Lyle were like to fall over or cry if pushed too hard.

To tell the truth, Jim weren't one for subtle revenge and if the offense purposefully bilious, which ain't always the case but in this one it were, he were less likely to hold yield in his body at all. Thus, Jim took part in an odious plot. The very next day as he embarked to school, Jim planned to intercept the key player of his plan, a one Miss Jodi Meaks, who if given even half the opportunity to spend any amount of time with a sort like Sweeteye Johnny, would no doubt find her way to the hobbled glory of his cock, 'cause that all she knew coming from a family like that, and given that, that always something welcomed in man's life, there wouldn't be much chance at reject by Sweeteye Johnny even if he weren't attracted to Jodi and better still considering he just as much a piece of shit as Grady, it wouldn't cause grievance for him to accept 'spite the obvious conflict of interest. Jim then planned, once bribing Jodi with the brain candy that he'd overheard Sweeteye Johnny praising her ever' waking move and that the only reason he even took up with Grady in the first place were to eventually get up with her, along with scrawling up some wildflowers out the back of his Granmommy's property over there on the other side of 'em bees, which when handed to purty much any country girl round, there's a guarantee offer up of a panty drop, paired with the instruction to meet up with Sweeteye Johnny outside by the shitter on Baker Hill, where Jim'd received all his beatings, today, at approximately twenty minutes 'fore the gang's supposed to meet up.

Jodi ate it up like fried liver. Face went to turning a hue while hands went a fluttering with the occupation of straightening up that nasty dress of hers down in feigned iron pleats. Poor thing didn't stand a chance. Damn near salivating after it 'fore Jim'd handed over the flowers, which meant she were in, but not 'fore Jim'd shared with her the best part. Where, from out his trousers came a particularly minty fresh canister of Granmommy's infamous lip balm, the batch set with four times the amount of peppermint doled usual. To which, Jim added that of all the times he'd heard Sweeteye Johnny speak on Jodi, it were 'em infamous puckers he'd mentioned the most, and how he'd heard, Sweeteye Johnny that were, that lip balm were just the thing he'd want his lady to wear always, 'cause there weren't nothing worse than a set of rough lips.

And boy didn't she go to the trouble of coating that shit on thick 'fore she went down on Johnny. Johnny just a standing there not knowing nothing nohow other than there's a girl fiddling with his pecker and he weren't gonna be the one to go causing stop to it now.

Needless to say, when Grady, Chubby Lyle, and Keller finally come round the corner on the scene, Jodie, Grady's sister, need it be reminded, were in a full-on throat fight with Sweeteye Johnny's battle stick, need it be reminded, Grady's, one and only love at the time. Damn thing were shoved all the way down her sternum looked like. And to go on and throw wood to the fire, 'bout that same time that peppermint'd probably started burning something fierce. 'Cause Sweeteye Johnny pulled outta Jodi's mouth faster than rabbits fucking, with a howl wailing out like he might die. All hands a fumbling and red face a welting and poor little Jodie not knowing why other than the wave of sick growing true in her belly, 'cause the one thing ya don't want to do with Granmommy's lip balm were to go ingesting it, not a lot least, and from the looks of it Jodi'd swallowed damn near half the tin. Skin all green and white, she turned to Chubby Lyle and ralphed all over the front of his fat little belly, spewing chunks of whatever the fuck 'em Meaks eat and as with most, once somebody gets a going it don't take long for the follow. Next thing Jim knew, there Keller was, spilling split pea soup and chunks of ham on the back of Grady's neck, as Grady'd moved closer in disbelief to Sweeteye Johnny. Hit him like an acid octopus with slippery green tentacles spreading all which a way over Grady's skin and one big center of snotted spitwad sliming down towards the top of his back.

Pissed him off so bad, Grady turned round and knocked Chubby Lyle into fucking next week. Bent that poor feller over on all fours and went to fucking town on his ass. Probably taking out a little aggression after seeing his sweetheart and his sister humming two steps on each other. And wouldn't ya know, little bitty Keller didn't want no part of it all. That loud mouthing dawg run all the way home, skipping the crowd that'd gathered and ever'thing. Oh, that's right, forgot to mention that Jim'd gone on and told ever'body at school that there were gonna be something worth seeing and it were in ever'body's interest to come out immediately and seeing as how that ain't something spoke very often, it'd drawn ever'one from their desks, including the teacher out to the yard.

As for Hellmouth James Daniel, 'fore that were what Jim, Connie's Daddy, came to be known as after, he were tickled pink by the whole thing. Carried his ass home back to Granmommy's with a Cheshire grin and walked right up to the apiary, on the north side of Breakneck Bottom, right where the land flattened for a spell, and she'd fit her boxes and waited for her to be done with the tending of the things so's he could tell her all.

She were gonna love it, that wiry sort. Widowed, two dead sons buried, a daughter-n-law gone, and the shuffle of earth falling on one of her granbabies 'fore she hit the ripe age of forty, Granmommy Daniell, that were her original name, she never found no use taking a man's name, and frankly weren't no reason for the ceremony of it in 1870 in a holler, where, needless to say, it shellacked in stone. Hard, mean woman, she were but loved a good story, didn't she. Wouldn't let nobody get up next her bees. Eliza, one of her two living daughters and Connie's Daddy's momma, said it were due to her getting hitched so young. Shoved out the door to a one Tumlin Scholl, who were arranged to take the hand of Granmommy Daniell solely 'cause it believed he an offspring of Daniel Boone and Granmommy's daddy, Dell, quite liked the thought of having his blood run through the family line. Course as it turned and as it were most like to occur, Tumlin were a sumabitch and Granmommy Daniell didn't take all that long to collecting her tears once he fell sunder to the dirt. Fact, as Henry told it, Eliza's brother, and Connie's Daddy's Uncle, Granmommy Daniell might've offed the bastard herself one night when he'd gone a little too far in front of 'em kids. Her three living children, Ada, Henry, and Eliza, Hellmouth James' Momma said it were mainly due to Dell being a shit storyteller. Said, she coulda weathered the beatings if he'd ever offered up anything smart to say.

Now what in the fuck any of this had to do with Hellmouth James Daniel straddling a tree on the backside of Albie Todd's property, with the scope of his shotgun playing mirror to Albie's wife—oh not much, just felt like the right story to tell.

40

FEBRUARY 3, 1960

THE HOUND

My head'd go to blank and light faster than a television set stripping ads over white sawdust stream, like when the signal cuts out and it in the middle of the show right 'fore the cowboy done what he come there to do, and the corner of the seat cushion'd just 'bout break from the grip, yar knees'd plunked down in 'em from where yar heart'd gone round the bend and weren't quite done with the journey yet, hadn't quite made it back to the veins.

Albie'd hisself a TV. That's how I knowed what it'd do. Stand outside that window over bone white Bur Oak that littered round me in broken corpses and watch him watch it. Scattered limbs sticking outta no-man's-land-dirt against my feet. Like trenches dug up somewheres with a man shell shocked, hollering out to the world over lost comrades.

First time I saw that box, I's hooked. Go down there even when there weren't call to. Fix up under 'em shadows and just view. His wife'd leave it on the whole damn day like a radio with constant chatter clanging against 'em silent beams of her empty but filled house. Always her and that box waiting. Wait 'til the sun'd rise at times just her and that box and no Albie on site. He'd not needed me then. Not when he's away doing the business. Come just for the TV then.

Felt like, when I's there and it were on, my head in that box way 'em things flashed on and off. Not like I's one of 'em folks in it. They's happy. Always happy. Always smiling and nodding and talking 'bout something in a kitchen or by a fireplace or in a yard or lab or something, all of 'em usually smile-glued. That ain't what I'm going after, what I mean, what I mean I ain't one of 'em.

My head didn't used to go like this. Didn't used to drop off, go blank, get 'em fuzzies wiping memory clean. One minute standing, thinking, carrying on 'bout something, the next just gone. Just dropped off. Head'd deemed time and thought'd go elsewhere. Didn't make one difference how hard I tried to put focus on it. Not one lick.

Got to be at times, if I'd stood long enough by that window watching, that screen'd hook in, 'em smolders of *then* popping embers on the *now*. Voices airing my thoughts right there into the dark.

Look here at the not so distant past where those damned Irish boys'd fought to the very end. Where Doc'd watched half alive half not. Stay tuned for the scenes to unfold.

Sound'd cut to something dancey, something worming round in the hip shakes, some greased back hair slicked down on a drawn parrot glamoring out 'bout what looked like razors. Dancing all 'bout 'til the screen went black and there grew from the nether regions of still'd come the "watch closely" broadcast of how 'em Irish boy's and Doc'd got got.

They'd pop up right there, right where I'd caught 'em down by Carol's plot.

Near a brown mound weren't no green clinging to yet. Right where her babies'd wailed all butterbean fat. Only two in Carol's brood left to claim the name. Friday'd passed with both sons hitting the ground. Ain't no room for ages when slugs go battering a crowd. She'd caught hers coming out the back of their place, that lanky sprout of a man lugging last rites as his body went for fail over cinder block stairs. Flesh raking off in slabs on the stone with Carol's tug on her sweetheart's arm.

Hated the waste. Good looking woman like that fighting after a sorry ass like Phil. A known deserter from their bed. Took girls to his old family farmhouse away from town. Plied 'em with funny cigs and bottled apple bright washed down with Bubble Up backs. Kept 'em there on benders. Hunting, suppose, the words filtering kisses on Carol's cheek as he left.

Died right there over top the somabitch in the house owned by the camp. Smoke still wearing out spurts of black from the entry in her head as 'em babies clung to their Mommy—dead.

We interrupt this broadcast for a special new's bulletin, coming live from the Hound's brain—Bur Oaks don't usually live this far east. More middle, up near Lexington. Where 'em mountains carry out in rolls, green seas mounding in crests. Big as damn rooms there. Some more'n six feet wide and hundred feet tall. Big enough to strike a thought, that's for damn sure.

They ain't white usually. That took some special caring after to happen. Doubt Mr. Todd thinks much on it now. This sad dripping fall-down of a tree on the corner of his lot. Don't like romping near these parts, suppose. Too close to the wild. Bet he don't give one shy to it. Woke up one morning and said to hisself, "that tree's gotta go."

Snarl in the blanket grown on too long.

He'd not knowed what it'd meant. That any boy with adventure in 'em'd made refuge on Big Ben Bur, what it named. Spread 'bout ninety feet and as a kid eyeing up, looked to be the whole world how far 'em limbs reached. Three hundred years old, Big Ben Bur. Three hundred years of towering over the southeast corner of land that'd one day become Albie Todd's. Gawddamn legend, that tree were.

This vacation really let yarself go, go Hertz class all the way back to where ya found the Doc and the damned Irish boys reloading breeches, hands steady as calm water. Faces buried in blood. Like buckets poured on 'em with potholes of white seeping through the background of red.

Fucking awful, they looked.

Suspect they'd thought I'd died. Probably shoulda. But I'd found the nurse in me somewheres and what I couldn't bind and mend, Mommy did. Best she could at least. Hard day for her when I's found. Daddy dead and the hog splayed wide for slaughter. Same day. Needed patch for skin. Had to come from somewheres and dead man flesh ain't like to fit nice on young boy face. Hog'd have to do. Daddy were kilt like all 'em rest. By men who'd not knowed the mouths behind slays their guns fed. Not the uncommon tale, afraid.

Weren't able to find his body for a fucking week, limbs intertwined like roots. One over top the other, half of 'em buried almost full right from the cut down of others. Like soldiers splayed outright over wire, their only job meant as boot maps for other feet.

Plop, plop, fizz, fizz, the alka-seltzer way—two men'd stuck dynamite in a coon hole, the smoothed center carved 'fore they'd took sip from mommy's tit, and damned Big Ben to smitherings. Shook the whole fucking mountain. Sent a frenzy of folks to the edge of Albie's lot foaming tight lip. Tiny hate claws burrowing in tired hearts.

Chunks'd swung all the way down to the river, some of 'em lodged up in a dam of sorts. Some believed it were Ben's way of holding true to the land, but it wouldn't take but one deluge to come and 'em sticks'd fall.

Existing for that long gonna tack soft spots, no way it can't. Big Ben heart strings carrying out all over 'em hills. Seemed ever'body a stone's throw from some story 'bout how they'd kissed a girl or found a frog or carved up sayings they thought the world needed heard on that bark. A right train of 'em trucking up the hill after that bang. Wet streams justa wallering down cheeks. Like after all that time, all that wrong done at the bottom of that bark somehow forgot.

She's got a man she's promised to love, honor, and keep house the right way—accident, that's what sisters and Mommy called it. Like there some sort of brushing off, some explanation for it, like the path leading out the knife gonna shorn forgiveness where loathe'd lived. Gawd love 'em all with their tending. Their attempts at Christian rights.

Four weeks and still Mommy couldn't hold her hand calm when she round me. Turned haint white stark, her son done buried. The image left not nothing any'd call their own.

Stood it as long as they could. Woulda maybe lasted a little bit longer. But weren't no need in making 'em suffer. World were doing a fine enough job at that.

Waited 'til the middle of night. Grabbed hold of a quarter of meat left for cure. Rest of the hog'd carry 'em out the winter if they's smart. Plus, far as rights go, the hog were mine, Daddy'd told me so 'fore the carving of my face, and I needed something for hold 'til a kill proffered and a fire built.

They'd, the blood red faces'd made quite a mess on me. Plied my forehead back like feathers planted in it and the meat needed clean 'fore the body spiked and laid over flames. Raked metal over bone with jagged licks, leaving tribal crags and dips, and stole down just above the eye in a wrecked broken flap, where even if there were a Doc able and equipped, easy on the eyes wouldn't never come from nobody's lips in a point towards me.

Left me so gawddamn ugly, fucking birds'd go for a walk on the wind when they'd eye me and I couldn't get within a quarter mile to a herd without alarm clamoring out. All braying and honk and crow and cry planting steel traps with ever' move my foot'd make.

This flat tire needs a man but when there's no man around—when yar young, grown notions come at ya in flashes of fancy dipped green, in clearly marked paths where lane A'll end up meeting lane B and they'll go for a bit 'til they wind up making

C. Like there's a box and once picked all 'em things, 'em decisions and points, fit inside and can't nothing else go in it, like once ya done crossed the frame where that path begins, things set, and there ain't never no going back and there ain't never gonna come no change.

Then once ya'r grown, 'em lines begin to fade and that box goes raw with tatter and there seems it not out of the ordinary for stuff to start coming in that ain't supposed to go and that were a round'bout way my working for Albie come to exist. I'm guessing that were one way the story'd go.

Come to where the flavor is, come to Marlboro Country—it were done, in a way, no one expected, suppose, Ben's falling. It'd gone on and lasted and existed round here for so long that it not standing no longer, shocked. Fucking just ripped it out from under folks. Their heads unable, ill'quipped for the rationale behind it.

The tree were man to a lot. What man's supposed to be. A pillar, carrying all things done 'fore to all things yet to come. But the ritual of man ain't nothing but fire and blood, ain't it? Rains down on those ill'suited to stand 'cause the muds too deep or the water too high or the wind too strong where their feet planted, the excuses countless if given moist tongue. The choice to uphold a matter of judgment on the leg's part. They's the one's carving the way through the grit, one black stone at a time.

In the dull and common place occurrences of day to day living, one thing stands out, Colt 45 Malt Liquor—last time I stood 'fore Big Ben Bur, sour pockets of raked skin matted grids on my face. The idea of death and three men scratching grinders in my gourd while smothered cold from where frost'd set in cackling witch throat puffs lumbered under my feet and somehow or another all of my head cradled Ben my redeemer, my structure of stone to anchor all that wrong done to me, to swallow it up, and take it away. 'Cause that tree existing long as it'd done musta known where to store such seeds of scripture, he musta known how to rid me of it so's living could commence.

But ya can't rid yar bones of memories like that. They remembered. Remembered how noon spewed dragon breath on my neck, making my joints swell and ache 'spite it being twenty years back. The whole of me just begging for a spell of wind but not even a crinkled leaf went to swaying, all 'em trees felled silent, their mouths plumb sewn shut. That hex of wrong that followed a killing frost. That black fettered touch tying all of an'thing that'd longed for sprout together in just one long death-chain working in fields through out.

Remembered the cramp of hunger as I waited all 'em years out in 'em woods by myself, how nine winters'd come and gone with the slaughter of deer and rabbit and squirrel and not none of it ever satiating enough, how this winter, the one of my recollecting woulda marked tenth since, the notch carved in my arm by a bowie knife, not that I'd ever unwrap the gift of forget—No, that weren't something I'd ever meet.

Remembered it all, the stumbling from out the hole, seemed one foot in-one foot out something of darkness-devilry-prove when home made in the remnants of a lizard cave ever since leaving the family abode, how on that day, that day I'd come to meet 'em men, the ones who'd carved me up, I's hurled forward from the smooth surface of polished-clean-once-ago-river-rock-bed almost without control, my nose pinned to a scent I'd soon come to know and remember as 'em, the men, how I'd happened on the clearing in a fever-dream-search, my ripping awake only permitted appear after animal-target-detect.

Remembered how my leg felt, that emptiness from where a chunk took from me, where the bone'd cracked from the pound after pound after pound of a set of brass knuckles, the consequence of a rope low-down-silent-creep-thrown over Cecil 'Doc' Hodge's head, the shelling dole of clicked-repeated-hit-give-to-me by Riley, the broder with fucked up ear, the mirror-matched-visage of hate gnawing venom fangs of rue into my skin. OH, I's haunted by it all, by the sudden latch down of bicep that'd caught full cattle-prod-death when a Marble Bowie cleared right through my bicep, grabbing hold of my ribs for a good, nice stick. Woulda contended against any proclamation of easy, that right arm of mine would. That this offense endowed after the mangling of my left forearm by the Christmas-ham-hew of one of Hodge's hatchets after he, Cecil 'Doc' Hodge, sought fight against that grand battle we must all lose, where the rope binding his neck round the trunk of a Poplar did unfortunately break, that cataclysmic ripping occurring after a dreadful disembowelment that'd betide him only seconds earlier with the cleaved jut, jut, jut, of what else, but a very jagged procured rock—No. My bones remembered the story quite differently, rawly in fact, as in the rawness of my wrists contending free when broder Cian'd captured and tied me down, wanting retribution hisself for the acts provided to his friend Cecil 'Doc' Hodge, how it were the dislocating of both shoulders that'd set me free, but the price paid dearly course in a couple choice placements of nails in my chest, the driving pierce of five inches not quite making it through breast plate, lest not entirely.

See, it weren't necessarily a cut and dry scenario that I'd found 'em men, called to 'em somehow, a ten year trot carrying that burden of what they'd made me, plotting and planning and gathering strength and skill whilst damning it all mean more than anything else, and it were true I'd made 'em suffer, finally cutting loose from 'em ropes, the dislodging of a nail so long it'd dug three inches into my side with a full five to spare free called forward for the cause, how I'd rived 'em broders stridently, bursting bloodless bounties into the night, and how after finding all dead, I'd bathed in their red, and I'd built a fire, and emitted dark, vile, nasty, things that'd long lived under the dirt of my insides, and that at a point in the night, feeding time'd come, 'cause the kills'd caused quite the appetite, but—No as the legend of it'd grown and spread and come to harvest many times over, there were a disservice to the truth, for rarely does the myth speak to anyone but the men who need repeat it.

Light up a Lucky, it's light up time— And thus it were, under Big Ben Bur and all 'em tales it'd seen that the bodies left there to rot. Worn so in the fall down of mulch and leaf and traveling ant under me, left still by heavied remembrance, the many markings of feet come to do the same, to give glance to that which'd stood and that which were gone, the disbelief shuddered in the leftover feet. What few who'd managed pause long enough without being shot on Albie's property'd affixed tributes to the ground, their scattered sprawling implanted along the frame of withered tree ghosts on hard cold dirt floor. If Gawd were good, which I ain't convinced either one way or another, He'd live near and under and on top 'em limbs with how much love folks'd dropped off. Lived right there with 'em crosses and stones and small spits of yarn and buttons and anything else poor folks'd leave round something they honored.

But just as Gawd tended so too did Devil render presence known and it were somewhere lulling between that my apprenticeship formed and took shape. Under such heading should the aftermath unfold.

Oops, now there's a happy accident, an accident that could lead to opportunity—

Right here where Ole Big Ben Bur'd stood. Roped 'em up right here. Right here 'fore there were a TV and a job and a man holding a gun on the other side of the lot, up there on a broke down tree, aimed right now, right now as I live and breath at Mr. and Mrs. Todd.

Funny, whenever work time starts, head sorts all things out mighty fine. *It's Raid, house and garden bug killer, both indoors and outdoors, Raid hunts bugs down like radar.*

41

1990

RONNIE FAIRCHILD

Listen up, ya dirty dawg, in the back of my head, on past the let out of red, on past that cramp in my back, my weight crunched odd against the metal of that Olds, lives the finger. That snapshot of messy splotch planted on stained and crumpling white. That smudge never noticed 'til it were, then forever after the only thing in existence. 'Fore ya come along, Mick, I'd lay up on 'em beams of Nanny and Papaw's, where brown bleeds from packed dirt, my tired feet still humming from a day of yard-monkeying round, and I'd look up at that finger, that perfect preserve sealed just for me over that battered floor.

Found it at three-and-a-half. That finger. Found it on a sunny midmorning day when they'd all gone out to walk the crop. Tend to the taters and cabbage. Make sure the "damn dears" didn't get up on 'em. Papaw hated 'em dears but Nanny hated 'em worse. She'd run out 'em, now. Withered age left at the sink. Butterbeans in the soak, 'maters sliced for eat up. She'd drop it all soon as one spotted. Go tearing out the front kicking up specks, her little patch of worn through dent waiting for her return by the window.

Wouldn't take the shotgun, though. Leave that by the door, said, "ain't meant for 'em creatures."

Amid that morning tear, I found the finger. Laid up on the floor in my box, assumed naptime my watcher. Can't recall how I found it. Laying there like that being young'll take the eye places, suppose. Getting used to the change of scene, perhaps. Mommy'd only just brought me up to 'em hills. It'd got too thick down yonder. We's better off here, what she'd said.

Liked to lay up at the base of Papaw's chair. Fashioned myself a little space, a little spot of my own. There, I found the finger. Ain't no secret what'd give cause to the finger. We'd only just all of us experienced it. But that didn't matter. Shit like that don't matter to a baby boy 'cause there's something to be made outta nothing always.

Contrary to other folks, my Nanny'd but one vice in her catalogue. Gave all too much cradle to the chew. She loved that shit. Loved ever'thing 'bout it. Loved that it sent fireworks through her mouth, that it planted mines up in the creases of her lips, the subtle shuffle of her tongue unleashing 'em.

Loved that she'd spend her days out in the field, out in the dirt, and that black'd be waiting for her when she'd come in all cool and ready. She'd planted down jugs all over the house. All four parts where the sheets hung. One by the bed. One by the can. One outside. Those nothing special, old throw away tins. But if she's peeling back skins or shucking out pods, she'd use that'n by the sink. Her dead Daddy's old shine jug. A small carved XXX plotted up mug ya'd like not to ever meet with bucked out teeth and worn through dents striking holes in cheeks and beady eyes by Nanny's sink.

See, Ole Grandad weren't never trained in no proper reading nor writing and X's went on to become his mark and ever'thing sporting 'em summed up as property of his. That mug, his finest possession, something Gawdawful ugly. Scare the shit out of ya. It's true.

Now, the problem with storing yar wad in a jug meant to hold shine were folks might go confusing the two. And when Nanny moved that favoritest of jars into the sitting area, that place where I'd lay up in between, well, Papaw made the grave mistake of doing just that. See, Papaw already done hit his own lightening and went on with that nightly tradition of telling stories 'bout how things used to could. Right in the middle—

"…that mule kicked the living shit out of him, sure did. Kicked his ass to kingdom come then drug him back down again."

You wouldn't know nothing 'bout that, though, would ya, Mick? All that sweet man and what he done for this family. For our Momma. You rightly wouldn't have a clue, would ya? Gawd Almighty I wonder if ya'd actually spent time with that man maybe ya wouldn't've been such a gawddamn disappointment. But, who's to say, there brother.

Anyway, it were his favorite. The retelling of his brother's mishap that'd resulted in the loss of his eye. One I'd heard dare twice a week ever since I'd the recollection of words. This were the part he'd get so tickled, "that look of pure shock, I tell ya, pure salt of the earth not believing," that'd send him into a fit that he'd pause. Take a sip. Then start it up again.

Well, Nanny'd done tired and wore herself out in the sun so that she'd already gone to drift in her chair and Papaw hadn't yet noticed. His focus being on the audience. My drooling over ever' sputter this jolly faced sweet man were like to tell. And when that set of heckling came drifting out at just the time of his pause and his fingers slipped down for a chance at slurping 'em back with a bit a fire, he happened on the wrong jug.

That slant of clay shot up, Nanny's dead Daddy's initials sending X's straight for my throat, stomping down any slipping of "Don't" in the floor. Papaw's throat pulled down a big, long slurp. The lining at the back of his mouth, bludgeoning a bell, "THAT AIN'T IT." Eyes went to watering all sorts of wrong and bad. Face went to steam. Lobster red. Heat signaling out smokestacks to get this shit out of me. Poor Papaw. Cocked back his head, crying out streams of damp down his cheeks, letting fall the nob of that cursed bottle to the floor, which were so gawddamn mean it didn't even break nor spill when hitting, and chalked out the biggest black loogie I'd ever seen.

Us just following the rise of it as it shot up. That sticky mass of thick juice and chud carrying play through the air. Fucker went propelling straight for the ceiling, straight for that spot where if I's to lay right smack in the middle of Nanny and Papaw's chair, its mark'd be the only thing to notice. Painted an imprint of three knuckles bent and a middle finger blaring CHARGE. Like some kid with freckles and a bugle calling 'em boys out to battle.

Now, ya can have a couple things going on in yar life 'fore time comes where they finally go at making sense. What that finger done for me were made that come on a lot sooner than most. Inked it down on paper and folded 'em up, sealed 'em right there behind my peepers. Taught that lesson some ain't ever like to learn and some never like to give care to, ain't that right Mick! Spend their time dancing round the issue like it don't apply to 'em. They ain't all fitting the mold but there's a lean extending most to be Thumpers and Christies. Well, there ain't a gawddamn thing wrong with having a little fear held up in ya from time to time. There's good word to things being done after the fire's lit but there's something to be said 'bout trying to fix that notion under a blanket and another thing for tending towards a prediction at what it's gonna do when. Ya'r like to run out of road. Case in point, brother, this right here 'tween ya and I.

What I'm cutting at, even though I's one to be directly participant or witness to the surroundings behind that finger, none of it mattered. 'Cause what were 'fore me were something different. An introductory fuck ya. A way of telling me there weren't nothing ever gonna be and nothing ever meant to be with the words SPECIAL pertaining to me. World gave all of zero fucks to my breathing. To my living. And I lay up there with my little goofy feet and my little head of messy hair and for some reason on Gawd's green earth I got that.

Weren't no reason for it to be touched on again but the fact of the matter that ya never did, there, dear brother…well, looks like it's gonna haunt us both ain't it.

42

NOVEMBER 3, 1930

JEB MURRAY

Rope shone simple and brown in my boy's eyes, swaying in the night wood all light, like a man not hanging from the other end.

"Enoch...Enoch...," I's waving fingers. "Enoch...hear me, boy..."

He were struggling, his head not firing right. His feet looking for a way to stand, for Old-Oak-firm to work into the ground. Watching water burn fossil fuel behind his eyes. They's all puffed and irritable, all waterlogged and he weren't answering.

"Enoch...hear me...hear me, boy..."

My wheezing more coming than going. More railroad rattling outta chest, metal jangling-screech. He's holding me up. Scooping loose meat in his hands.

Dirty smudges wrapped his cheeks, his fingers rushing to dry the age away. Damn near led the charge, my boy. Not breaking from me once. Not even when we found 'em men.

"Enoch...boy...boy..." His ears trained deaf. His head lost. Ever since we took the camp. Just lost.

Come up on a roundup of three, we did. Near the north ridge. Half mile east of Windsor's Peak. Bodies all pressed flat over that limestone. Where the tree line waned and dried brush went wild.

Company men. Brought in. Train still ground on ‘em, coal black stringing up their boots.

They’s smart. Made no fire. No light ‘cept the glint of metal as they trained eagle eye down rifle shafts. Stumbled on ‘em due to the boy. My boy knowing this ridge, this crow’s nest overlooking Hazard. Told me, “ain’t no better place for spotting.”

Ever’one knew of it, even ‘em Irish but my boy’d believed it his, his place to give. Owed that right. A right to hisself, to getting to know the land. Understanding why it important. Where he belonged.

He’d knowed something wrong soon as we climbed, my boy. Soon as the line broke between land and sky. Soon as three mounds of something lived where nothing ought to be. Boot heels and fine coats there for our greeting. No cause for concern to what lingered behind. What crept from ‘em woods. And in the distance were why. Once our feet hit dirt-wall-stop-from-skid, sounds of the valley climbed up.

Screams. Horrible, pitiless bucks of firearms crushing babes awake, of doors splintering Mommas from their beds, of country men and boys rallying arms, the suckled plead of mules, and chickens, and dawgs for quite to come again, for the pitched crack of glass to stop smashing daggers of little broke faces on the ground, for the smoke to lay still, to not creep so close to bedroom boards, those haunting silent rushes of barren hopeless holds on life scooching for cellar doors; inside that valley, riling aimless in the dark, folks were clawing, and biting, and taken up rocks, and they were dying. In unison. On both sides. One faceless long descent with death. He who’d not seen it would know not what to call it but they’s Killing Fields true and true.

Dawned on us then, ‘em men weren’t there to prevent those from coming down, they’s there to prevent ‘em from coming up and we took to ‘em fervently. All of us in turns of ill, we went at ‘em, ‘cept for the boy. My boy who were locked froze, that bit of revenge not quiet born yet.

Fifteen when Hazard switched from lumber to coal. Crewed up on the very first build out with Mr. Davis. Very first digging of 'em tunnels. Coal promised double pay what cutting trees did.

Foreman Williams placed me as pillar man. "Steady working with wood," he'd barked, when I come to his desk for assignment.

Whole slew of us standing in line 'fore the sun come up only to head down to the ground where it don't live. Coal Co'd gone to working on 'em mines for two weeks 'fore we's allowed in. Brought in cars full of Chinamen off the train to blow rock for tunnels. Laying dynamite. Machines, they was. Woke up. Came to work. Killed mountain. Went to bed. All they did. Didn't talk to nobody. Didn't bother nobody. Just there for the work and once they's done, hopped the train. Mountain carved.

Davis'd men burning 24/7 first leg of the mine. Kept the tools down there so's all needed were a drop-off of bodies to pick up where 'em others left off. A man for ever' job and a job for ever'man, what Williams'd belt.

First time I went down. Not the second. Not the third but that first, ground liked to swallow me. Given two buckets from Williams. One for us. One for 'em posts. 'Bout a four by four, 'em buckets. Carried three men or nine posts, not much else. Jackson, the Framer, a black man from down off the coast, who'd come via Savage Mountain, and Thomson, the Dirtman, a sunken-faced pale Scot who'd cut his teeth at Crestline Ridge, all of us packed on top each other like sardines and the shit between Jackson and Thomson thick even 'fore we saw dirt.

Leather whipped "giddap" as we filed down behind the white ass of a burro-pony-mule. Tracks wouldn't be placed 'til wood up. We's the wood. The Haulageway men. In charge of planking post to beam for the ½ mile they needed 'til it sound enough for veins to shoot out the sides.

"Gee, Gee," spit Thomson. Mule clocked right and in the tunnel we went.

Two minutes in, black swallowed us. Poured molasses rich in

sticky tar fog. Mule clickity clacking over broke rock. His hide disappearing behind inked curtains.

"Aye, hold da rope, boys," Thomson slipped.

"Where?"

Thomson tapped my right shoulder, shuddered going down my arm. Led me to the slacked feed of fiber trailing through holes in metal stakes posted to our right. "Lifeline," he called it.

"Duh us to lit de match in a pace," Jackson asked.

"Aye."

Rock seethed. Hissing. From ever' plot round ya. Like it taking air. Like ya's resting in a beast's belly. "Bin hissing des rocks long time, gots to tame dem. No worries boy," clopped water like from Jackson. "Need wait for da beast. Let air go mixing round ya. Make sure it fit…"

"Pipe down," sledgehammered from Thomson's way.

Jackson kept on, "wouldn't want no light nothin' with da bad gas pouring on ya. Fires."

Mule drove forward creaking 'em cars toward cold breath. Each thud leaking lean air out while lungs clipped baskets full, knowing not if they'd gasp again.

Plod.
Clunk.
Plod.
Clunk.
Plod.
Clunk.

"Whoa. Duh us no worry, de beast smell might fine." Jackson grated a match, blinding light on us, and tipped his head down, bringing flame to that candle on the front of his hat. "Whu dum say, dem walls," Jackson asked not quiet whisper like and not quiet talk.

"Ain't said not'ing, and I'd keep it down, 'fore 'em walls start lending ear." Thomson's face peaked glow.

Roof hung low. Maybe a hand taller than that mule. 16 hands in all. Not even enough for stand. Crouched outta 'em buckets and went to pulling wood.

"Time gwine creep by no dem words." Only Jackson's eyes and teeth showed, his face bleeding with the coal.

"Ya know what don't go to care for time," Thomson breathed through gritted teeth, "the dirt over back us."

Pointing to his chest, Jackson broke, "Da big black, him no bit'uh."

"Oh, we's all black down here, aye. Now grab me a board."

Our jobs were to lay posts at midpoint of what already carved. Then work our way back, and for ever' beam grounded we's to add one in front. One in back. One in front. One in back. One in front. 'Til there a solid bridge.

"Ah, Mister Thomson…"

Jackson bullied up to Thomson all blowed out chest and rolled up sleeve and curled from his lips, "Da duh big big buckruh up dey bit yem yent yiddy down here."

Thomson dropped his tone, shuffled right up to Jackson, a man who if the stone weren't topping out at 16 hand, woulda stood easy at 20, and wired up right next his ear, "fuck off, ye cunt, and grab me my board."

"Um Mister Thomson, there's a....seems a…"

See, not only were Thomson the Dirtman for our crew but he were the Dirtman for the company, which meant we's the first to start laying wood, which meant we's deep in the mine, which meant we's one of the first to chug air in the dirt since 'em Chinamen come down. No one ahead of us 'cept black.

Trouble with going deep in a mine, 'specially when there ain't no support, when it just carved, 'specially when there's a group of stubborn asses pushing air round a set of rocks that ain't seen none for hundreds of years, where if dug deep enough there's seashells mixed up with that coal, speaking of a time when water ruled, where if given true head and enough want, there might could peak dinosaur bones, mixing man up in a place like that, where it argued he'd no place to be, where even one simple thing, like a group of foreigners, a mule, and three flames could threaten fucking anything, could change the place so much, even if there only a couple of minutes, that the dirt'd want to just close up so's the nuisance handled and the slate wiped clean, and it were becoming apparent that's the trouble we's wading in.

"Who dis man here? Charging dis big wud, I axe. T'rowing dis small weight round." Jackson's hands balled tight.

Now, only mule I'd ever known were a sweet Bessie, my great Aunt Dierdre brought up. A Clydesdale work horse blend and the sweetest thing one could know. But Bessie, this white beast were not and in the middle of Thomson and Jackson's braying and biting at each other, that fucker'd got right ill with contempt and tromped his ole white ass deeper than he should in the tunnel and slowly pulled our buckets with him. 'Em posts, that transport out, and that fucking mule thudding straight for hells door, and that mixing, that pairing of air with earth gas, with man's pride, with dirt that would rather rid its core of us than be bothered any longer, were 'bout to throw the towel in.

"Mister Jackson, Mister Thomson, the…"

"Oh ye fucking fuck, kick yer fucking head off yer body. Cut ye fucking down to size, son." Thomson cranked, the makings of rage spilling gutteral down his chin.

"Dat so," 'fore it'd even spilled full right from Jackson's lips, his hands wrapped tight round Thomson's neck. Pinched that boy up like a turkey, he's so strong.

Felt the charge of something not right hanging over us and blasted, "THE FUCKING MULE." Voice lit dynamite wedges in the roof, and walls, and floors, and Thomson and Jackson's lamps turned side cocked my way and slow mouthed "Go," as earth began to move.

Ground'd gone to swell, boiling hisses and pops, tremoring overhead, rumbling threats of a break, threats of a slide off, of whole slabs smashing to the floor, crushing us underneath. Swift like, Jackson kicked back sooted dust, going for the mule, nothing but his light giving hurried glow deep in earth.

"Leave it," Thomson yelled, "Leave the fucking t'ang. Murray, grab hold the rope. Git out. It's coming down."

Cradled by the rock's edge, the rope swayed, the earth's shiver crumbling in pebbled specs, our feet stomping forward, just two orbs tracking heavy breath to the surface. Behind the braying whine of something wrong, the clampdown of fall, avalanching boom in loud rift, that black dust tearing at our heels. Shift of land screeching out, deafening our heads with jagged cotton. Chug, chug, chug, like gears, Thomson and me moved, crashing out the mine just as the lip closed, as the mouth collapsed. That rope whipping back.

Survived all that. Years and years of going down that shaft, risking it all, and now it'd come to this. Me. Above ground. Sky overhead. Staring at my boy with air gurgling out my lungs on borrowed breath. My boy caught fiddle string thin, his eyes locked on that rope, locked on that thick twine, trying to make sense. Realizing it us or 'em. Realizing it a Gawdsend Cecil'd carried that rope on him, that once 'em Irish'd got done crafting heart-ache on 'em men's bodies, after Cecil'd chawed hatchet chunks from their arms and legs, littering Jack the Ripper stills all on the ground, after I'd gone rabid dawg mad on the one left standing, on the one who'd cocked .22's in the air, who'd curdled white soiled spill all over mountain dirt when I'd bashed my shotgun through his chin, seeing now that one of 'em slugs charring death through the night'd struck flesh, that it'd spread black lung lumps from his daddy's chest, that it only natural for that rope to find its way to my boy's hands, that that white oak back aways granted more than just invite to its fibered threads, that he needed no showing how to tie the knot, that it lived in him 'cause I'd showed him, that he needed the man strung up just as much as I did, as we all did, that there strength he'd not knowed of living in his legs, and that a boy motivated just right can soon become a man. So's while I gulped back my last, while Cecil paid head nod and respect, while 'em Irish cleaned their blades, looking over the valley for what's next, while my boy wrangled hurt, lassoing war dawgs from his chest, while my shotgun rested cool near my leg, and life leaked from his Daddy, my boy stared at that rope, and allowed slaughter growth in his head.

43

NOVEMBER 3, 1930

ALBIE TODD

The first attempt on Albie's life, though it not something a man even begins to recognize at the time, more a matter of tortoise plight isn't it, happened upon him not as one might think, by the eager nature of retribution for ills wronged, but perhaps if peered from wider stance, it enlightened as so; instead, our dear Albie faced the peril of man's great gift, that destructive, trusty, effluvium of violence that springs forth so richly when inspired right, due to of course a misunderstanding of place. His misunderstanding of place.

Conferred with the underpinning of what can only be called consumptive doubt, that bloomed righteously in his lower abdomen, percolating a particular orifice best reserved for privacy and God willing Annabelle's absence from the house, Albie paced his bedroom floors. It was a rather unfortunate unsettling that wrought plague on him ever since the morning's coffee, leaving not even water a savior from subsequent constitutional frequency. Appeared ever since the "friend's" arrival last night, an uneasiness about him that would not wane and no matter what distraction, Albie tempted fate at, it was something that could simply not be ignored.

What began as a restless itch in his bottom right shoe, the very singular act of merely removing boot and sock and garnering scratch on his big toe the remedy, became an overall regalias production beginning with the thrusting of a fine wool jacket on the floor and the unlooping of a wire hanger, for he'd already dressed and there was no sense in unlacing, chiefly because his nineteen eyes laced all the way to the top and his coarse pants tucked therein. It was of course a day where things might occur and that called for the proper attire.

The itch, which Albie'd proved uproariously inefficient in leading the hanger's steel to the right spot, expanded, its blatant refusal for proper scratch begging, then pleading, until it pounced recourse on his left leg, as if an invisible string of ants allowed passage between the two. Why Albie imagined the discourse quite disconcerting as he rushed, vexed by the new arrival and tore down yet another wire hanger. This time a set of slacks crumpled atop the jacket along the floor.

Try as he may, and what an effort placed forth by Albie's flustered hands, a pinched hook in right and left, aching metal down his tall boots, with the left leg bent daintily forward, the toe pointed down, his back slightly arched, what phrases he might inspire if onlookers at hand, the itches evaded all relief, and it simply would not due to keep the boots on. And thus, the grand disrobing.

Naturally, as soon as his laces loose and the boots yanked, and his pants pulled high to his knees, revealing a somewhat brash bushy display of rich reddish-blonde leg hair, the irritations gone. Vanished. As if never existed. And how infuriating such a thing can be. Working up a sweat and what not even before the descent of stairs and specifically separate from that of husband-and-wife encounters. It was most assuredly not something our dear Albie appreciated in the least. Not to mention all the activity'd further aggravated that rumbling of bubbles down below and nearly forced a trip against Annabelle's nightstand as he rushed for the facility's closed door.

Once reposed and repositioned, Albie proceeded to practice again in front of the long, standing mirror adjacent the closet door. The one Annabelle'd shipped from New Orleans due to it carrying a baroque charm she simple couldn't live without, which is exactly what she'd said upon spying it from the street. "Darling, I simply cannot not have it, simply couldn't live without." Albie'd immediately procured it with the help of remarkable bargaining skills as he'd argued the merchant from $30 down to $20 and took much pride in standing before his achievement whenever he got the chance. He thought what might inspire, or assuage, whatever actions his "friends" might do, best delivered with a modicum of decorum and thus the oratorically recitation of a speech he'd prepared in case the men restless.

He anticipated being met, perhaps irrationally so, by angry discourse, these interruptions planned for accordingly at particular phrases throughout his speech, subtle stops of silence where the jeering acceptable. He'd give this to the men, their time for proper rebuttal and then strike up once more, inspired by the promise of enterprise and common good. That was what Albie referenced, of course. The common good for the town and for these people and for Mr. Davis and subsequently for he and Annabelle.

He'd gone over each word, making sure emphasis on the right things, and like any true politico would, that his finger timed with his cadence to rest assurance on the crowd and garner favor with his genuine appeal. Colloquial flavor thrown in, sprinkled over a few choice sayings, stirring bile in his throat, but he was beginning to learn to smile at the unpleasantries of such things. He felt that despite his inability to savor such crossings along his tongue that the "folks" down there, the ones dressed drabbly in hand me downs and owner-sowed attire, might gestate it for him, and that more the point. Hence, after the third delivery, and the taste of foul dissipating behind his lips almost entirely, he decided he would finally join Annabelle downstairs for breakfast but as soon as his foot crossed the bedroom threshold, he felt the mingling of what would soon manifest epidemic unrest commence again, this time in the pull of his back legs, which led to the tremble of his gut once more and yet Albie simply refused to be a man dictated by such things at such a young age and dismissed the inconvenience entirely, that's how it to be referenced from now on, an inconvenience he pushed down, choosing commitment to the fight ahead instead.

They were waiting for him already, his "friends," at the bottom of the hill, some daring knighthood display of city dusters and thick pants not unlike the ones Albie'd tucked into his boot. Come to think of it, the very idea of such a thing borrowed when Custer James stepped on the train platform last evening, a discernible limp in a bad knee, results of an accident at Blair Mountain, though to be fair, it wasn't so much an accident as a sign of survival, in that, he had, and were it not for the fact that Albie convinced at times that ideas appear to him through divine intervention, such as tucking his pants into boots this morning, and not thus, led to him by other influences, their planting in his mind silently until time appropriate for their recollection, which when presented forth some sort of blossom only he could have thought, needless to say, at this point in Albie's life, he was a rather maneuverable man, and in this fashion, having seen Custer James dressed in the same way just last night, had dawned similar attire himself, thinking not why. One can only imagine the stifled snicker hid beneath Custer's mustache, fashioning his face like some disappointed Giant Schnauzer, when Albie came trotting along.

"Nice boots," Custer chewed the air, not maliciously, more, so none of the other five men standing might say it first, granting offense with less cushioned delivery.

"Yes." Albie remarked, missing entirely the hidden meaning. Yes, operating more as a greeting then acknowledgment more a bridge for him to cross so he could talk straight business, continuing to ignore the unsettling waft pining the air. "I've prepared something and think it best delivered in front of the mine."

But through no acquisition other than his own, it dawned on Albie his sudden outnumbering, the thought amalgamating from the very same place his speech had earlier, with a quiet and inconvenient displacement that rang both true and horrifyingly false at once. The men looked not unlike those down at the mines and this placed a certain level of distrust in him, dividing them into a rugged category separate from himself. A distrusting masculine coarseness at their chins jutting forth in all manner of direction and styles, leading fuller in scale the farther down the line in pecking order it appeared, for if the Schnauzer led the pack, then it was the Affenpinscher who prevailed thick in blackened goatee, heralding the name Tobias Adler behind him. It was standing next him, ripened with a down word groomed Welsh Terrier beard, Connor Blevins, a man so stout, one doubted whether or not his capabilities of running someone down, however this assuredly part of his charm. It was to the right of him, a short Brussel Griffon, gifted in the virtuous stride of chawing on enough boot heels to prescribe him with the name Biting Bernard and as if the brush not full enough, there stood amongst the last two the viscous Chow Chow clopping down in wide stance, a hidden nasty intent lurking behind his grin, introduced by Custer as, Calloway Adams, and yet of all their barbed bristle, it was the pencil thin bare faced Affghan, Lorne Waters, who quaked most alarmingly, for he the closest representation to Albie, himself, and he, this Lorne, a scab, a traitor, frowned upon and yet needed all in the same breath.

It was, of course, him, this Lorne, to address Albie next. "Ain't gonna be no speech."

"You will have to excuse my friend, Lorne, here. I'm afraid his customs still a little raw," Custer swiped, washing away the mess. "A speech is a fine thing to have prepared. Sure it sounds real nice."

"Yes, thank you." Albie's yesses were starting to flap out like wandering tape in the wind.

"I do hope you get to say it," Custer said stepping from the others, "Mr. Todd, what we've come to do here today is probably not going to go like you think it might."

"I may not be well versed on your exact methods but there is certainly something to be said for propriety and I believe it within our abilities to extend such favors to the men—" but even as Albie said it, he knew it to be false. He knew exactly how it would go, how men like the miners would act, how the dogs carrolled around him would act, he knew from being placed in close quarters with such men, from being shoved and tempered by whatever oscillating presence his father'd played in his life, he knew it in the way, that as soon as Lorne spoke, his words dripping truth down the back of Albie's brain, titillating his spine, prickling the hair up on his back, he knew it as his hand mindlessly crafted perfect cursive'd ideas on paper, how even when he spoke them aloud in front of the mirror, his eyes smiled back slits that yelled, liar, in the way his pants'd drawn tight just beneath the front buttons with the thought of violence. Knew it because he secretly wanted to know it, secretly wanted anger to writhe free, that was what the unsettling about, the itch in his foot, the unease, just as now, in the moment of his lost thoughts, or perhaps those increasing in distinction, he could feel the channeling of what he wanted, remembered, buried, those glimpses only in hiding.

"Mr. Todd, what is it exactly you think we've come here to do?"

So transfixed now on these feelings, these inconveniences, Custer's mouth merely moved in front of Albie, the words passing over him, registering empty. Or not empty but indistinguishable, he understood they were there, that they meant something, that when strewn together they would carry weight but the imperceptibility of their belonging in a question, in that question, and that question having an answer, the answer causing consequence, conflating into, dare say ramifications, for even Albie couldn't deny that. Not unlike man viewing fire for the first time, watching the flicker dance on his eyes, feeling the heat trickle candied licks upon his skin, disappearing in the yellows and reds, that feeling all at once ever so down deep that this somehow where he belonged, with that preternatural flame, but because he, trepidatious and curious all at once, not ventured hand towards it, he'd not felt the singe nor smelled the burn nor seen the visceral expression of fire's faculties, how then could Albie ever make sense of it?

He, thus, followed the men, pressing down the inconvenience that now splayed havoc in the recess of his back, a large saddlebag cramp enveloping both stomach, side, and nethers, for as mentioned before, Albie would resist all pursuits against his conquering the day. Besides, that what was really going on here—competition. Dismantling, mounting and dismantling, tearing apart entirely, crushing even. Oh wouldn't Albie like to crush something, just completely eviscerate it. Why, he'd start first with Annabelle's hydrangeas, walk right back up to the house and break the chair on the front porch, slam it down right there on the steps and rip the leg from it, throw the bits not splintered over the railing, and jump down, not caring at all. Yes, didn't that rile Albie up ever so, straight Capone jump start the event, after all he'd plotted their demise from the beginning, watching from the window their puffs blowing in the wind, their blue hedge sailing savage threats, all the while him, donning disguise in his head, a gardener, of course, the sheers merely instruments needed for their upkeep. He'd whack off bud after bud after bud, smack the smell of blue from them, rid the hill, his hill, his overlook, his mountain, entirely. Eradication.

So automatic, it was, that Albie's boots fell in tune with Custer and his crew, it appeared almost immediate. As if this recent mental splurge'd weighted down his step, sealing the necessity of industry in ever' crumpled break of dirt. If ever there was an image of a suppressed grin idling, of a new man springing forth, there too, would it belong upon Albie's visage for like never before had he pierced the morning air so. Why, doubtful at all, that Albie saw what his companions did, the peeking heads just up from morning brew stumbling from their beds, curiously entertaining the morning's rays, sleep still resting below their tired lids, their eyes gulping the strangers in, knowing not who or how they'd soon affect their lives, perhaps knowing not all they were strangers, after all the town full of rail men passing on and off, dropping packages there only to pick others up here.

How dubious of Albie indeed to misunderstand his inconvenience, that spilled from ever' tip of his body now, that stung his insides like electric veins, like rambling hornets buzzing in his chest and fingers, and feet, like his circulatory system one large nest, until now as he passed the houses, as he walked behind Custer and his men, he, Albie, some sort of masthead overseeing all the damage to be listed after. Not until the revelation of the box by Lorne, the pulling aside by Custer, the conversation transitioning from him yipping orders, to them barking cues to each other, to the fact that Mr. Davis'd no intention whatsoever for talk. Not by him, not by these men, and certainly not by Albie. That rules, those of valuable life extension, dictated that Albie exist here, in the pit, where the meat prepared for dogs. He was there for liaison, as bridge to Mr. Davis who, of course, could not be present. That Connor Blevins'd positioned Albie out back behind Randi's, not as Albie secretly hoped in the field, or better yet at the crank. The crank, yes, the mere acknowledgment threatening his inconvenience to break from the sausage casing of his skin and drip to the floor. Or more delicious still, Albie'd wished he might be the metal itself, the shot to pierce the air, travel through the Gatling, splitting, siphoning seconds from the men's lives, compressing time to a minuscule part, a particle of black.

And for the first time conjoining these signs, this nervous wash rushing through Albie, this pinning frenetic twinge, he entered into the agreement, jubilantly. The morbidity of it striking vociferous against his inner cage, compressing his lungs, he felt, to a place they'd never been before, to that exalted inhale of high, yes, that indeed was what Albie felt, a high. The excitement fueling necessity, that it necessary he looked, that he gulped it in even, that the cataclysmic winding of bullets and blood and gore and men proffering the air for only him, for his eyes only, so that he could basque in the horror, watching, changed and anew, that inconvenience relenting to quiet, fulfilled, and at peace. The wonderment of it all better than anything he'd ever held. So glorious a thing, Albie'd never even felt the Model 620 rifle press his back but there certainly was no escaping from the sound it made when Mr. Davis pumped it.

44

JANUARY 30, 1960

GARY

Tunnel's mouth grew plumb out from the side of the mount, come out all wonky like, with jagged boards fitting round the edge like teeth, and swear to Gawd, ever' time we went a walking to it, that there wind'd get right airish. Hot and airish. Today weren't no 'ception.

"They don't want us having nothing, tell ya, that's the gawd honest truth there brother. Just nothing. Probably take that from us too." It were what we's all thinking. Corbin Brighton'd just said it.

Gawd knows he felt it worse than most. Already wore on him, it did. Poor bastard'd started pitching over at age fifteen. Back all cameled up, hump causing his chest to fold in. Boy'd done time in the mine since ten, working small rooms. Wouldn't even dynamite the full thing out yet. Just send 'em children in and get to picking. Feelers, ya hear. See if the room even worth the build out. Made it so's, pretty much ever' single one of 'em who'd gone down to the black so young stood with their arms pitched back just below the elbow to offset that upper body slant. He and ever'one of his brothers'd the same build. Like walking round with a bunch of ole tired men.

"Just got to sign 'em papers, boys. That's what they gots to do.

Just sign it up." Eisle, Corbin's twin, weren't no better. Fact, he might have the worst of 'em. Walked damn near on all fours, way his back'd gone to hang high.

"Ain't gonna sign shit."

See what it was, and I'd a feeling on it now for the last couple days, ever since Kieran'd got all puffed out when the lot of us got together, how in the hell that man'd ever got voted in as speaker beyond me now, there were to be a hold out. In that, no matter what we put forth, Kieran were gonna find some way, some excuse, to cause a delay. Couldn't go no way other. Weren't gonna take nothing for nothing, 'em men running things. How they saw it anyway but how it done now were the short end of the stick. And they's surely not gonna go changing stuff just cause the men they's profiting from wanted it. Gawd honest truth spoke to that. If it didn't, we'd have ourselves some running water up through 'em houses now, wouldn't we.

"What'd Enoch have to say on it, Gary," Wayne asked, Corbin's eldest brother.

"Ain't said much. But there's a plan a coming. Know that to be true."

Enoch'd gone underground twenty odd years back. Lived further in 'em hills than 'em Meaks did and were just 'bout as mean with all that shine running through him, wet half the county out his still and threatened hell bound assured if ya's to go for a walk'bout anywhere close. Had to YAWL the door from a half mile back and that were still placing a purty steep wager. Gawddamn pickle to get word to. Been waiting for a week with nothing but crickets chirping in my ears.

"Expecting it to come soon." Gawd, I hoped.

Myrtle piped up, "It better," as he felt after that finger he'd lost last spring. Damn thing clopped off right at the nub.

Mine'd swallowed up little parts of us all suppose. Took out Lannard, Blevins, Connor, O'Malley, and 'bout a dozen others a year ago. Fucking gasket blew in an air line and spewed out a river round ‘em boys in a room not befitting to hold it. Coal seam too thin, see. Course, ‘em bastards'd found out to late. Went to working like nothing wrong at all. That's how it got ya. And when one of ‘em boys or the other, don't know which and don't matter, ‘cause it woulda ended all the same, went to hitting a wall and let loose a rock that shouldn'ta fell, that's how ‘em Brighton boy's put it, they's a suspicious lot, WELL—might be, we all got our things, but ‘em Brightons wouldn't go near a rock or wall that held a speck of green in it. That's where they said paper coal lived. How the hell they liked to see a speck of anything other than dark and darker, couldn't say. But they'd walk right out the room if it breathed a glimmer of it. Say, “green's where ‘em knockers hole up.” Wouldn't go near a knocker, oh no.

Now, whether or not that rock done spilt green, ain't my truth to tell, but that room let loose a whole helluva a bad mixture and it believed a spark born from the gas that were leaking once it hit, and well, charred ‘em boys up. Blew O'Malley's fucking head right off. Didn't find it ‘til three fucking days later when there were a host of mice making a fuss in the corner. Fucking thing straight from a horror movie, crisp as fucking BBQ.

And it ain't like ‘em boys who'd gone down there after, for the cleanup and more picking, were any safer. Afterdamp'd got ‘em. First set of relievers, plumb went down there all shaky and riddled, having probably said an extra coating of “Let me just git through this one Gawd,” thinking that some sort of saving grace. But the worst part of a fire ain't the fucking fire. Honest to Gawd, I know it sounds backasswards to say, but it just ain't. Worst part's all that bad air sandwiched in ‘em walls once that flame squashed.

For five days after, there'd be whole rooms of men that'd just laid down. Their heads stopped working. Their brains saying sleepy time. Mean, just huddles of men who were picking black, who just laid down, the will of life done left ‘em. That gas taking the shit straight out of ‘em. And it weren't something that just went away neither. That Afterdamp'd ride through now. Get an itch to go deeper, and go deep, have a change of heart and come back up, get into 'em rooms most heavily trafficked and just a sit there, fucking waiting for more men to come in, malicious shit. Ya just never knew, ya know, when that shit were gonna find the mouth of the mine and spill out.

Lost five fucking teams of three to that.

Hell, just last week, we's high kicking through groundwater that fissured outta room 5B. We's in room 4C, which were a good room. Good coal. And if ya ain't ever gone down no mine, let me give ya an idea. If level A were the attic, then B'd be the main, and C, the basement. So's when that water got hit loose, it dropped right down from 'em rock floorboards and puddled up in the cellar where we's at in the corner. Took out a thick slab with it. Slivered right the fuck off. Damn near took Eisle with it. If it weren't for Corbin, who were a jumpy sort to begin with and downright fright-ridden when he's in the black, not feeling that drop plop on his helmet, and pushing his brother out the way, the both of 'em toppling out into the main tunnel, there might be another box needing carve.

And I'll tell ya something else, ya ever wanna see grown men turn white, ya go to making some noise underground after a ceiling's dropped rock. 'Em Brightons might be Chatty Cathys when theys above ground but down in the mine there weren't hardly a word shared between 'em. And when Corbin and Eisle fell out and that slab of rock come crushing down, booming sonar raddlers to all 'em other slabs of rock in 'em other rooms, mocking it to "fall too," there were one mighty fine quench come ever' asshole in there. All of us just a holding our breath, saying our things to folks, if ya gathering my meaning. Sure did. Buncha "shoulda told her bye" and "fuck, this can't be it," cranking tight lip in our skulls while hope for some bastard up in there to have a lick of luck still stuck on him and that it might carry on over to us.

Fucking waded shin deep through that shit rest of the day, all of us waiting for rescue 'cause we felt sure any step'd bring a full fall through. Know what that does to a man, boots all full of gawd knows what water, rock above ya feeling like it gonna break at any time, rooms closing in on ya in a space that couldn't spare not even an inch to begin with, that'll sure as shit make some evaluating go through yar head. That's a fucking knee-slapper of overwrought how we's risking shit and we ain't even got no fucking running water. Mean, the water we's standing in could pump through half the fucking houses in the town as far as plumbing goes.

"Ya really think Kieran's gonna give 'em demands over," Myrtle spit, knowing full well like the rest of us—weren't no way in hell. "Nah, he ain't gonna do nothing but sit in that chair and act like he's doing something. Bastard, just like all the rest of 'em."

"Probably right."

"Know I'm right, Gawddamnit. Seen Albie Todd, hisself, carrying on with the fool just last week. Real chummed up the two. Laughing and ever'thing like there weren't a care in the world. Fucking pricks."

"Now, Myrt, just 'cause they's socializing don't quite mean pocket holstered."

"Shit it don't," Myrtle ripped his hardhat off, bowed up hotter than steam on Eisle, causing all of us to take a pause in the dirt. "Listen here, brother," Myrtle forced hat to Eisle's chest, "much as ya like to believe things gonna get better, that there ain't an angel in Heaven gonna allow 'em men to continue doing what they done, that somehow or another they's gonna start looking at things...ought to slap sense in ya, boy. Fucking look around." Myrtle panoram'd his head-bucket, paying very close attention to the two sturdy motherfuckers beating trouble on us all by the tipple.

There, backed by three train carts and 2 stories worth of coal waiting to be heaped out, stood brothers Chester and James Swarthout. Made foremen through family. Made asshole by power. Sort that'd kick dawgs just 'cause they could. And their views on the Union a secret to no one. Bloodied two Spaniards and an Irishmen, who weren't doing nothing but walking back home, weren't even walking together. Just sorta close is all. 'Em Swarthouts and their long handlebar mustaches and well fed pot-bellies and wide blue sky eyes, riled up on Gawd knows what, accused those three bastards of conspiring. 'Bout took all threes fucking heads off. Blacked ever' eye, broke all three noses, and splintered ever' pointer finger useless, yanking it almost clean off. Left 'em out of commission 'til it healed, 'em Swarthouts did to 'em boys, and that were if they even stood a chance of getting their jobs back in the first place, which ever'body knew they didn't 'cause Swarthouts answered direct to Albie Todd and him alone.

"Brightons. Gary. Let urs holler at ya for a srec." Tobacco settled coal lump heavy in the bottom of Foremen Swarthouts' lips. Stole r's from their mouths. Placed 'em in odd places that caused a whistle to slip. Fucking voices forced cement to our toes and sent scorpions down our spines.

"Y'all going to room 1A today," Chester hawked.

"Like hell we are," Myrtle shot.

"First floor ain't spit nothing worth a damn in two months, Swarthout." Corbin slapped, his hat flinging to the ground, clicking gun fire threat over rocks.

James Swarthout laid it down, glopped chaw with his finger and plopped it on Corbin's boot. "Well, suppose, ya better pick real hard then."

"Shift starts in 2, gentlemen." Chester Swarthout peeled shit from his grin. A head nod motioning Mine-time ain't to be wasted by no man.

Seen it 'fore, this sorta shit. Punish, that's what they's doing. Weeding out, wear us down, get it so's the fall-back-in-line automatic, so's the lip don't even consider bite back, the hope docile and calmed nerves. That's what they meant when they now said Coal Men.

Tried to prevent it. The repercussion of Myrtle. Channeled steel holds on him. Wayne on one side. Me on the other. Corbin venting Charlie Brown teacher horns, the useless, noiseless barks, registering empty to his brother's face. The scene getting heavier with ever' scuffed char spun from under Myrtle's feet. With ever' audible "Bastard…ya can't fucking do this…ya can't fucking get away with this…families…we got families..." chugging bullhorn loud in the air.

But there weren't no controlling Myrtle. Not now, not never. Whole reason part of that finger of his missing. Weren't no Mine accident that'd caused that. Not in the slightest. See, he and Solomon Johnson used to go swarping together 'fore Solomon got married and Myrtle musta got smart with him or something down there in the tunnel. Said a thing to a man he'd not knowed no more. And Solomon turned round and whipped a pick down on him. Didn't catch nothing but that finger, Solomon did, but shit fire, he sure caused a helluva an aftershock to his person once all 'em brothers crawled up out that deep.

OH, 'em Brighton Boys were a bad batch if ya's to cross just one of 'em 'cause ya weren't gonna get out of the affair without facing 'em all. The most accommodating folks that could ever exist but they'd blast straight wicked if the tables turned on 'em. Per exact, their shooting of Solomon's ass outright. Weren't no waiting on it either. Carried their lunch pails, hats, and dusty coveralls straight to Wayne's truck and pulled a rifle off the rack and walked right back and put a full metal jacket through Solomon's leg. Took him outta work for six months and caused a limp for eternity. Only reason there weren't no payback come to 'em Bad Brighton Boys due to Ina Johnson begging her sister to take the family in over there in Morehead. Wanted to stuff the plug 'fore the torture get chance to begin. Couldn't go having none of 'em Clay County feuds up in Hazard when there's all that fighting going on already. Sense enough, that woman, to send 'em kids and herself on over, Solomon and his brother Samuel, there for assisted travel, were to light out the following week once checks collected, but, course, Solomon wouldn't have known of that, planned on a stopover at Momma Brighton's house where Myrtle and all 'em others still lived, a come-out-the-yard-let-me-holler-at-ya-for-a-few moment.

WELL, it didn't go down like it were framed, did it. No-sir-re-BOB, it did not. See, due to all the commotion going on at the Mine and 'em visitors prowling for REASONS through camp and 'em men going missing in the night, rustled out of their shelter 'cause suspicion'd placed targets on backs, and 'em rumors milling 'bout, painting black over doors, declaring Enoch friendly behind 'em boards, 'em Brightons paranoid-forced for round the clock watch and checks, so's when Solomon and Samuel brother-dear came up to Brighton abode-land, Eisle, there, who were staged up like a window bandit with barrel pointed did what any man with Matewan and Blair Mountain running through their veins would, shot.

That .12-gauge ramrodded fire sticks through night air, stacked truck beds of repo-man-fucked on Solomon and Samuel Johnson skin, scalpel scraped twenty ounces of flesh from off Samuel's shoulder, neck, and face, rug burned freckles out his cheek, tooth-tied-to-string-and-doorknob-yanked his back molars from his mouth. As for Solomon, WELL, that bullet went straight through. Licked the top strands of his eyebrows and passed pork shoulder thick through his skull. Woke ever' blazing gun on the street up. Ever' fella and lady coming peak to see where's trouble, what's next.

And despite what one might think, giving the history of the land, the murder of Solomon Johnson went untested 'til late in December where disguised as a woman, Samuel Johnson came back for his vengeance in bonnet and full-blown Sunday dress, his grievance, a .22 long rifle colt diamondback, held in a Bible, the knowing that Ms. Brighton carried her boys with her to service ever' week heavy in his heart. All of it set to expire right when service let out. Thus, standing in the middle of a well-maintained grassy knoll, he made his move and when the service doors opened with Preacher McDaniels leading the way and all 'em Brightons behind, as 'em boys wouldn't sit nowhere 'cept the last pew, Samuel Johnson ripped metal from verse and chunked a bullet right for Eisle Brighton's chest.

'Course that shot were took from a man who hadn't never shoot and when that release of the trigger pulled back, that barrel's end kicked up on him popping that metal in an arc up in the sky and while most eyes went to follow that, including dear Samuel's, brother Mrytle's there did not and he barracuda ripped through that Preacher with all his brothers following and they went to a grand smiting on that Samuel. Bashed his head in with a rock right there 'fore the entire congregation. A full slew of folks mouth breathing at the shock of it all least. 'Til. That. Bullet's. Landing. Finally. Came. To. Be. Known. Spiraled ever'one of 'em naysayers into leaders of the pack, into blood thirsty curmudgeons. That bullet'd killed the Preacher and ever'one standing needed retribution now, which were why in the wake of this little Johnson vs. Brighton episode there weren't no Law brought in due to ever' witness there declaring the pair'd died from natural causes.

SO, suppose it a rather sticky spot in the here and now, with all 'em men huddled round, unrest shoving fighter jets to their brains. Bombs hidden for years knocking loose from their shoulders, landmines popping up like weeds at their feet. Ya could hear it. Hear the whistle, the alarm pulling sleepy men awake, bashing clocks against walls. Could see it, the flames getting higher, 'em Swarthouts loading logs into a hearth that didn't need no fueling, brown threats churning from their teeth.

Room A meant no wages for the day. Even if something could get picked, scale wouldn't read it. They'd say we'd knocked nothing. Ten hours wasted just to come back and have it done again.

Swarthouts didn't even know what they'd done. Too drunk on what's supposed to happen. That we's just to get it out our systems, have ourselves a little bitch fit, that's what they thought. Saw it in their eyes, in the play of, "ya ain't gonna do shit," glint animal tracking us. Couldn't feel that fight boring holes in our caves, hammering pride from our souls, could they? Didn't know that thought, the thought circulating through all our heads, chanting, "let Myrtle go," yearning finger slip. They'd not knowed that burning "Fight fire with fire," restless in our legs. Not heard the shouting of now, now, now, boom. Not seen our hands suddenly release the beast, our heat wafting that wildfire of "let it begin" set free.

45

1930

EARLY IN THE MORN ON NOVEMBER 4TH:

12:30 AM FOR EXACT

PELL-MELL

"Ya shoot, boy..." Voice chawed in the early morn rise, his forehead plated and hoed blood pink like a Cherokee. "...can ya shoot, boy, can ya shoot the gun?"

Shotgun bucked hefty like over my slumped arm, laying there like a sleeping snake just waiting to be woke. Daddy growing cold at my side.

"Said, can ya shoot gawddammit...Enoch, can ya shoot?"

Daddy'd taught me last fall how to hold a gun. It weren't long like this'n though. Showed me on a shotgun, yeah, but the barrel stopped just shy my shin. This'n carried on. Almost a foot farther than my toe's reach. See, I's too small to shoot it regular, that other'n. Ain't no telling what this'd do. Shoulder-breaker this one. Knew it soon as it fell from Daddy's lap. All worn with the handle grooved near rabbit felt, all 'em prints that'd handled it, that storied long nose throwing down extra weight only yar bones sense like their's Daddy's Daddy that'd died while holding it.

Shooting cans, how Daddy taught me. Out yonder in 'em woods.

Old soup cans Mommy'd done used twice. He'd go to setting me down like I's waiting for the sun to set and rise just breathing next to me, hot air filling my ear, while that shotgun lodged. Placed me like I's a toy soldier or something, with one knee down, sturdied by my other leg, and my body stationed somewheres in the middle. Still weren't enough weight on me to go taking the smoke full on. Learnt that'n the hard way, didn't I. Like to a blowed my cheek off when I shot that thing standing. Knocked my ass three feet back and put a damn blackberry on the whole right side of my face. Learnt real quick what rubber banding meant. How ya gotta be rigid and loose at the same time. But not too much of neither, just right in between. How I needed a lean on me and a definite boot planted. And that gun needed a move through at the end of the shot, let it guide me like I guided it. Otherwise, I's to end up just like I did standing, with a dirt hulled face. 'Til my leg went sprouting out man size, that were what it's gonna to be, a little toy soldier planting shots hours in advance.

Song birds'd gone to get up round us, their pittering chirps pillowing niceties, like that somehow gonna cover up all the bad. All that bad dripping wonky dew off my fingers, red looking forever clamped in grooves, like 'em lines ain't ever gonna come clean, what they looked. Only time I'd ever seen such dye where when I'd picked strawberries with Mommy this summer. Hands coulda stood trial for a town's slaughter. Didn't come clean for three days and then there were spots that wore the death for months after. Soap never granting Gawd's true touch.

Donnie and Tate'd gone to say I's carrying the mark. Had me believing I's gonna turn or something, like something's gonna come out my pinkie where light red still lived and go to murdering folks. Post up on me in the middle of the night, whispering shit in my ear 'bout how witches'd planted that strawberry bush just there last week 'cause they'd knowed Mommy and me'd go for the hankering. Follow it up with something or another 'bout how there's one nasty little Knocker they snatched out the mine to do their dirty work, lure in mangy kids when they needed handled, that's what they'd say, "that Knocker gonna fucking handle ya, boy." How that Knocker come round and tattooed red on me when I's sleeping, said 'em witches'd placed him inside one of 'em berries, and once we picked it up, the one they'd put him in, he went to prick, prick, pricking blood on our hands. How 'em witches knew which ones to come get when the time right. Hands looked sorta like that.

Suspect, I'd let it alone as long as I could. "Yeah, I can shoot."

Ain't felt sorry for myself but three times in my life. Once, when Robbie, my pet turtle got crushed by a Mule, once when I stumbled in front of a purty girl in town and Donnie and Tate'd went to mocking me so bad I thought my head gonna explode from the red bubbling, and now, sitting next my dead Daddy with blood on my hands from going to town on a fucker while Cecil 'Doc' Hodge faced me down. And in ever' single instance, I forced stop on my self-pity 'cause I'd never seen Daddy go to waller over nothing. Not once in his life. Not when the mine'd started to turn, not when his Mommy died, that sweet woman being the closest thing we's ever to get to an angel, not when little brother jack died in Mommy's belly and we's forced to bury him near the well out back, and not when life'd finally left his eyes after being smoked by a couple cocksuckers playing lookout. Now maybe that were due to his not being able to process the whole of it or maybe it were to him having principle enough not to let it get a hold of him. Either way, it wouldn't be something he'd want me to entertain very long and even though there were a spell of numb and empty renting room up in me, couldn't let sorry burrow up there with 'em.

"Good. Let's go." Cecil'd hunted down the rest of the scalps he needed to go ahead and pack up a bundle on his belt and with each pelt he'd stuck there, the red grew on his face from where 'em drippings wiped.

Meantime, 'em Irish'd busied 'emselves with the strip of two dead men down to their nethers. In the process of quiet a fuss, in fact, picking and choosing who were gonna wear what. Each of 'em, well, the talker of the two peeling coats back here, smelling shirts over there, looking at whether or not the blood dripping from off 'em bodies' heads were gonna be a containable stain or not.

"Still Riley, just look at these trousers," Cian went to dancing, spider legging over all 'em dead like he'd caught some treasure. "Rathher fierce, I'd say. Oh, and look at ye, a right copper ye is. With the hat and ever'thing. Girls," Cian poked Riley in the ribs, "gonna go wild fer ye. Right deadly. Ye'll see, we'll be down there just wilding along, and betting there'll be one lassie who can't peel her eyes from ye. Wait and see. Wait and see."

"Time to go," Cecil barked.

"Not a pinch of fun, that one," Cian boasted to his brother. "Ahh, yes the boots, Riley, would ye look at the boots." Cain didn't hold a care at all seemed, certainly not one that spoke to Cecil's wanting speed. Ignoring instead, he went to struggling after a boot, the yank prying loose an ungawdly swath of air that smelled of old cheese and sulfur, a bell-hop of noise scattering morning glories charming dawn in the bushes with the pull, their bodies lifting with buckshot speed. "Just can't seem," Cian tugged, "listen ye, gonna pull ye off," he tugged and tugged and tugged, "fucking ting, won't…won't…won't…"

Wager it, Cian didn't even feel the swoop of Cecil's hatchet, that severing of that dead man's leg coming off surprise entirely, boot sliding off, happenstance. Probably didn't even know it'd happened 'til Cecil chipped out, "Gawdammit, let's go."

"For fucks sake, I's in the middle of somet'ing there. Still, look at what ye done Doc, poor family'll have to bear a closed casket now for sure. Coulda pasted some hair on him but…and look at what ye done to me broder, got him all riled up. Just chomping at the bit…

…No, Riley, Riley, now ye listen to me, Doc didn't mean not'ing by it…sure we're gonna do some grand t'ings down there, sure."

Cian hurried with the boots. Throwing his old shoes down near the man's numb and straightened his pants, bunny popping up and sprayed with a tug to all the finery, "Look mighty fine, if I don't say meself," pausing only momentarily to give that head nod to his brother, who were already making his way down to camp, "Alright, let's go kill some men."

Cian and Riley'd bowling ball dropped from Windsor's Peak in two trail blazing tracks of fire, both of 'em bumping heavy grid 'bout a thirty-foot distance from the other while me and Cecil'd hunted down opposite trail, his snout pinned on Randi's, me tramping shotgun over my shoulder, that look-back to the past snaring—tempt, at metal's end. Past Holly and Hemlock, through thickets of Bladdernut, our elbows breaking Ninebuck buds in the wake, our boots trapping Farkleberry jam to the ground, we hustled, me not knowing what's gonna charge at us next, and Cecil looking ready to end any and all that came in his way.

"I'm to leave ya on the roof." Cecil'd not even stopped when he said it, the kickback coming more from the wind slicing up and over his hatchets as both of 'em'd come out soon as we hit Buttonbush leaf. Hacked down half the shrub with a wide step, he did. Whipped back a three-inch branch on me that liked to a took out my eye if I'd not ducked.

When we'd come up to Butner's Pass, we's both crouched balls, our knuckles snarling dusty fingerprint on that bridge, and that sun playing accordion fan in the sky, our heads bucking thankful peak in and out of low hanging fog streaking window-curtain-horizontal, we seen 'em Irish peacock out. Cain playing close buck against the back of building brick. Riley trained forward, patrolling open and wild in the sun, the clippings of the former owner's duster fitting small and hackneyed on his back from all the stabbings the bastard'd took. They moved, one another, in a zigzagging course. Dispersing like fireflies. Popping up random, without understood course. But always followed up, one to the other, the brother never too far if aide needed yet far enough that the snake struck at both ends.

When I used to think on fighting, real fighting, things other than cans and rabbits and squirrels, there weren't no sun up ahead, no dead Daddy, no not having my brothers by my side, no boulder of tight sitting cattywompus on my chest, squeezing the air from me with ever' cranked step. There were a code to it, not order, today'd proved that, even when I's clipping fake Engines in the woods, it chaotic. Code spoke to something or another 'bout if a man's down, how ya'd go to take a second for him to get back up. Like honor supposed to be tied up round yar neck when ya go to fighting. Like somehow that'd be the takeaway once it's done—the honor—the "he fought with such dignity didn't he," they'd say. What'd I'd seen today, weren't no honor up in that. Watching what I done watched, a boy's faced shived off, a battalion of men shot down, what I'd done to that man after he killed my Daddy, ain't no place for honor round that. And once I's on top that roof Cecil'd planted me on, the tale-end of "Choose yar marks" and "Shouldn't none of 'em come close," beating barricades in me, doubted honor and the code were gonna somehow magically spring up, and sure enough, from atop Sterling's Hardware, it didn't. Tucked there, up where that namesake spelled in big red letters, just over where the metal awning dipped so's it could come down at the right angle, the end of my dead Daddy's shotgun muzzled out with me surely suited for hellfire. Code be damned. No room for it nohow. Not near me. Not with all I's 'bout to take in.

And. Here. We. Go—

Riley took the first of 'em, didn't he. Claimed folly on a couple of saps walking in a group of three, all of 'em sporting similar wear as him, and none of 'em thinking twice 'bout the fella coming their way 'til it too late. 'Til they saw that scab of an ear, that creep of crushed youth and battered soul smiling at him from under the Irishman's eye. Stepped out from behind Colby Dan's Coffee and took one out with the mere smack of his face hitting Riley's big brawling burly fucking chest, knocked that boy, for that's what he looked by compare, right on his kisser, and sent the other two into a barrel of "what the fuck's" and thumb-torched-safety-holds, all fingers involved by way of the gun thugs bearing down, now, on that bit of metal that'd save their ass from a man the size and force of Riley.

Needless to say Riley didn't take to the threat, lifted his size sixteen boots over that bastard's head and smited down with a Gawd's fury, squashed it like fruit, like it some fucking melon picked out the garden in Mommy's yard, he did. Bear clawed 'em up, pressing steel against the back of their sponge throats. Poor fucking bastards not knowing what to do other than contort, all fucking pinched-white-bugged-eyed-out, with bodies tensing repent, repent, repent, for any and all the wrongs that'd caused 'em to end up Riley's whooping boys. All of it, this affliction towards right to live. Did they have it and would that beast Irish fucker give? Certainly, seemed not. For even as 'em boys went to muscle twitching fingers towards triggers, Riley head battered and box-cutted 'em up, rammed both their cheeks against each other and played pick-up sticks with their passed out vessels, their bodies taking a beating from Ole Danny Bowen's brass knuckles that left minced pies of flesh on the ground after Riley's one, two, three's.

Within ten minutes the alert'd gone out. Forty dusters cramming blacktop, boots marching out of ever' crevice in town. All of 'em wanting those responsible for the mauled bodies on top the ridge, their relief no doubt mired by the greeting of disfigurement. They came from ever' quadrant surrounding the mine, rifles heading east down Main Street, muzzles coming north from Happy Hollow, others coming west down Oakhurst, all of 'em parading. Unified. Armed with clubs and pistols and orders of mean. All of 'em hankering for a bash-in, a body so's a lesson could be shown, so's ever'body might see what a statement looked like, something to place bruises on, something that'll spew high when bullets went to chew. Looked to be if it were up to 'em, they'd drag, quarter, and hang any man found who even second guessed 'emselves responsible, and it wouldn'ta took much to go to stating one might be, with how hard a bargain they's driving, looked to be like they'd beat verdict outta ya no matter how far from the truth it lay. But let me tell ya something else now, that outfit they got down there roving along 'em streets were visiting, not born and bred, stop-overs, see, and what 'em men didn't know, what they couldn'ta understood, no matter how many they done up and faced 'fore us, no matter how many similar towns they done gone up in, there weren't a one of 'em marching nor ordering boots that coulda factored in that hornet's nest sworming round.

Hell, it's hard to tell exactly what came next. Or who shot first. But soon as I seen Cian spread-eagle-goosehawk-diving from up top Hazard Drug store, his hands Jesus-hanging in a T with crucifixion nails clawed up between ever' finger, and not one good gawddamn care to the second floor being the jump-off, figured, I needed go ahead and pick me a target and yet weren't no time for it. No time at all 'fore Cian'd taken out a line of four, each of the maurading-cotton-swaths-slurping-Pinkerton-plight-in-ruffles-of-dusty-fabric-felled-crush under the weight of this unimaginable fallen object, their knees locking faulty cock between the linings of bone and muscle, the joint disbelieving of the pressure, snapping suddenly, their bodies ill'quipped to understand the shredding, the mauled propensity of an Irish man pushed, well, pushed ain't quiet how it needed put, more inclined, as in his face pleased with the outcome of bloodletting. Took to 'em all at once, Cian did, didn't he, talon grating ten inch nails through cheek, back, arm, leg, belly fat, groin, looking all kinds of a haint with hummingbird fast arms swiping down, picking up clips of flesh here and there like pinned, hooked, ready for grilling meat, and then upon finding the men left stunned, their eyes lodged out by the prick of Cian's spikes, he left, filtering back into the mid-morning ground fog that'd fallen just-so, making 'em streets seem plumb swallowed up.

And I'll tell ya something else, once 'em brothers got started, the two of 'em working as they were back and forth like they's hacksawing a gawddamn redwood, 'em men they's hunting and that town that weren't theirs went into a of fucking-no-other-way-to-put-it state of terror. Bludgeoned through 'em streets with fire held under their palms, just fucking plain dislodging things, just battering through meat and bone and flesh like they's swatting flies out the air. Cian running west, picking old kerchiefs from his pockets that he'd throwed coal pebbles in and putting flame to package, underhand pitching 'em devils out to crowds of bastards. None of 'em dusters knowing from where it came or where the giver went. A fucking ghost, Cian were. Threw 'em from ever' direction, constantly swerving in between buildings, constantly changing sides of the street and in his wake, in his spiraling web of nowheredom, that brother Riley, that sumabitch marched right down the middle. Butchered 'em in plain sight, he did. Clawing out teeth where mouths wanted scream close, clopping men down like sacks of flour, reached up from round the back of 'em, Riley's big meat hooks ripping throats straight out, that set of brass knuckles with teeth on the end clipping full metal holes through 'em dusters. They's moving so gawddamn fast that by the time I tried for a shot on a fella, 'em Irish'd done rectified the wrong right out 'em bastards, just fucking ripped it out. A full-on cock-kick sent straight from the Coal-Miner-Redemptive-GAWD, were what's playing out underneath me in 'em streets.

And good Gawd Almight, if they's not bad enough, Cecil sure as hell were giving it to 'em. Locked up right at Elm Street, that bee-line of East Main leading straight to the foot of the mine and Cecil delivering communion to any sicko stepping foot in his path. Plain cut 'em the fuck down. Planted right there in the middle of that cross-section belting out the horn of the end, the fucking four horsemen grooved in both 'em battle axes, 'em hatchets coming alive with all the action. Had 'em blades curving round 'em duster's arms like they's snakes coiling, up and over and through and round, leading 'em, he were, leading 'em straight to their takedown, their fingers not fast enough to go to bat against the dance, too busy trying to fight 'em hatchets hooking polls over breeches, hoping for avoid, 'cause looked to be 'bout all 'em boys'd got from up here were hope 'em hatchets wouldn't knock metal from their rifle snouts, knock 'em straight outta their hands. Course weren't no helping it. Gunblast kept cranking black fire out too late. Cecil'd already shifted and cleared it, only smoke left, buckshotting ears silent. Worked 'em bits through bone and flesh, that red face of his searing meet-yar-maker burns into all 'em bastard's eyes.

Might coulda kept on like this, me scouring bullseye on marks, 'em Irish and Cecil down there, two blocks away from 'em Killing Fields, bringing death to the town, folks getting both wiser to the ploy burdening their blacktop, lone peepers scooping back sneaks from behind curtains, legends soldering names in the back of their heads, all the things that's taking place 'fore 'em, coulda kept up with all of it but don't suppose three men and a boy granted bulletproof for all that long, is they? Naw, there were but 'bout three more seconds of this existing 'fore I's to feel just how much damage that shoulder breaker I's holding could do.

46

NOVEMBER 3RD, 1930:

LATE IN THE EVENING 11:30 PM FOR EXACT

GUT SHOT

"Read it," said Mr. Davis plain as day.

"Why?"

"Cause it's what's asked."

Mr. Davis' veins might not've bled blue like all those dying round Albie and him, but he were Philly born and that were a state line closer than Albie'd ever get, come their eyes, and as it stood, steeped as Mr. Davis was in the dripped cleanse of Country Christian nature, that charlatan ever ready for the peddle at one's backdoor, Mr. Davis' tongue'd adopted the trill of colloquial banter in such a way as to be almost indistinguishable from the town, as if he'd lived nowhere else other than. Even now as the barrel burnt between Albie's shoulders, the wonder of when and where exactly Mr. Davis'd dropped his Y's and began languidly unfurling his I's in long fiddle length threads from his mouth, frothed bile up the burp lane of Albie's sternum, for when they'd first met some years ago it most certainly were the refined contrary that'd greeted him. So—given then that behind Albie, this man, Mr. Davis, who'd found useful need to go on and change certain mannerisms to fit in with the natives at the toss of a coin, it would appear, it then quiet understandable Albie's dalliance in wishing to know all that a finely folded piece of paper, slipped steadily—not even one waver of a wiggle in that paper's edge, over Albie's shoulder by a man, who wanted or so Albie believed, to not be tied to the incontrovertible assassination of unarmed coal miner's at Davis and Brother's Mining just over yonder way, who coincidentally decided, for no apparent reason whatsoever that Albie could deduce at the moment, he would then show face near, and who at this very moment crunching barbarous over cloyed morning dirt where calloused grooves of rushed feet'd only minutes earlier thought well to take in the sun's calm rise, carried a rifle and pinned it on his second in fucking command. Why indeed would Albie care for the contents of something like that and yet compelled by Gawd knows what or why, he asked, "What does it say?"

"Ever'thing."

How could it be, that something writ presumably no more than a week's time ago, contain that of ever'thing? And were it true, shouldn't the decency of an envelope exist. Mean, surely the contents of ever'thing if given spy by some unknown, some nowit, inspire repercussions. Mean, couldn't just go spilling out to ever'one the knowhow of ever'thing. Ain't there no privilege left in society no more, just handing the goods that takes years—lifetimes even to acquire out for free. Even if it contained most of ever'thing…no, not even then, Albie thought. "Can't say ever'thing, letter's too small."

"Say's all it can and all that it should."

Slight bit of difference then isn't.

"Ya wanna know the main reason why Matewan didn't work, Albie," Mr. Davis asked, his head engaged in the runoff of red sowing rivulets across ruffs of browned limestone at their feet like it some stream of rain.

It occurred to Albie then, the morality he might soon face, the proposition of Matewan and what he knew of it's unfolding, the here and now of just round the corner calamity, both their newly minted miraculous nature perforating the insides of his lips with sweet sallied driblets of salted saliva, that the phrasing of Mr. Davis' sentence misleading and heavy handed as if the correction to come as some parable, some riff pertaining to the essence of WRONG. It wrong. This wrong. He would not have it. Would rather read the note. Yes, the note and its ever'thing. That better than this.

Albie tried after the unfolding of it but Mr. Davis refused silent mediation on all the world encompassed and continued on perhaps moreso to himself than Albie. "They had the brought-ins doing the dirty work of the already hired. Ya can't have an unfamiliar come in and do what a friendly known face can. Not how these people work."

These people, what calm reflection Mr. Davis took in the cradling of "these people," in the cotton soft swath with which he laid down the words, as if "these people" his people and thusly not Albie's. Mean, why else aim the gun? Turn the screw? Oh, Albie got quick with it indeed. The things not said, that's what's going on here, the in between the lines, the secret decoding. Didn't even matter what the note said, did it, Albie thought. Note wasn't for him. It was for them. For "these people."

"Ya don't have the brought-ins do what the already there's can, Albie. Surely ya see, ya understand? Face of a thing is ever'thing. It's whole existence packaged. Had they only the gall to do it 'emselves, how the story woulda gone."

It was nonsense. A spew of something that stood for nothing, a mirage, an attempt at misdirection, that's what Mr. Davis was doing. Had to be. A deflection, yes. A deflection from what settled down the street. From the acknowledgement that was happening, the fierce outpouring of unmitigated rage, of misunderstanding looped in chaotic shrill cries, the syllables wrangling mad cattle, their long horns shying from the lasso, their faithful avoidance of the snare leaving holes where words should've gone, so that all imagined with their absence, the floating bobbling of mismanaged heads, the bodies of the beast still yet to be formed in the wearied mouths of those coming to the scene outside Randi's store. The crippled unknown just left there in sounds debased with the question of what comes next?

"Had the Chief of Police not interfered, meddlesome ninny..." Mr. Davis now assuredly carrying on solely to himself. The full of it purposefully left out, purposefully shielded from Albie's eyes. So much so that Mr. Davis's diatribe dissolving right before Albie from words to clicks, to sounds, mere sounds meant at meaning yet holding none of its grand apparel.

"Click, click, click, click....clickety-click-clickety-click....clack, clack, clack, clack..." Mr. Davis went on like tabs of a language not understood and the more Albie thought on this while being led, that's how Albie referred to the interaction now, led, which was far better than pushed, which was exactly what it was so as to give full transparency of the act, but led will do for now, and when Albie left off that part about the metal muzzle ripping sanity from his flesh, it almost clamped pleasant along his shoulders, yet not to get distracted from the point, that part where Albie wondered how it might all play? The note? Mr. Davis? Him?

But a man as Mr. Davis was, a man never once in his life in need of justification, couldn't and wouldn't be bothered with a such a thing as the thoughts or wants of men less than, that's what the gun was saying after all, Albie less than, that's what the end of a barrel does, doesn't it? Cordoned off those in fine quarantined categories of shouldn't exist any longer tropes, these going away, so that those don't or won't have to lay swirlies on them anymore—the digression could go on—lay witness back instead to Mr. Davis as he walked our dear Albie beyond Mr. Bird's Café, past Lula August's Room and Board, a place where even the most miscreant vagabonds granted shelter, the same place, no doubt, the officially head-holders for their "friends" who'd spearheaded the cleansing Mr. Davis'd ordered, and over to the clearing of where the dusty steps of the Court House crept meritoriously towards Heaven as if honor laid there in the very nail beds placing board against and along board. Perhaps it here that Albie finally granted see the rise and fall of where this path might end and no more so were it on the tip of his tongue that Mr. Davis continued the illusion of his grand orchestration.

"How familiar are ya with Philly," Mr. Davis asked brushing the gun further into the small of Albie's upper back, which pushed in turn, Albie to step atop the Court House stairs.

What could Philly possibly hold claim to that which would be relevant now? Mean truly—how and why would the bringing up of a town Albie'd never visited nor held yearning to venture to, bear any strip of nohow to the occurrences spoiling soon-to-be-vulture-meat in mangled-body-limb-garden out front Randi's anyhow? Not to mention how the choosing of the Court House as personified glory-hole to the unveiling of the gawddamn thing somewhat insulting and assuredly functioning in no way anything other than Mr. Davis perhaps getting ready to tell some bastard to get fucked, and course that bastard smelling more and more like an Albie Todd hot pie with ever' slip of buttered flake coming off Mr. Davis's mouth.

"Take a seat, Albie. Gonna need reserve in 'em legs once all's said and done with."

This, however, did not translate to Mr. Davis taking a seat with him. Rather it mere gun shift from back to front head, that rifle proned locked and loaded on any threat Albie seemed like to commit.

"For all its downfalls, which innumerable if given the right time, Philly's truly the only city to prepare a man for the modern world. Some might believe differently but their thoughts'd lead them wrong after full disclosure and reflection."

The lecture'd begun. Bastard'd taken to the pulpit before Albie'd even a chance to get through the doors and take to the greet. Mean, isn't customary for a handshake to a stranger before the preacher got going and considering Albie's religion not something to be engaged in lightly, as in he didn't, as in he wouldn't, as in he didn't believe, it were quite frankly fucking unconscionable that this man, his boss, a one Mr. Davis, who KEEP! IN! FUCKING! MIND!, for all Albie knew, might very well go through with the heinous act of dislodging a bullet in his skull right there on the Court House steps. And somehow this struck gold for Mr. Davis as prime time sermon of the mount as he'd sought nothing-like-the-now-momentum to give Albie a life fucking lesson right then and there, which, as if the gun weren't enough, there were indeed gonna come barreling any moment some sort of mountain justice straight for the eye and the head, and that combo sitting and standing as they were all willy-nilly probably not the best idea if anybody might care to check the facts. And honestly, the combination of the day, from the early morning to the now and to whatever in the world lurked next, Albie felt that bile he'd tried hold at was liable to come up at the next hint of trouble come his way.

Never-mind-you, that Albie'd felt somewhat assured that there wasn't any way possible to get out of a day like this without flaring up a little bit of the craze on even the most stable of men and considering it still up for debate what category he fell in, all this nonsense Mr. Davis spouting didn't really amount to anything but horse shit. Of Matewan, as in the series of events that unfolded there and the coincidental slaughter of individuals during and some that'd followed the week after, Albie would agree with Mr. Davis on this, it mismanaged, drawn out, and missdone by all parties involved, he would, however, and could not condone no matter what homily of Philly or connection of bridged similarities between there and Matewan or here and Matewan or here and Philly or better yet the connectedness of people in general and how experiences in Philly led Mr. Davis to have foresight into things here or that somehow they informed his view of Matewan—Albie wouldn't have it at all. That this, this experience, this happening going on down the street, this gun in his face, this man bearing note before Albie in any way the same to those others, in any way like those others. Chiefly and solely because Albie was not in fact present there. No, this was different. Albie was not a bad man. Couldn't be. Simply wouldn't be a bad man. After all, it wasn't him who'd called the action down, nor him who'd brought the friends here. No. He was acting on behalf of Mr. Davis, on Mr. Davis's account, informed by and for the merit and extension of Mr. Davis. If there was anyone to blame, anyone to cannonize devilish opulence, it was certainly, unwaveringly, absolutely Mr. Davis. And God Almighty if Albie listened for much longer to this long-winded-snake-oil-salesman, it wouldn't just be the bile he worried about containing.

But the court looked to be held despite the yearnings of lesser men and Mr. Davis'd not missed a beat in the earful he's giving the world. "Simply, in no other place was the game rigged to win and fail so simultaneously, Albie. Ya see, there is always someone willing to do the work, that's the foundation of it. Always. Signs at Elis Island, down at the southern ports, near the border of Mexico, men and families will come. They will work for nothing because American nothing is better than ever'where something. The problem arises..."

Replaceable. That was the mark, the thing Mr. Davis hinted at, the thing that all this based on. His little rant. His little tie-in to Matewan and Philly and now most vehemently and with utter certainty some sort of long wooden hook careening over Albie's neck just waiting to yank him off stage and send his replacement on, someone perhaps more in line with Mr. Davis' views. His resignation, that's what this about, Albie was meant to resign on the steps. In front of a crowd. Yes, of course. He would take his pay and go. Take his Annabell and flee this place. Perhaps he would go west. Seek out gold and the promise of California. Annabelle's Aunt lived out there in the Bay area, certainly she would love the company and a chance to start anew. Why, could Albie really ask for anything more in life than a padded exit with a velvet hand.

Thus, he began to look upon the direction of Mr. Davis's rifle barrel with new light, he thought it all some sort of ruse wherein the gun more a covered bridge of choice, in that Mr. Davis was funneling Albie towards the decision come the other side, that part hid just yonder the bend of the wood's curve, where all this would come together and make sense, that he, our Albie, would look upon it with a chuckle from some cigar parlor later in life and be thankful for the forced exit and that he and Mr. Davis would no doubt still keep in touch, meeting perhaps once a year in some fine fancy restaurant to discuss how far Albie'd come since his days of working at Davis and Brother's Mining. So entranced with the idea and with the cadence of Mr. Davis voice which split intermittently between Albie's thoughts with words like, "these people" and "violence" and "it all rather misunderstood," it seemed almost automatic that he, our Albie, felt over the note that'd rested, no, waited, patiently in his hand for the right time and the right place to be read, often his fingers tracing the press of its declared fold, often his heart fluttering with a caffeine charge at the thought of it's contents and what it indeed had to do with him, he, our Albie believing, no wanting, if nothing else to be peppered in practiced measure as to where the words would land once clipped from his tongue, why, it seemed Albie could barely help himself but to read it, to take this opportunity of Mr. Davis' affording, and scour the white.

Of course, as ever' aspect of the day'd withered and riled just beyond our dear Albie's control, so to were the words incensed. It appeared what Albie needed the note to say purposefully left out as if he, in fact, handed the wrong paper. As if the note corresponded to someone else. Meant not for him at all. And to the extent that a person can have at that particular moment, now, when suddenly all the effort put forth towards shifting the meaning of what a gun held to one's head really indicated, in this case Albie realizing unfortunately, no matter how he spun it, its taste sour, and that the note undoubtedly was written by the very person the subject matter portended to—a one Mr. Davis.

Flashes of confusions what it was, of words not meant for Albie at all, of phrases not connected to eyes but coming instead from head. Blaring bosh spit from tyrannical pen, slipped through no vessel of filter and indubitably baring no connection to Albie whatsoever other then the constant unfortunate repetition of "I, Albie," here and "I, Albie" there as if it some legal document meant for Albie to sign 'cept a dedicated hand and mind'd already overseen the deed. Frankly, by the time Albie's eyes'd made it down to that part where the black'd run out, that devastating sea of white drowning near ever' thought in his head, there appeared only one way of rectifying. And yet how could he and what with and to what end plagued and trolled in circle around what needed to be done, what needed to be handled because there simply could not be any other way because to do so would mean to face "those people" and Albie knew all to well where that lane ended. Matewan told the story of that. Bled out like stuck pigs all over that town, with men coming in trying to do things townies'd not wanted and townies following suit with responses the men'd not asked for and all of it starting with a fucking ambush in the middle of a town square, with townies holding guard and wait while the men sought out particulars with the heads in charge and there wasn't, not one of those bastards who wasn't trying to actively double cross the other, each and ever'one of them were playing an active hand. The only thing that mattered to Albie most about the story was the fucking Mayor was shot first. Can it even be imagined. Mean, the fucking Mayor, followed shortly thereafter by the lead man who'd come to town, followed then by the hunt down of another and the wasting of a couple bystanders and then followed by hit on the last lead man in charge in his second in command a week later on the court's steps and what all this told Albie, what the grand lesson of the day looked to be—by God, he better make his move first even if it forced, which was why throughout all of Mr. Davis's clicking, Albie'd noticed and remembered.

Number one, from the vantage of a bird's eye view of that scope aimed at first down Albie's nose then next to Albie's chin and finally now to Albie's chest, Albie'd noticed Mr. Davis was either growing tired of trucking that 620 pump around or he'd got lost in all that jabberwocky he's spouting and gravity'd naturally settled in, and number two, Albie remembered that amongst all the planning into his outfit today, what with the boots tucked so and the shirt pressed in and that a gentleman such as himself would dare never dream leaving the house without a fine tipped pen, even on a day when their belief things might happen and happen indeed they did, he consequently began ever so cautiously slow to nip his hand down into his pants pocket and retrieve the Waterman left therein and clipped loose the heavy cap's head and pulled the small metal bayonet up the length of his thigh and began crafting the story he would tell to any who asked afterwards. He would, of course, pause often in this story to caste believable character where none lived, laying it out in golden pamphlet as some homage to the time he'd spent with Mr. Davis, to the time before and to the fictional time after where they'd shared drinks in a parlor room of fine fancy things, he would of course, burn the letter promoting false ownership to the atrocities of the day under his name at some later date and tucked it, now, where his pen once lived in the safety of his pants pocket. He would rectify over and over again just as he did now the reasoning behind his actions, the fact that the clock must strike eleven an hour after it hits ten, how this the way of world, and how Mr. Davis'd set the course and Albie merely reacting to that which laid before him, almost defenseless, as in there was no choice but this, yes, no other way it could've gone, no way it could be, but here and now with the pen, the Waterman he'd received from his Annabell on their wedding night, with the inscription on the back, "A great pen for a man bound for many great deeds!" He would of course start the story the same way in ever' instance when asked after the happenings of today, with a long grieving pause, a stillness of warranted reflection, and say with the tone of a Reverend at a funeral to people he respects, "There are times when even the greatest men are led astray, it was unfortunate that Mr. Davis sought residence with such mired company as those who would kill rather than resolve."

Thus Albie, with the narrative set in stone in his head and the Waterman firmly grasped in his hand, simultaneously knocked Mr. Davis' rifle from his chest and struck with snake speed the end of that golden tip into the meaty side of Mr. Davis' neck over and over again until the great man who'd brought coal and enterprise to the town of Hazard, and with it a slew of other misdeeds, geyesered blackish red over the once sanctified Court House steps.

47

1988

RONNIE

—

A BOY KNOWS HIS FATHER

'Bout the time that college boy got laid out and all 'em White hairs showed up, I'd a slow-clap-peripheral-fade-out-John-Hughes sorta epiphany, ya know somewheres between that Sixteen Candle cake on top the table scene, me dressed all in pink like the bell of the ball, that purty boy eye goggling 13-year-old-leave-room-for-Jesus-type-of- slow-dance-touches on my skin and that Breakfast Club fist pump closing shot, where were I one for theatrics, I might've thought Gawd shining down on me and this my special moment but that woulda made a gawddamn fool of me for sure. Seemed there another plan ahead and weren't none of it laying down templar at my alter.

Punch to the face sprawled that message loud and clear. Cheese graded metal strands down my skin with meat hooked brass that'd come from black-and-white-nowhere to-hurdled-fuck-ya-face-spew and not one of it marking nowhere close to part of the plan. Granted ya'd have to be hanging on more than the shifting overhead heat lamp of asshole dangling off the end of yar name to go round expecting something like that. Weren't no reason beating myself up over it, not when there were cold-cocks serving lunchroom whoppers straight from the dock. Gawddamn knuckles sent me DIRECT from front seat gala to middle-of-the-ring knockout. Deposited the whole hunk of me right down. Right there. And me not none the wiser to where it come from or where to go next other than lights the fuck out. But I'm here to testify to this by Gawd, there's to be some retribution coming off a slug like that and I's ready to stand Judge, Jury, and Gawd to whoever planted it.

My suggestion, best hold on to yar dungarees, we's 'bout to hit up high-octane- variety-speed and that first bumps gonna be right uncomfortable. Follow close as ya can, folks.

If it please the court, exhibit A: Willard, the man rooting up all that confusion yonder, shall be hence forth referred to as the nail. Ya know the one stuck in the jock's beefed up Bronco at the beginning of The Breakfast Club, best keep with continuity, right. Don't matter ya can't see it, trust me it's there, right there, right smack dab buried in that rubber as 'em wheels come screeching halt at the beginning of ever' kids worst nightmare, Saturday detention, a place so reviled and yet so cosmically necessary that finding oneself elsewhere merely not cool, why I'd bet there were a fucking uptick in attendance after that movie came out, a bunch of retards soulesssly map-charting their identities in various positioning round the room, though ever'body knew that even the squarest of 'em all secretly prayed that outlaw'd fit best. A fucking-Willard-metal-stalactite-jutted-there after a, let's say drive for argument's sake, past a construction site for an asshole relative ya'd like to forget but can't and come three days later ya'r tire's flat in the middle of rush hour traffic on a six lane HWY and yar in lane three, smudged right between two semi's that've leaked petrol and are sure to blow up-incinerating yar stupid fucking off tan/brown bronco that squeals masculine will ever' where it fucking goes. Yeah-the fucking nail sent to not only ruin yar day but yar gawddamn life if not checked after. In this microcosm shit storm of life that's exactly who the fuck Willard is—the nail buried deep unbeknownst to the audience in the bronco in the beginning of the Breakfast Club, where only after the movie's ended does the real horror begin. Why if told truly the Texas Chainsaw Massacre wouldn't hold up a flame to the wreak and havoc a simple Willard Nail could plague.

So then—who the fuck am I? Natural—I'm the cigarette burn in the criminal/outlaw's arm, a nuisance left over from a father who'd perhaps once cared but can't deal no longer with life, partly 'cause his son reminds him of his failures or moreso, failures such as his can't live nowhere but right underneath the skin like a rash ready with only the slightest rush of air where ever'time a mirror passed or his tired-ass-used-to-be-purty-wife-but-life'd-caught-up-fast-and-hard-and-smokes'd-turned-to-two-a-pack-days-and-the-liquor'd-gone-on-and-set-in and shit there were tanning beds now and she weren't above a romp in the sun to make 'em legs look skinnier, which just 'cause ya smother it in pineapple scent—pina-colada it don't make, her shorts'd attest to that, but when she would peak up from her whatever-the-fuck-trash-mag and go to stare on him, disappointment's what it'd be. Disappointment lurking round ever' turn, just dripping like bad curtains thumbtacked up in a trailer 'cause they couldn't afford the luxury model that came with room for a rod.

Surely this can't be a stretch, the two facing off. Pinned at opposite ends and yet tied by the same mongrel twining, that of unaware father, the one and the two both holding tether to that same line and yet neither knowing fully the repercussions of its pull. Simple, ain't it, that they'd fair hate on each other despite being born from the same place. Ya see, the problem passes down the line regardless, it, this knowing and yet not knowing, blooms despite, the matter not caring in the slightest after the operating of the one to the other, for how far should the universe truly bend to a man's wants—it is a problem padded first in the phrasing.

But these are things better left unsaid, ain't it so.

Misdirection, that's what any good lead needs, right. Misdirection and a strong face. Good jawline. Make way for a boy playing a man playing a boy, ya know someone who's still containing baby fat on their face to air on the young side of 16 but has enough weight behind their eyes to look like they know what the fuck their doing and by proxy what ever'one else is doing too.

And the story line follows as such: Stay with me folks, here's the tricky-yet-fun- yet-tricky-part: feast yar eyes on the nebulous never 'fore seen boy who actually knows what the fuck is going on, the ne'redoweller roving the outskirts of the crew*, the one who'd wanted the lead but couldn't quite make the cut, 'cause smart-ass-looking-right-side-of-the-track-rich-kids make good villains, Nordic-3rd-reich-fuckers scream even better villains, and HOLY SHIT, slicked-back-Russian-goons, clear the aisle kids, bombastic-tackle-the-fucker-quick-Red-Dawn-types make great villains, BUT, s l o w i t d o w n, BUT, slightly average-mussy-haired-wouldn't've-got-the-lead-'cept-for-in-Goonies-never-say-die reels, and this ain't that, *fucker who, course, believes the director doesn't know what he's missing not casting him, if only the director'd just open his eyes and see him for who he really is then he'd know like they'd all know (LOUDSPEAKER INTERRUPTION: INTRUDER ALERT, I REPEAT INTRUDER ALERT, ALL FACULTY PLEASE BE ADVISED ARMED MAN ROAMING HALLS) right, mean how could they not see him (CHANNEL SIX NEWS: TOP STORY TODAY: MAN OF 35 STUNTED IN GROWTH BY THE MEAGRE PROSPECTIVE OF UNDERSTAND TOOK HOSTAGE EARLY THIS AFTERNOON A DIRECTOR, FOUR CREW MEMBERS, AND A SLIGHTLY SLOW BUT NOT QUITE RETARDED PA ON THE SET OF JOHN HUGHES LATEST ENDEAVOR: THE NEW KID) do not. I repeat do not make very believable villains, which is why, and this is gonna probably make more than one head spin, hold on there's something going on over there, yes there, on the other side from where he's standing.

Folks if it please the court, I present Exhibit B: That part in the run where the obstruction comes in, ya know the thing or person or group that's gonna prevent that cigarette burn from meet and greeting that nail, see ‘cause they got to meet at some point in the story right, otherwise what’s the fucking point, who’s gonna take the girl to the dance, ya know, who’s gonna be the one to win out on the end credits with a fist pump and a cake scene. Two main’s gotta sort it out and find their common ground so they can live happily ever after in the halls of Hollywood land. So then who’s it gonna be? Gonna be that bottle neck fuck, that supercharge-red-waiting-to-explode-Toby.

Nah, fuck Toby. Toby ain’t shit. Toby’s just a pile of loose Salisbury steak smooshed up that ain’t worth a damn, sort ya wouldn’t even feed yar dog but ya’s forced to take it ‘cause a blue hair from the church’d cooked it when yar Mommy died.

Guess that a part left out.

Died March 4th. Year of ’86. Middle of the day. Fresh cup of coffee poured and steaming on the kitchen counter. Body’d give by the sink. Found her in that dirty robe she’d dawned when it were face time in the morning. Fucking thing coulda stood for a Sears beauty manual from all ‘em splotches she’d wiped on it. Last thing she’d bought for herself and the damned thing were ten years old come January.

All I’m gonna say on her for now.

So then who’s it gonna be if it ain’t Toby, or ‘em white hairs sprawled ‘bout, though they’s for sure gonna cause a shit storm of something, hard not with that many assholes lurking ‘bout. Look at ‘em over there, bobbing ‘bout on ‘em John Boats like a bunch of “come holler at the mount disciples” all of ‘em dripping gory-goo-goody-gumdrops at the hair pin chance of gnawing flesh, a ragtag team vagabond troop of salvaged souls brought up from the depths of deep cavern bog just ready for it. All of ‘em fucking-Fright-Night-Children-of-the-Damned-fuckwad-weird.

So then ya gotta ask yarself right, what the fuck is going on and why were we just speaking on a pudgy boy who thinks, no, is a man, no, wait, I forget entirely how it goes now, if I could just get…take a breath—anybody else feel woozy up in this bitch.

Point being, there's a lot a knock to the head'll do to a man. Let's just take a pause and backtrack for a sec, what ya say.

Think.

Think.

Think.

Out of the corner of my eye, suppose the meat claws clamping jaws of life tight in a wad for my face coulda perhaps, maybe they were, been something else. Yeah. Now that I come to think on it, shrugging off all that glamour and glitze, that ball of fire that squared me crooked, looked to be more paddle wood brown than white, and that spiked slap that charred asshole and bastard in my skin all at once came from and upward swing for the fences type, and the only person close to me at the time, like perhaps the sort holding sway over that piece of wood a tad bit shorter, and considering the only person standing even remotely close were—

Sally, my brother's long ago wannabe girlfriend and former tiddlybit holder in a neon yella suit, who'd moments early graphically declared pole riding a national water sport, turned out to be a tried and true cumdumpster cunt with an agenda all her own, a Molly Ringwold jollyrancher red gatorade disaster spew, 'cept in this frailed yarn, Molly Ringwold's a manipulative whore who runs a side gig with the Mason family and ain't nowhere close to American's darling sweetheart. That, just-a-ticket's-shy-of-ride-free-on- the-cock-carousel-girl'd picked up an oar off a discarded John boat that probably ain't seen no real water since Nixon got on a plane and bid the public farewell and fucking jack-hammer-sledged that wood to the side of my face while all 'em cocksuckers where watching the commotion over yonder on the opposite deck.

Remember the nail. Oh it's there even if ya can't see it now.

And so the plot thickens: Apparently, not only was this little bespoke river rat angel in the business of cock-hobbling the unsuspected dopes on Cocktail Cove but she were also mighty fine tuned to then transport these sad saps back over to where her boyfriend stayed, a one (unregistered first name) Mason, over to Highland Terrace. It were there, of course, that the predictable shakedown ensued, the threat of something held overhead with the cure of money unlocking the solution. Sure it'd probably be more than any of 'em sad fucks owned but it were just close enough to where if a relative's house mortgaged or family title signed over, that undocumented case of syphilis and herpes the poor fuck'd soon find out he had wouldn't be splayed up all over town by way of Joannies' Print Hut, Joannie, course were married to a Mason and saw nothing wrong with a little extortion. None of 'em did.

But what she didn't know and what seems apparent neither do y'all, were, Sally WAS the exact person I's needing to meet. Oh, ya think it just happenstance, that I traveled all the way to boomfuck nowhere Georgia and spent time on a terd-stain body of water like Lake Lanier for just nothing, huh. No-sir-e-Bob, simply ain't true.

Time for a little back tracking.

I knows…might be asking yarself, how many gawddamn gears this boy got left in him, now?

Like to be three more. Just hold on and I'll get ya where ya need to go.

See, like any hard-hitting basket-case such as Sally, there's a scent give off her for, I don't know, let's say, couple miles, where any two time hustler'll get pulled too. A fucking neon zapper on a hot summer porch. Squeeters just come. So's when I's taxed with finding the bastard who'd spit me out—running on nothing more than gambling and a vague sense of tracing myself, I went to all 'em places where 'em stenches live.

Soon as I crossed over the South Carolina border after following a shit lead fed to me by a one Mr. Boyd Fowler, a real tall fucker with a little bit of a PROTRUDE coming out his front side from where 'em beers'd fit mighty white on him over the years, who'd stated, and I motherfucking quote, "Best game goin' in

Cackalacky… happens over at Monroe's place…a mile marker in past Hartwell," where when he were done spinning that thread, it weren't quite discerned whether he were asking me the fucking question with how much wet he'd let fall down to that endless pit of his. Shoulda known there, he were fuller than a septic tank.

But I'll say this for him, were it not for that bastard's passing out and only 'em flies and that fat boy sweating bullets and cracking beers behind the bar left to keep me company, I might not've gained access to the sportsman-like interest of helping a brother out that fat boy cracking beers were willing to give.

Seemed, according to Porkbone, his Daddy'd a sense of humor what he said as that were a Gawd given title, there's a family come 'bout an hour from where we set that were just fine with taking any man's money willing to put ass in chair. Told me, he said, "Oh yeh, 'em Mason's only one's holding down a tent in the wind. Years they'd gone at it. Just drive on down to Lanier, now, and y'all spot 'em. Ain't no way ya can't. Devil done ripped they's soul from ever'one of 'em. Ripped the color right off their hair, now. White as cotton they is."

FASTFORWARD—to the not quite here and now but better side of a week ago to a BBQ joint off Holiday Road just a hair lip spread from the lake: Took all of four minutes at Old McDonald's for me to spot Sally sitting in the corner, her ripped cut-off's oozing nethers all out over the chair and that bright pink tank top that even Andi woulda found off putting in Sixteen Candles, stealing second base in front of a bunch of drooling high school boys playing side eye so their Momma's friends lunching two tables over wouldn't go back with a story to tell 'bout how 'em boys got caught up with a loose girl, which were exactly what all of 'em woulda traded their left nut to do at the moment. Type of pink that haunts ya when ya close yar eyes 'cause that dancing spot of bright dares not die down. She were all high-school-drop-out-used-to-be-middle-school-pageant-Queen chowing down on ribs with BBQ sauce spilling on her tits 'cause maybe that's just what's bound to happen at a roadside joint or maybe it were due to that pink tank top damn near bordering nipple town. Ya know, one of 'em bona-fide country whores with a heart of gold 'cept ya gotta remember this ain't a movie, folks. Meaning, she's rotten to the fucking core and I knew right then and there she were the mark and sitting there flanked by two white hair fucks who looked to be boyfriend to her and brother to him and both of 'em already pining bullseye on me only confirmed it.

Cue to NOW: interior. Shitty interior. Shitty-soap-scum-filled-peeling-porcelain- finish-drop-in-bathtub-interior with hair swirls holding court in between mildew filled tiles and a strong case for black mold blooming out of a Head and Shoulders bottle with a faint smell, NO, strong smell of stank hanging 'bout, like come the other side this shower curtain, unnatural green and purple stains abounded, there lived an old shit in a commode that lost the dignity of a lid when the dinosaurs roamed.

Cramped.

Hogtied.

Not the good kind. The bad kind. Kind where yar feet goes numb in the first ten minutes. Kind where yar face's so busy holding a defensive line against pube splotched soap that's threatening a fall from off the bathroom ledge that ya almost don't notice the hole in the wood panel'd wall that offers all reprieve. There redemption lived. There, a plastic pink flamingo holding a smoke outta it's mouth with a sign drooped round it's neck charging "If ya ain't Highland Terrace, ya ain't shit," proved all the pain and discomfort worth it. Sally'd got me in. And not only that but she'd parked me in the trailer cross from the main stage 'fore just as my face'd got all too familiar with the hair loss of another man's unders TWO doors opened: the one just cross from me in that tropical shit box and the door to…

Interior: a beat to hell bathroom. Smoke floods light through a marlboro thick hallway. A man enters. On his frame a particular age and build that suggests dying ain't no longer a problem. The hogtied man in the tub clinches as the man who entered shuffles through discarded nothings crumpled on the floor. Come in for the can. Why else? A twelve pack of pee lodged in his tank for the last two hours wouldn't hold no longer. He stops shy. Something changed his mind. The stench virus infesting the bowl perhaps.

A shower curtain peels back, the stick of gross clinging for dear life at the bottom to the tub and:

"Afternoon Willard."

48

FEBRUARY 3, 1960

FIGHT FIRE WITH FIRE

Cold'd shoveled snowbanks of frost up on their skin and they'd not moved from their post for over an hour and yet their blood were wood-stacked-furnace-mad, all five of 'em steam engine puffing against freezer burned midnight ruin. No big deal some'd say, just a bunch of Brighton boys and Gary but it's downright hard to tell when men are chainsaw teeth packed to the rim in cannonade fusillade fucked with a directive that romped all sour and chthonic in the hollows of 'em. Damn hard to tell indeed. 'Specially when that sense of brandished hell burrowed round a camp of unsuspecting, well that can't rightfully be touted true for all, but for the most part, unknowing lay-me-down-to-sleep-dwellers of particularly not-belonging-round-here-fools and a fair smattering of families who'd not got word, not that there were much word give, seeing as how that's the sorta thing that'd land a bullet in yar skull or a rope round yar neck or worse if handed over to that nefarious clarity imagination'd imbue, no need for thanks here for 'em tight lips, fair say, doubt there were a soul who woulda called it at all, the intents of 'em five's souls, which don't truly equate to much, ‘cept perfect conditions for things made and set to go on and become undone.

See ‘em tents’d come once doors burdened with hardened knocks, the wood broke down, laying invisible vacancy-here twinge in the middle of the night as bodies shuffled “don’t matter love” sentiments and home-is-where-the-heart-is dirt bunnies round stampered tired feet, lost families now figmenting routines where hearths and stoves and spare chairs’d gone missing almost overnight, their bodies seeking found under canvas cloth, fighting live against fuliginious naught, the trade of cot and dirt and fire pit not existing long enough in their minds for memories to trigger muscle hold, like life resided somewhere else and they’s all just ghosts waiting for the real world to let ‘em back in.

Fact, were it not for all ‘em dirty-browned-boot-splotches running between tent after tent after tent, their form spelling nothing but just-landed-from-a-train-ranger-squads, ‘em five’s reasoning for why the crate and ‘em and there needing all align might not’ve made a lick of sense at all.

Closed up there with cold working stitches through chattered fur coats aiming warm on their teeth, ‘em five did. Their hands flint-rubbing thermal thick, hoping bite and frost not meant for meet, that angry wind bulleting down, picking rock outta limestone flesh, covering their hearts with the iciest of intents, they stayed rowed up there as they were the four and the one and the crate, with Corbin and Eisle’s humpbacks wallering like pigs unrest, the sway catching back and forth as they rocked that bleak crass gelid sting away, they stayed. With Wayne fighting fire out his brain ever’ time that needle of regret bashed bone along his chest, the figments of lives once lived playing puppet shadow behind dirty white tent, they stayed. With Myrtle’s, to his brothers and Gary, Mryt, 1000-yard stare down at that crate, his eyes holding driven and detached tight-like over the bridge of his nose, they stayed. With Gary calling shots and the clock’s time not set to right just yet, they stayed. And when buckshot kicked back in the distance, by gawd, ya guessed it, they stayed.

Wayne slipped, "Shotgun…up on the hill."

Now there weren't a one of 'em that didn't know what a fucking shotgun sounded like nor how to tell, once that spit of metal blew air turbid, riling out like shit-spew-slou, where, in general, that barrel cocked might've dislodged, nor were it beyond a single one of 'em hardened bastards to know what a slug coming from off the hill meant but there were a damned character witness proceeding stand over all of 'em with a tight death grip demanding that for some reason or another ever'thing decried mention as if this were something that'd hold their boots upright throughout the events to occur ahead.

"Ain't our problem," pipped Gary.

"Not yet, ya mean," simmered low-like from Myrt, his pot already done tipped way back, that fire inside him licking high flames at any chance for that burn to begin.

"Gotta be ten fucking degrees out here—"

Charred black smite gurgled, "Ain't never met nobody who'll go to complaining 'bout weather more than ya. I'll be just gawd-damned, mean 'course it's fucking cold, Eisle, it's fucking February."

To be fair it weren't all Eisle's fault he'd go on 'bout the weather like he did, the boy were a runt if ever there were one. Mean even Corbin, who weren't even a solid ten pounds over his brother, wore it better and it still fit him like a loose hanging suit on a sad sapling and in all honesty it were fucking cold as hell outside but ain't nobody a sitting duck in this here venture and fair were an illusion shred long time ago, and quite frankly, there were a side bet going on in another room, if ya garner my meaning, that Eisle knew exactly what'd rile his brother Myrt up and well, when one's left without a sense of control in a situation, ya'd be surprised how that might extend out of nowhere and go to hang in the air.

"Ye ain't got to be gawddamned, Myrt, ain't like it's gonna do ye any good. Keep yer fucking voice down," slow-roll-pace-sludged-out from baby twin brother number two.

"What the fuck that mean, Corbin?" Myrt scooted up close to the twins, the shelf-live of locked, stocked, and loaded near past due on that stink breath of his flowing all hot lava like out on the wind.

"Thought that tooth woulda fell out, there, Myrt," Gary puffed, busy at the wipe of cold-water creek streaming out his left eye 'cause the smell so gawddamn raw.

See, that bad tooth'd gone on and set up dead in the back of Mryt's mouth for better part of a year. Turnt his breath fucking mean and that cold seemed clasp on it the worst. Sliced the air like rotted cheese and played curse to any who'd garner courage enough to come up on him.

"Too gawddamn close for all that—" Wayne relief pitched a red tin from his pocket, the savoir to all five huddled there like a bunch of fucking coons taking over a fox hole, and when that metal hit drive-in theater bright as the moon stole third from under a cloud's nose, there were a brief come to Jesus moment for 'em all.

Wayne shoved the tin to Mryt's face, "Eat one dammit."

Now, not taking the mint meant Myrt'd face the unholy blocking out of all things going, a promise wrapped round a threat Wayne'd give him once that tooth'd took a left turn at worse. Told Myrt there were plenty enough things clamping discomfort on all their lives, they weren't 'bout to add one more by choice. And seeing as how Mryt didn't go nowhere Wayne didn't and how Wayne, hisself'd, grown more then accustomed to the company, feeling Myrt's presence more like the extension of an arm, in that it belonged at Wayne's side, Wayne went on and made habit of the mints being readily available when the time came for their dispersion.

And once all well in the world again, well, certainly a stretch but something 'em men'd seemed donned control of, Nervous

Nelly, Eisle, sought out some reassurance like something'd done changed in the two hours since they'd stood post outside 'em tents and asked, "What'd he say again?"

"Said finish it." Gary pulled back from his pew, his ears burning hot from a sermon come the other side that tent. Pastor-Sheriff-Bastard-elect Kerian Sterling atop the mount, his disciples itching and ready with snake handlers slithering faith formed by way of rifle metal, with demonstrators feeling the rile of the Spirit move 'em so that tongues'd took over near half in one baritone bullet chomp, these mongrel few, who would no doubt, take pride in their due-diligence-of-soon-to-be-fuck-this-coal-camp's-world-up, and Gary's mind stopped working out for a sec the how-to of what really comes next, that gathering of exact and when cohorting to now, and he turned and vetted over to Wayne who stood by Corbin who stood by Eisle then Myrt then him, and then down to the crate double checking 'em "t's" and dotting 'em "i's" of what Enoch'd said, and he realized "ain't no other way."

"Bullshit, Wayne." Eisle yanked after his brother's arm, that face of his set to high roll boil with red chugging hot steam out into the night. "What 'bout 'em families, Wayne, ya gonna answer for that?" Eisle slapped ahold his eldest brother's arm, jostled Wayne's bear grip on the crate and begged the turn back now 'fore "too late" settled in.

"Let go my hand, Eisle," splayed calm and stern in front of his brother, the table setting itself for a full-blown dynamite spike if the request not met soon and to Wayne's liking.

But his baby brother, misunderstanding the message behind the message, that there existed no other way, that this the only thing that could and would be done, that this not something meant for hearts as his, not meant for hands that'd scooped slugs off the path so lives don't end, that's what his baby brother Eisle'd do when one spotted on a rock, its slime seeping out in a steady trail of tiny haint feet, Eisle'd avoid all chance of damage done, by pick up, redirect, and let down of the small gooey creature, his hope the "too late" for it to never come, just simply could not see past. And that's alright in all honesty 'cause there ain't a lot who can. And Eisle knew that deep down too, his make and theirs, and the divide in between, that grand bit of space growing farther and farther apart as the clouds ticked SOON overhead.

"Just let me send word, Wayne," Eisle's plea favoring the back-end of a Dear John letter with the closing of let's still be friends.

"Can't be done."

"But I could make it, Wayne, I could get in and out without no one noticing."

"It's too late," Wayne said, eyeing his brother's bird grip.

Too late carried far over 'em Brightons, that mountain-pass-Dommer-party already set and snowed in, their steps seeming always a few feet too slow, with their Mommy laying closest example to their fault. Her death a crossfire between men arguing outside their homes with suits sent there to kick 'em and their families out, cause "sympathizers won't be tolerated," that's what they yelled for all 'em soot covered faces and runny nose children to hear, an example, an example little Mrs. Brighton just couldn't stand hear no longer. All her might forced, trudge forward, her late husband's shotgun flung over damn near bone brittle arms as she went for the load—Cocked that sucker back and shoved through the front door of her log abode and clicked out a double shot and that little ole crinkly voice of hers, "May the Lawd curse yar fucking name," traveling lightning speed right after it. Shot one dead. A Plinker, through and through right there where he stood and began the reload of another but her little ole arthritic hands weren't fast enough and she were sent to meet her maker in the same place she'd raised her boys in a one bedroom shack she'd never even owned 'cause the Coal company wouldn't never let her forget, she and all 'em others digging black, filling gold coffers of the few, that replaceable tenants all they'd ever be.

And thank Gawd, 'em boys'd thought at times over the next following weeks, as fight after fight after fight ended with another of theirs, "Sympathizers," dead, when women and babies were thrown from their homes in the middle of the night, 'em savages plundering through their belongings vandalizing fucking yarn and buttons and heirlooms those folks'd held dear to their hearts, when men plain fucking TOOK only to be found days later bashed up and in and some sorry excuse 'bout drinking and having a fast fat lip, when ever'body living woulda described 'em fellers as Gawd fearing mutes, 'em Brightons were somewhat fucking grateful she'd not lived another day to go viewing all that. And that were 'bout all Eisle could hold tether to now as he eyed his brother and that grip of his went from tight to loose and that barrel chain-ganging "ain't right" and sorrow round his heart spiking down one last iron of "thank fucking Gawd" his mommy weren't alive on the day her boys handed out the innards of that fucking crate, and he whispered "ain't right, Wayne," more to hisself 'cause wouldn't no one bare hold truth in their hearts 'bout what's really 'bout to be done. But, the yarn already bent full circle round as it were, that too late meeting where crate once lived and stood, the box now moved.

A matter of perspective really, ain't it, guess that'll hold on to the lot of most anything. Mean, Wayne were carrying the crate 'cause his brother Eisle and Corbin wouldn't and 'cause Mrt there, shouldn't, all the hate in the world didn't need no favors coming off that one, and 'cause Gary couldn't, nah, see he needed stay, needed process what it were coming off that cocksucker Kieran Sterling's lying lips, 'cause it weren't 'til then, 'til that moment after he'd feasted on 'em dirty fucking words, that endless crockpot of shit bubbling out from Kieran Sterling, that he convinced, that Enoch right, that the crate necessary.

See, there were a part of him that went for the agree with Eisle. It were cement mixing between his shoulders, dropping anchor into the sea of "what if" at his feet, that unknowing of right, fat washing his veins ya know, threatening a block, threatening a fucking hike back up the hill to that fucking monster, the Hound, up there, 'cause at least with him there weren't no second guessing why. The monster does, 'cause the monster do, hear. Naw, Gary stayed when 'em Brightons went. Right there pigeoned up against the back of that tent, waiting for 'em boots to stop shuffling come the other side and for that grand monster that all men face but don't no one ever go to mention its haunting, to fucking kettle ball move from out his gut.

In the last minute, Kieran'd flipped and fumbled his thumb and finger over that coin in his pocket fifty-two times as he awaited the words needed for the right response. That persistent trail of its tracking down the fat of his finger, wiping away, he hoped, the not-so-distant path that'd brought him here. Why in time, he felt, it perhaps something to be forgotten entirely where not even those who'd drawn straws against him would remember the grayer parts of his ascension to Sherriff from appointed Union man and seeing as how one could not hold both the same, it were course the better position to go with maintaining the peace with advocacy for the Union dangled on his sleeve, so to say.

In his current plot, not something, need it be reminded held for very long, Kieran'd made a name for hisself as none other than liaison. Least that's what he felt and if he felt it, than it most certainly must be true, right. In the last two weeks alone, were it not he, who'd greeted ever' single, and I mean ever' single family who chose to be removed from their humble abodes, 'cause that's what it really were, weren't it, they'd chose to act up, and acting up garnered reaction, and reaction came in the form of men sent and meant to carry out other things. Sure enough did, greeted ever' single family. Spoke with all of 'em, writing down in that little notepad in his pocket, the one opposite where the coin lived, all their concerns, all the things 'bout "what's to be done next" and "how's it gonna go now." Made a big to-do of it all, sitting there as he would on boxes, and recovered chairs and sometimes just the floor, rather awkwardly though when that the position offered, couldn't quite master the political leg cross there, no ye couldn't, so's Kieran fashioned the closest form therein, a pinnacle of earnestness with both feet crossed underneath him, some child ready and eager to learn all that they'd give. And forever and always a study of man, a lesson delivered to him from a former partner in a former life some time way back ago, he took those little words unsaid, those mere utterances of perhaps could be and he stored 'em in checks marked by men's names and over time, say within two to three visits with all 'em families, Kieran'd gathered all that he need right there in that little book.

And the beauty of it all, he'd not even asked one question to find the answers. It were just give to him, like little gifts from Gawd. After all, he'd done it for the greater good no less, least that's what he'd convinced hisself of and MY what things can be accomplished when that the case indeed. Come to it all on his own, though there were talk it'd happened otherwise. Fact of it were, Kieran didn't rightly need that much convincing to do anything that'd place he and his ahead. That ain't to say he weren't hit with a spell or two at times of what've I done, that's bound to happen, but that's why drinks invented, ain't it? Take a slip off that ole wagon and there ye go right there in forget-yer-troubles-company.

See our fair broder here, Kieran'd become all too comfortable with the notion of TAKE when opportunity presented. Thus take he did. Took that very favorable moment of granted entry to all 'em families' homes as grand-count-his-lucky-stars-chance to glean fat from the top, a classic pinch-hit-one-two. See, there'd proved no true movement for common ground and the Davis and Brother's Mining Company'd obligingly inferred to him that they'd only continue lining pockets for so much longer unless rope give. So's in the fashion of any man vested in the ideology of gain, our broder Kieran here, sought to make a deal and deal he did. Met with dear Albie just three nights prior, the very evening after an unfortunate reaping give to him via Connie at a Union gathering, with a list neither asked for nor expected, a gift he'd later claim, of all those known to be sympathizers and supporters to the Union's cause and what better person than he to deliver such things seeing as how he'd officially taken over the post of Sherriff just this January past.

And what fine and gallant deed this translated to, why our dear friend Albie. Oh, he were plumb overcome, regalias in fact. Invited our broder Kieran into the house, he did, not to say this were the first encounter of the two, certainly not, but never to the house, and certainly never inside. And my, didn't Albie ever unroll the pageantry. Oh, fine tea from a fine kettle, brought out no less on silver platter, reflecting the beauty of none other than Mrs. Todd all shimmer and sweet for him, all don't-mind-if-I-do take a biscuit, and "Oh no but I couldn't have another, Mrs. Todd...oh very well." Stuffed it up right proper and left assured what's done were right when Albie ushered Kieran out with the shushed happy calm phrase, "What bright future bore ahead indeed."

And yet once Albie's door closed and the night black settled in, for Kieran'd certainly waited 'til the cover prime, there were the unsettling notion of watch—as in being watched—as in someone knowing and sizing Kieran up in the exact same manner he'd done to all 'em families down below the hill, shredding bare their skin right there as they stood to pierce the heart's inner mysteries and then leave without a man the wiser. It were something, Kieran'd not care for at all and adding insult to injury, it were something he'd not invited, which to him landed damn offensible at his feet. After all he'd lent the common courtesy of a knock when robbing souls. Not to mention did a man truly want to live in a world where thoughts stole right from ye with no safeguard at all? Damned savagery if council truly imparted and not nothing nowhere near to where Kieran Sterling likened hisself to be, 'cause do remember this were the right thing to do. No. In fact, the ONLY thing to do. That's right, no choice other than this, that's what were held close inside Kieran's little beating heart.

Could then it be somewhat expected when Kieran went to glancing over his shoulder to where that cold gaze portended, and glancing there friend, a loose wrapping, for it were more scant eye peak and a very hurried shuffle along that our broder Kieran here, spotted in the black decay of naught, a beast of a man, a Hound, an imperial dragon of doom, a face to which he wished never revisit again but the only face forever implanted in the fertile futility of his mind from now on, as in the quietude of solitude brought this image forth and this image forth alone, and it were this very ruination of hisself that'd sparked his speech to the National Guard, the men, the soldiers, who'd arrived after various occurrences, that's what Albie and anyone from Davis and Brother's Mining referenced it as, occurrences. Not deaths. Nor fires. Nor attempted feats of retribution. But occurrences. All of those culminating with the unfortunate crossfire accident of two children, two children caught up in the way, not of course aimed after and picked just last evening. No matter though to the actuality of things, as far as Mining Men circles'd go, as in those that owned it or worked high up therein, they'd, as in the children and all those other unfortunates and sympathizers who'd got in the way, would remain nameless, 'cause where there were no name no accuse could exist.

It were after this settling as one might call it, this resolution of right, as in, on the right side, as in, whose side are ye on—the right one of course, that Kieran abandoned his pausing and fiddling with the coin, that coin give, well give's a rather loose term ain't it, as in—if it were not give then it were took but took rarely gets fair play in the day of light and certainly not in hindsight, curious if noticed how most all things are gifted in the history of lives, simply a better spin PERHAPS, needless to say the coin arrived, yes that's good, arrived in the ownership of Kieran after the unfortunate decision of his former business partner to not understand the facilitation of certain funds as necessities, thus the parting of ways and the coin GIFTED to Keiran as favor for the trouble of course, stopped its swivel.

"It pains me to imagine this place, broders, to conceive a time where this the necessary path, but what else good can we do," Keiran took a pause, a seasoned professional pause, as in this the driving force of it all, this the thing he'd repeated over and over and over again 'what else can we do,' "then bend our will to the path for which we've been driven. It's truly a disgrace what's happening here. This week, this hellish grappling week delivering the gate to Satan's mouth direct here to Hazard." He moved his hands to his face, "Calcified lock-jaw on all our throats, has it not?" Ahh he were good indeed. And a little bend now too, a little pitch over with the back aimed high as if carrying weight, "Have we not all felt the boot heel raking cross our backs with the promise of endless strife." And right back to a powered up stance, a finger pointing to all 'em hungry followers, "And I'll tell ye this, we do not want such men as these, these dejectors, these abolitionists, that's right, let's call 'em what they is now, they's trying to halt a way of life here," that finger 180ing right back to Keiran's chest, with a tap of three for emphasis, "halt what we've all worked so hard to build. There's money aflowing mountain deep in 'em hills, justa flowing, waiting to be picked, waiting for this here to be done and over, for order to come back to 'em men and this here glorious town and there are those that just can't see beyond it like I sees it, like the neutral sees it." Oh how high and mighty that soapbox musta felt. "'Cause that's what I am here, neutral, for the Union and the Mine. For ever'one in this town. But how can this be, ye ask, the Union and the Mine, how can it be when there's those that's dying, perishing disastrously?" And, oh, what a long pause here he took, parallel parked a 1960 Cadillac de Ville in that long spot of silence, he did, "'Cause I'm an optimist. Always have been. Faith led, we are. In the flood, what did we have? Nothing but faith, faith and each other. Just as then so is now, faith. Faith that all this can be mended, and a bridge built within the divide. That the Union and Mine can go hand in hand with each other and that all ye standing ready able to make it happen. Let us do what's right here, let us settle the storm and batten down the hatches so that when it passes, we can begin again. Let us realize all that has been accomplished between the two, the Union and the Mine and all that will be done in the future no doubt. But for now it is order we seek, order where order is needed. With upmost confidence, I'll leave ye all to it, gentlemen."

Course this the speech handed out for the masses, the one he needed prying ears to hear, a message of hope, of contained control, of faith, tenants of an organized society, of a democracy, yes, that's what it were DEMOCRATIC for the National Guard to be brought in, democratic of Kieran to liberate those in need of liberation even when they 'emselves unaware of the things holding 'em back. After all he were merely the liaison, the messenger, what anyone did with the information couldn't be tied to him. Certainly not. 'Sides he'd not even mentioned the list and if it weren't mentioned then it almost didn't exist, and this list he'd give to Albie which were, of course passed along to the Guard weren't nothing but names nohow. Just ink on paper.

With the crate opened, 'em wires looked down right out of place, their black led-pencil-thick jutting outta brick red candy sticks like they's something docile. Something that weren't gonna cause no effect.

"Here." Gary pickaxed the dirt aside with his fingers, hollowing out a bed for a bundle to go while 'em Brightons stood full attention turned in ever' direction 'cept for down at what Gary were doing. Well all of 'em but Wayne, who were trick-or-treating out that crate with angel soft touch, 'em sticks just cotton ball landing on the ground in seven piles of five.

"Ya reckon that shot hit meat up there on the hill," Eisle asked right quiet like to his twin.

"Couldn't say."

Mrt gritted. "If he shot it, it hit. Ain't no wondering on that."

"But who'd he shoot," asked Corbin 'fore Eisle'd the chance.

"Don't matter right yet. Now start unraveling that spool." Wayne pointed out the marks to his brothers, the lay down of where 'em presents soon to go.

"I'm just wondering maybe this already over, ya know…like maybe we don't need to be doing what we's doing…like maybe what happened up there on that hill's gonna change things…like maybe we don't need to be doing what we's doing… like maybe we don't need to be doing what we's doing…like maybe." Eisle'd go on like this for hours, just stand there spiraling outta control saying the same thing over and over again, 'til somebody, usually Corbin, were able to quiet him down, somehow pull him outta the tunnel so to speak. Nerves. Product from getting separated in the Mine when he's six. A boy just lost down there in all that black looking for comfort couldn't none of 'em walls give. Corbin'd were the one to find him, course. Somewhat of a marvel to tell the truth like one twin ought always know 'bout the condition of the other. It were why 'fore Eisel'd even gotten started, Corbin'd tried to brush it off, feeling the hair stick up on his own neck for no reason and realizing it weren't his nerves they's speaking too.

"Eisle," Corbin grabbed his brother, "Eisle, ya gotta quiet down now. Quiet down. Listen to my voice. Listen to yar brother Corbin. That's right, it's me. Yar brother Corbin and that there's yar brother Mryt and Wayne and Gary and we're doing something right now that can't not be done. No….no…up there on the hill doesn't matter. It doesn't change anything down here. Ya know that. Ya know that 'cause I know that. Cause the man who watches up there doesn't let anything happen. No….no…there's no but's here, there's no might be's or perhaps could, there's only real. Real. And. Now….no it doesn't matter, the shot doesn't matter to us. The Hound doesn't miss. He doesn't loose. Don't ya remember the stories. Listen to me…listen to me, Eisle….that's right, the stories, the stories of The Hound. He doesn't miss, Eisle. The shot changed nothing. Now go on and help Gary dig holes at the marks, sky's gotta light up at midnight and it's half past eleven. That's what Enoch told Gary and that's what we're gonna do."

49

FEBRUARY 3, 1960

THE HOUND MEETS HELLMOUTH JAMES WITH A VISITOR TO BOOT

PART I

Another fire burned out below, the trailing zipper of smoke blacking Hazard, leaving two beady eyes to stare out in the night.

Don't no wind go shushing coal flames, the Hound thought. Don't matter how hard it'd hankered after destroying the night prior, building fury down from Iowa to Illinois and flushing heavy through Hazard on straight-a-way to Matewan no doubt by middle of night, ain't gonna silence no coal. Knew coal ain't like to burn out less effort put forth. Sure as shit ain't gonna silence two outta four, he thought. What'd happened in the last hour, two outta four fires dead in the valley, dead where company men'd carried torch down the marching ground of the camp and lit 'em. The Hound doubted men cut like that'd let blind sit for very long on their watch.

Felt it all the way from up on the hill, the Hound did, that vestibule brimming with can't-contain-here-woe, a maddening affair of silent enclaves moving afoot, their burrowing venturing closer and closer to the hive and it's Queen as if her sundering might quiet the ill inside 'em all, but the Hound'd no time for the subtle buzz clamoring up vengeful puffs of "we will be heard." Weren't no room for that, not with the frost paving crunch on that grass under his feet and the wind shaving skin off his face, just rawhide welts on already turnt sour looks—No. Reckon the Hound didn't give one gawddamn to nothing like that, less it stepped foot on Albie's hill and set up there on a Loblolly Pine with a scope turning heat towards his boss. Cared a bit 'bout that right there, what'd caused that walk of his to take special care now as he crossed over towards the man perched, bleeding in and out of the dark on the far ridges of Albie's lot lion hunting the figure from behind. And a sight it were, the Hound, moving with two hatchets secured tight at his belt, both knobs crossing X just below his belly so's that it the second thing a man spied if he could ever tear his eyes from that Gawd-awful face. Carried a rifle with him too, bucked down as it were, some horse ready and waiting to be rid of its load, justa gnawing away at leather for that back to perch up light speed fast and kick out the end of something—No. Suspect, it were the exact opposite of a sight for sore eyes.

Suspect when that gun of his finally brayed up and bit air, that barrel nibbling metal hold to back of head skull, that man on the Loblolly Pine meeting breadth-of-life-left-worry for the first in some long time were not how either of 'em envisioned the day'd go.

"Know who I am?" The question more an annunciation, more a can't-quite-wrap-yar-head-round-what's-just-begun, that sudden collapsed compendium of life wickedly grabbing after footing so's the body might stand chance at erect, it, the voice crafting finished chisel on that grand question all of existence posed, almost as if it bore not from the want of answer per say at all, and yet it'd done demanded regard, and regard it now or else, that were the rigid sprawling of rustling Eastern Cottontails awaking from their early morn slumber, their driving out from under forest brush upsetting a Dark-eyed Junco who'd stumbled out onto the wooded floor, his just-trying-to-survive-black-hop hastily dragging wrong way down the fairway of the food chain, the soon-to-be discovered faulty turn jutting out from Weasel-territory-tunnel-home, that

Ermine striking on double down mode, that clamored crunch perhaps continuing out in the wood, that natural order proclaiming a-thing-begot-a-thing-begot-a-thing, enough chaw-marks in the stiffened cold that'd attest to that.

Hellmouth didn't answer at first. Weren't no need. No mystery who it were that watched the man on the hill and weren't no mystery to who'd be calling after Hellmouth being there. But ain't knowing and facing two very different things.

Hellmouth gulped, that cold restless wind fighting knock against his cavity door, the threat of disappear training his skin on the lesson of accept and reckoned suffice not something he'd want dine with today, so's he spread out his answer in a stream of slow molasses drip, "Yep. Know why I'm here?"

"Don't matter," the Hound quipped.

If Hellmouth were afraid, his voice spoke not of it nor did his frame as he were saddled out over that Loblolly like he expected it to move any second now, like 'em targets in the distance gonna go to hightailing out and he's gonna need a quick kick to giddyup after 'em. Not even once did he look back to the Hound who towered over. Heard enough tell how that face looked. Weren't no reason to go viewing 'til the need necessar, he reckoned.

See, age'd not treated the Hound kind and if his face horrific in young years, it categorically worse now—No. The thirty years since he'd melted ruin from Cecil 'Doc Hodge's blade while two crazed Irish broders watched on with chant foaming "yes" off their mouths'd claimed more than just skin from him and when Hellmouth took a long hard gander, 'cause there weren't no way round it but, fear were gonna spread over him with an ice blanket—No. Suppose that slab of pig's skin sewn there all 'em years ago never did stand chance at took, as in it hadn't, sat there all country-cured-ham-salt over the Hound's face, sticky-glued down daily, that faint smell of pork hawk-eyeing just above his nose—No. Suppose 'em pot marks left from where the Hound'd tried over and over again at sew and stay riddled Bubonic-plague-black along the left side of his face, all 'em tiny yarn threads buried in shallow-what's-left-face-skin-grave not something wanted view for very long. And the cleaved nose that'd split from a rock splintering stone on his face'd never healed, hung so wrong that it made mention to falling off at any moment entirely with the bit of rot that'd gone on and set in. And this all fit under the track of splotchy mown grass that sprouted backasswards and incorrect from the top of the Hound's head in pared blips of blondish white tufts seemed altogether unearthly, truth be told—No. The entire affair of the Hound's face from missing teeth, what'd seemed ever' second or third spot, to hardened-latched-with-string-mask would provoke the grandest of stirs inside any man, stun 'em cold, 'til the echo chamber of recall bounced back.

Reason for his employ, ya see. Men like Albie could and would do whatever they wanted but for the few things that needed remain Preacher like when their name mentioned, well that's what the Hound's for. What he done just earlier this morn. Carried down the edict round the coal camp at 9:05, just in time to spot the company men busy laying rock circles, how he'd know'd of the fires and their placement. The yearnings of Albie then carrying and setting him up in the west far enough out not to get seen but close enough in to watch after those that needed watching.

Twice, the Hound'd done a swoop round that post, moving through the pigweed attempting a ladder to Gawd, finally finding rest amidst a blanket of poison oak that'd swallowed the small patch of land between four yeller poplars. In his hand, a stack. That very same stack of white paper that'd fallen from Albie's window grate and into the bush. That the Hound'd then salvaged and looked at only once, just long enough to plant little black seeds in the back of his head. From then 'til now, 'til 'em sprouts'd near full grown, he'd held 'em names inside his mouth, sucking his tongue over each letter 'til their taste molded behind his teeth and his belly done swoled up with ache for the meat to finally drop. It were there, squatted in amongst that bane sea of green, that he let their names drop finally from his mouth and fill the palms of his hands, each letter dripping lather of wanted-call-wash-me-clean, that's what Albie'd asked for, a cleanse, a please return these lost souls back to the dirt. And there in the Hound's hands, where soon 'em fitted hatchets'd go, he let the sprouts call out their visitation rights, let their names spread roots over top him with something of a double check duty, so's there weren't no room for confusion to exist.

"Matters to me," Hellmouth bit.

"Bet it does." Snot bombed the ground, the aimed sentinels stringing threats in lifelines that hung from out the Hound's nose. "What ya planning on doing, there," he asked clearing his throat, wanting rid of that cold working through him.

"What the situation calls for."

There were a long pause between the Hound's asking and Hellmouth's answering, a working out and sizing up. A grand spell of extra consideration give to the fell of words slicing courtesies off their tongues.

"Best let it be, maybe." Wind'd carried it more as WARN than plea, slathered it out over top the two of 'em like kerosene on wood, both of 'em just awaiting for 'em flames to get up, felt like.

"Man can't just go round doing whatever he wants." Hellmouth dropped, that metal spark flinting right close up to where 'em logs the Hound'd just put, lay. "Todd's gotta answer."

And just like that, the kiln tipped over, the coals spread, the rocks no longer charged with the duty of contain, that sound of muffled spurts that comes with high octane gouging middle of the road blood lines starting to harp on REACT as that skin went boa-constrictor tight, as 'em sounds muffled out in spurts of blipped cotton ball dives off the mount of don't-no-one-make-a-sudden-move-rope, that heavy load of not-hearing-what's-done-gone-on-and-got-said plowing crators of unease over head and neck, bumping that BEAT, BEAT, BEAT of rush for who's-gonna-act-first-and-how-will-the-other-recover-after-and-soon over Hellmouth as the Hound cracked knowledge on Breakneck Bottom Schols. That's what Hellmouth caught. Spilled words drum, drum, drumming over rushed pulse, over the Hound's spotting of Hellmouth family line. That watchful gathering of who and why and what the fuck nailgunning Hellmouth's trigger finger tight, that promise of shootout lingering END over both, all, and ever'thing, with one sudden squeeze.

"That so?" The Hound shifted, his eyes scanning the Pine and Poplar laden drop where Albie's hill tumbled into the belly of Hazard below, his snout SNIF...SNIF...SNIFFING the smoldering air, charring his barrel with something's just not right. Oh, they'd go at it, wouldn't they? Why, both of 'em full set filled up in Marie Curie buckets behind 'em chompers in the here and now of speak, understand. Already that ringing come to him, that syphoning through, locking and clogging 'em ear spouts, with only feelings left to say and what to do. That's what'd happen to the Hound always right 'fore that leash let off, 'fore that clank of chain ripped down and dropped, that hearing of his gone by the wayside. Which were why 'em hairs gone to stand and 'em goosey-bumps perked right up, that knowing of Hellmouth's claw clipped close coming to the Hound in underwater vibration zones, that twist of Hellmouth's hand over the wood forend of his rifle courting big blue whale charges, announcing action to come. Hold tight. Not.

Just.

Yet.

That drilling of BOOM shockwaving decide fast and decide soon right down the core of him, leaving only that clock's clicking hand to slow roll that plotted hole Hellmouth's head'd were gonna wear once that melon blew. And while that image went on and gave a little perk to that meat down below, it weren't something that'd grant a deep enough wound, so's the Hound decided against it.

"Gotta answer for something," Hellmouth said, "gotta pay for what he done."

"That might be," the Hound spit, "but ya likely ain't the one to give it today, there brother."

And so's the fire 'tween 'em grew. Sunk that gripping dirt of pins and needles that'll come when that shoe's finally 'bout to drop on over Hellmouth, sharpening his ear for that hint of blaze that'd come off the Hound's breach when the bullet born. He coulda turned then, coulda lifted up off that log and switched back and met the Hound. Splintered buckshot all through him maybe 'fore he's peppered but the thought of that window going unwatched and Albie Todd drawing breath for another day while he were dead, knowing that he coulda kilt that bastard if there weren't a turn, if he'da just stayed forward, minding his business, casing his mark, it were a raw enough deal that he didn't. Tarred him up real good that conviction did, made it so's even though that garrote of what the Hound'd do next were clamping his windpipe shut and his tongue were turning to sandpaper raw, that taste of iron already brushing the back of his teeth, he kept his chart forward, his breathing calm.

Should've pitched up closer when there were a chance, Hellmouth thought, cased it out better, spotted the man who he knew watched, but ain't much place left when rage is filling full pipe led. Need take it where the taking could get got. So's he sat half-accepting and half not the chances that shot gonna come 'fore the Hound tired of looking at the back of his head and just as the scale tipped and there seemed a shadow 'bout to cross that window's edge, a sudden-THUD-of-metal-DROPPED behind him as the slow slither of wood handles removed—rubbed against leather.

In the midst of what seemed forever Hellmouth turned. His gun's barrel battle-shipping to that Gawdawful crisis of fucked that were the Hound's face. But just as that blaster's snout were primed and ready, the Hound's hatchet fucking fighter jet cross swiped, caught metal, gripped down, and pushed off that bit of ole Daddy rifle. Hammerfisted Hellmouth's gun, arm, and hand straight down to hell. Throwed the world's axis off, changing the course of that would be shot. Nothing but bucking bits of crunched up dirt biting back at would be closers now for it'd be hand to hand ever after.

And just like a man who's seen a thing men ain't meant to view, i.e. that pound of broke down meat that were the Hound's face, Hellmouth went to double-time-hop-move-two, aiming for the rework, the charter back to get ground lost. Changing his weight, he looked for position, for angles, for some spot of gain, some way of get out and fight as 'em hatchets went to swinging all booby trap launch from hid up marks, from run-through-yard-don't-die-yet-stomps of Hellmouth boot, his feet grappling underneath, making that Gumby bend driving forward and reverse a tad shakey so's that the full spot of him one big drunken picture of over, snake, move, cross, duck, do. Came out from the BLAH. BLAH. BLAH. of the Hound's wooden handles and backend hatchet spikes sporting that tucked in tight body hold, that beware the boxer's tightrope line tide down the ring, with Hellmouth stepping, squat, go, while the Hound's flesh spreaders sliced, cut, countered, and blowed.

And thus, the gathering of the two in FREEZE-still-inpesctor-zone-view, forged by the cross body throw, switch grip, catch—glue of Hound blade to Hellmouth boot pulled knife. But the locked and loaded chambered hand loose near Hellmouth's face, the lucky lady dice, for the DECK. DECK. DECK. Right smack into Hound ear resulted in the fallback, hatchet arms down temporarily smart-man-move followed by the hidden-annie-mountain-blast-UP of elbow to throat delivery. But with that, oooohhhh, how the torment grew. The Hound u-turned from play-with-yar-food-fun to direct death overdrive slicing 'em big ole purrties straight for kill zone marks, kicking boot to Hellmouth chest, stepping over, then SHAVE. SHAVE. SHAVE a little off Connie-daddy edge as Hellmouth carried blade up and over Hound forearms. BLAP...BOOM...verdict SAYS...point to Hellmouth....hit stopped by Hound face, a ringer of Hellmouth palm shoved up and through to go-for-the-eyes-gouge.

BUT the Hound shook it off, tiger teeth tearing CONTACT instead to Hellmouth lower arm, bit-up, spit, spewed, a chunk of white landing on that cold spikey floor of country dirt below distress signaling out Hellmouth-yar-gonna-die-flares into the night, which course in turn shot down all chances of not being heard from 'em tenants in that house over yonder to big fat chicken egg 0. Now, not that/that were really that much of a concern anymore seeing as how the price of living surged right the fuck up to beat the Hound down 'fore Hellmouth ever meant to see a chance at end-Albie-game, which coincidentally sent the spiral meter of pissed the fuck off to right through the gawddamn roof resulting in what's more like described as a bad'n-meets-bad-gear-change-one-screw-loose where Hellmouth somehow kicked it up a notch, yanking the Hound close, shoving that pig skin towards eat-shit-boots and went on ahead and conveyed a air dropped via balled-up-fist-round-knife-handle-hard-fuck-ya to all of the Hound's vital organs with a wrist-to-elbow-to-chest-to-thigh BONG-STAB-BONG-MOVE, and for that shitpile-cherry-on-top-Sunday-finale a slammed head to head granite spark act.

And once it appeared maybe the Hound down for a three-count-begin-there-can-only-be-one-duel, Hellmouth legged it the fuck outta there. Jumped that loblolly and trained his ass right straight for lock-in-the-finish-Albie-door, his knife flipping as he went, that hand reaching out over top it, cuffing it against the palm, leveraging out CONTROL. CONTROL. CONTROL, shushing down that hurt football piling up on him from that HIT. HIT. HIT. He'd took off 'em wood handles, which unfortunate for him made that noticing of WHOOSH-WHOOSH-WHOOSH of metal turning behind as it topsy turvery'd divided I-don't-think-so-commands from out the Hound's hand. And quick as shit after potluck chili, a gusher anchored into Hellmouth rived leg, butter splitting muscle and bone at the seam, and sending Hellmouth barrel forward into unexpected dirt sandwich town, in a MAN-DOWN-the-ankle's-been-took.

And just so's we's all here on the same page, a layout of the scene—Hellmouth feeling right primed and pretty for a little revenge resolution'd milled his ass away from the pale-rider-death-dawg-team and almost managed a sign-me-up-clipboard-moment with Albie's front door, which were the whole point 'member, but like any dirty bastard hell bent, the Hound weren't the cowering type and even though he stunned still by some fancy knife footwork, he'd organized enough gump to crank that ax thirty feet forward to that running-man-murder-get-away and that there's right on point to where we need to be, hence—carrying shitbricks of how the fuck, the Hound went to'a cranking after that which shoulda already been done, as in eye-on-the-prize-crumpled-Hellmouth, all that nonsense of red river oozing out his neck and arm, a don't bother affair, a forget 'bout that alarm ringing and latch hold to that picture of Hellmouth climbing for a stand, falling, then going toil at it again. Always were a little glutton for some pain, weren't the Hound. Ergo, the ripped shirt, the tournequit made, the tower of survive and proceed propelling him forward with jerkey'd heart strands so mean, dictating moves automatic—Naw, ya couldn'ta stopped the Hound if Gawd were pushing and fate'a pulling, that'n there's veins were as rigid as Roman roads of last-forever-strong, of 1098 AD brassed on 21st century bones, the Hound wouldn't stop 'til the resurrected came back for the call and he weren't gonna pick up the phone 'til he's damn sure and ready!

And just like that, the gate let up, and the beast sent out, plowing full steam ahead all bug eyed ready for a fuck-shit-up-fiasco, the Hound got right close and comfortable with the makings of that stick in the goo situation, bashed his boot heel direct over top, sending that tip of used-to-be-'Doc-Hodge-biters all the way through to cold crunch ground, staking Hellmouth there as they lived and breathed, then clopped forward in one big mountain lion hop so's both feet landing either side of Hellmouth ears and drove his talons in a SNATCH down Hellmouth gullet and went for the pull, yanking Hellmouth tongue clear the fuck out with 'em not-today-sir-crushers. Left that man looking Mississippi red and Colorado boulder blue from the shock of it all. It were a grunting and struggling and a fight-to-the-death-ward-the-other-off-in-whatever-way-ya-can, with Hellmouth still splitting BAP. BAP. BAP. in the air behind, up, and round him as the Hound went 'bout the quarter and the disembark, 'em hatchets too fast and furious for Hellmouth reach.

See, for ever' swipe Hellmouth took into ghost night air, he found another opening left on him, another spot of bleed out making it's way underneath, turning his innards into outards quicker than he could manage a goal of stuff back in and even though he caught the bastard behind the knee and in the thigh, it weren't gonna be near damn enough. No-sir, this here were the GRAND grapple fair, the tote-yar-youngins-mom-dad-aunt-uncle-cousins-second-third-fourth-and-fifth all in the damn car and make a day of it 'cause we gonna pinch ever' single bit out of this here viewing by GAWD, which were the reason for the Hound jumping and yanking all to high heaven on top of Hellmouth, squashed him into the ground like a set of wild hogs that ain't been fed for years, all of it just a big ole gnawing mess. And seemed to be there wouldn't a come no stopping to it neither. Mean, the Hound were in it for the long fucking haul. Mean, mince 'em bones, ya know, break it all down. And sure as shit woulda maintained the fervor if there weren't that scent coming on him from somewheres, that little bit of SNIFF-distraction drifting in from naw-that-don't-seem-just-right-over-yonder-smell, which will STOP a man sure-fire-true right where he stands, tricky part of it though were hardly ever does that translate to the CLICK. CLACK. BOOM. of a shotgun's snout from a direction undiscovered and unknown.

PART II

Which brings us now to the particularly measured placement of the Visitor, crouched as he were behind a Bottlebrush Buckeye only ten feet away for the majority of the fight.

Now for those not privy to what a Bottlebrush Buckeye portends, let's lay down a little snapshot. A Buckeye's a bush and it'll get up there. Lounge out on a spot like a fat ole sunbather. Grow as far and wide as it allowed, and if there ain't no tending to it, that gawddamn thing'll reach up twelve feet tall, 'em bushy-spirals-of-white-peacock-fanning-in-bunny-rabbit-tails-all-cathedral-point towards 'em Heavens. But that's prime-time summer now, and it ain't that. We's dead set in middle of winter with snow threatening fall and witch's-titty-raw-clipping-skin-froze and that Bottlebrush Buckeye looked to be more like a skeleton fence, with browned wiry twiggs standing up man's size tall all whirly like, and were it not for a Virginia Pine begging question on why it'd not shown Christmas tree bright in Albie's living room, the Visitor'd probably done been spotted by now. But as it were, he'd not.

How the Visitor came to stand the other side that Bottlebrush Buckeye with a Virginia Pine playing backup and his dead daddy's shotgun logged over his forearm, all started with a visitor hisself. 'Bout a month back. A one Gary Noah Lynn, and if court charged that same Gary Lynn who attended disorder with 'em Brighton boys down below.

Now, that Gary'd climbed up into 'em hills on a-needle-in-the-hay-sack-search for a man rumored to be dead and that rumor done kicked under dirt for some fifteen odd years and he weren't going on much more than an Old Timer's whisper that meat-hooked a name to his chest and that there a fair amount of skeptical consideration to the notion that once arrived Gary might actually get granted audience and convince this man, who'd held private consul for thirty years—in the woods—by hisself, were a little more than a traditional leap of faith. Might be better suited under the heading, Covenant, in fact, with a side bet on Gary's middle name tethering the entire damn affair together.

Needless to state, it'd not gone as intended when the parties met. Not at all. See, Enoch Murray, the man Gary were clipping dirt for, wanted no part in bearing FOUND anywhere close to his name. Fact, he'd done just 'bout ever'thing he could not to. Tracked up in 'em hills further than any bastard round. Four damn days to go finding him, what it'd take a man, and that were with a compass and a scout. Never mind if a fool could even get close up enough to go tripping all 'em traps Enoch'd set up. Ten ways outta ten to go dying near Enoch's shack and if a man made it past that he'd have to face Enoch hisself and that were a whole other issue weren't it.

Well not for nothing, Gary'd done it. Pinched hisself in a situation more than twice but weaved past all 'em bear clamps, jumped over ever' pit covered in leaves, found ever' rope and snare and deadfall and mesh Enoch hid. Took a whole fucking week with two hours held just on watch whenever Gary cleared and came to a new plot of land. And there for the greet when he'd finally spotted wood wall, a small shack that looked worse for the wear but stood up fine and well due to the damn thing existing built off a limestone palisade, Enoch stood, some four inches short from six feet. His head woulda met Gary's tit if either of 'em'd got close enough for the initial greet, which they didn't, course. 'Bout like the size up of two animals met in the wild, where one'd face down more than the other, and there were a helluva pot of suspicion on brew, that caldron blistering WHY and FUCK YA HERE out.

See, Enoch'd faced down a black bear few years back and the event'd robbed his left eye from him and caused a permanent crater ridge down his cheek from where the juice'd let out, so to say he were in ANY WAY wanting companionship of, well, anything WERE fucking wrong. That dusty ass motherfucker picked up a rock 'bout the size of a baby apple and hurled it right center Gary's face 'fore Gary could get out the way. Knocked him out right there where he stood. And Enoch perhaps spending a spell too long up in 'em hollers went to casing his prey back and forth, justa panting there in a line, all fur-trapped-clothing-wild-eye'd-hoof-marked-man.

Made plan on agree to something, though. Couldn't a worked out no way other 'cause Enoch'd spent the last two days slogging down that spongy forest floor after something. Same reason suppose he were standing where he were now behind that Bottlebrush Buckeye come way of a Virginia Pine and certainly the same reason he'd surveyed and participated in, as in he'd not stopped the terrible acts, in the slaying of six separate men. Six men who'd he'd never met but who'd all fit snug like in the recesses of his mind with all 'em other Unionizers, as in he one of 'em and 'em sum parts of he, that scar of the last man culled by the Hound already etched so far down in him it were round up by his tail bone now.

Oh indeed, how that poison oak'd shown polky dot red when the sun'd full grown, how the Hound'd left his post between 'em poplar one by one and yanked the men from their yards and porches and some even beds, right out from slumber, and dragged 'em all back to the oak and dismantled 'em, butchered 'em in quarters, ripping hearts from meaty red cages, folding 'em up in small hankies so's that the white cloth granted sanquine spot from where the pump'd gone to clear, how after ever' hatchet whack that'd split flesh logs onto that ground Enoch shared with the beast, the Hound'd wiped his blade, like reverence bowed only in the glorious marking of CLEAN, and even after each one razed, the ceremony not done 'til the Hound'd placed a piece of white paper in his mouth and chewed, the next man only collected after the gulped swallow cleared, this continual loop touting capable, as in what the Hound could and would do, as in ANYTHING, scored into Enoch's very spine as he stood watching the Hound and Hellmouth go at it with their grievances behind that Bottlebrush Buckeye.

Ah yes, the hunter come after the Hound, it appeared.

All the bells and whistles of righteous ruin just come the other side a Bottlebrush Buckeye. And what of the man who'd lugged chart on it? What of this Enoch who'd acted not when fellas much like hisself granted front-of-the-line-greet-to-hatchet-city-mad-man-show, what of his part and plan? Why, the subtelty to which his hand fitted over the butt of his daddy's shotgun'd enact a route not unlike the two spied upon, and not unlike those two busy dismantling the confusion of when will death actually arrive, Enoch too accorded compunction, for were it not his very same thought. The stock pitched into his shoulder woulda gifted special rise of end-this-all-here-and-now wouldn't it've, seeing as how the gun bore the acquaintance of four men who used to could, now cold, dead, and gone.

Ah, yes, why indeed would Enoch, a man who claimed allegiance with the Union, who'd perhaps bled the color from birth and without choice and therefore never claimed thought on it all, for is that not the passage of most and all men, bestowed-believed-bereaved-then-die, who'd waited for thirty years far enough up in 'em hills for most to forget the burden of his name, 'cept a solitary few, that revelation perhaps affecting Enoch the most, how it'd took the uncovering of a crate long shuffled away in a dark corner, the many years of soot slowly peeling off the letters of who he once were one coat at a time as he opened up and peered into that passed down relic which'd finally ignited that pitiless monster of gutted sorrow, how it were only after living with that open crate staring him down, carving remember on ever' splotch of skin on his frame, did the chaos begin to bleed out from order.

This Enoch, who'd held private consul for thirty years up in 'em hills not a "stone's throw away" according to mountain talk, from the Hound, never did traverse the ten miles over to his neighbor and gain retribution, 'cause that were the only visit ever paid to the Hound, most never living beyond first-foot-on-property-plant, rightly due to the anger burrowed inside him never organized enough to lay blame. In that, his seclusion both his damnation and salvation at the same time and yet there came a calling on him that month ago, Gary Noah Lynn with CHANGE fitted round his neck, the time finally coming forth for all things righted wrong and what a wondrous showing did Enoch have in store.

Ergo Enoch proceeded to go ahead and put some powder out there in the game. Had enough marbling 'em rough'iens play 'bout, ya see. Places he needed be up in soon. And he'd made it all the way cross that foot bridge of steeps with intentions paved in gold standard. Weren't gonna come another chance. The proclamation done give down. And considering he'd spent his day watching that meaner of the two butchering folks that weren't doing nothing but trying to live their lives, WEEEEELLLLLLLL, it didn't sit right with him did it, so's when he see'd the Hound mule-a-jerking that other, he went on and lever-action-pulled that shotgun. Sighted it straight out and through the Hound's shank. Aimed it right for that thick vein that'd loosen up the dam in the thigh. A bleed out for sure.

But by GAWD, what he'd not counted on were that fucking bullet going clean in and shitting right out. Not factored it in at all. And seemed the only way Enoch were gonna be able to go 'bout the rest of his business were if he stopped the Hound from freight-training direct for him in the yeller-line-next-stop-Enoch-death-by-Hound-station. Which hokey pokey'd out just like this.

Full wolf sprint ahead, the Hound stormed the field, clipping Indian burial mound clumps of dirt behind him, shooting desperado rock bodies into the night, that muzzle of his huffing smoke signals of pain into the early morn air, those hacking hatchets just a going after glory, all thumb-spinning handles and blades forcing up with diagonal slashes, all blood-man's-modern-marvel-of-how-the-fuck-he's-still-turning-gears-after-all-'em-gashes-got-got 'til finally contact happened—SKIN IN THE GAME.

And here we have an uptick—SURGE of things, where Enoch just as fast bit by bit met 'em hatchets with shotgun handle HIT, with cross, defend, cross, 'em blades pricking nicks on top that burdened metal three fold at a time, with the Hound curving spikes over Enoch's head, once, twice, catching jutted wood shotgun butt instead. His hand switching the hold, the hew, the huck, the pull, the clip it by Enoch's ear, carry it over, swipe-face go, catching the hunter by blood in the eye gusher surprise. WHERE, that guttural knowing of live-remain-here-die, traveling off the mount Jesus crucifixion fast to end of Enoch's hand it's time for a blast, he, this man battered blocks off Hound's flesh, the hack, hack, hack of fitted cleavers missing land.

From down to up to punch to back, the Hound worked against Enoch's defend, his arms pummeling hatchet handle punches to uppercut chin, shoulder wrapping snakey eights round, shoving up then pulling down, delivering target cuts and big daddy bastard blows, running death-activity-collect all along basic motor skill mode. With Enoch crushing shoulder to Hound hunched-down-and-buried-into-body-head, the reciprocation, a swipe of Enoch planted leg, with one over the other, with Hound arms barging full peril dread as his fingers went midnight rider searching for eyeball sockets instead, for rip-the- face-clear-the-fuck-off, end it all now, be done with it, let him lay there dead, he rounded out hatchet tip for temple dip, spreading blades mighty high and right overhead, he juddered POW. POW. POW. 'til tendon turned to slush, 'til Enoch vacant eyehole caved into mush, and when that last hooray look to be'a hollering NEAR, when that cut him down moment'd done landed and come clear with the Hound pinning Enoch and Enoch bear clawing up the front of him and down the rear, with a looksee to where his gun knocked then slipped then booted free, Enoch wrestled up and caught the Hound's mighty hatchet swing, his hand making prayer book calls just above his chest, then knee'd up, dick-crushed-lift, punted Hound off, overset, grabbed hatchet spike end, flipped handle, sundered down for dead-Hound-dawg-dead.

50

1988

MOTHERFUCKED OR RONNIE AND WILLARD'S COME TO JESUS OR A REDNECK TWO-STEP WITH 40 ANGRY DICKS READY TO SWING

Monkey-wrenched-booze dick-jerked the high school drum line awake that'd clogged assembly in my noggin with a bad version of "Under Pressure." A cadence left over and imprinted from the reign supreme of SHUT DOWN that'd steam rolled spikes on the lawn of me the night 'fore. That reel going full speed ahead at ninety miles an hour with no stop in sight. Fucker on repeat the whole beating. Straight out a boom box the size of a fucking fat-fed-coon, where that ear cannon first fired. Hauled up and fastened by bungee cords anchored round two nails that were just fucking drove so many times through that interior wood paneling that old trailers always got for whatever fucking reason that the damned nails'd loosened up at least a couple centimeters on either side so's that there were a threat to fall ever' time that kick drum hit and Bowie chimed in.

Apparently somewheres or another there existed an interior designer that equated taste for the poor to be chic-shit-brown-wood-paneling, and not 'em long square blocks like they got up in 'em fancy library homes but terse stacked slats were what we's talking on here and frankly that person ought to be shot for the amount of fucking ugly brown that plagued the less fortunate with early coffin walk-throughs. But besides that point, better back-track on to that falling stereo and the hope that Gawd woulda took to its smiting down 'cause turned out, I liked getting the shit kicked outta me less and less as the years'd stacked up.

But, alas Gawd were busy, the manning of the ship naked as a jaybird. Only thing left were the assholes and cocksuckers living and breathing, some barely if current affairs accurate, in a cold-e-sac in the middle of Highland Terrace under the watchful eye of white-hair-Roy-Batty-looking-motherfuckers that all ended their name with Mason.

And by Gawd, 'em cocksuckers kept tempo, didn't they? Etched that fucking song under the skin with ever' welt formed. And I'll tell ya this right here, Freddie Mercury might be DIVINE to some but after a while, think even he checked out. Got his shit and went on to find what ever' hungry mouth he were gonna double dip Rhapsody in and let that B-team go on and step up. Mean, after the fourth encore, it's all a count of closed eyes swaying, ain't it? Don't really matter what version of "Under Pressure" tremored out after that just as long as

DA-DA-DA DAdAdA DON DON DA-DA DadAdA KISH

...in tow.

And what a sadistic set of ramrodding zit-stains were left once Main-Man-Mercury-and-the-band gone. Justa bunch of tired leftovers and wannabes heaving beat next, clunking Krispy Kreme glaze where cock-hard-gold'd stood. Fucking clawed up from the dirt hangover aftershocks of getting beat to shit blues. True fucking bastards. Mean, ain't nothing worse than a truly NOT earned headache, ya know, as in pound after pound after pound not counted in drunk beers but by blows absorbed. Fucking defectors from the holy shrine of just-get-it-together-and-hit-the-day-sweat, as in run out the Under-Pressure-head-beats. Oh but can't do that with these, not this hidden hoe-hoe-moonpie-crowd, this poor man's substitute, this betrayal of Mr. Mercury's hard work in keeping the band together one high pitched kick at a time. These not earned head thumps can't get drowned out. Nah, this set seemed clipped special from the memory's backlog, edited just right so's 'em late cymbal clinks the reverberations of BEAT DOWN, of ghosts' drums

DA-DA-DA DAdAdAING

...on the sidelines deflecting the necessity to move.

Or so it seemed. Seemed, ain't that the operative word. Seemed to me, there weren't no real break from then to now jangling in 'tween 'em ears of mine, as in the fakers damn near synonymous with the real thing like I's getting a lesson in PTS from a fucking headache and a song that weren't really playing but ghost prancing inside the ooey-gooey padding of my head, and all of it asshole enough to go on and block me from getting the fuck up and out of the shithole situation I'd climbed in. But there were only so long it could last, right? Mean sooner or later, the head's gotta figure out 'em silly-puddying punches it still believes it's getting ain't happening.

Mean, this B-rate gaggle of fuckwads blindly drum dolling beats can't last, ya know. Gotta fucking will to power that shit away. But I'll tell ya this right here, head'll go to sparking all kinds of crazy misfirings now, 'specially if it meat cleaved over and over again. And better still, getting yar temples smashed'll go ahead and unlock a whole slew of other grievances one'd not known they'd got. That endless crank of

DA-DA-DA DAdAdA DON DON DA-DA DadAdA KISH

...echoing inside, never meeting up with the fucking Under Pressure part just amplified that purgatory prelude now didn't it. Just beat the fuck down, just praying perhaps some kind soul'd "Push Play" and ignite the fucking chorus, bring Mercury back to center stage for the final sendoff so's we could all get up and move on with our fucking lives.

But that just ain't like to happen, were it? Better chance of that reject high school drum line comingling with that iron-pump-crowd dick jocking the field. Not like to mix up, 'em two. Not in 'em halls or locker rooms or Friday night after parties. Wouldn't know a thing 'bout that if it jumped up and bit 'em drummers in the ass. Oh, they'd dream on it, wouldn't they. Corn maze cocks round elbows to get a peak of how the other lived. Cut S's from the top of driveways and bushes to neighborhood backyards just to see the highlights of Jenny Maller (not her real name, cause ain't none of this happening nowhere 'cept in my head) get double dog dared to show her cuss to a crowd after they'd fed her enough hunch-punch that girl's belly'd not knowed what up from down ('cause ain't a girl round that's gonna turn down a purple drink with gummy bears floating in it out a cooler...whole thing just airs too close to exotic, and ain't that what ever' high school girl aims high and bright for, EXOTIC, AS-IN-NOT-FROM-ROUND-HERE-NEED-TO-HAVE-SPECIAL) but sure as shit that hooch'd enlivened the love she held in her heart with ever' minute of 'em boys wanting knowledge of the look of her slant. That were for damn TRUE.

All that drum line ever wanted were a girl to drop-trou and let 'em dear dive on her. But it just ain't like to happen were it, least not with the girl they wanted. Probably'd have to settle for Jenny Maller's cousin Tammy who were a slut in a half in the first place and a good, I mean, goooood country fed hundred pounds heavier. She'd let 'em dive now, but she'd also let yar brother, daddy, and uncle dive too so's the demand ain't all that high, if there's meaning to impart.

Wait, hold yar horses there folks, something happened a second ago that needs a little reverse 'bout...believe a WILL TO POWER mentioned somewheres, as in butt-fuck-the-game-up-change-the-course scenarios, as in that other side's breaking in, fuck-blasting-Heeman-take-over-the-world-pleas from through a hole in the trailer wall, and they's igniting a "clear the gawddamn field fuckers" anthem to 'em band geeks, as in we's 'bout to get MOVING here.

Now, that the squadron of fighter jets flying over came in the form of "Eye of the Tiger" speaker-barreling napalm bombs all over the cold-e-sac of Highland Terrace shoulda ignited a fire under both Willard and mine's ass. Lawd knows it'd riled up ever' white hair with a cut off t-shirt from their roost right quick. But unfortunate as timing'd have it, it did not in the slightest do nothing for comatose Daddy out cold next to me. Fact, if anything it just kick started the best gawddamn gun's-blaring-bare-knuckle-brawl-ready-to-fucking-drop-kick-the-shit-outta-fake-Freddie-Mercury's-b-team-brigade-DREAM a motherfucker could have, but to state the call to arms a little slow to go for that action to actually get kicked up'd be putting it light. And to state that sat well at all for me, considering the only reason to go fucking cock-trumpeting—

DUN
DUN DUN DUN
DUN DUN DUN
DUN DUN
DUuuuuuN

...probably meant we's both 'bout to face Part II of beat down city, 'em bastards out there's just getting a nice good stretch in 'fore they come storm the grounds and gather up the prisoners i.e. us, and I don't know 'bout y'all, but I'd long outlived fairy tales by this time in my life and that right there were just 'bout the biggest fucking tall tale living since Paul Bunyan and Blue Babe i.e. weren't no time for a-catch-some-z's-snooze. Not with the firing squad spraying—

DUN
DUN DUN DUN
DUN DUN DUN
DUN DUN
DUuuuuN.

Fuck, even I felt the bulge tighten when that first line kicked out all smooth and shit 'spite my broke down body of a man near beat to death laying fucking useless on the floor. Oh 'em fucktards'd Snake Plissken seized the "quartz stone peel-and-stick vinyl flooring" of the trailer bathroom in Bloodsport gore, ripping pounds of flesh from Willard and me and arrow-spearing 'em in tiny horror shows all over the grime of carnage-clopped-gew the night 'fore. (Remember. Mercury. "Under Pressure.") Poor health'd put it light, what we were. Both of us. Took to us with kicks and stomps and belts and buckles and welted-angry-at-the world-mean for don't-know-reason-why-but-'CAUSE-hurt. Dixie Dukes'd rained grapefruit hail on both of us, no tarp in site. 'Em boys'd only settled 'em slugs 'cause a cooler that'd held two cases of Bud heavy'd gone empty in the rush. Just stopped what they were doing right then and there, right in the middle of Mercury's little bedside melody and peddled their grievances elsewhere.

Point being, beat to shit really can't be emphasized enough, and when my own puffed portholes slitted open as the velveteen gush of Dave Bickler cock-grabbed the sun and beat it to a pulp with that second phrase 'bout faces and heat—the injection of junkie adrenaline to my veins forged a cesspool of recognition. And as the light adjusted, and the smell of soldered iron rose and settled from the marshland of hair and blood speckled 'bout, a weight'd formed on me. And there, while my chest heaved from all the factors mentioned, the resemblance of the face across from me roused my own garrison of meatheads. The sort that didn't truly care for the peak of Willard Tell's nose, how high it marked his face, how the eyes, when they weren't swole probably drooped some on the sides, the extra fold of skin cape-like, how behind that fat lip of his, the mouth probably etched down. Nah, the meatheads burrowed deep down and within did not take kindly to these images at all as that fucking banger of a chorus tigered outta that Survivor song

Now, bonding's found easier places for a man and his son to happen but throw 'em both in a meat grinder and there's gonna be a spell of kinship to follow regardless of the years separated. Or so it thought. BUT…AND THAT'S A BIG BUT, mired as we were, the two of us, all dishrag discarded on that fucking floor, all hangman's gonna come soon positioning, there couldn't be no denial no longer, that wall of sour'd done gone on and broke off in me, that gut-rot of Willard spilling wrong all along my innards, staring down that ugly fucking mug, that face that'd belong to me in twenty years only put kindling to the pit. So's I did what any Red, White, and Blue American'd do, I whipped back and socked that motherfucker right in the nose like he'd name me Sue.

PART II

That Willard's rousing came simultaneously with a meaty press-up of 300 on the bench were a fucking Gawdsend 'cause were it not for that iron-crowd's rough and riled squawks just outside 'em paper thin trailer walls, that pep-rally of squealed calling after some good ole boy named Cody made country-flesh-fed-big by a heaping of beat taters, chops, peas, and biscuits ever'day since the sprouting age of ten, where it were dutifully noted by a high up Mason that, "this'n here's gonna stand chance at real muscle," hence the crafting of front porch gym takeover with cock-hard Survivor swinging leather tight dicks on a morning get-big pump, paired with Cody and his goon squad sounding like a bunch of hyena's circling prey as they shrieked out demands like, "metal to tits, Code," and "don't ya dare fucking buck, boy," as if lending know how to something their own body's could never know, that scrawling of AUTHORITY something of an inferred title by 'em shouts only, and were it not, it should come repeated, for that constant loop of…

DUN
DUN DUN DUN
DUN DUN DUN
DUN DUN
DUuuuuuuN

…Willard's re-entry to this world from cold death to fire hot mean after I'd firecracker'd that snout of his into a leaky faucet of red, they mighta, all 'em Masons round, heard the leather-crack-whip of "WHAT THE FUCK," come fastball hurling outta Willard's lips.

And yet, they'd not. Not even when Willard's forearm spread barbs over my ear, the deafening slug fitted with a silencer that pole-vaulted outta the dusty dank tub like a ninja hammering bone apart. Kinda arm that'd grazed devil showdown more in its lifetime than it'd care to talk on and the kind that either couldn't care or plain fucking didn't that it kin meat at the other end of 'em thrashings. Fucking slaughterhouse dived on me, rolled out the tub in one big mass of not-quite-working-yet-but-still-could-go-on-and-lay-it-down-old-man-tank-big and pinned his elbow in the nook right under my chin, locking in with that other titan forearm, and went on and SQUEEZED the turkey neck out of me like he's 'bout to fucking go to plucking Thanksgiving feast. Just plain pressed down on me so hard there weren't no where for my mitts to go 'cept right claw-mark-grip on 'em fucking Popeye cans. Landed 'tween a rock and a hard place with only seconds left 'fore that sleeper took hold.

Willard countered, razor bladed, "Gawddamnit boy," from his mouth. The falling drip laying bare his wishes of "quit now" over my skin

Needed to shutdown the pump driving red to his pythons, stop the flow to down the beast. All started with pivoting 'em hips, drop the knees, pull back the arm, get some leverage on him, then roll. Keep him on his side though, can't go flying 'bout overtop him, gotta stay grounded. Needed planted roots in my back leg, throw over the other, lock some lumber right on his jawline, then latch and skin-saw that motherfucker 'til he yelled Uncle. Problem with that dog though, it's gotta come full commit to that race in order to catch the rabbit and just as I began the set 'fore that gun blew DING, Willard hustled quick with it, switched grips, hasped his talons just under my elbow, yanking my arm up and close to that hard belly, and kept that other paw sowed right under my ear, right so's that when he lifted 'em hips, FUCK OFF'D come quick. Deflated the air right out of me. Placed bone crushers on my ribs. Shocked ice streams of DON'T MOVE all over me.

Now, I'd shouldered lots of shit kicks in my life and wouldn'ta knowed fair in any of 'em but if pushed come to shove, probably only count three cheap shots in all. Deserving at the time, I might add, to ever' single bastard who'd received 'em. Fourth weren't gonna grant no different, suppose.

See, apparently in the fuss of throwing weight round over top his son, a bit of a conscious clamped over Willard and suppose there were a little come to Jesus 'bout how all this actually set and Willard there, feeling perhaps moved by the Holy Ghost, or the ancestors past, or what ever the fuck might dissuade a man from continuing to kick the shit out of the son he abandoned 'fore that boy could even talk, went on to slack up. And in that loosening, 'tween 'em big ole run-down-horse-breaths he were panting out, Willard went on and waved surrender with, "Boy, let up now."

And with that his fingers broke their braid.

"Gonna let go now, boy."

Boy raked gravel over me. Ownership sounding in a way that cracked ill inside my bones but the wind began filling the tank again, 'em crawlers retreating from the front lines 'til they's finally gone and that BOY part not so loud.

"On three…"

He landed chair back to the tub with the roll-off, his legs straight out in front of him with me curled up just left his feet getting reacquainted with my neck. That and figuring out how I's gonna leave my mark on him. Didn't do hisself no favors when he asked, "She dead?"

His knee pitched up when I didn't answer. Suppose he felt the gut needed protecting or maybe it'd weighed just like it intended. "Only reason to meet. Sent ya here even after she's gone, huh. That 'bout right."

I nodded. Couldn't go to talk on her. Not to him. Not without that ball growing fat in my neck.

"Gawddamnit. How?"

Might as well've asked why. Just as impractical as the How in this case. "Heart…" cleared my throat, "heart give out."

"Big one of those, that woman. Didn't like to show it much. But in my time of knowing her, all I saw."

"Ya's shit at acknowledging it."

Willard were silent.

"She coulda used you. Coulda had good use for a man round."

Weren't nothing he could say, suppose. Mommy's dying wish, a fucking forced trudge through shit. Hated him for knowing her so well even though he'd been missing in action for thirty fucking years, for knowing immediate why I'd come, that she'd sent me, that it the only thing she fucking asked of me in her will, that she even wrote a fucking will that included his name, that she'd scribbled with her own hands in broken cursive: Willard Tell's yar daddy. Find him. That any of this, this bullshit, this sitting 'cross from a man who left her, who didn't even have the decency to write, checkup, see on her. And that fucking blood just went to boil on me, just fucking step-ball-changed the mood, just grilled me hot, made it so's all I saw where red.

Weren't nothing to do but what I did. Fucking three-point finger planted in that shitty bathroom floor and power drove through that motherfucker. Took the one-piece-shower-tub-snap-in-modern-component with us, just fucking dropped the shoulder and knocked the shower, Willard, and me right through the goddamn wall of that rotting trailer.

PART III

The redneck two-step with forty angry dicks swinging took the main stage to headline the show just as Willard, the bath, and I crashed ass to grass in the middle of the cold-e-sac, in the maze of Highland Terrace, while Survivor's tenth loop of repeat were just wrapping up and weren't a Mason round who didn't drop weight to take note of the crash-pad-landing.

Cody's spotter slipped digits on the bar, the fifteen or so standing 'bout dropped dumbbells were they stood road-side-traffic-jamming the brawn-built-white-haired-freak-show, three toddlers that were air pumping to their daddy's tunes slapped down their arms, the cries from not knowing what-the-fuck ruffling the feathers of momma-bears to come out on make-shift-porches, four old timers cracking jokes over morning-Joes let coffee mugs slip, the brown sludge watering weeds at their feet, causing the four dogs napping in the morning sun to go ahead and clap out hounds-of-hell barks, which started the alarm of ever' gun willing and ready to get pulled from truck racks, closet doors, bedside perches, side harnesses, weight bench hiding places, and under trailer sequestering to come forth in full bloom like this the gawd-damn standoff at the Alamo, and all of it waking the grand honcho of Gerald Mason to come angry-mean-giant stomping from out his lair and cold-war-pull a rifle and aim it at Willard and me, declaring the Red Scare back on. All it took were two fingers held up from his sun-drenched-butcher hands to file the troops in appropriate rank.

And what pray tell does a man do in such situations when he's staring down the breech of a thing like that and that thing backed by forty angry dicks ripping and ready, just after Willard's whispered to him 'bout a shotgun buried on the backside of the property, though it ain't doing one bit of gawddamn good currently, but since the sole trajectory of this entire mission according to Willard, a one Mr. Gerald Mason, who currently crushed gravel under his work boots not three feet from our heads, were in fact present—well SMILE, of course. Willard certainly were as he blood gargled, "sure do appreciate the expedient audience, sir."

PART IV:

MAW:

1990

"Ya wanna know Nanny's favorite story, Mick? One she used to tell me when ya'd go to teething and cry yarself to sleep, waking me up in the process. Just being an altogether nuisance to the household. She used to pick me up, take me downstairs, set me there next to Papaws boots, that shine jug of his getting eyed full view the entire time, couldn't trust the damn thang, and she'd tell me of Nov. 4th, 1930, 'bout a boy, left fatherless, who mighta held fear in his heart but he'd a gallon of blood in his eyes. Nanny'd go—

"See, Ronnie, she'd say, back up round his molars, the soldier's tongue knife picked a lower case x. A tick that befitted the entire legacy of Joab men. In particular those lodged in Munfordvilles. Seemed a wicked set of cuspids haunted that legacy with a fierceness and where it not for the feverish tracing of the Joab men's tongues over and over again behind 'em sharp canine teeth, that tongue'd face the unfortunate lockup of CUT, as 'em fangs destined with a mind of their own. Evidence'd shown wearily in their mouths for as long as most the Joab's could recall and war weren't no 'ception. Flared up in the Battle of Green River in 1863, and the War of 1812, and of course the Revolution in 1775, where Ebner Joab, being pillar and point in the Boston Colony, proved integral in orchestrating The Suffolk Resolve, which'd parlayed favor on the family's name 'spite the hushed whispers of madness swirling 'bout, mad kooks 'em Joabs, and that cavernous gap where 'em cuspids donned OWN, admitted a most frenetic environ. One riddled more ichor existence than pink gummed flesh so's that during the battlefield march each Joab men toted a jaw full of dark red along with their armament. That this Abner Joab, the one currently transfixed with the outline of lower-case x's as he marched beside wooden wheels, were not made aware of the family tradition perhaps the worst horror of 'em all, for how could a man truly know hisself if he ain't never knowed of his families beginnings."

"She'd go on like that, that ole muffler rattling out hot breath over me and me not giving a damn 'cause she coulda told me her grocery list and I woulda took a seat just to hears it. Captivating ole gal, Nanny were—

"Such were the situation then, Ronnie, she'd say, that entombed need to mark the world in accordance with the Joab family tick, that a Joab transposed lower case x's into that very same set of wooden wheels that lugged in front of Abner now, claiming divine edict ever after and for always that wherever they landed, it exactly where they's meant to be. Can't hardly buy that sorta publicity, Ronnie, least not one with a story like that and not with a journey that'd tracked just as much territory as the Queen and Crescent cross the state and that were just in the two years since their carving on 'em wheels, let alone all 'em miles marked when Davis Mining Brothers'd procured it in 1930. Hell by then, could come argued there weren't a town in the southeast of the state that hadn't worn 'em x's. Least not no place on the border and surely not no place carrying black gold in they's hills. 'Em x's'd gone straight for those when Company took hold.

"Ronnie, she'd say, don't never go underestimating the want of a man to stain the world, now, it'll fang ya ever' time.

"Suppose it weren't no wonder then, they'd rounded out and cut up tracks in Hazard. Started all the way back at Lovern Street. Back up yonder by that courthouse. Up on the north end, like they come up from Main then settled on hold for a spell by 'em courthouse steps and musta prospected a change of course called for. Reckon, they followed that trail of blood that'd leaked outta Mr. Davis when he were still warm 'til they found that stuck corpse dead as a doornail and more than not that the impetus for the reroute on over to High Street. Specially, come to find out, Mr. Davis the one orchestrating the whole damn affair, behind closed doors of course. Bit of an obligation floating to see the damn ordeal through, understand, Ronnie.

"And 'em x's didn't come just by 'emselves now—shit no. They carried a gawddamn brigade with 'em. Any tracker worth a damn woulda jumped ship right then with how many stunk spoors were pockmarked round and out. And if that weren't the spear poking yar ass down the plank, the fucking scars smearing HEAVY, as in whatever it were getting carried, well that's exactly what it fucking were, HEAVY, round that trolley of footprints sidelining 'em lower case x's spoke to the notion that it probably very well should get considered that this ain't the train to come calling on. Fact, if anything, Ronnie, could come derived from such an affair, suppose it were that the calvacade'd arrived and it were steamrolling straight for a shit storm.

"But never mind ya that, 'cause there's a boy aiming FOUND down his dead daddy's gun on top a roof in the middle of Main that wouldn't knowed stop unless bullets buried. This the good part, Mick. Oh Enoch'd plan alright, rooted down in that spare room holed up inside him where his daddy used to fit. A sign neon blaring lost, as in that's more how he felt than anything else, over that room's door. Well, lost and alone. Likely couldn't come no better motivators in the world now, least not something a boy could hold onto for all that long. But a dead daddy, that'll go to rubber-cementing for life, and if a boy's not careful to peel back on some of that WRONG and let it go, there's a road of hardship up ahead that'd settle ill on ever'thing it touches.

"Now, the best anybody'd could gather, 'cause there weren't all that many that'd survived the ordeal, Enoch couldn'ta heard 'em wheels getting pulled down High street. Just no way 'bout it. Mean, Mick, had Enoch or any of 'em others known 'em x's were coming, that a proper hollered HELLO butted out 'em wheels, well, the day woulda probably resolved itself in a much more hurried manner. But as it were, it'd not. No—that wood made silent death speed, muffled and wrapped in all 'em throats already slit on the ground below like it playing home-field advantage. And I'll tell ya this right here, Mick, don't matter how much dying a boy's ears get exposed to, that sounds like to enter through different doors ever' single time. Mean, 'fore any of this, 'fore Randi's store, and his daddy's slaughter, and 'fore Cecil 'Doc' Hodge and 'em crazy Irish men down below spilled blood, Enoch'd thought all dying sounded like hogs in their letting, with squeals and gasps, but this'd shown cries the day 'fore and hushed splurts the day after, that lost land of "why" and "don't" banging deaf. Fact, once all said and done, death just sounded like limbs dropping in a storm, Ronnie, she'd say. That strike falling KNOCK against a window pane, like that broke-off piece of wood just not right strong enough to stand hold against nature's fury.

"But ain't no use to go focusing on that too long, 'cause Abner Joab and 'em lowercase x's'd just pulled round the corner of Sterling's Hardware. Right there, not but a block down, Mick. Mean, were it not for Hazard getting quick with it 'bout that bit of hubris they's trudging 'bout, 'em x's mighta made it just that hair further down that they'd wanted too, but 'em pot holes'd a different yearning. See, craters plagued all of High Street. Any bastard stepping but not looking'd attest to that, blow yar knee out right where ya stood and just like any sort not knowing what they's doing in a place that screams it get knowed, they'd got caught. A bastard furrow the one to do it, that wheel fitting just snug tight against worn dirt that'd dipped an inch lower than what 'em x's'd like or hold, type of hollow that any born and bred folk'd known from the age of five to not go stepping in nor round, type that'd bit Jim Bate's feed wagon right in two, fresh spread of corn and collards toppling dusty and mired all out in front Major's Market where he aimed to make trade, and type that'd took down Russel Dodd's entire family one Sunday morn when they's on their way to Providence Baptist not a year later, damn near broke Granny Dodd's hip with the fall and Russell Dodd's eldest, Elijah, ain't never scoped right since, and type that'd tripped up Sheriff Stone not once but three separate times which'd finally landed a cast and a set of crutches on him and endless shit talking over at Mincy's Lunch Counter, that's to say if there were ever a seat open and waiting for him, which ever since he went to regulating Unions, there were NOT. Damn pothole even brought mean Ol' Bastard Meaks to his knees when he come off the mount, and it were for damn sure there weren't a soul standing nor watching that gave even the slightest pause to his inconvenience, so's to think that depression gave one shit to a Gatling Gun and Company men's desires to be rid of the pothole were a fucking long shot. IT. DID. NOT. GIVE. ONE. SOLITARY. SINGLE. FUCK, RONNIE. Fact with all the rushed driving forward over and over again into that wall of mud by Abner Joab, only thing 'em x's done were drive that brand deeper down to hell.

"Now, believe there needs a little bit of extra attention paid to that prize jewel of Main Street, Mincy's Lunch counter. In that, it undenied, the best meat-and-three round and by gawd the only spot that'd send ya out with a bottle of hooch if ya knew just how to ask, but the real beaut of the place were the man serving it, Mincy's husband Mr. Blevins. And between the two of 'em, both truly living the Lawd's path due to Mr. Blevins treating and believing a small black board placed under the counter opposite the flat top were just as good as script when the Mine went to holding wages and her, that sweet little plump Angel by Gawd's side, allowing up to four marks by a person's name 'fore she shut off the food valve, and that included as many mouths as needed feed, which meant hungry babies could sometimes eat twice if set there long enough, and there were a story circulating that spoke to both of 'em, Mincy and Mr. Blevins hearing Gawd speak to 'em, which were the reason why they'd put Mincy's Lunch Counter right there in the middle of the flow of folks on Main street, which meant it nuzzled two storefronts down from Sterling's Hardware right in between Bonnie's Boarding House and Merle's Getting Store, and it were on Mincy's very roof, Mick, that Enoch'd stacked odds with his one-man-regime. And if that don't speak to Gawd twirling the pot, reckon there don't stand nothing that does. Hear me now, Mick.

"Not to mention, Mincy's Lunch Counter were the only other building in all of downtown Hazard that held a sign over top it's front wall, a big to-do that'd come custom from Lexington, and 'course that holding of an awning, of which Mincy's one of five in a row that sported such similar attire, granted just ample hiding in the event one needed do so, but most important of all, were Mincy's Lunch Counter sat at that precious spacing where High Street met Main. See, 'em two roads, which ran one on top the other through the course of downtown Hazard met up just east of Jacklot Hollow on the north end of town so's that if Sherman, hisself, were to've made campaign through Hazard, it woulda probably followed the loop of High and Main that the burning occurred and if he were to've stationed a faction anywhere as lookout, it woulda granted no better vantage than on Mincy's roof, as it the birthplace of sight for all things coming and going down either street. So's guess there could exist better lending then, that it just downright good business that Enoch'd chose such an point for that breech's spoke.

"And being that by dawn's break on Nov. 4th, 1930, Abner Joab's tongue'd started in on 'em teeth real good, the habit born almost without his knowing at all, as if with ever' dead duster he and his company shot past, the detection of NOW firealarm'd out, as in NOW'S the time for Abner to join the rank and glory of all 'em other Joab men 'fore him, and that unfortunate and rather unsettling accompaniment rearing rancid red throughout his mouth, coating not only his gums and cheeks but forming spill NOW in beacon bright from between his lips so's that Enoch couldn't do nothing but beeline his dead daddy's gun straight for Abner. Mind ya, Mick, there seemed not only two but a third set of forces propelling that yearning for NOW nearby, so much so that Mr. Blevins'd decided step out from Mincy's Lunch Counter and venture his sweet Christian disposition out into the wild with a plea for, "Don't none of this need go no further" and "Don't nothing come undone by the end of a gun, boys." And seeing as how Abner Joab took it upon hisself to rectify what he saw THREAT, and decided crank on that lever that'd sent men to meet their maker a day ago at Randi's store and that continued in its ill advisement to pursue such similar endeavors that day, there splayed a most awful interaction when that Gatling Gun'd ripped Mr. Blevins into shreds basically at the bottom of where Enoch'd made hold up.

"Now, I don't believe that I need express to ya, Mick, what sorta effect this took hold in that boy, Enoch, up there on that roof. Nor do it need come examine all that hard how Abner Joab hatcheted up delight in finally attaining familial camaraderie with the battle. Believe it might better stand to just go ahead and projection assail the matter 'bout how fire shockwaved smoke outta that metal anteater at the end of Enoch's arm. How that butted wood craned hard against his shoulder, anchoring that nook in the hold of his jaw, and how that boy's face who'd-seen-a-fair-share-too-much-already slang back just the tad bit it needed not to go breaking bone, as he head-hunted that barrel-blown-arch slicing the air in a straightaway aimed DIRECT for the meaty protrusion of a Company man's shoulder just to the left of Abner Joab. And once butter spread outta that hefty boy's frame, Enoch moved. Jutted two letters over to where that N marked the latter part of LUNCH and ducked his little ass down and loaded up again. The belief, Mick, what can't be found, can't be hit. And by gawd it were a good thing too 'cause there ain't like a bite from buckshot to go sparking the flame to MOVE on a set of men.

"No—'em boys down below, showering the sky dark with all 'em slugs kicking out, took to heart real quick the flattening of one of their own. The man to Abner's left fell to the back of the rank, the one behind him stepped up and in, and Abner hollered out "LIFT" to that crowd back behind. And just as Enoch settled into his new position up above, that Gatlin barrel'd gone on and got pitched up to the Heavens and went hell hath-no-fury-quiet-like-revenge against that L of Enoch's previous standing. Blew that fucker and all its glory from big-city-Lexington right in four, Mick, just plain busted out fourth of July style with sparks going this-away and that, sending direct the message that come hell or high water there's gonna be a bit of compensate for one of theirs taking heat.

"But Enoch there'd, gone on with a little bit of suspect that might shine true, and cast up again and shot out the left eye to the feller to the right of Abner Joab, then hit ass to grass and crawled back over to where that L'd just got splintered and by Gawd he didn't stop there, Ronnie. He picked up one of 'em big chunks of shattered neon delight and he pulled that fucker in the air so's that it'd rain down smite on 'em bastards below and sent bullet right through it. Fucking dirty dawg shred it. Flecks of burnt school bus yeller arrow-spiked down on the Company. Tore and hit and flamed 'til that Gatling forced to pause its release and redirect.

"'Em fellas got so sour 'bout it they just went to unleash, Ronnie. Peppered the makings of Mincy's roof with enough seasoning the joints of the building started to swell, bricks just popping off left and right, that U N C and H taking hit after hit after hit so's that 'em letters limp-fry-fell, and Enoch were forced to crouch up near the back part of the roof's ledge and wait out, search for a plan. But ain't no sitting ducks in this story here, Mick—hell no—Enoch army crawled his ass, shotgun in hand, and ya wanna know what that boy did, what only he coulda done from his vantage, what he knew were the only chance of getting away from that hell blaze down below, Mick, HE shuffled over to that big vat in the corner where Mr. Blevins kept Meak moonshine and he rolled that heavy fucker on over to the lip of that roof's ledge and he tipped it up as that Gatling went for the reload and pushed that motherfucker over RIGHT when that first clip went to move out that metal bastard snout below. And that barrel of grade-A-fine-Kentucky-shine fucking exploded and carried down streams of fire with it, blanket-baby-swaddled 'em men, Mick, and once that fire soaked down to the roots of where 'em lower case x's lived, the whole operation went lights out. Abner Joab and his men carried out in spasms, their limbs searching for FREE, for anything other than burning hooch, and in all the confusion of their hustling 'bout, Enoch perched up there where that L U N C H once set and he picked off ever' one of 'em bastards that didn't just lay down and die, leaving Abner Joab last. Sent a signed-sealed-delivered mail shoot straight to his gullet, cracked out ever'one of Joab family teeth straight out that fucker's mouth, including 'em lower case x's that'd sought defile on all things tradition and Hazard, by Gawd.

"And ya wanna know what that boy did after that, Mick. Simply got down. Didn't wait for no thanks. Didn't wait for no apologies. Just walked straight past over 'em bodies right down Main Street. And disappeared in 'em woods. Gawddamn patron saint of Hazard, far as I'm concerned."

"And when she were done, Mick, ya know what she'd said? She'd said, ain't nobody gonna make things right for ya, 'cept ya, Ronnie. Moment ya go to blaming others 'bout yar plight, that's the moment ya might as well die, cause ya already done give up. Sometimes wonder if she ever told ya that story, Mick. But I highly reckon she didn't."

51

FEBRUARY 3, 1960

GARY'S STEEL TRAP

They'd not put no plaque up where 'em bastards'd died. Town'd not wanted memory on all those that'd come after. Like somehows or another that lettering over yonder where Randi's used to could'd salted the wound, like it'd brought on all that other that'd followed. More like than not, just weren't in the interest of the Company to bare mark on a bridge that'd end up at we's-involved-road. 'Cause case could get made, the death of Mr. Davis and the suitable snatching of Davis and Brother's Mining by a one, Mr. Albie Todd thereafter, who certainly weren't related to the Davis family, and who certainly probably wouldn'ta never landed on first pick were any of the Davis family stationed in Hazard other than the late Mr. Davis, and who, that opportunist, Todd, no doubt knowing full good and well that if his historically loathsome position placed alongside that of Davis dynasty, no favors woulda come his way in aiding nor attaining a position such as he got, and when Mr. Davis left this world to meet the Heavenly Father above, it quite frankly left as good timing and right place in Todd's mind to go on and make Davis and Brother's Mining his natural calling, thusly and such it became his interest too, to not go having the whole affair revisited. In fact, doubt it were something hardly any would want to recall on at all.

But ya can't just rightfully go suppressing what's done already got mashed up and smothered inside hearts, now can ya? Better luck next time, I says, that know-how of Enoch's involvement, 'spite his name not adorning no silver nor rusted metal, were holed up behind ever'one of 'em ribs willing to seek and know the truth. It were hung in notices just under they's necks as they carried stomp into Mincy's Lunch Counter on days when the clouds'd hold shadow just right and 'em Old Ones, after they'd married 'emselves in ham, and taters, and peas, and biscuits would cleave to his memory, allowing the meat of Enoch to stick to their bones with want, and when they'd got right full on him, when they'd felt that ball of warmth fire up inside, that sense of pride building up, they'd lug it on over to the back room of Merle's Getting Store and there they'd share his story over a jug of shine 'cause can't go quieting justice in men's lungs no matter how hard there's an aim try.

In 'tween sips of Meak's gold, batches that were now cranked up so high in proof it'd go to blocking light from yar eyes, well light and dark and anything else—see, ever since Old bastard Meaks'd met the hapless ending of getting shot by one of his own coming back from a battle-with-a-bottle drunk and loud as a gawddamn gang of buffalo, and his boys seeing fit in that time after to go ahead and double down on the hooch, deciding only way product gonna get moved were to make it so damn lethal it's bound to send a shallow grave to most who harped on it for too long, and that paired with how shine ain't necessarily something hard to come by no more, it understandable there a little bit more attention paid to having an edge as some folks'd go, and since 'em Old Ones just plain didn't give a damn to when their daises gonna get pushed up, they took to it 'til damn near all of 'em slumped down in a chair drunker than a cooper's cat with dying embers of little boy Enoch fighting off hundreds in their heads, 'cause that's how they'd knowed it and told it to be, and frankly ain't that how legends get passed on anyhow, rotting out from the core of drunk men who HADN'T 'bout men who DID. Least that's how it always told to me.

And if I's to tell it straight, which most won't, February 3, 1960 couldn'ta come 'bout less November 4, 1930'd a happened and I'll go even that much further and state, were it not for that troop who'd marched against Enoch way back then, that mountain ordnance getting shoveled ant hill deep all up round that camp by men who's bones were heavy dripped-dried-and-doused in a right proper serving of what Enoch'd spouted and lived and that's including yars truly doing the narrating, wouldn'ta never got done. Gawd knows, I sure as shit wouldn'ta got yeller-belly-bright tinged fingers the way I got now nor would I'a knowed the type of damage a hurled smoke'll do to the push button of a pile of dynamite. And yet I fucking do.

Tell ya what, when that blast came, it plain fucking ripped the roots right out the ground. I mean, macraméd sledgehammered slabs of rubble that hung like burnt broke plains on ownerless flattened hangers. Crazy ain't even close to doing it no justice, it were all just this big mess of thick tanned hides grappling after other men in pyro'd-flashes, the backdrop of some monster called up from the deep shuffling dusty dirt and darkened red bastard babies out into the world just far enough so's they could get a taste but not all that far they couldn't rubber band back by a finger twitch pull on momma's part, and that charge fueling nit-ro-glycerin in a maddened mass of "fuck-ya-and-move-time," were stampeding out like a team of horses broke off from the coach, and all that course, were proceeded by that poor bastard who'd stepped off the beaten path, landing all that bit just too close to where 'em Brightons and me hid, damn near blowing hisself in two, boy'd split his leg clean off right at the base of his hip and peeled that other calf like a torn hem, flesh just spilling down off the bone like it'd seen roast time, and there MOST CERTAINLY were a shore-fire-build-up of scrambled that came out after that, as in we's and 'em doing nothing but, with Mryt going to work over yonder, dipping and diving to the next closest fire sticks buried, Eisle and Corbin flipping down and out to that other side where 'em Company men now seemed holed up, and me charting super-fly-fuck-ya-lightening-speed after Kieran and all that bullshit that were starting to seep out the bottom of his trouser leg and I'll just go ahead and SPELL-IT-OUT for those of y'all up there in 'em cheap seats, there weren't fiber living nor existing in my being that wanted nothing but destruction with a capital fucking D.

Needless to say a couple hours ago, there were a drive in me that woulda watched it all come down if that were to be the case rather than have another one of 'em Company men go to taking something else away from Hazard and by Gawd that meant anything that were born and bred here, anybody that'd grow'd up hard and tough and mean with mountain blue blood here and that included ever' fucking tenantry of existence. So's then it probably ain't gonna shock nobody, why I didn't even wait for 'em Brightons to go firing up the rest of the payload, cranked up that ole-git-er-done spirit and stormed through that little bit of flap that were left hanging on that tent 'em Company men and Keiran'd made shelter in and lobbed right over top that sumabitch and dragged his little soft Irish ass right out from under 'em Guard's noses.

Wink and bear it as I says, but ole fiery Keiran didn't take a shine to that now did he, no-sir-e-bob he did not, went to hissy-fitting back in paltry balled fists that'd no business striking licks even back when school days woulda granted it good, damn fool crying out something or anothers 'bout how the "Union board's gonna hear on this" and how "captive ain't gonna garner shit." And ain't that the grand rouse, "Captive," he kept shouting it out like it something of a safe word, like it gonna stop what's coming.

"Captive. . . ." like there's gonna be somebody barreling outta of the dark to come save him. Says it again, damn fool. Ain't nobody coming for him. Not with—ahh, wait just one second...and...

NOW...that little ole flare up of TNT night-lighting over yonder. Can't help but go for the guts and glory now, can he, clobbering out Cassius Clay wannabes in the air like 'em mitts of his gonna do some damage to something, but I done knocked back **ONE, TWO, THREE** on him, clamped down on a real bad bloodsucker of a pound on that nose of his, settled out a stream from 'em starries that woulda made the five year old me possibly go to feeling bad but ain't no time for playground antics here, not today folks. Not with the two of us hustling past the 3rd set of sticks with Dizzy Dean clamoring out a play by play:

*Kerian Sterling making a play for it folks, hoping for a line drive if I could guess, lace it right over top the ground ...wishing for any sorta grip he can as long it connects—and here's the pitch...swing and a miss...seems the ash didn't want hit just yet...Gary sets Keiran up again...wants a cool clean knockout no doubt...Keiran steps up to the plate...shaking off the last blast absorbed...and heeeeerrrrre's the pitch...Keiran bunts the bender straight down the line...ball bounces twice 'fore Gary gets hold of it...and right behind him to second base they go, friends...gut shot after gut shot after gut shot...and get this with three strikes, one after the other it looks a stalemate to come, friends and neighbors...**BUT NO**... Keiran goes for a steel...**IT'S GONNA BE CLOSE**, and Gary'll have none of it. Just **COMPLETELY** shuts him out...a knock to the head, jaw, and chest, and the coast seems clear for goodnight and goodbye...BUT wait one second...**UNBELIEVABLE**, Gary's dropped it, he's dropped the ball, **CALAMTIOUS**...Keiran's going for it, going for gold, running to the hills...a breakaway...why, **HAVE YA EVER** in all yar years seen anything like it...**HOLD ON**...there's another push, Gary's got hold the ball again, **HE'S PICKED IT UP**, he's running after Keiran **AND** he's got **HIM**...knocked him down right there on Memorial Drive...that's right, folks, looks like Gary's got the secured lead—*

—The trail off kindling-crackled 'em fires quiet and when the sparks happened to fall, the camp, disaster-still-froze, a Paths of Glory tracker, Kirk making his way down the tunnel of shocked men as geysers of dirt blasted the fucking Star Spangled Banner heavenly, a fucking grounds crew cover up on a rain delay, men crunched low on all haunches protecting 'emselves from a wash out, a fucking no-fear-this-is-what-we-came-here-to-do collaboration of strife, the stage-side pyrotechnics at the ready for the curtain to drop, for Gary to hop front and center, and for Enoch to come down off the hill and start stirring the pot, and in 'tween the settling of ear drums and unclenching of teeth, when that DYNAMITE'D felled dormant, that next hiding place haunting ever' living soul left breathing in camp, there's a fine banjo twinge of WHY that pangs off 'em limestone hills. A look 'bout spoke to it, that massive misfire of "how the fuck" and "don't understand" as it crossed the Guard's faces, Keirans'd shared it too. Good. Distractions protected plans. Things'll ground down to 'em basics now, abler men grappling over the weak, a shuffleboard tactic of move or get displaced, a panicked know how reverberating survive in heads that just frankly wont. It were the makings of a rough-and-tumble-fight, of dirty sideswipes of bullets in the dark and it only took Mryt's lighting of 'em candy sticks near L O Davis Dr for 'em skeeters to get shot.

And my oh my, what a fucking rat pack of dirty deeds came a-dodging for 'em men hired by the Company. Lewlynn Pointer, who's participating in the Union'd amounted to barely a toe dip in the shallow end of the pond, steamrolled out his hut, which sat directly in front of where that last blast'd kicked off, and stepped off that Company lent half-blowed up porch and kicked back buckshot in a straight away, blitzkrieging bullets into that fucking confused crew's line. Broke up the three Company co-ops busy blenching "where the fucks" from under hot "find me a target now" breaths and went to boot-scoot-and-boogying on over to Amos Jones' place, who were just 'bout as much affiliated with the Union as Pointer were, hollering out, "whose side ya on, boy" with a bang, and the fucking brush fire took off from there. For ever' zinger shot from Government guns, there appeared another set of coal drenched black boots on wood toting whatever ammo they'd hid up that woulda got-got if they'd stayed on indoors. And that little shindig only seemed to grow. Why, any who dared poke their head from the shootout, found that within the entirety of that tent city, there weren't a step not brandished by some cuss or another holding up his family's history in steel and wood claiming, "ain't gonna take what's mine nor his no more." And for a moment, though it briefer than that probably when all's said and done, when I'd dragged Keiran up the ridge, past Main and High, past the Courthouse, and all prospects of civility and we's at the bottom of the North end of the Mine, waist high in a slab of fog, it looked like we might actually make it through 'fore that counter attack occurred, but just as the thought untethered inside, that sky went up Vegas-light-bright with a whole fuckton of shi-bangs.

Mortar collapsed, hailing shatters of Sterling's Hardware over top the Sidewalk, pinging chips of brick off Mincy's and Merle's like they's a set of vandals with hands caught in the cookie jar, plaster spewing sheetrock and wood siding from Bonnie's, sending baby WHY'S out to the streets, crackled loose spider veins on glass windows, sending scratches all on 'em seafoam green and dusty rose appliances, engineered for maximum destruction, 'em bullets, woulda crushed it down in its entirety in one viscous bite were it not for 'em men under overhangs and alcoves, their firepower poprocketing reprisal, Yosemite Sam'ing gutter grenades against the battered front, refusing defeat, death, and the drudgery of OWN 'em Company firecrackers meant. They's hell bent on not only getting out alive but blowing up any and ever'-gawd-damn-thing that moved in the meantime.

Oh, they's in on it now, Jones and Pointer'd joined up with a right motley crew, with Harold Billchomp, the burliest somabitch to ever live off one helping of meat and taters a day, damn man coulda turned over a truck if he'd the yearning and enough 'shine in him to go ahead and show it up, and Compton Turner, that Compton part belonging to his Momma and that Turner airing on Daddy, and neither of 'em fucking feuding forebearers knowing nothing 'bout "give a little," something that frankly most round these parts couldn't quote no verse to any how, just naming the bastard two last names, which ain't worth that much mention less compared to his brother, Elm Turner, who musta worn favor from the womb, 'cause Momma Compton and Daddy Tuner'd picked his lettering from the Bible as if preordaining that youngster to a life of more, which in turn'd propositioned, of course, Elm to be just 'bout as mean as any of 'em Meaks and as viscous a drunk as any Hazard'd seen, and that didn't cut off the cur neither 'cause they's both followed in fact by four fucking Meaks, who'd no horse in the race to begin with but who'd seen opportunity to go ahead and shoot some shit and came a-running down. And they's, all of 'em, busy making one helluva case for the power of 'shine and all its capabilities.

For ever' Company man that donned breathe out that canvassed foxhole, "fire in the hole" scourged flare cross that early morn sky as 'em four Meaks visited reigns of orange in the form of burning-lit-over-proofed-hooch on 'em boys. And I'm telling ya loud and clear, it were a gawddamn assembly line of pick-off, as in scurry the troops, as in let 'em riflemen go on and target practice up 'em motherfuckers scattering outta the blast. Funneled 'em right over to death's door, 'em coal mining boys. Sure enough did, placed 'em with bogged down backs up against that new Company store, that'd got pitched up like some gawddamn quilted revival after the last time there were a mini-revolt. Oh, they'd got 'em moving all right. All the way over on Broadway, that buttered slab street sandwiched 'tween High and Memorial, got 'em so's that they parked right there in the lot of "get fucked."

Fanned out like marauders heavy with the stench, with bundled groups wreaking havoc fully equipped and ready to follow 'em bastards anywhere they might go or flee 'til they got what they wanted. And by Gawd, they wanted blood. And they were greedy somabitches. That's for sure. At one point, hell, looked to be 'em boys'd a wing devoted directly and solely to the utter purpose of climbing atop that lavish bastard store, which, mind ya, didn't really need all that much push for folks to go on and hate. Not with the way they'd set it up. Throwed the largest white bed sheet to ever grace anyfuckingwhere over top that motherfucker ever' damn Sunday like it some sort of fake bullhorn calling the folks in. Took two damn turns 'fore folks figured out they weren't gonna come no closer to Gawd by visiting it. Mean, just imagine—little Ole Biddys 'dorning their Lawd's best coming down off the hill, only to find it the fucking Company going for the sell on 'em. Downright haughty. And weren't no mercy present up nowheres when 'em boys finally climbed up on that Jerkinhead, 'em old spike lumber boots of theirs tacked into that gable. Hell naw, kicked that hornet's nest that resides in most ever' man called rage, and ripped that motherfucker up. Mean, lit it up. Tore 'em eaves to drips, bored slugs right through that ridge, leaving tunnels a small boy could rip his hand through and go down for the borrow, and when they weren't in the business of pressing the trigger, their fingers pried as many shingles off as they could, dropping the leftovers on the Company down below. Roof ain't seen that much action since Earl Tompkins crawled up there and took a piss off the side back in December.

But can't no mind get paid to none of that now, least not in whole. 'Cause standing clear as day and twice the Christ Messiah BIG, Enoch bulked ahead. If only Keiran coulda seen him, seen the man Hazard wouldn't soon forget, not that they ever really did in the first place, but I'd smashed purtty hard on 'em swole little slits of his. Orbs just didn't have much to show no more to be frank. Hell, Keiran woulda harped shit company nohow. Thumped three teeth out his mouth and finally sent him to mercy snooze just for shut-the-fuck-up-from-the-wailing-relief. Carried him the rest of the way up the hill to the foot of mine over my damned shoulder. But that didn't stop me from dropping him and trou to go on and take a piss on his head for the wakey-wakey now did it?

What ya take this for, some sorta holy-roly morality tale.

Now, piss'll do a whole lot of things but a cleanse for the soul ain't one of 'em, just ask Kieran here, his thoughts on it…*"damn ya"…"captive"…"captive"*…got up with that word again. Made me wanna knock out the rest of his teeth so's that spewer of his'd go ahead and shut the fuck up. Ya'd think a man in his situation'd have a sense of the brevity we's harping on here, mean the man has risen—ENOCH's holding three pounds of dynamite in a fucking chicken coop in front of him…wait…oh, poor bastard sees it now…*"ya can't go"…"but they's"…"and they's"*…he's got it now, tacked there to his forehead—S-H-O-R-T, as in on time, as in KABOOM SOON.

Keiran'd cared not in all his time presumed negotiating between the Company and the Union to examine what his betrayal'd surely mean to all those that would succumb to it. It were the biggest gawddamn lie he'd ever tell hisself. A damn fool to believe such nonsense, I says. But ain't it easy to get lost in one's mind when perspective not heard from that other side, egh. Hell, we's classed among the damned perhaps all of us, and how deserving we stood, waiting for the ravenous revenge of our souls as Enoch went to work, with Keiran and I paralyzed as we watched him auger red sticks all along the timber collar of the main entry of the Mine. Play a hand at Gawd, I says, what it looked and what it seemed, wash away the sins of the earth with fire, I says, blow Davis and Brother's Mine to fucking smithereens. The count to begin with Dizzy Dean again in………1………………2……………..3…………

Bottom of the ninth here folks and Gary's still on the mound... making quite a show of it here, folks…two strikes down…seems Keiran's not to be phased…steps up to the plate…Gary…looking for the sign…looking for a fastball appears…Enoch with the windup… and heeeerrrrreeee's the pitch...and it's up…whacked the fucker into the GAP*…Keiran's scrambling for a catch…scampering loose Gary's grip…running for the safety mark of free and clear the blast of Enoch's fire…and what a finish this could be, folks…but wait* *one second…there's interference on the field…what looked to be an outta-here-blast has a partner…no correction—the gang's busting down three…that's right three bundles of dynamite planted…three reasons to run hell or high water…doesn't look like Keiran's gonna get it here, no Sir…not a cold chance in hell for this to fall on the flattened hope of* AVOID*…timber tried a strong stance…but couldn't hold on to the bindings…no hold in sight for it…friends and neighbors, the simple truth of the matter is the sky is black…the smoke is thick…and the three men are presumed dead…what some might've called a victory…an outta of the park hit has left the stands stunned and in silence.*

52

1988

RONNIE — PAY THE PIPER

When that dust'd settled from all 'em roughnecks bull-blazing their heels with hellfire snort, there were a feeling paint-thinning battery acid off my insides, a hyped-up stench of dried sticky Mountain Dew spelling OFF like kids running wild for way too long feral, like a wrong in the crust of yar mouth that keeps getting picked over by yar tongue dribbling AWFUL down along yar chin, a smothered nohow that the gavel's gonna drop, that the mizer holding time's chimed DONE and OUT, and that the cocksucker popping the can, unloosing the spray of slowed-assured-death is none other than the bastard Willard's come to see, the motherfucker Gerald Mason chalkboard-grating, "who the fuck are you," in the form of twisted barbwire warn, and buddy, I got news for ya, there ain't but one sure fire way to go ahead and rouse up a hornet's nest nearby faster than spilling a spot of turnt-bad-sweet on the ground.

Twenty-five things—that's what stood between me, the cocksucker, Willard, and freedom, and with the two just mentioned, better dress it up to twenty-seven just to be fair, that's twenty-seven head-on-a-swivel-dirt-dungeon-throw downs, twenty five separate bouts of thunderdome-two-men-enter-one-man-leaves-Mad-Max-pulverizations, one bought of slaughterhouse-blues, and one Ronnie's-gotta-gun-showcase that's bound for headline news at eleven on some sorry for nothing channel that spouts out worrisome bother 'bout pets getting caught up in trees, which speaks to a gawddamn bet-yar-bottom-dollar-guarantee that the sorta sport I'm gonna need to work through all 'em twenty-seven things'll get the prime-time thirty minute slot. And hell, ya go to counting that gun Willard fucking mice-chirped 'bout while we's roller-derby sprawling on the fucking front lawn of somebody's-bound-to-get-a-bag-of-dicks-shoved-down-their-throat-country-time-jamboree, might ought to go on and call it SQUARE at twenty-motherfucking-eight things. And that's a one-time-no-do-over-show-pony-affair, if ya catch my drift, as in go ahead and fucking forget 'bout that $200 bounty ya's expecting once ya rounded the board. Only thing assured by this little Grand Experiment were a sure-fire sprawl of defeat cross somebody's ass that'll more like than not result in a body bag. Ever'body presents just trying not to get plastic-zipped.

Best to pay close attention now we's bout to get FIRED UP—And that goes for #1, 2, and 3 of the blockade, the mangy mutt fur fence presently aimed at soon-to-clamp- throat-removal-monopoly, cornered the market in the winter of '83 when the father, the son, the other son's show-down-death-match included the perilous faltering of a toddler, two fat ten year olds, a dumbass teen, and the scantily clad Loretta, who'd found 'emselves, (the folks) a little too late, in the close proximity of one of Senior Mason's cookie jars, hence the hound's (the father, the son, and the other son's) categorical MAULED MAYHEM that came to follow next, and who now (the hounds) were let loosed by a one beafy sweat clamp of a red faced feller in a Lynard Skynard cut-off-T that I'm purty sure went by the name of Dwight or Wyatt, least that's what it sounded like when that Cocksucker yelled his name.

FREEZE.

Could it not be forgot even if one aimed try that the hounds probably the least of the worries in all honesty, seemed Highland Terrace'd their very own vagabond team of lineman racked up and ready, with defensive tackle #4 Randy White come by way of Cody, that meathead fucker power lifting on that bench, who were surely looking to "Manster" some shit that ended in the letters ME, and who came fully equipped with a beastly crew to boot. That spotter, #5, of his were as big as a gawddamn tank with enough meat-fat on him to go ahead and move a fucking dozer if need be and buddy that's exactly what looked to be the case in this instance. That blowhard came to play for sure, woke up this morning and garden trimmed that military high top he'd probably sported since fucking Vietnam and looked his self straight in the eyes of that metal mirror he'd just windexed down (if ever there's a way to turn a man a clean freak, its fucking service that'll do it), and said, "Self, there's a bit of collecting that preens apparent today and if nightfall don't come with the offering of broke, as in I've done—to someone else, don't reckon the day'llve proved nothing," and then he might like to've taken a big ol'breath, allowing hisself some room to measure the sort of failure that might appear to him and then, go at it again likely, "and if there's one thing I despise," grinding up 'em teeth, buddy, "it's a waste of fucking time."

And shit if that ain't enough, can't go discounting the rest of the fucking special teams that numbered 6 through 21, the fucking fifteen dumbbell-chunking-standing-by'ers who'd looked more like a cranked-up-redneck-cohort-of-mean-albino-vipers with the way their heads went to swerve at the vow of any sort of action that involved FUCK IT UP. Shoulda seen 'em, lit up like a gawddamn Christmas Tree, their eyes did. And the breakdown of 'em now, wouldn'ta won nobody no first prizes neither, ugly fucking bastards, they was, with three of 'em sporting what seemed to be a shared (direct blood line) hair lip, two with a set of sonar ears poking out wider than Dumbo, one shaped like Humpty Dumpty (just plain pitiful little bitty ol legs on him), and then there were that troop of real-get-with-it-motherfuckers, who were built 'bout like smaller versions of Cody, but that ain't speaking to no normal size neither, Cody reached 6' 7" and probably tugged round a whopping 320 for how big 'em arms and legs were now, meaning 'em others were USDA Certified Bullion-heavy-weights, with four of 'em wearing fresh black eyes like they's a set of glasses, like they'd just got done duking it out in one of 'em trailers and settled on, "well, Murv, Jake, John, might do well for a spot of fresh…outside," then all four of 'em concurrent nod…(HUDDLE UP), like when they met up with their COMPADRES out front in the yard they's all of sudden unburdened, deciding better yet, "Murv, give us a hand with a SPOT," and Murv just being that sorta guy, ya know, sort that'll plumb knock a fucker into next week 'cause… well…suppose, "just felt compelled," and then saddle up with a icebox of beer and wanna talk the world with ya, gargles, "what the hell," under his breath and drifts his happy ass on over with a "give me ten."

And it'd just sorta domino'd out from there, ya know, with #16, 17, 18, 19, and 20 ranking up there in the legendary Good Ole Boy's Hall of Fame, all five of their stats reading 'bout three pages long but the only sledgehammer pounding IMPORTANT were the same for all of 'em: KILLERS, ever'one of 'em. Contract Killers. Part of the CK faction of any good outfit, as in: they would, they could, they have, and by Gawd, they will again. To lead off that kill list, there were Todd "Tomahawk" Reynolds, a skinny shaved short balled motherfucker with not one set of chompers left in his mouth, hacked 'em all out so's if he ever found dead there wouldn't exist no way of identify, but don't get it wrong, now, that motherfucker'd a set fake teeth made outta nails that he'd flip in if need be and by Gawd he'd gum yar ass to death if that the only option. Absolutely gnaw yar face off in chews. Second, were "Lacy" Levi Tanner, a man so good looking it were said and believed he could woo a nun from Gawd's hand, but who were compelled perhaps by that very fact to go on and make ever'thing else in the world down right vile by comparison and the only reason he ever got on long enough with the lot of 'em, 'cause he'd done his fair share of ripping and raiding, but moreso due to his relation to "Tomahawk," that being his cousin on his Mommy side, which thank Gawd for Todd 'cause were it to come that other they'd all'a died.

For slots #3 and #4 on that bandwagon, the twins, Isreal and Isaac, set of Biff-wannabe-bad-guys with the brawn and build to actual bust yar ass and, as noted 'fore, bury ya, better known as the Bludgeon Boys, revered that way by the entirety of the Southeast, unless course ya get up there by Virginia where they's noted as simply Devils, which were due to 'em being exactly that and the alleged line to Devil Jim, their purported Great, Great. And finally the worst of 'em, the filthiest cunt ever to cross the Atlantic, Dick Daniels, a fucking-bucktoothed-bug-eyed-Skeletor-wannabe-doublecrossing-backstabbing-corpse-fucking-(it were a yarn that went round)cunt, who found hisself indebted to a one, Tellmore Mason, after Dick got bit by a copperhead gallivanting 'bout in the woods looking for a tree to piss near in the middle of a three day card bender where sleep weren't likely an option with the amount of dough getting flung 'bout—not to mention the fact that, that green he were flashing didn't actually belong to him but were instead a stake from some operation outta Kentucky looking to dirty-dick Mason waters and when this revealed to Tellmore after Dick rushed back into the small cabin in the middle of the woods where that game'd stayed steady for three GAWDDAMN DAYS, Tellmore agreed to help Dick if he gave up the name of said Business, to which Dick being a Dick did, and this having only transpired last week, the two became fast friends in close quarters as Tellmore, course, insisted on escorting Dick to said entreprenuer, kindly uniting the other Hall of Famers mentioned prior with Dick and the businessman, who consequently is presently following the lead of four more rogues rounding out the end of the list #22-25.

Ya can call 'em the Cuthroat Collective: it's what they did and what they'll do, a lean mean ragtag team of real rowdy runners from Raleigh, who came replete with a blood contract and rousing response time of IMMEDIATE, as in will handle all things in that fashion to completion, so diligent that the Masons called on their abilities often when their a containment issue at hand, which were what the Businessman they's carting were...something that needed containing.

And pray tell how did I come to know all these details... weeeeeeellllllll...let's just say two years ago I worked alongside all three of the Famer's, that were, ever'one 'cept the Dick, who at some point if ya got up long enough with 'em sorts became familiar to yar tongue even if it in reputation alone. And if ya worked with the Famers then ya'da worked with the Cuthroats too. How I'd avoided the Masons 'spite these connections were the true "lost on me moment." And to complicate matters further, 'cause why the fuck not, the businessman they's fucking to-and-froing were my brother Mick, as I fucking live and breathe.

Mick, that same motherfucker who'd fucking turd tarnished ever' gawddamn thing he touched, and course, that same motherfucker, who were gonna likely lead to me dying in a rusty ass trailer park owned by a family that, if he weren't present, I mighta could bore favor with somehow given the connections already listed. This motherfucker here, the fucking scorch of all creation, I do declare. And when 'em Hall of Famers and Cuthroat Collective's decided to bring out their high-hat-surprise-businessman, as in "look here boy, look what we's aimed to do to ya," sideshow freak and that motherfucker eyeballed me, he made matters all the more worse by camel spitting in the dirt, "Ronnie."

Now, I gotta tell ya, a wave of fucked'd all 'bout swallowed my ass from the beginning of this little venture but when that dumb fucker loosed 'em lips of his, Gawd Almighty help us all. Mean, shiiiit, how that boy couldn't get it through that mashed tater face of his, oh they'd took for a walk'bout sure enough, peeled and popped both his peepers into real shiners and looked to be just straight knocked his nose clear off and telling by the just-ate-a-bee puff the whole left side of his face were sporting they'd gone on and knocked a hinge off that jaw, musta done something to that brain of his 'cause how he didn't clue into the lifted eyebrow my way, were the exact wrong move to make were a gawddamn metaphor for that boy's sorry fucking life. Not to mention that back-asswards bend Willard went to making when there a perceived bit of ya-mean-to-tell-me-ya-just-so-happen-to-know-the-fucker-that's-beat-all-the-way-clear-down-to-hell-well-shiiiit-ain't-that-convenient-look and when I traded back in a burnt BBQ sear that barring-separate-daddies-he-oughta-know-when-he's-seen-another've-Connie's-kids, he finally got quick with it and both of us laser-focused in to exactly what it were that's to come outta Gerald Mason's mouth next 'cause it more like than not gonna end with a scenario where we either get to continue drawing air on Gawd's green earth or not. And since that sprawl of bad-mean-tore-up-fuck-wad-machine of a man didn't very much like the notion of SET-UP, which were exactly how it looked my knowing the businessman and him knowing me and as Willard's starries pointed out, the fucking convenience of that, Gerald fucking lifted up that Remington 870 he'd kept trained at his hip and kicked that birdshot straight for Willard's thigh, which clipped in there on purpose 'cause as evidence'd show 'em Masons weren't real big on letting folks die nice and easy.

Maim more their speed, understand.

And sure enough when 'em little bitty pellets went for the disperse in that old man chunk of mean, it did not end well for either party involved. Bit of a hazardous scenario with Dilbert or whatever the fuck that tall pasty nut job were named standing next to Gerald Mason, who looked like a Dilbert, as in the only one standing and breathing who might contain a lick of sense 'bout him and who in another life mighta made quite the number pusher in a legitimate business but were born in the wrong bloodline hence his yammering in Gerald's ear the one thing that coulda slathered avoid on this entire situation but that now were gonna cost him the unfortunate loss of more than a couple of men—mumbled: "that there's Ronnie Fairchild…run with some of the Famers and Cutthroats way back when," to which this here circle existing in a rather tight noose, in that if yar in it, ya bound to know ever'one even if just by namesake alone, which were why that fucker, Gerald feeling the severity of what's just done motherfucked back at Dilbert, "who's it I just shot?"

Which got answered in an equally daunting manner, "can't quite say but there's more than a fair share associate 'tween 'em faces wouldn't ya say, might could come argue a paternal sharing," and that right there were what Krispy Cream glazed ain't that good cross Gerald's face.

Which purty much brings ya nice folks right BACK UP TO SPEED with that numnuts Wyatt or Dwight, whatever the fuck his name were, letting that dawg loose…that big-headed-not-knowed-no-better-fur-block-of-muscle came flying squirrel jump direct from his handler to three inches shy my torso, 'em chompers of his spare-ribs-wet-nap-salivating at the prospect of meeting a full belly's dinner 'fore it even time for lunch, that cock toting bag of fleas liked to take out my innards right there on the front lawn, jaw spread Grand Canyon wide did not, I repeat did not take too kindly to my shit-kickers jamming leather down it's throat. No—it did not. And I gotta tell ya, what come after were less of likeable dose to any of 'em other fuckards standing 'bout. It were true Willard down for the count for the most part, that bone of messy red, white, and gooe splaying HARD LOT on trying to fit back into his leg but that ain't to say that if I didn't channel 'em over to where he's laid out Willard weren't mighty resourceful with a bit of old-forgot-and-discarded-mowing-chains he found in a patch of weeds. Tell the truth, couldn't come no other way than to describe Willard's utilization of that there bit of metal as EFFICIENT and as that Reader's Digest put it when the Walkman hit the market truly INNOVATIVE—what a pair indeed.

Now, what were it I said, 28 things…sounds 'bout right… well here it goes—the Puncher's Chance portion of this evening's program: snake eyes darted off 'em beady buckets of needing to prove braggarts of dumbbell lifting die-hards, 'em 2 hair lips, 2 dumbos, and one humpty dumpty tearing their way from 'em weights straight as a crow flies towards us, and standing nekid, as in unarmed, a three point stance only thing to do and by Gawd when that lot got close enough to steamroll drive ahead, that's exact what I did, put my shoulder through the pins of hair lips 1, 2, and 3 and bowling ball redirected their featherweight asses on over to Willard, who promptly settled their charges with the Tell and Fairchild household by towel snapping that chain in all three of 'em shit's eyes knocking loose more than one from their sockets and sending that lot into a frantic Operation game redo of 'em parts back into their rightful slots. As for 'em real-get-with-it-motherfuckers, they came full regatta speed out the deep with shiv flailing octopus arms and dynamite dipped heat, it were all DUCK. DUCK. Butt to the head, speed jab at the teat, fresh gash of spilled cheek. MOVE. MOVE. MOVE. Dip down, shoulder to hip—connect. LIFT. Bulldoze bone, explode. HIT. HIT. HIT. Chicken piccata pound flesh, take it—the scrape, the tear, the slash, the bash, the clip, the clobber, the crash, come out that other end bloodied, black, battered, and beat but thank ALMIGHTY GAWD above still standing panting like a fucking dawg who'd got lost too long in the heat.

And as for 'em Good Ole Boys and Cuthroats, well the beaut 'bout that bastard fucking lot were they couldn'ta give one good gawddamn to any of the ruckus playing out in that yard. See, they's contract. Ever' single one of 'em. Which meant less they got paid for the job, they ain't doing the job and I knows firsthand at least that they's mighty peculiar 'bout how all that negotiated, as in there weren't no tag-team-jump-in-for-the-green-ring-side chance in hell one of 'ems gonna move and start bashing skulls but that sure as shit don't mean 'em fuckers can't get provoked. And that little diddly-do-dandy came by way of one Cody git-real-big-meathead-cunt who came full press charge after yar's truly amidst that clusterfuck. Threw that press bar weights and all in a shortcut path that butter sliced that lot of Good Ole Boys and Cuthroats that'd made their congregation in a little huddle of don't give a fuck on the left side of the yard right up next that bench and the porch where Gerald, Dwight or Wyatt whatever the fuck his name were stood. Believe maybe that meat fat boy, Cody, thought he could've cleared 'em, 'em muscles bulging the way they were and all but DARE say there weren't all that much thought put into that move 'cause the bar barely made it past three of 'em contractors 'fore it smacked 'em twins, the Bludgeon Boys, cracking both their heads in a real nasty affair that domino'd into the spiral staircase to hell with Isaac and Isreal cow-tipping-fall right into "Lacy" Levi Tanner, who as mentioned 'fore were not the one to go tripping round and who certainly were not in favor of getting knocked down into the dusty dirt of trailer park yard and WHO in retaliation whipped out a Crocodile Dundee knife and went to honey- backed-ham slicing parts off 'em twins, which did not in any way whatsoever endear civility to take over.

Au Contraire, it called out the animal kingdom song of doom with all and ever' fiefdom present up in arms and ready to defend it's home turf, which meant the Good Ole Boys or what were left of 'em and the Cutthroats began a gladiator brawl of smashed and crushed limbs, a tug-n-touch-topsy-turvy of fucking free-for-all, a grab the nearest thing this redneck rancho's got available and give ever'body in the near and dear vicinity a walloping that ain't gonna end nowhere but hillbilly carousel body dump zone, with all four of the Cutthroats making use of a couple discarded gardening tools: shovel, ax, and a hoe, leftovers from a 'mater garden just to the right of the trailer while two of the Good Ole Boys making arms of the leftover smatterings of what once were a purtty good workout session. And don't mind if I do, this all seemed to work in our very favor for the DISTRACT, as in not paying attention to the Businessman, my brother Mick, no more and not paying attention to Willard nor me, which allowed for a private audience with the renowned Gerald Mason, hisself, well that were if ya didn't count the brawl and the fact that ever' woman in Highland Terrace currently held enough arms like there's 'bout to come a rally through the park with a threat at taking 'em.

Well, beggars can't be choosers, right—wrong. Apparently Willard could. Spotted the once renowned but currently wasting away wreckage of a John Dear riding lawn mower, probably where that chain he'd made handy-man-weapon come from in the first place, and proceeded to salamander slide his bullet assailed body over to what he no doubt viewed as Salvation incarnate, as if this whole little shindig here were gonna end with a closing shot of the sun setting and a grand ride-off into that bleeding orb of orange like the fucking Duke of Highland Terrace, and frankly I don't for the life of me know'd what got into that bastard, how he thought 'em women weren't gonna start popping off slugs soon as his hand touched that wheel were beyond me but when yar partner makes the move—ya go along with it by Gawd, and seeing as how he the only friendly I got in the crowd, 'cause brother Mick over there weren't gonna do shit all, that for damn sure proven, I followed after. Went for that majestic prowess of a gator chasing a fish on a lore, waddling and curving round all that muck 'em brawlers were tossing 'bout, dodging a boot heel here and shimming over and past the Bludgeon Brother's groping meat paws there, edging arms and feet past that yelping dawg that took another mouth swipe at my leg 'spite still carrying the full taste of crocodile boot leather from 'fore when I shoved my heel down its throat, and broad shoulder gripped onto the back of that rusted green deer that Willard'd managed a tug, hold, and mount onto and just fucking went for it. To hell with the Grand Teton Gerald and all 'em biddies sporting shoot on us and the businessman, Mick, who probably deserved ever'thing that were coming his way…

EERRRRRPPP…*wait ya just left him there, left yar brother to the hands of a bunch of maniacs and the likelihood of…* Yar gawddamn right I did. Whatever it were that got him to where he were, it were traded on fucking fools gold, AS IN, now this just a guess but bear with me and I doubt I'm that far off...the business Mick were purportedly running outta Kentucky that'd some sort of stake in personally fucking with the Mason family dynasty all the way down in GA, which were revealed, lest we forget, to Tellmore Mason via Dirty Dick Daniels way back in that cabin where promise made concerning some sort of favor-repayment-plan after a snake bite, were the gawddamn epitome of over-reach if I ever saw one, AS IN, swimming in the deep end of the croc-pond with a set of floaties tied to either arm and a wish and goal to get to that other side in one full piece but the lacking wherewithal to've learned how to swim in the first fucking place prior to fucking diving in sorta over-reach, the type that would dictate the right move to make after falling into a little spot of money, which Lawd knows how that even happened probably a con on an old fucking widow or a robbery that by the luck of the draw'd finally gone the right way somehow, a man'd go to hiring out a couple of roughnecks to go down and hit up an operation he didn't fully know all that much 'bout but sure did sound like a real fucking good idea after a bottle and slow and wide ride of a fat country whore, (it'll set more than a few men astray—trust me) sorta devices, WHERE it only surprising to my brother, Mick, the same man who orchestrated this cock-heap-palooza that he standing with a 12 gauge double pump pinched into his back currently. So fuck yeah, I left him, 'cause the only thing good ever happened round the sumabitch were when his head hit the floor after the bottle emptied.

But just like August of 1978 and ever'thing else Mick touched, that motherfucker just—Could. Not. Let. It. Go. and 'fore we's even able to get where Willard were trying to get, probably that fucking gun he'd buried out somewheres, a flashback of me asking, *where the fuck we going* and him clipping back *gawddamn gun* during this haywire shit show of cosmic fucking coincidence, Mick reached out those greedy sausages of TAINT and belted out, "Ronnie Fairchild, ya just gonna leave yar brother here to die," and boooooyyyy didn't that go to interesting the likes of all 'em Masons who now definitely viewed this as AMBUSH on the highest authority. That fucking cock-gobbler just signed our death sentence 'cause he couldn't stand the thought of me getting away, of me getting out and escaping, frankly of me leaving him at all. Been holding it against me since 1978 and apparently the years'd not done nothing to alleviate the burden, this just existing as his first opportunity SINCE to act it out in the world—fucking bastard.

And I'm just gonna lay it out plain as day what happened next 'cause even if I were to go to the embellish on it, doubt it would make it any more believable than what actually did verifiable occur—Willard kicked that lawnmower up to high gear saying fuckall and to all a goodnight, which bucking-bronco threw me off the back end, smacking a face full of gravel, mud, and blood right at my chompers, and causing three of 'em Mason bitches to shoot out slug—double pump—slug after him. But I tell ya what, that crafty sumabitch drove that mockery of misused engineering straight through the yard of our former holding cell, knocking over the flamingo, the lawn jockey, ripping ass over that bud light blue kiddie pool with dirty resort style 'squeeter water that consequently sent a little deluge down and out over the bottom of that there deck, and flipped a bitch just as 'em tune-town-roger-rabbit-bullets spewed overhead and stopped, dropped, and rolled off that motherfucker into a row of shrubbery that let out into what would come to get know'd later as the rightful resting place of that there shotgun he'd gone popping off 'bout. Mean out of all the places for it to be, underneath the trailer just down from where we's held up were gawddamn resolute GENIUS.

Meanwhile, all that brass firing outta 'em breechs'd finally alerted 'em goons to look up from their melee and with all eyes attending, Gerald Mason decided it time as well to go and side-glock the end of his 12 gauge right through Mick's temple which sent him dummy diving down 'em front steps, his head pitch-clipping the rusty side of a nail leaning outta banister and then face-planting not three feet from where I's kicked off that mower so's that the both of us looked like some sorta sorry spelled out large L, that missing H E and P of our SOS-deserted-island-sheet-game-not-notifying-nobody-no-time-soon, fruitless effort to say the least.

WELL, with the full court's attention that beat down didn't go to stopping there, now did it. No sir. My sorry brother and I found ourselves at the bottom of gutter sandwich, both of us trying best we could at centipede ball up roll while the rest of 'em bastards left still standing took turns punting our insides. A fucking football pileup with me cursing 'em, him, and myself for being dumb enough to be in the wrong place at the wrong fucking time sorta fella, which I ain't. Not never. Which were why I'm gonna stop and pay a little acknowledge to how ridiculous the next thing I'm gonna say sounds, I know how it sounds but that don't mean it didn't happen just as I says it does—that crazy motherfucking sumabitch Willard Tell, my daddy who left my sweet Mommy and me just after I's born for no good gawddamn reason came Wild Bill Hicocking out from under that trailer right down the main drag of Highland Terrace with a Winchester 1897 pump action arrow pointing direct at Gerald Mason's noggin, seemed there some unfinished business left between the two of 'em that Gerald didn't know, which were illuminated by Willard hollering out just that, "got's business with ya needs tending, Gerald." And when one of 'em women got trigger happy setting off a warning round down towards Willard, he put her ass right through the trailer wall with buckshot. Mean, ice cream scooped four fucking helpings right out her insides and NAH he did not stop there, went on ahead and shot ever' other snatch standing round so's that there wouldn't be no contending no longer.

Well, as ya can imagine that went ahead and ended that there beating brother Mick and I were taking, scattered 'em men out like a piñata smack over that yard with a warning to any others considering HERO to come following the end of their name to fucking plain NOT. And Willard didn't waste no time at all bull horning that message and just so's ever'one were clear he William Munny'd out, "I'm here to kill ya, Gerald. Buried this gun up under that trailer two years back. Gone biting at the thought ever since."

To which Gerald big-man-burly-beard-smiled out, "I don't even know ya sir, never seen ya's 'fore," his eyes scanning losses, "fact, willing to let all this slide, willing to let ya turn and walk right out yonder to the main. Forget 'bout the whole thing."

But Willard knew like we all knew, weren't gonna get no forgetting. Not something like this. Nah—this'd go down the line of generations to come if not handled.

"Drop it," Willard cracked, motioning at that 12 gauge still locked in Gerald's hand."

"Done," metal melted like butter, disappearing from his possession, clanking down the steps 'til it stopped at good ole brother Mick's feet.

"Walk down here…SLOW."

"Sure, Sure," Gerald said, the feel of a politician 'bout to woo an angry mob slipping from his lips as he took to the steps of his porch.

"Get right up close here…" a click pinched Willard's ear, the cock of metal shifting gravity in the gaggle of men standing to the left, a stupid move, the Winchester 1897 redirecting for two seconds—BOOOOMMMM—spreading bits of leather and blue jean like feathers in a field, dropping the sorry cocksucker who'd sealed heartbreak on his mommy's soul when he were stupid enough to think this not the day he's gonna die. "…anybody else? Nah. Good. January 28th 1957…"

"Now partner…"

"I ain't yar partner…" Willard shoved that Winchester 'til its mouth met Gerald's forehead, "…three Mason's…eastern Kentucky…card game…"

"There's a slew of us now, Mister, I can't…can't go accounting for something that happened 30 something years ago."

"They's ya blood ain't they…Bobbie Mason, Randi Mason, and yar brother Jimmy Mason."

"Shit, Jimmy died long time ago."

"I know…I's the one that did it."

"What?"

"Killed 'em all."

"Ya Sumabitch."

"Careful there," Willard lifted the barrel, slamming that metal snout into Gerald's cheek, and locked back on his forehead, "don't want ya dying 'fore story time's over. Thirty something year's right, how long it took me to track 'em names, find y'all out, then two years ago gain entry to a game on Highland Terrace," Willard nodded his head back to the trailer the gun come from, "that trailer right there. Don't remember me 'cause I didn't wanna get remembered…but I do now. Gerald, ya gonna die, I'm gonna kill ya, and I'm kill any fucker who tries to stop me…HEAR THAT…," Willard hollered out.

A gun's hammer clicked again, the sound not distinguishable other than general direction of grouped men, Willard jaguar pounces the Winchester past Gerald's ear and a railroad tunnel where 'em men once stood, three bodies falling pickup stick style. "Yar blood 'caused me to miss out on my boy's life, Mason. Now yar gonna answer for their wrongs."

"Now, I'm sure we can come to some…"

BOOOOOOMMMMMMM—Gerald's gourd exploded like hit fruit, white hair dandelioning in the breeze, cherry pie dribbling overflow off his neck and down his chest, that frame of him not quite knowing yet it were time to fall, that the dynasty just got a reboot and there's a new sheriff in town gonna come take over soon.

53

1988

RENEGADE

Stone barbs squished and crunched, sounded like chewed glass spreading chunks of flesh with ever' boot's landing. I'd cattle-hauled both Willard and Mick under the ripe swelter of Georgia Summer dawn where three digits seared scold on the skin even 'fore ten o'clock, drug the brother by his nape, his boots and back cottonmouth swerving over top that gravel, that snubbed pull of rocks slinking under his weight, cherry ripping cowbell bruises and cantaloupe knots over the railroad track of already existing scrapes on his arms and legs, hauled Willard over top my back, the busted bone blowed out by buckshot anchoring WALK impossible. We moved low and slow like lions on the hunt, ever' periscoped glance of Mason babies charring our wrongs in the back of they heads, the curses of what we done spoiling the milk lining 'em bellies that's more like than not already shifted to that grand leap towards burdened men.

They'd not budged as we left, bunch of banshee bandits peppering 'em trailer porches, crow picking over their fallen, hawkeyeing when it were the three who'd combed full terror in their plots'd be done and gone from their land so's the keening could begin and the rightful buried in the family plot down by that Lanier outlet, the fitting view of six-pack plastic rings playing carnival toss over tree roots and fallen branches where there stood more markers of downed Masons then there did shrubs and grass and in that aftermath of boiled body parts, suppose we shoulda counted ourselves lucky for the shock and the haze. Course it'd only take one of 'em, one of 'em branded Masons to get that venom back in their grill, rest'd follow suit, hunt us down, do worse to us than we did to 'em. Maybe even worse than that.

Couldn't carry Willard all that much farther and it only took ten steps once we finally rid our stench from Highland Terrace 'fore brother Mick there started to waller 'bout that rake of rock. Sitting ducks ain't ever been my style so's I dropped the payload off right there on the side of Hwy 369, grabbed hold that Winchester 1897 pump, trained the barrel down, checked the chamber—one—fuck, lined it up anyhow, felt the PHEW...PHEW...of eighteen wheelers whiz by, 'em chains and mud flaps shocking out pebbles of mayhem onto the side of the road...PHEW...PHEW...spotted out a red chevy dually streamlining it's haul five cars back, marked up...PHEW...PHEW...PHEW...PHEW...stepped out onto that black top and bullseyed that barrel right for that driver, little prayer to Gawd lifting up outta my chest there weren't no rack behind that seat.

Watched as 'em tires skid, screeching *what the fuck* over government road, waited as the old woman in the passenger seat knocked air down her jowl with a set of passion pink stick on nails to her chest, the disbelief of *this isn't happening* starting to work electric nods over her crepey loose skin, walked over to her door 'cause PHEW...PHEW...PHEW, 'em cars kept coming along that other side, made sure that shotgun full privy to any drivers coming up behind, who immediately veered EEEEEEEEEERRRRRRRRR, redirecting their efforts elsewhere, tapped that snout of metal up against that vintage-roll-it-down-glass and spit blood and a loose tooth that my tongue'd-gone-busy-with-the-wriggle out on that needed-mowing-country-curb, and motioned to that soft grandpa working the rig, who looked decent enough that he weren't gonna stand stranded on the side of the road for all that very long, and booted his and his little ole wife's ass out the cab, hollered back to Mick and Willard, who were coiled up like a set of pit vipers up against each other in a pile of dirt and clipped, "Get in the back of the truck," training that muzzle with enough Peckinpah pluck weren't no second guessing a full chamber of slugs waiting to blow little ol' biddy and farmer Joe to high hawg heaven, and crawled up inside that cab and set off for a place in the woods where men go to disappear for a while.

The barn, a squatter, a forget-it's-on-the-land-once-ya-hit-that-mark-of-12, a double-aught practice ground, with barrels of hay lining ever' wall to prevent target practice from getting bloody. Tucked back up off 211. Nothing more than bones. Probably due to that fire that'd hit it at some point. Wood still carried the mark on the southern wall, a hole eat outta 'em boards with scorch framing the bite and a tarp nailed over the top of the mouth from where some fella at one point made promise at fixing but never quite got round to that part—done. Served as perfect lay in wait spot. Dropped the sloppy Joe mess of Willard and Mick off, their bodies and brains mushy enough for sleepy baby naps and drove out again, calculating the likelihood of a Tennessee state line getting crossed sometime in the near future. Stopped on over there at the Golden Pantry up off 53, stocked up on beenie-weenies, white bread, beer, and kerosene, ignored the big woman with fire-plug splotches of frontier plotting her face who rung me up, each hit of her sausage stoppers on the register drilling cannonballs of *hurry the fuck up* as she observed the inability of my blood blockers to prevent the occasional geyser of spew to come out the five skin breaks on my face, and got the hell outta dodge, bunkering down for the not-get-found-mode.

Course wouldn't none of that matter when I got back, 'cause just like a cunt, brother Mick there'd other plans in store. Barely brought the bag in, arm still setting down the kerosene in the grass by a pile of tires come the other side that blue tarp, 'fore a fucking 2-by-4 t-balled the bottom of my jaw. 'Bout cracked my head right off from the neck and sure as hell spliced a Kirk Douglas smoosh square into me. Damn groceries went flying, kerosene can went tipping, and my big ass went falling, chopped down like a gawddamn tree.

DING:

Ladies and Gents, our Main Event—happening here LIVE *in the middle of a converted hideaway house/barn,* DIRECT *from the woods acreage belonging to the Turner family, a family who have no idea that their grandfather's barn, a structure that once operated as house and home to Papi Turner, hisself, is housing one of the most touted events of the last ten years, not since 1978 have these two opponents faced off....30+ years of pent up aggression brought to you by way of one dead Momma, one bought with a Mason family dynasty, one barely standing Father of a son he's just met, and a Cain and Abel reckoning that's as old as Father Time—3 rounds of fuck ya up* GLEE*—our older brother in the bluuuuueeeeee corner just introduced to the battle via hardwood lumber, weighing in at an astonishing whiskey-4-barrel-load of* GET FUCKED....RRRRRROOOOOOOONNNNNNIIIIIIEEEEEEEAAIIIIIIIRRRRRCHILLLLLLLLLLLLLLDDDDDDDDDDDD. *And fighting in the yeller corner, the younger brother, weighing in at an equal amount of sauce and jeer that's just as fucking rotten as his older....*MMMMMMMMIIIIIIICCCCCCCCCKKKKKKAAAAIIIIIIIIIIIIRRRRRRCHILLLLLLLLLLLLDDDDDDDDDDDD.

Ya know the backstory between these guys is just astonishing...

Is that so...well, I can't wait to hear 'bout it....

DING: *and that's the bell, folks. Let's see how the punches are gonna land.*

Head powers to overdrive, a Mack Truck of RESPOND, RESPOND, RESPOND, of whoever pile drove that splinter in an uppercut ain't just gonna stop after one and done—naw, fuckers gonna come at me. Gonna come at me hard. So's open yar eyes ya dipshit, get ready, get guarded, get yar provisions right so we can fucking Donkey Kong our way outta here. That's right…let the light slip back in…let the flutter of 'em lashes spread open so's the lookout of the pupil can go on and Schwarzenegger detect, can spot the ass wipe that's gonna get a full fucking payback of that IOU I just wrote when his meat paws decided to fucking send me out to tinsel town. So's I'll say it again…open yar fucking eyes, Ronnie, ya hear me, this-me talking to me, open yar fucking eyes.

And he's back…well, I tell ya…thought the fight was over 'fore it even a chance to begin.

Nah—not Ronnie Fairchild. Wrestle the Devil outta hell if that's what the fight took.

Is that so?

Ya bet yar ass, there Jim.

Mick's fucking dark hair hangs over me like a scythe, madness in his eyes, rabies foam in his mouth, that 2 by 4 pole vaulted up like the strike gonna come from Gawd Hisself. Got to bring him down—switch hips to the side, right hand down—LIFT motherfucker, get it so's that left arm's up for the protect, so's when he shoots that blunt-force-trauma-scenario down like he's 'bout to do in 3…2…PEW—that motherfucker stakes right through the mud then boot that bad boy yonder, send it-the-fuck-away, battle star dodge all 'em stomps he's sending at my forearm…just keep it tight, keep moving with him, keep switching from left knee to left arm rolling back like a half saucer to right knee and right arm… don't think 'bout how I need to stand up, the stand'll come soon enough, watch out for his hammer fists, for 'em Thor thunderbolts he's sending down on my collar bone and neck, position it right for that raw to take over, that forgetting he's my brother and family, treat him like he's threat, don't go easy…fucker entered the ring on his own and by Gawd he's gonna have to earn the right to leave it. Ya wanna fucking mash it out little brother. Fine.

Shred his fucking knee. Boot. Heel. TATATATA. Hit it 'til the fucker falls. Send that knee cap right through to Ostrich city—body down—avoid the wailing octopus flail of disbelief, that bullet train of pain shooting black ink down his left leg, sending that right one up just for spite, for Major Tom to Ground Control check in, but there ain't no safety there brother when the beast's engaged—feed 'em sledgehammer POUNDS, bear claw the back of that turkey neck and MASH…MASH…MASH his cheek, don't let him squirm away, deflect 'em arms pinning hooks after eyes and mouth, tell 'em to BAM…BAM sit the fuck down. Fuck yar face—WHAM, mountain climb that knee up to his groin and HIT…HIT…HIT, fucking shatter any chance at offspring falling off that tree. Watch the arms settle loosey-goosey down, the eyes cabbage patch kid puff up, and wait for that knowing of stay the fuck down to brush-fire-spread over him.

And by Gawd, pray that's the last spot of stupid that's gonna find me today. Buuuttt, seeing as how there ain't come a single peep from the other side of that tarp 'spite all the hooting and hollering, it were a doubt settling in a little too close to home that the case. Sure enough once I hogtied that fucking boy up with a set of jumper cables procured from the back of that truck and went on and crowbar'd down on that plastic, moving that blue over just the smidge I needed to see 'em bloody boots and that fucking rorschach batch of fresh smeared beat down that were DEATH to my-newly-not- necessarily-reconciled-with-Daddy-but-certainly-someone-I-thought-might-exist-for- longer-than-two-days-and-an-afternoon scenario, ya best believe I stomped over to that cab, eyed that Winchester that'd parked sun-bathe next to me in the front seat, and sloughed that motherfucker off 'em cloth buckets seats, and planted that metal meet-yar-maker right up against brother Mick's face with a James Earl Jones slip of, "WAKE THE FUCK UP."

DINGDING DINGDING:

While we wait here for the official's decision, let's take ya back to that Kentucky Fall evening all those nights ago. Waaaay back to

1978 where the bad blood originally formed between the Fairchilds. A legendary snafu, one of which is said to've furthered both their interests in a life of crime and misdealings, in violence and mayhem, the tightrope between square and outta sight beginning with a disagreement, a small thing that can quickly snowball into something four walls, a roof, and a bloodline no longer can contain, the A-bomb decimating whatever chance there stood at NORMAL, *pulverizing the ground, shaking both the Fairchild's core—the revelation of Mick's father's identity, the one and only Albie Todd, the controller of Davis and Brother's Mining, leaked to him from the squirrely scoundrel with fast lips and no sense of true self, Mac, who'd profiteered off the back of Mick's stupidity for years, the destitute trail a scab that wouldn't heal bleed-off, a younger bother's wanting to follow in the footsteps of his big brother's pipeline* OUTLAW *dream leaving him blind to the wolves in his very own backyard, the same wolves who'd covered up the knowing of a rape—*MAC, *and the one who'd done the pillaging for sport, hisself—Albie, which'd resulted in two boots on the ground gaping* DISBELIEF *over the envelope of money Mac were handing over with a pat on the back of* JOB WELL DONE *very soon after the reveal, but commerce is commerce as they say, and the latest venture in conning-the-poor deemed a success, hence the fat stack.*

But in the wake of a fever dream, when the dough started feeling dirty and the bottle started hitting hard and the boy could no longer face the truth—that the money handed down to him from MAC *was actually raining from the dreary faucet of Albie's well, for it common knowledge the one worked for the other and how else could money get gained other than through coercion after the Mine's explosion in 1960, that this burden too much for him to bare, and that loneliness and time'd allowed the eye of the storm to brew over him to just the right point, that when his brother finally visited three months later for his annual birthday hooray to their Mommy, the storm right overhead, that on that evening as the crickets quieted in the trees on their Papaw's farm, who's death now carried more weight and sense than Mick could withhold, Mick unleashed his frustrations onto his brother. The one who'd left. The one only born a bastard but a bastard outta love nonetheless. Mick did what any man ill'quipped to put into words their frustrations does—grabbed a beer bottle, drowned his sorrows, decked his brother over the back of his head, bloodying Ronnie's noggin in two shades of crimson, then left him there to either survive or die, as he traipsed off to do what Hellmouth James Daniel failed to do so long ago. But as with anything lacking control, the goal loomed just beyond Mick's grasp and the young man who so desperately wanted to be a part of the* **GANG** *fell short, passing out piss drunk on the front of Albie Todd's lawn with Nanny's old battered shotgun bulletless near his arm, the cartridge box in his jacket pocket empty 'cept for one.*

This then followed naturally by big brother's courtship of Mick out into the wild, the welcome matt more accommodating to the experienced Ronnie, who knowing the only place a bastard can find peace is through the willful killing of that which made him a bastard in the first place, followed the drunken tracks of Mick all the way to Albie's abode, found the drooling mess of a man and did what he thought would finally set his brother free. A mercy under fire. Ronnie picked up his Nanny's gun, tracing the footsteps of his Papaw Hellmouth James Daniel and walked up to the front porch passing those lovely big blue azalea bushes, knocked on the door, loading that one shell into the chamber he'd found in brother Mick's pocket, watched as an old woman attempted venture from her seat as her fella intercepted staving off her pursuits with a gentle hand to her shoulder, that this fella, who ransacked the air from that very room soon as he turned from her hobbled to the door, his frame sunk to a mere 120 pounds, the meat dried right off him, were of course Albie Todd, hisself, which endeared Ronnie's want to go on and be done with it all, thus 'fore the door could even swing open, Ronnie blasted Albie Todd right straight to hell.

It was said years later, after the brothers parted ways, that this the straw that broke the camel's back.

Carrot sky frames the burning barn backdrop, the Apocalypse Now swelter of a full can of kerosene dumped and swished 'bout, Master-Blasting the flames in crooked picket fence points. Makes the bulletless Winchester seem eerie in my hand, dwarfed and useless, like fire the only true eliminator that's ever walked the earth and it's this thought that sits snug-like in the back of my throat as I cross the ankle high grassy field. In the end weren't no other way for it to go. Suppose I'd gone 'bout knowing that for a long time and suppose he were justified but that don't mean I needed make any more time in my life for the bastard. Took my pound of flesh and rid myself of him for good.

1990

LEGEND'S MOTOR INN
—
ELIZABETH JOHNSON REPORTING LIVE FOR CHANNEL 5 NEWS

They're calling them the Fairchild Boys—two brothers found dead early this afternoon at Legends Motor Inn off of I-77. A shoot-out that resulted in seven bodies.

The Fairchild Boys, believed sole perpetrators of the violence. The bodies within two feet of each other. What the detectives have noted as a standoff with one, what is dubbed as the younger, being shot down from the roof, the landing of brass and subsequent tumble to the ground resulting in death upon impact and the older, the firer of that shot, receiving an equal slug in his gut, his body pitched against a Cutlass, who died an hour later. His hand, extended out as if waiting for the other to grab hold.

The Police are investigating whether or not a previous wound on the younger brother, a "mound of flesh" missing from the body's chest has anything to do with the skirmish. There are no other persons of interest at this time.

However, a clown was found asphyxiated in the vehicle registered to the elder Fairchild as well as a decomposing tongue wrapped in a white cloth underneath the body. The only identifying marker a coroner's tag nailed to it with the name MAC *written in sharpie. How something like this happens is beyond the fine "Christian" folk of West, Texas, who for all reports and measures...*

ACKNOWLEDGMENT

I've either sipped whiskey with ya or we've shared a long chat, either way ya know who ya are.

Daughter to an American and a Kentuckian as she used to say when she was knee high to a grasshopper, Ashley Erwin grew up in a nowhere time in North Georgia spending the majority of her time looking for trouble and the latter part finding it fit better than it should. When she weren't hip clipped to her Daddy listening to tales of the "Old Place," she were reading or working. Born out of the natural yarn spinning of the most animated round the fire gets the biggest pull of the jug, it weren't a surprise she found her life lending itself to the peddling of drinks and the slinging of whiskey.

Ashley Erwin is the Southern Pulp author of A Ballad Concerning Black Betty or the Retelling of a Man Killer and Her Machete, with shorts appearing in Cheap Pop, Shotgun Honey, Switchblade, Revolution John, and Cowboy Jamboree's "Grotesque Art." An avid reader at Noir at The Bar traveling across the country with some jaunts over the pond for debauchery in England, she is the Woman to a Man and the holder of two cats and she bides her time in sunny Los Angeles cranking out bangers whenever she carves the time.

SHOTGUN
HONEY
2012 • 2022
CELEBRATING 10 YEARS OF
FICTION WITH A KICK
THE ROAD IS JUST BEGINNING
shotgunhoneybooks.com